The Gate of the Sun

Derek Lambert

HarperCollins*Publishers*

HarperCollins*Publishers*
1 London Bridge Street
London SE1 9GF
www.harpercollins.co.uk

This edition 2018

1

First published in Great Britain
by Hamish Hamilton Ltd 1990

A catalogue record for this book
is available from the British Library

ISBN 978-0-00-828768-9

Typeset by Palimpsest Book Production Ltd, Falkirk, Stirlingshire

Printed and bound by CPI Group (UK) Ltd, Croydon CR0 4YY

MIX
Paper from
responsible sources
FSC™ C007454

This book is produced from independently certified FSC™ paper
to ensure responsible forest management.

For more information visit: www.harpercollins.co.uk/green

The Gate of the Sun

Derek Lambert was born in 1929. He served in the RAF for two and a half years and then worked as a journalist for local newspapers, becoming a foreign correspondent on the *Daily Mirror* and then the *Daily Express*, travelling the world to exotic locations that later inspired his novels. The *Express* sent him to Moscow, where he wrote his first novel, *Angels in the Snow* (1969), based on first-hand knowledge of his material. It was his authentic tales of espionage that made him a household name and best-selling author of more than 30 books. He spent the later years of his life in Spain, where he died in 2001 at the age of 71.

By the same author

Angels in the Snow
The Kites of War
For Infamous Conduct
Grand Slam
The Chill Factor
The Twisted Wire
The Red House
The Yermakov Transfer
Touch the Lion's Paw
Grand Slam
The Great Land
The Saint Peter's Plot
The Memory Man
I, Said the Spy
Trance
The Red Dove
The Judas Code
The Lottery
The Golden Express
The Man Who Was Saturday
Vendetta
Chase
Triad
The Night and the City
The Gate and the Sun
The Banya
Horrorscope
Diamond Express
The Killing House

CONTENTS

ACKNOWLEDGEMENTS

I could not have written this novel without recourse to the following books. Any mistakes are my copyright.

CIVIL WAR: *The Spanish Civil War*, Hugh Thomas; *The Passionate War*, Peter Wyden; *Images of the Spanish Civil War*, introduced by Raymond Carr; *The Distant Drum*, edited by Philip Toynbee; *Blood of Spain*, Robert Fraser; *Homage to Catalonia*, George Orwell; *The Forging of a Rebel*, Arturo Barea; *And I Remember Spain*, edited by Murray A. Sperber; *Personal Record* and *The Spanish Labyrinth*, Gerald Brenan; *The Assassination of Federico García Lorca*, Ian Gibson; *The Spanish Pimpernel*, C. E. Lucas Phillips; *Behind the Spanish Barricades*, John Langdon-Davies; *March of a Nation*, Harold Cardoza.

THE FRANCO YEARS: *Spain Under Franco*, Max Gallo; *Spain: Dictatorship to Democracy*, Raymond Carr and Juan Pablo Fusi; *Spain: Change of a Nation*, Robert Graham; *Franco*, Brian Crozier; *The Face of Spain*, Gerald Brenan; *The Moles*, Jesús Torbado and Manuel Leguineche; *The Franco Years*, José Yglesias.

GENERAL: *The Spaniards*, John Hooper; *Spain*, Jan Morris; *The Spaniard and the Seven Deadly Sins*, Fernando Diaz-Plaja; *A Stranger in Spain*, H. V. Morton; *Well Met in Madrid*, Archibald Lyall; *Unknown Spain*, Georges Pillement; *Spain on £10*, Sydney A. Clark; *Both Sides of the Pyrenees*, Bernard Newman; *Iberia*, James A. Michener; *The Spanish Royal House*, Sir Charles Petrie; *Spain*, Yves Bottineau; *Spanish Holiday*, SPB and Gillian Mais; *Spain Everlasting*, S. F. A. Coles; *Or I'll Dress You in Mourning*, Larry Collins and Dominique Lapierre; *Spain As It Is*, Helen Cameron Gordon; *Ambassador on Special Mission*, Sir Samuel Hoare (Viscount Templewood).

My thanks, too, to my old friend Laurie Lee for the help and regenerated pleasure I obtained from *A Rose for Winter* and *As I Walked Out One Midsummer Morning;* to the archivists of the National Geographic Society in Washington DC; to Ian Gibson who forsook *García* Lorca for a day to show me a battlefield; to Ed Owen, Bill Bond and Tim Brown for their journalistic acumen; and to Tom Burns, a professional and articulate writer on Spanish affairs who cleansed the book of its more obvious errors. Tom is, among other things, an associate editor of that polished and comprehensive English language magazine about Spain, *Lookout*, which is published in Puebla Lucia, Fuengirola (Malaga), and I should like to place on record my gratitude to Ken Brown, publisher and editor, and Mark Little, senior editor, for the articles that have over the years provided sustenance for my novel.

I am also indebted to my personal word processor, Marjorie Ellis, who was sadly forced to abandon the book three-quarters of the way through because of illness, and to Sue Gallacher who finished the job.

Lastly my thanks to Jusèp Maria Boya, *Conservador del Musèo dera Val d'Aran*, who enlightened me about a small and little-known war in 1944. How many people know that Spain was invaded that year? And a final note of appreciation to a gracious lady, Pat Dally, the most youthful octogenarian I have ever met, who granted me access to her Spanish library.

AUTHOR'S NOTE

There must be an element of masochism in my nature because it would be intimidating enough for a Spaniard to write a novel about the labyrinth (Gerald Brenan's apposite choice of word) that is Spain, let alone a foreigner. It may also be interpreted by Spaniards as an impudence. What possible pretext can an Englishman proffer for chronicling in fiction 40 years of Spanish history beginning with the outbreak of the Civil War in 1936? My only justification is that I wrote the book because I love Spain and its people, and I seek forgiveness for the mistakes and occasional liberties – the over-simplification in the Civil War of Fascist and Republican was perpetrated in the interests of clarity – that inevitably occur. I would like to believe, however, that I may have arranged the words in such a way that the vibrancy of Spain rises from the pages to obscure such infelicities.

For Jonathan, *mi hijo*

1975

PROLOGUE

Every morning the old woman in black packed a Bible in her worn bag, walked to church and prayed for forgiveness.

At first, newcomers drinking coffee and Cognac beneath the hams hanging in the Bar Paraiso questioned her fragile intensity but soon, like the old hands, they accepted her as part of the assembling day, as predictable as the arrival of Alberto, the one-legged vendor of lottery tickets and the screams of abuse from Angelica Perez as her husband scuttled from their apartment above the bakery.

None, unless they could cast their minds back 40 years, would have suspected that she had once set a torch to pews and vestments dragged from another church and spat upon a plump priest as he ran a gauntlet of hatred.

As for the woman she cared nothing for what they thought – scarcely heeded them, or the muted roar of traffic on the M30, or the squawk of the rag seller, as she made her way down a narrow street off the Marqués de Zafra in the east of Madrid.

She was 68 years old but she had spent her passions early and did not carry her years easily. Sometimes she mistook the boom and crackle of fireworks for gunfire, occasionally she confused the uniforms of the city police for the blue *monos* the militiamen once wore, but she did not dwell in the past. She lived rather in a suspended capsule in which the lengthening years and changing seasons were scarcely acknowledged.

Her hair was a lustrous white, combed tightly into a bun; her gaze, although the focus was remote, was steady; and her face had not yet assumed the fatalistic mask of the old and unwanted.

This bitter winter day she walked at her usual pace that never varied, whether the city was sweating in the heat of August or cowering before the snow-stinging winds of January. And such was the remote authority of her gait that the crowds parted before her as nimbly as pecking pigeons.

When she reached a corner lot, where children played basketball, the walls were daubed with fading graffiti and geraniums hung from pots crowding the balconies, she turned down an alley where, at the end, stood the church, its dome like a blue mushroom.

As she made her way down the street its occupants set their watches by her. A solicitor practising the scrolls of his signature, a purveyor of religious tracts scanning a mildly pornographic magazine, a greengrocer polishing fruit from the Canaries . . . At 9.18 she would enter the church, pray in the last-but-one pew and emerge at 9.23. What prayer she held in the chapel of her hands no one knew, only that it had been thus for 10 years or more.

But today she walked straight past the open door of the church without so much as a glance inside, causing consternation in this modest thoroughfare. What none of the inhabitants knew was that it was vengeance that had imparted that air of impartial arrogance for all those years and that today, instead of a Bible, she carried a gun in her worn bag.

PART I
1937–1939

CHAPTER 1

Difficult to believe on this February morning in 1937 that, as a new day was born in the sky, men on the earth below were dying.

Tom Canfield lowered his stubby little Polikarpov from the cloud to take a closer look, but all he could see were swamps of mist, broken here and there by crests of hills – like the backs of prehistoric monsters, he thought – and the occasional flash of exploding shells.

He nosed the monoplane with its camouflaged fuselage and purple, yellow and red tailplane even lower, as though he were landing on the mist over the Jarama river. Hilltops sped past, vapour slithered over the wings; he had no idea whether he was flying over Fascist or Republican lines, only that the Fascists were trying to cut the road to Valencia, the main supply route to Madrid, 20 miles north-west of the beleaguered capital and had to be stopped.

Three months ago he could not have told you where Valencia was.

Despairing of finding the enemy, he raised the snout of the Polikarpov, known to the Fascists as a rat, and flew freely in the acres between mist and cloud, a tall young man – length sharpened into angles by the confines of the cockpit – with careless fair hair that gave an impression of warmth, and the face of a seeker of truths. The mist was just beginning to thin when he spotted another aircraft sharing the space. He banked and flew towards it and as it grew larger and darker he identified it as an enemy Heinkel 51 biplane.

Enemy? I don't know the pilot and he doesn't know me. Why should we, strangers in a foreign land, try and shoot each other out of the wide sky? He adjusted his goggles which were in no need of adjustment and, with the ball of his thumb, touched the button controlling the little rat's 7.62 mm machineguns.

Wings beat in the cage of his ribs.

He thought the German pilot of the Heinkel waved but he could not be sure. He waved back but he had no idea whether the German could see him.

His chest ached with the beat of the wings.

Tom learned to fly in the good days, in his father's Cessna at Floyd Bennett Field, before his father was wiped out on Wall Street in the Crash of 1929.

Those were the days when, without pausing to spare good or bad fortune a thought, Tom had lived with his parents in a 32-roomed mansion at Southampton on Long Island, an apartment overlooking Central Park and a cabin at Jackman in Maine, near the Canadian border, where there was a lake stuffed with trout.

One day's dealings on the Stock Exchange had erased these visible assets, and a lot more besides. Harry Canfield, self-made and bullishly proud of it, had suffered a stroke and his wife had mourned his convalescence with stoic martyrdom; the Cessna had been sold and Tom had quit Columbia Law School to earn a living.

Unprepared for routine labour, he had not prospered, succeeding only as a bouncer in a speakeasy until five Italians beat him senseless and concluding that period of his life share-cropping in Arkansas. By then he had lived in accommodation no bigger than a garden shed in a coal town in West Virginia and subsisted on soup made from potato peelings, and he had stood in a line in sub-zero temperatures in Minnesota waiting for a meal that had evaporated when he reached the head of the queue, and he had shared a brick-built shack in Central Park with commanding views of the blocks where the more fortunate citizens of New York still resided. And he had become rebelliously inclined.

When civil war broke out in Spain in July 1936, he and

some 3,000 other Americans identified immediately and passionately with the Republicans – the workers, the peasants, the *people* – and crossed the Atlantic to help them fight their terrible, fratricidal battles. Some went through the Pyrenees, some reported to the recruiting centre of the International Brigades in Paris on the rue Lafayette.

Tom was interviewed in Paris by a chain-smoking Polish colonel with a shaven scalp and pointed ears who was reputed to have fought for the reds in the Russian civil war. He made notes in an exercise book with a squeaking pen in tiny mauve lettering.

What were Tom's qualifications?

'I can fly,' Tom told him.

'Aircraft?' The colonel stared at him through the smoke rising from a yellow cigarette.

'Boeings,' Tom said.

'Stearmans?'

'P-26s,' Tom lied because Stearmans were trainers and this shiny-scalped Pole with the exhausted eyes seemed to know his aircraft.

'Age?'

'Twenty-five.'

'What's the landing speed of a P-26?'

'High, maybe 75 miles per hour.'

'Politics?'

'None.'

The colonel laid down his chewed pen. 'Everyone has a political attitude whether they realize it or not.'

'Okay, I'm for the people.'

'An Anarchist?'

'Sounds good,' said Tom who had not thrown up on a cargo boat all the way from New York to Le Havre to be interrogated.

'Communist?'

Tom shook his head and stared at the rain-wet street outside.

'Socialist?'

'If you say so.'

The colonel lit another cigarette, inhaling the smoke

hungrily as though it were food. He scratched another entry in the exercise book. 'Why do you want to fight in Spain?'

Tom pointed at a poster on the wall bearing the words SPAIN, THE GRAVE OF FASCISM.

'Tell me, Comrade Canfield, are you anti-poverty or anti-riches?'

What sort of a question was that? He said: 'I believe in justice.'

The colonel dipped his pen into the inkwell and wrote energetically. The rain made wandering rivulets on the window. Lenin smiled conspiratorially at Tom from a picture-frame on the wall.

'You were born in New York?'

'Boston,' Tom said.

'Why didn't you go to Harvard?'

'I went share-cropping instead.'

'Please don't play games with me. You see I, too, lived in New York. You're no peasant, *Mister* Canfield, not with that accent.'

'My father went bust.'

'So why does the son of a capitalist want to fight for the Cause?'

'Because bad luck is a two-edged sword, *comrade*. When we were rich I saw only the sea and the sky; when we went broke I saw the land and I saw people trying to make it work for them.'

'And did it?'

'I lived in a shack with a married couple with five kids in a coal town in West Virginia. Know what they paid them with?'

The colonel shook his head.

'Coal,' Tom said.

'What were you paid in?'

'Ideals,' Tom said. 'Do you have any objections to those, comrade?' thinking: 'Watch your tongue, or you'll blow it.'

'Why didn't you join the Party?'

'Which party?'

'There is only one.'

'You don't reckon the Democrats or the Republicans?'

'There's not much to choose between them, is there? They're all capitalists.'

'What do you believe in, Colonel?'

'In the class struggle. I believe that one day the slaves and not the slave-drivers will rule the world.'

'*Rule*, Colonel?'

'Co-exist. But please, I am supposed to be asking the questions. Do you believe in God?'

'I guess so. Whether he's Muslim, Buddhist, Jewish, or Catholic. Or Communist,' he said.

'The Fascists believe they have God on their side. Maybe you should fight for the Fascists.'

'Perhaps I should at that.'

'I'm afraid we can't allow that.' The colonel almost smiled and his pointed ears moved a little. 'You see, we need pilots.' He leaned forward and made a small, untidy entry in the exercise book.

At first Paris was a disappointment. The inhabitants of the arrondissement where he was staying resented penniless mercenaries on their streets and the other foreigners taking part in the crusade, particularly the Communists, were hostile to an American who, although he had picked fruit in California and collected duck shit at the east end of Long Island for fertilizer, still possessed the sheen of privilege. He was either slumming or spying.

When one Russian on his way to Spain as an adviser – they were all 'advisers', the Russians – accused him in a café of being a spy he resorted to his fists, a not infrequent expedient when his tongue failed him. The Russian, a Georgian with beautiful eyes and a belly like a sack of potatoes, fought well but he was no match for the middle-weight champion of Columbia.

'So,' the Russian said from between fist-thickened lips, 'if you're not a spy what the hell are you?' He picked himself up from the wreckage of a table.

'An idealist, I guess.'

'With a punch like that?' The Russian shook his head tentatively and touched one slitted eye. 'Are you reporting to Albacete?' Tom said he was. 'Maybe I will become your commissar,' continued the Russian. 'I would like that.'

Followed by other advisers, he walked into the rain-swept street.

When the Russians had gone the sturdy bespectacled man in the corner said, 'So you pack your ideals in your fists?'

Tom, who was beginning to think that ideals could get him into a lot of trouble, said, 'He asked for it.'

'And got it. Where did you learn to fight like that?' His accent was Brooklyn, as refreshing as water from a sponge.

'Columbia,' Tom said, sitting at the table. 'Where did you learn to talk like that?'

'A rhetorical question?'

'Rhetorical, Jesus!'

'I come from Brooklyn and I mustn't use long words?' He beckoned a waiter. 'Beer?'

'Fine,' Tom said, examining a bruised knuckle.

'You a flier?'

'Am I that obvious?'

'I can see it in your eyes. Searching the skies. My name's Seidler,' stretching a hand across the table. His grip was unnecessarily strong; when people gripped his hand firmly and looked him straight in the eye Tom Canfield looked for reasons – he had become wise in the coal fields and the orchards.

The waiter placed two beers on the table.

'Are you going to Spain?' Tom asked doubtfully because with his spectacles and the roll of flesh under his chin Seidler did not have the bearing of a crusader.

'To Albacete. Wherever the hell that is.'

'Why?' Tom asked.

'Because Spain seems like a good place to fly.'

'You're a pilot? Wearing spectacles?'

'For reading only.'

'So why are you wearing them now?'

'And for drinking beer,' Seidler said.

'Okay, stop putting me on. Why are you going to Spain?'

'Isn't it obvious? Me, a German Jew, Hitler and Mussolini, Fascists in Spain . . . Or am I addressing a punch-drunk college dropout?'

'I used to collect duck shit,' Tom said.

'Guano,' Seidler said. 'Best goddamn fertilizer in the world.' He took a deep draught from his glass. 'So your old man went bust?'

'How did you know that?'

'Instinct,' Seidler said tapping the side of his nose. 'Who interviewed you? A Polak with pointed ears?'

'He told you?'

'Said you were a flier, too.'

'A very stupid flier,' Tom said. 'Eyes searching the skies . . . Didn't you have your eyes tested before you started flying?'

'I'm short-sighted which means I can see long distances.'

'So?'

'I keep crashing,' Seidler said.

After that Tom Canfield enjoyed Paris.

On 28 November Seidler and Canfield departed from the Gare d'Austerlitz on train number 77 on the first stage of their journey to the Spanish city of Albacete which lies on the edge of the plain, half-way between Madrid and the Mediterranean coast.

There were many volunteers on the train, French, British, Germans, Poles, Italians, and Russian advisers. Tom felt ill at ease with the leather-jacketed Russians: he had journeyed to Europe to fight injustice, not espouse Marx or Lenin or, God forbid, Stalin. But, as the train paused at small stations he was comforted by the crowds on the platforms waving banners, offering wine and, with clenched fists raised, chanting, *'No pasarán!'* – they shall not pass. He was also cheered by the knowledge that he and Seidler were fliers, not foot soldiers; there is, as he was discovering, a pecking order in all things.

'Tell me how you became a flier,' he said to Seidler as the train nosed slowly past ploughed, wintry fields. Wine had spilled on his scuffed flying jacket, much shabbier than Seidler's, and he felt a little drunk – happy to be here in Spain.

'I wanted to join the Air Force,' Seidler said, chewing grapes that a well-wisher had handed him and spitting the pips on the floor. 'Actually volunteered, would you believe? I mean, do I look like Air Force material?'

'It's the spectacles,' Tom said, but it was more.

'They were polite. "Not quite what we're looking for, Mr Seidler, but thank you for offering your services." So I went back to selling books in a discount store on 42nd Street and learned to fly in New Jersey and waited for a war some place.'

Tom pointed at a miniature haystack on a church. 'What the hell's that?'

'A stork's nest,' Seidler said. 'Did you leave a girl behind?'

'Nothing serious,' Tom said.

'Parents?'

'My father had a stroke after he was cleared out. They live in a small hotel in upstate New York. They didn't want me to come out here' – the understatement of the year.

'And you're obviously an only child.'

Obviously? He remembered the house on Long Island and he remembered avenues of molten light on the water with yachts making their way down it, and men dressed in shorts and matelot jerseys drinking with his father, fierce moustache trimmed for his 60th birthday, and his mother dutifully reading to him in bed. She had been beautiful then, an older Katherine Hepburn, with chestnut hair piled high. He had never told them that he hated boats and, when he was lying on his back on the deck of the yacht, he was imagining himself at the controls of a yellow biplane exploring the castles of cloud on the horizon.

'But you're not,' he said to Seidler.

'Two brothers, one sister, all gainfully employed in the Garment Centre.'

The train which they had joined at Valencia stopped at a station, little more than a platform, and a dozen militiamen climbed on board. They wore blue overalls and boots, or rope-soled shoes, and berets or caps – one wore a French-style steel helmet, and two of them sported blood-stained bandages. Although the war had been in progress for only four months they conducted themselves like veterans and one carried a long-barrelled pistol which he laid carefully on his knees, as though it were made of glass. They were all young but they were no longer youthful.

Seidler spoke to them in Spanish. They were, he told Tom,

returning to Madrid which had miraculously held out against the Fascist onslaught.

As Seidler talked and handed out Lucky Strikes, which were taken shyly and examined like foreign coins, Tom spread a map on his knees and tried to understand the war.

He knew that the Fascists, or Nationalists, were drawn from the army, the Falange and the Church, the landowners and the industrialists; that the Republicans were Socialists, trade unionists, intellectuals and the working class.

He knew that, to protect their privileges, the Fascists had risen in July 1936 to overthrow the lawful government of the Republic, established in 1931, which was being far too indulgent towards the poor. He had read somewhere that before the advent of the Republic a peasant had earned two or three pesetas a day.

He knew that the Fascists, led by General Francisco Franco, had, with the help of German transport planes, invaded Spain from North Africa and that in the north, led by General Emilio Mola, they had swept all before them. But great swathes of Spain, including the cities of Madrid, Barcelona and Valencia, were still in the hands of the Republicans. *No pasarán!*

He knew that the Moors fighting for Franco took no prisoners and cut off their victims' genitals; he knew that the heroine of the Republicans was a woman known as La Pasionaria.

He knew that on the sides of this carriage where, on the wooden seats, peasants sat with their live chickens and baskets of locust beans were scrawled the letters UGT and CNT and FAI, but he had no idea what they meant and was ashamed of his ignorance.

The plain rolled past; water and smuts from the labouring engine streaked the windows.

'So what else have you found out?' Tom asked Seidler.

'That Albacete is the asshole of Spain but they make good killing knives there.'

The militiamen, Tom reflected later, had been right about Albacete. It was cold and commonplace, and the cafés were crammed with discontented members of the International Brigades from many nations drinking cheap red wine.

The garrison was worse. It was the colour of clay, the barrack-room walls were the graveyards of squashed bugs and the floors were laid with bone-chilling stone. Tom and Seidler were quartered with Americans in the Abraham Lincoln Battalion – seamen, students and Communists – but France was in the ascendancy: the Brigade commissar, André Marty, was a bulky Frenchman with a persecution complex; parade-ground orders were issued in French; many uniforms, particularly those worn resentfully by the British, were Gallic leftovers from other conflicts.

He and Seidler complained to Marty the day the commander of the Abraham Lincolns, good and drunk, fired his pistol through a barrack-room ceiling.

From behind his desk Marty, balding with a luxuriant moustache, regarded them suspiciously.

'You are guests in a foreign country. You shouldn't complain – just think of what the poor bastards in Madrid are going through.'

'Sure, and we want to help them,' Seidler said. 'But the instructors here couldn't organize a piss-up in a brewery.'

Marty fiddled with a button on his crumpled brown uniform.

'You Jewish?' He sucked his moustache with his bottom lip. 'And a flier?' – as though that compounded the crime.

And it was then that Tom Canfield realized that Marty was jealous, that fliers were different and that this would always be an advantage in life.

'We didn't come here to march and clean guns: we came here to fly,' Tom said. He loved the word 'fly' and he wanted to repeat it. 'We came here to bomb the Fascists at the gates of Madrid and shoot their bombers out of the sky. We're not helping the Cause sitting on our asses; flying is what we're good at.'

Marty, who was said to have the ear of Stalin, listened impatiently and Tom got the impression that it was Communism rather than the Cause that interested him.

'I want your passports,' Marty said.

'The hell you do.'

'In case you get shot down. You're not supposed to be in

this war. Article Ten of the Covenant of the League of Nations.'

'So what about the Russians?' Tom asked.

'Advisers,' Marty said. 'Give me your passport.'

'No way,' Tom said. Then he said, 'You mean we're leaving here?'

'To Guadalajara, north-east of Madrid. You'll be trained by Soviet advisers. There's a train this afternoon. On your way,' said Marty who could do without fliers in his brigade. He flung two sets of documents on the desk. Tom was José Espinosa, Seidler Luis Morales. 'Only Spaniards are fighting this war,' Marty said. 'It's called non-intervention.'

'Congratulations, Pepe,' Seidler said outside the office.

'Huh?'

'The familiar form of José.'

Tom scanned his new identification paper. It was in French. Of course. But he still had his passport.

At the last minute the Heinkel from the Condor Legion, silver with brown and green camouflage, ace of spades painted on the fuselage, veered away. Tom didn't blame the pilot: the Russian-made rats were plundering the skies. Or maybe the pilot was no more a Fascist than he was a Communist and could see no sense in joining battle with a stranger over a battlefield where enough men had died already.

He banked and flew above the dispersing mist, landing at Guadalajara, which the Republicans had captured early in the fighting. Seidler was playing poker in a tent with three other pilots in the squadron's American Patrol. He was winning but he displayed no emotion; Tom had never heard him laugh.

Tom made his reconnaissance report to the squadron commander – he was learning Spanish but his tongue grew thick with trying – debating whether to mention the Heinkel. If he did the commander would want to know why he hadn't pursued it.

'No enemy aircraft?' asked the commander who had already shot down 11.

'One Heinkel 51,' Tom said.

'You didn't chase it?'

Tom shook his head.

'Very wise: he was probably leading you into an ambush.'

Tom fetched a mug of coffee and met Seidler walking across the airfield where Polikarpovs, Chato 1-15 biplanes and bulbous-nosed Tupolev bombers stood at rest. It was cold and weeping clouds were following the Henares river on its run from the mountains.

The trouble with this war in which brothers killed brothers and sons killed fathers, he thought as they walked towards their billet, was that nothing was simple. How could a foreigner be expected to understand a war in which there were at least 13 factions? A war in which the Republicans were divided into Communists and Anarchists and God knows what else. A Communist had recently told him that POUM, Trotskyists he had thought, was in the pay of the Fascists. Work that one out.

They reached the billet and Seidler poured them each a measure of brandy. Tom shivered as it slid down his throat. Then he lay on his iron bedstead and stared at his feet clad in fleece-lined flying boots; at least fliers could keep warm. He had once believed that Spain was a land of perpetual sunshine . . . Sleet slid down the window of the hut and the wind from the mountains played a dirge in the telephone lines.

Seidler sat on the edge of his own bed, placing his leather helmet and goggles gently on the pillow; only Tom knew the secret of those goggles – the frames contained lenses to compensate for his bad sight.

He stared short-sightedly at Tom and said, 'So how'd it go?'

'Okay, I guess.' He told Seidler, who had already recorded one kill, a Junkers 52 on a bombing mission, about the Heinkel. 'I'm not sure I wanted to shoot it down.'

'Know what I felt when I got that Junkers? I thought it was one of those passenger planes in a movie, you know, when Gary Cooper or Errol Flynn is trying to guide it through a storm. And as it caught fire and went into its death dive I thought I saw passengers at the windows. And then I thought that maybe it wasn't a bomber because those Ju-52s are used as transport planes, too – 17 passengers, maybe more – and maybe I had killed them all. Kids younger than us, maybe.'

'What you've got to do,' Tom said, 'is remember what we're fighting for.'

'I sometimes wonder.'

'The atrocities . . .'

'You mean our guys, the good guys, didn't commit any?'

Tom was silent. He didn't know.

'In any case,' Seidler said, 'I'm supposed to be commiserating with you.' He poured more brandy. 'I hear that the Fascists have got a bunch of Fiat fighter planes with Italian crews. And that the Italians are going to launch an attack on Guadalajara.'

'Where do you hear all these things?'

'From the Russians,' Seidler said.

'You speak Russian?'

'And Yiddish,' Seidler said. The hut was suddenly suffused with pink light. 'Here we go,' Seidler said as the red alert flares burst over the field.

'In this?' Tom stared incredulously at the sleet.

They ran through the sleet which was, in fact, slackening – a luminous glow was now visible above the cloud – and climbed into the cockpits of their Polikarpovs. Tom knew that this time he really was going to war and he wished he understood why.

The Jarama is a mud-grey and thoughtful river that wanders south-east of Madrid in search of guidance. It had given its name to the battle being fought in the valley separating its guardian hills, their khaki flanks threaded in places with crystal, but in truth the fight was for the highway to Valencia which crosses the Jarama near Arganda. On this morose morning in February the Fascists dispatched an armada of Junkers 52s to bomb the bridge carrying this highway over the river.

Tom Canfield saw them spread in battle order, heavy with bombs, and above them he saw the Fiats, the Italians' biplanes which Seidler had forecast would put in an appearance. He pointed and Seidler, flying beside him, peering through his prescription goggles, nodded and raised one thumb.

The Fiats were already peeling off to protect their pregnant charges and the wings were beating again in Tom Canfield's chest. He gripped the control column tightly. 'But what are you doing here?' he asked himself. 'Glory-seeking?' Thank God he was scared. How could there be courage if there wasn't fear? He waited for the signal from the squadron commander and, when it came, as the squadron scattered, he pulled gently and steadily on the column; soaring into the grey vault, he decided that the fear had left him. He was wrong.

The Fiat came at him from nowhere, hung on behind him. Bullets punctured the windshield. A Russian trainer had told him what to do if this happened. He had forgotten. He heard a chatter of gunfire. He looked behind. The Fiat was dropping away, butterflies of flame at the cowling. Seidler swept past, clenched fist raised. *No pasarán!* Seidler two, Canfield zero. He felt sick with failure. He kicked the rudder pedal and banked sharply, turning his attention to the bombers intent on starving Madrid to death.

Below lay the small town of San Martín de la Vega, set among the coils of the river and the ruler-straight line of a canal. He saw ragged formations of troops but he couldn't distinguish friend from foe.

The anti-aircraft fire had stopped – the deadly German 88 mm guns could hit one of their own in this crowded sky – and the fighters dived and banked and darted like mosquitoes on a summer evening.

Tom saw a Fiat biplane with the Fascist yoke and arrows on its fuselage diving on a Polikarpov. As it crossed his sights he pressed the firing button of his machine-guns. His little rat shuddered. The Fiat's dive steepened. Tom watched it. He bit the inside of his lip. The dive steepened. The Fiat buried its nose in a field of vines, its tail protruding from the dark soil. Then it exploded.

Tom was bewildered and exultant. And now, above a hill covered with umbrella pine, he was hunting, wanting to shoot, wasting bullets as the Fiats escaped from his sights. So close were they that it seemed that, if the moments had been frozen, he could have reached out and shaken the hands of the enemy pilots. But it had been a mistake to try and get under the bombers; instead he attacked them from the side. He picked out one, a straggler at the rear of his formation. A machine-gun opened up from the windows where Seidler had imagined passengers staring at him; he flew directly at the gun-snarling fuselage, fired two bursts and banked. The Junkers began to settle; a few moments later black smoke streamed from one of its engines; it settled lower as though landing, then, as it began to roll, two figures jumped from the door in the fuselage. The Junkers, relieved of their weight, turned, belly up, turned again, then fell flaming to the ground. Parachutes blossomed above the two figures.

Without looking down he saw again the white, naked faces of Spaniards killing each other, and reminded himself that among them were Americans and Italians and British and Russians, and wondered if the Spaniards really wanted the foreigners there, if they would not prefer to settle their grievances their own way, and then a Fiat came in from a pool of sunlight in the cloud and raked his rat from its gun-whiskered nose to its brilliant tail.

The Polikarpov was a limb with severed tendons. Tom pulled the control column. Nothing. He kicked the rudder pedal. Nothing. Not even the landing flaps responded. One of his arms was useless, too; it didn't hurt but it floated numbly beside him and he knew that it had been hit. The propeller feathered and stopped and the rat began its descent. With his good hand Tom tried to work the undercarriage hand-crank, but that didn't work either. Leafless treetops fled behind him; he saw faces and gun muzzles and the wet lines of ploughed soil.

He pulled again on the column and there might have been a slight response, he couldn't be sure. He saw the glint of crystal in the hills above him; he saw the white wall of a farmhouse rushing at him.

CHAPTER 2

Ana Gomez was young and strong and black-haired and, in her way, beautiful but there was a sorrow in her life and that sorrow was her husband.

The trouble with Jesús Gomez was that he did not want to go to war, and when she marched to the barricades carrying a banner and singing defiant songs she often wondered how she had come to marry a man with the spine of a jellyfish.

Yet when she returned home to their shanty in the Tetuan district of Madrid, and found that he had foraged for bread and olive oil and beans and made thick soup she felt tenderness melt within her. This irritated her, too.

But it was his gentleness that had attracted her in the first place. He had come to Madrid from Segovia because it had called him, as it calls so many, and he worked as a cleaner in a museum filled with ceramics and when he wasn't sweeping or delicately dusting or courting her with smouldering but discreet application he wrote poetry which, shyly, he sometimes showed her. So different was he from the strutting young men in her *barrio* that she became at first curious and then intrigued, and then captivated.

She worked at that time as a chambermaid in a tall and melancholy hotel near the Puerta del Sol, the plaza shaped like a half moon that is the centre of Madrid and, arguably, Spain. The hotel was full of echoes and memories, potted ferns and brass fittings worn thin by lingering hands; the floor tiles were black and white and footsteps rang on them briefly before losing themselves in the pervading somnolence.

Ana, who was paid 10 pesetas a day, and frequently

underpaid because times were hard, was arguing with the manager about a lightweight wage packet when Jesús Gomez arrived with a message from the curator of the museum who wanted accommodation for a party of ceramic experts in the hotel. Jesús listened to the altercation, and was waiting outside the hotel when Ana left half an hour later.

He gallantly walked beside her and sat with her at a table outside one of the covered arcades encompassing the cobblestones of the Plaza Mayor and bought two coffees served in crushed ice.

'I admired the way you stood up to that old buzzard,' he said. He smiled a sad smile and she noticed how thin he was and how the sunlight found gold flecks in his brown eyes. Despite the heat of the August day he wore a dark suit, a little baggy at the knees, and a thin, striped tie and a cream shirt with frayed cuffs.

'I lost just the same,' she said, beginning to warm to him. She admired his gentle persistence; there was hidden strength there which the boy to whom she was tacitly betrothed, the son of a friend of her father's, did not possess. How could you admire someone who pretended to be drunk when he was still sober?

'You should ask for more money, not complain that you have been paid less.'

'Then I would be sacked.'

'Then you should complain to the authorities and there would be a strike in all the hotels and a general strike in Madrid. We shall be a republic soon,' said Jesús, giving the impression that he knew of a conspiracy or two.

Much later she remembered those words uttered in the Plaza Mayor that summer day when General Miguel Primo de Rivera still ruled and Alfonso XIII reigned; how much they had impressed her, too young even at the age of 22 to recognize them for what they were.

'My father says we will not be any better off as a republic than we are now.' She sucked iced coffee through a straw. How many centimos had it cost him in this grand place? she wondered.

'Then your father is a pessimist. The monarchy and the dictatorship will fall and the people will rule.'

On 14 April 1931, a republic *was* proclaimed. But then the Republicans, who wanted to give land to the peasants and Catalonia to the Catalans and a living wage to the workers and education to everyone, fell out among themselves and, in November 1933, the Old Guard, rallied by a Catholic rabble-rouser, José Maria Gil Robles, returned to power. Two black years of repression followed and a revolt by miners in Asturias in the north was savagely crushed by a young general named Francisco Franco.

But at first, in the late 20s, before Primo de Rivera quit and the King fled, Ana and Jesús Gomez were so absorbed in each other that, despite the heady predictions of Jesús, they paid little heed to the fuses burning below the surface of Spain; in fact it wasn't until 1936 that Ana discovered her hatred for Fascists, employers, priests, anyone who stood in her way.

When Jesús proposed marriage Ana accepted, ignoring the questions that occasionally nudged her when she lay awake beside her two sisters in the pinched house at the end of a rutted lane near the Rastro, the flea-market. Why after nearly a year was he still earning a pittance in the perpetual twilight of the museum whereas she, at his behest, had demanded a two-peseta-a-day pay rise and been granted one by an astounded hotel manager? Why did he not try to publish the poems he wrote in exercise books? Why did he not join a trade union, because surely there was a place for a museum cleaner somewhere in the ranks of the CNT or UGT?

They were married during the fiesta of San Isidro, Madrid's own saint. The ceremony, attended by a multitude of Ana's family, and a handful of her fiancé's from Segovia, was performed in a frugal church and cost 20 pesetas; the reception was held in a café between a tobacco factory and a foundling hospital owned by the father of Ana's former boyfriend, Emilio, who fooled everyone by getting genuinely drunk on rough wine from La Mancha.

Emilio, whose black hair was as thick as fur, and who had been much chided by his companions for allowing the vivacious and wilful Ana to escape, accosted the bridegroom as he made his way with his bride to the old Ford T-saloon provided by Ana's boss. He stuck out his hand.

'I want to congratulate you,' he said to Jesús. 'And you know what that means to me.' He wore a celluloid collar which chafed his thick neck and he eased one finger inside it to relieve the soreness.

Jesús accepted the handshake. 'I do know what it means to you,' he said. 'And I'm grateful.'

'How would you know what it means to me?' Emilio tightened his grip on the hand of Jesús, becoming red in the face, though whether this was from exertion or wine circulating in his veins was difficult to ascertain.

'Obviously it must mean a lot,' Jesús said, trying to withdraw his hand.

Ana, who had changed from her wedding gown into a lemon-yellow dress, waited, a dry excitement in her throat. The three of them were standing between the café where the guests were bunched and the Ford where the porter from the hotel stood holding the door open. No-man's-land.

'It means a lot to me,' Emilio said thickly, 'because Ana promised herself to me.'

'Liar,' Ana said.

'Have you told him what we did together?'

'We did nothing except hang around while you pretended to get drunk.' What she had seen in Emilio she couldn't imagine. Perhaps nothing: their union had been decided without any reference to her.

Emilio continued to grip the hand of Jesús, the colour in his cheeks spreading to his neck. Jesús had stopped trying to extricate his hand and their arms formed an incongruous union, but he showed no pain as Emilio squeezed harder.

The group outside the café stood frozen as though posing for a photographer who had lost himself inside his black drape.

'We did a lot of things,' Emilio grunted.

The porter from the hotel, who wore polished gaiters borrowed from a chauffeur and a grey cap with a shiny peak, moved the door of the Ford slowly back and forth. Fireworks crackled in the distance.

Jesús, thought Ana, will have to hit him with his left fist – a terrible thing to happen on this day of all days but what alternative did he have?

Jesús smiled. *Smiled!* This further aggrieved Emilio.

'You would be surprised at the things we did,' he said squeezing the hand of Jesús Gomez until the knuckles on his own fist shone white.

Finally Jesús, his smile broadening with the pleasure of one who recognizes a true friend, said, 'Emilio, I accept your congratulations, you are a good man,' and began to shake his imprisoned hand up and down.

'*Cabrón*,' Emilio said.

'God go with you.'

'Piss in your mother's milk.'

'Your day will come,' Jesús said, a remark so enigmatic that it caused much debate among the other guests when they returned to their wine.

The two men stared at each other, hands rhythmically rising and falling, until finally Emilio released his grip and, massaging his knuckles, stared reproachfully at Jesús Gomez.

Jesús saluted, one finger to his forehead, turned, waved to the silent guests, proffered his arm to his bride and led her to the waiting Ford.

From the bathroom of the small *hostal* near the Caso de Campo, she said, 'You handled that Emilio very well. He is a pig.'

She took the combs from her shining black hair and shed her clothes and looked at herself in the mirror. In the street outside a bonfire blazed and couples danced in its light. Would he ask her about those things that Emilio claimed they had done together?

'Emilio's not such a bad fellow,' Jesús said from the sighing double bed. 'He was drunk, that was his trouble.'

Didn't he care?

'He is a great womanizer,' Ana said.

'I can believe that.'

'And a brawler.'

'That too.'

She ran her hands over her breasts and felt the nipples stiffen. What would it be like? She knew it wouldn't be like the smut that some of the married women in the *barrio* talked while their husbands drank and played dominoes, not like the Hollywood movies in which couples never shared a bed but nevertheless managed to produce freckled children who inevitably appeared at the breakfast table. She wished he had hit Emilio and she knew it was wrong to wish this.

In novels, the bride always puts on a nightdress before joining her husband in the nuptial bed. To Señora Ana Gomez that seemed to be a waste of time. She walked naked into the white-washed bedroom and when he saw her he pulled back the clean-smelling sheet; she saw that he, too, was naked and, for the first time, noticed the whippy muscles on his thin body, and in wonderment, and then in abandonment, she joined him and it was like nothing she had heard about or read about or anticipated.

It is true that Ana Gomez only encountered her hatred during the Civil War, but it must have been growing sturdily in the dark recesses of her soul to show its hand so vigorously.

When, slyly, was it conceived? In the black years, when one of her three brothers was beaten up by police, losing the sight of one eye, for rallying the dynamite-throwing miners of Asturias? When, at the age of 62, her father, a gravedigger, bowed by years of accommodating the dead, was sacked by the same priest who had married her to Jesús for taking home the dying flowers from a few graves? Or because the same fat-cheeked incumbent had declined to baptize her first-born, Rosana, because she had not attended mass regularly, although for a donation of 20 pesetas he would reconsider his decision . . . Ah, those black crows who stuffed the rich with education and starved the poor. Ana believed in God but considered him to be a bad employer.

As the hatred, unrecognized, fed upon itself. Ana noticed changes in her appearance. Her hair, pinned back with tortoiseshell combs, still shone with brushing, the olive skin of her face was still unlined and her body was still young, but there was a fierce quality in her expression that was beyond her years. She attributed this to the inadequacies of her husband.

Not that he was indolent or drunken or wayward. He cooked and scavenged and cleaned and Rosana and Pablo, who was one year old, loved him. But he cared only to exist, not to advance. Why did he not write his sonnets in blood and tears instead of pale ink? wondered Ana who, since the heady days of courtship and consummation, had begun to ask many questions. It was she who had found the shanty in Tetuan, it was she who had found him a job paying five pesetas a week more than the National Archaeological Museum. But his bean soup was still the finest in Madrid.

When the left wing, the Popular Front, once again dispatched the Old Guard five months before the Civil War, Ana understood perfectly why strikes and blood-letting swept the country. The prisoners released from jail wanted revenge; the peasants wanted land; the people wanted schools; the great congregation of Spain wanted God but not his priests. What she did not understand were the divisions within the Cause and, although she reacted indignantly as blue-shirted youths of the Falange, the Fascists, terrorized the streets of the capital, she still didn't acknowledge the hatred that was reaching maturity within herself.

On May Day, when a general strike had been called, she left the children with her grandmother and, with Jesús, who accompanied her dutifully but unenthusiastically, and her younger brother, Antonio, marched down the broad *paseo* that bisects Madrid, in a procession rippling with a confusion of banners. One caught her eye: ANTI-FASCIST MILITIA: WORKING WOMEN AND PEASANT WOMEN – red on white – and the procession was heady with the chant of the Popular Front: 'Proletarian Brothers Unite'. In the side streets armed police waited with horses and armoured cars.

Musicians strummed the Internationale on mandolins. Street vendors sold prints of Marx and Lenin, red stars and copies of a new anti-Fascist magazine dedicated to women. And indeed women marched tall as the widows of the miners from Asturias advanced down the promenade. The colours of the banners and costumes were confusing – blue and red seemed to adapt to any policy – and occasionally, among the clenched fists, a brave arm rose in the Fascist salute.

After the parade the hordes swarmed across Madrid, through the West Park and over the capital's modest river, the Manzanares, to the Casa de Campo, a rolling pasture of rough grass before the countryside proper begins. There they planted themselves on the ground, boundaries defined by ropes or withering glances, released the whooping children and foraging babies, tore the newspapers from baskets of bread and ham and *chorizo*, passed the wine and bared their souls to the freedom that was soon to be theirs.

Ana pitched camp between a pine and a clump of yellow broom where you could see the ramparts of the city, the palace and the river below, and, to the north, the crumpled, snow-capped peaks of the Sierra de Guadarrama.

Her happiness as she relaxed among her people, her Madrileños, who were soon to have so much, was dispatched by her brother after his third draught of wine from the *bota*. As the jet, pink in the sunshine, died, he wiped his mouth with the back of his hand and said, 'I have something to tell you both. A secret,' although she knew from the pitch of his voice that its unveiling would not be an occasion for rejoicing.

Antonio, one year her junior, had always been her favourite brother. And he had remained so, even when he married above himself, got a job, thanks to his French father-in-law in the Credit Lyonnais where, with the help of the bank's telephones, he also traded in perfume, and mixed with a bourgeois crowd. He was tall, with tight-curled, black hair, a sensuous mouth and a nimble brain; his cheeks often smelled of the cologne in which he traded.

'I have joined the Falange,' he said.

It was a bad joke; Ana didn't even bother to smile. Jesus took the *bota* and directed a jet of wine down his throat.

'I mean it,' Antonio said.

'I knew this wine was too strong; it has lent wings to your brains,' Ana said.

'I mean it, I tell you.' His voice was rough with pride and shame.

There was silence beneath the pine tree. A diamond-shaped kite flew high in the blue sky and a bird of prey from the Sierra glided, wings flattened, above it.

Ana said, 'These are your wife's words. And her father's.'

'It is I who am talking,' said Antonio.

'You, a Fascist?' Ana laughed.

'You think that is funny? In six months time you will be weeping.'

'When *you* are taken out and shot. Yes, then I will weep.' She turned to Jesús but he had settled comfortably with his head on a clump of grass and was staring at the kite which dived and soared in the warm currents of air.

Antonio leaned forward, hands clenched round his knees; he had taken off his stylish jacket and she could see a pulse throbbing in his neck. She remembered him playing marbles in the baked mud outside their home and throwing a tantrum when he lost.

He said, 'Please listen to me. It is for your sake that I am telling you this.'

'Tell it to your wife.'

'Listen, woman! This is a farce, can't you see that? The Popular Front came to power because enemies joined forces. But they are already at blows. How can an Anarchist who believes that "every man should be his own government" collaborate with a Communist who wants a bureaucratic government? As soon as the war comes the Russians, the Communists, will start to take over. Do you want that?'

'Who said anything about a war?'

'There is no doubt about it,' Antonio said lighting a cigarette. 'Within months we will be at war with each other.'

'Who will I fight against? A few empty-headed Fascists in blue shirts?'

'Listen, my sister. We cannot sit back and watch Spain bleed to death. The strikes, the burnings, the murders, the rule of the mob.' He stared at the black tobacco smouldering in his cigarette. 'We have the army, we have the Church, we have the money, we have the friends . . .'

'Friends?'

'I hear things,' said Antonio who had always been a conspirator. 'And I tell you this: the days of the Republic are numbered.'

Jesús, eyes half closed, said, 'I am sure everything will sort itself out.' He had taken a notebook from his pocket and was writing in it with an indelible pencil.

'You were a Socialist once,' Ana said to Antonio.

'And I was poor. If I had stayed a Socialist or a Communist or an Anarchist I would have stayed poor. How many uprisings have there been in the past 50 years? What we need is stability through strength!'

'And who will give that to us?' She took the *bota* from her husband, poured inspiration down her throat. Her brother a Fascist? What about their brother, the sight knocked out of one eye by a police truncheon? What about their father, sacked by a priest with a trough of gold beneath his church? What about the miners, with their homemade bombs, gunned down by the military? What about the peasant paid with the chaff of the landowners' corn?

'There are many good men waiting to take command.'

'Of what?'

'I have said enough,' Antonio said.

Jesús, licking the pencil point, said, 'Good sense will prevail. Spain has seen too much violence.'

'Spain was fashioned by violence,' Antonio said. 'But now a time for peace is upon us. After the battle ahead,' he said. 'Join us. The fighting will be brief but while it rages you can take the children into the country.'

She stared at him in astonishment. 'Have you truly lost your senses?'

'Life will be hard for those who oppose us.'

'Threats already? A time for peace is upon us?'

Jesús said, 'The milk of mother Spain is blood.' He wrote rapidly in his notebook.

Antonio poured more wine down his throat and stood up, hands on hips. 'I have tried,' he said. 'For the sake of you and your husband and your children. If you change your mind let me know.'

'Why ask me? Why not ask my husband?'

Antonio didn't reply. He began to walk down the slope towards the Manzanares dividing the parkland from the heights of the city.

When he was 50 metres away from her she called to him. The diamond-shaped kite dived and struck the ground; the bird of prey turned and flapped its leisurely way towards the mountains.

'What is it?'

He stood there, suspended between distant childhood, and adulthood.

She raised her arm, bunched her fist and shouted, '*No pasarán!*'

The militiamen came for the priest at dawn, a dangerous time in the lawless streets of Madrid in the summer of 1936. Failing to find him, they turned on his church.

The studded doors gave before the fourth assault with a sawn-off telegraph pole. Christ on his altar went next, battered from the cross with the butt of an ancient rifle. They tore a saint and a madonna from two side chapels and trampled on them; they dragged curtains and pews into the street outside and made a pyre of them; they smashed the stained-glass window which had shed liquid colours on the altar as Ana and Jesus stood before the plump priest at their wedding. They were at war, these militiamen in blue overalls, some stripped to the waist, and a terrible exaltation was upon them.

Ana, who knew where the priest was, watched from the gaping doors and could not find it in herself to blame the wild men who were discharging the accumulated hatred of decades. Since the Fascist rising on July 17 the 'Irresponsibles' in the Republican ranks had butchered thousands and invariably it was the clergy who were dispatched first. Ana had heard terrible tales; of a priest who had been scourged and crowned with thorns, given vinegar to drink and then shot; of the exhumed bodies of nuns exhibited in Barcelona; of the severed ear of a cleric tossed to a crowd after he had been gored to death in a bullring.

But although she understood – the flowers that her father had taken from the graves of the privileged had been almost dead – such happenings sickened her and she could not allow them to happen to the priest hiding in the vault of the church with the gold and silver plate.

The leader of the gang, the Red Tigers, shouted, 'If we cannot find the priest then we shall burn the house of his boss.' He had the starved features of a fanatic; his eyes were bloodshot and his breath smelled of altar wine.

Ana, to whom blasphemy did not come easily, said, 'What good will that do, *burro*, burning God's house?'

'He has many houses,' the leader said. 'Like all Fascists.' He thrust a can of gasoline into the hand of a bare-chested militiaman who began to splash it on the walls. 'What has God ever done for us?'

'He did you no harm, Federico. You have not done so badly with your olive oil. How much was it per litre before the uprising?'

He advanced upon her angrily but spoke quietly so that no one else could hear him. 'Shut your mouth, woman. Do you want that scribbling husband of yours shot for collaborating with the Fascists?'

'As if he would collaborate with anyone. No one would believe you. They would think you were trying to take his place in my bed.'

'The olive oil,' the leader said more loudly, 'is 30 centimos a litre. Who can say fairer than that?'

'I asked what it *was*.'

'So you know where the priest is?' he shouted as though she had confessed and the militiamen paused in their pillaging and looked at her curiously.

She stared into the nave of the church where, with her parents and her brothers, she had prayed for a decent world and a reprieve for a stray alley cat and for her grandfather whose lungs played music when he breathed. She remembered the boredom of devotion and the giggles that sometimes squeezed past her lips and the decency of it all. She stepped back so that she could see the blue dome. A militiaman attacking a confessional with an axe shouted. 'Do you know where the priest is, Ana Gomez?'

And it was then that Ana Gomez was visited by a vision of herself: one fist clenched, head held high, the fierceness that had been in gestation delivered. She told Federico to drag a pew from the pile in the street and when, grumbling, he obeyed, she stood on it.

She said, 'Yes, I do know where the priest is,' and before they could protest she held up one hand. 'Hear me, then do what you will.'

As they fell silent she pointed at one young man with the tanned skin and hard muscles of a building labourer: 'You, Nacho, were married in this church, were you not?' And, when he nodded, 'Then your children are the children of God and this is their house. Can you stand back and see it burned?' He unclenched one big fist and stared at the palm in case it contained an answer.

'And you,' to a white-fleshed man whose belly sagged over his belt, 'should be ashamed. Wasn't your mother buried in the graveyard behind the church barely two weeks ago? Do you want her soul to go up in flames?'

'And you,' to a youth who had filled his pockets with candles, 'put those back. Don't you know they are prayers?' She paused, waited while he took back the candles which cost ten centimos each.

When he returned she raised both hands. 'Our fight is not against God: it is against those who have prostituted his love. If you take up arms against God you are destroying yourselves because you came into this world with his blessing.'

'So the priest who grew fat while we starved should not be punished?' Federico demanded.

They looked at her, these vandals, and there was a collective pleading in their gaze.

Again she waited. Raised one arm, clenched her fist.

'Of course he must be punished. So must all the other black crows who betrayed the Church. Beat him, spit on him' – they wouldn't settle for less – 'but don't degrade yourselves. Why stain your hands with the blood of one fat hypocrite?'

They cheered and she watched the muscles move on their lean ribs, and she saw the light in their eyes.

'Where is he?' demanded Nacho.

Another pause. Then, 'Beneath your feet.' They stared at the baked mud. 'In the vaults. With the gold and silver.'

'Who has the key?'

'The fat priest. Who else?' She placed her hands on her hips. 'Don't worry. I'll get him.'

She went into the church. Long before the priest had started to squirrel the altar plate in the vaults he had given her father a key; she had it in her hand now as she made her way through the vestry to the door. The key turned easily; in the thin light filtering through a barred window she saw a kneeling figure.

The priest said, 'So it has come to this,' and she thought, 'Please God don't let him plead.' 'Here, take this.' He handed her a gold chalice. 'And help me.'

She distanced herself from him and said, 'This is what you must do. When you emerge in the sunlight they'll beat you and scream at you and spit on you. Run as if the wrath of God is behind you' – which it must be, she thought – 'and make your way to the old house where I used to live.'

'They'll kill me,' the priest said. As her eyesight became accustomed to the gloom she saw that his plump cheeks had sagged into pouches. 'And make me dig my own grave.'

She wanted to say, 'My father could do it for you if you hadn't sacked him,' but instead she said, 'Give them the gold and silver, that will speed you on your way.'

'It's a trap,' the priest said. He bowed his head and gabbled prayers. 'How can they hate me like this? I have been a good priest to them.'

'That is for God to decide.'

'You are a good woman,' the priest said, standing up.

She handed him back the chalice. 'Take this and the other ornaments and follow me.'

He said, 'I wish I were brave,' and she wished he hadn't said that because it made her think of her husband.

'If you believe,' she said, 'if you truly believe then you need not fear.'

'Do you believe, Ana Gomez?'

'In a fable? A black book full of stories? Angels with wings and a devil who lives in a dark and deep place? Yes, I believe,' she said and led the way out of the vaults.

In the vestry she ripped up a surplice, wrapped it round the leg of a shattered chair, dipped it in gasoline and lit it with a match. She picked up a green and gold vestment, soaked that in gasoline and, torch carried high in one hand, vestment in the other, emerged into the sunlight.

The mob stared at her, confused. She threw the vestment on the pyre; the gold thread glittered in the sunlight. She applied the torch to it. Flames leaped across the cloth, swarmed over the gasoline-soaked fixtures of the church. Thick smoke rose and sparks danced in it.

She turned and signalled to the priest lurking in the church. He had removed his clerical collar and he was wearing a grey jacket and trousers and big black boots, and was more clown than cleric. His eyes narrowed in the sunlight, his dewlap quivered.

He threw the altar plate at the foot of the flames and began to run. She spat at him, threw the torch on the pyre and ran towards the gold and silver.

The crowd hesitated; then those at the front made a dash for the booty. Federico, the leader, held aloft a gold salver. 'And we had to count our centimos,' he shouted.

Then they were after the priest as, weaving and stumbling, he reached the edge of the poor square. Some made a gauntlet in front of him; rifle butts and axe handles smote him on the shoulders. He tried to protect his face with his plump hands but he uttered no sound. Ana reached him and spat again and hissed to him to run down an alley to his left.

She blocked the alley. 'To think we obeyed such a donkey,' she cried and indeed he looked too absurd to pursue.

She listened to the receding clatter of his boots on the cobblestones. The pursuers hesitated and, frowning, looked to each other for guidance.

Federico pushed his way through them. 'Out of the way, woman,' he said. 'We must have the priest.'

'You will have to move me first.' She folded her arms across her breast and stared at him.

He advanced upon her but as he reached her a burning pew slipped from the pyre belching flames like cannon fire, and smoke heavy with ash billowed across the square.

Ana raised her arms above her head. 'It is God's word.'

As they dispersed she returned to the church, locked the door and made her way down rutted lanes to the house where the priest was waiting for her.

She had listened to La Pasionaria broadcasting on Radio Madrid. 'The whole country throbs with rage in defiance

... It is better to die on your feet than to live on your knees.'

And on 20 July she had stood ready to die in the Plaza de España, where Don Quixote's lance pointed towards the Montaña Barracks in which Fascist troops were beleaguered – Fascists later pointed out that Quixote's outstretched arm closely resembled a Fascist salute – and she had moved inexorably forward with the mob as they stormed the garrison.

She had watched the troops being butchered, although many, it was learned later, had been loyal to the Republicans, and she had watched a marksman drop officers from a gallery high in the red and grey barracks on to the ground.

She had heard about the Republican execution squads, the bodies piled up in execution pits at the university and behind the Prado – more than 10,000 in one month, it was rumoured – and she had wondered if her brother, Antonio, had been among them because although the bourgeoisie and the priests were fair game there was no more highly prized victim than a Falangist.

And she had heard about the inexorable progress of the Fascists in the south, under the command of General Francisco Franco with his Army of Africa – crack Spanish troops in the Foreign Legion whose battle cry was 'Long live death' and Moors who raped when they weren't killing – and General Emilio Mola's four columns in the north.

To Mola fell some of the responsibility for the killings in Madrid. Hadn't he boasted, 'In Madrid I have a Fifth Column: men now in hiding who will rise and support us the moment we march,' thus inciting the gunmen, many of them criminals released from jail in an earlier amnesty, to further blood-letting? He had also boasted to a newspaper correspondent that he would drink coffee with him in the Puerta del Sol, so every day coffee was poured for him at the Molinero café.

She had doled out bread to refugees roaming the capital, in the sweating alleys of its old town, on the broad avenues of its heartland, and when the first aircraft, three Ju-52s, had bombed the city on 27 August she had organized air-raid precautions for the *barrio* – shatter-proofing windows with brown paper, painting street lamps blue, making cellars habitable.

So what am I doing drinking coffee in my old home with the enemy, a priest?

Her brother, a street cleaner whose eye had been knocked out long ago by the police, railed. 'What is this fat crow doing here? He should have been crucified like all the other sons of whores.'

Salvador harboured a bitterness that was difficult for anyone with two eyes to understand, Ana thought. The patch over the socket stared at her blackly. Salvador hosed down streets at dawn but often his aim was bad.

She said quietly, 'He baptized you and he married me and he listened to our sins.'

'Did he ever listen to his own? Did he ever do penance?'

The priest, cheeks trembling as he spoke, said, 'I did my best for all of you. For all of my flock.'

'For my eye?'

'That was none of my doing.'

'Did you pray for the miners in Asturias?'

'I pray for Mankind,' the priest said.

'Ah, the Kingdom of God. We have to pay high rents to occupy it, father.'

'Jesus was the son of a carpenter. A poor man.'

'But, unlike us, he could work miracles. Why did you only educate the rich, father?'

'We have made mistakes,' the priest admitted.

This took Salvador by surprise. He adjusted his black patch, good eye staring at Ana accusingly. The three of them, and her father who was dying on the other side of the thin wall, were the only people in the house. The house was a hovel but that had never occurred to her when they had been a family. The patterned tiles on the floor were worn; the whitewashed walls had been moulded with the palms of plasterers' hands and, since her mother's death, dust had collected in the hollows.

Salvador lit a cigarette and puffed fiercely. 'I shall have to report his presence to the authorities,' he said.

'Which authorities?'

This bothered him too, as Ana had known it would. Before July he had supported the Socialist Trade Union. But now he suspected that Communists were infiltrating it – Russians who had forged tyranny instead of liberty from their Revolution. And they in their turn were at odds with the anti-Stalin Communists.

So Salvador was beginning to move towards the Anarchists, who believed in freedom through force, and didn't give a damn about political power.

Already families were divided between the Fascists and the Republicans. Please God, Ana prayed while the priest shakily sipped his coffee, do not let the Cause divide us too.

'The police,' Salvador said lamely.

'Which police? There are many of those, too.'

'Stop trying to confuse me,' Salvador said. 'Get rid of him,' he said pointing at the priest.

'Kill him?'

'Just get rid of him. I don't want to see his face round here.'

'Since when was it your home?'

'You think our father would want a priest, *that* priest, here?'

'I don't know what our father would want,' Ana said.

'You realize,' he said, touching his black patch, 'that we are now the revolutionaries?'

'Weren't we always, in spirit?'

'Now we are doing something about it and we have the Fascist insurgents to thank for it. We are taking over the country.'

'Do you think the Fascists know about that?' Ana asked, and the priest said, 'We are all God's people,' and Salvador said, 'So why are we fighting each other?'

Ana and Salvador looked deeply at each other but they did not speak about Antonio, their brother who had betrayed them. Had he managed to reach Fascist armies in the north or south? It was possible: certainly Republicans trapped behind Fascist lines were reaching Madrid. Salvador pushed back the top of his blue *monos* exposing his right shoulder. 'Do you know what that is?' pointing at bruised flesh.

'Of course,' said Ana who knew that he wanted a distraction from their brother. 'The recoil of a rifle butt.'

'The badge of death,' Salvador said. 'That's what the Fascists look for when they capture a town. Anyone with these bruises has been fighting against them and they kill them. In Badajoz they herded hundreds with these bruises into the bullring and mowed them down with machine-guns.'

'You have been firing a rifle?' Ana looked at him with disbelief. 'With one eye?'

'Think about it,' Salvador said. 'When you fire a rifle do you not close one eye?'

'Where have you been firing a rifle?' she asked suspiciously.

'Not, who have I been shooting?' He smiled, one eye mocking. 'Don't worry, I'm not a murderer. Not yet. There's a range on the Casa de Campo and I have been practising.'

From the other side of the wall they heard a moan.

Ana, followed by Salvador, went to their father who was dying from tuberculosis. He looked like an autumn leaf lying there, Ana thought. His grey hair grew in tufts, his deep-set eyes gazed placidly at death. On the table beside him stood a bottle of mineral water and a bowl in which to spit. His prized possession, a stick with an ivory handle shaped like a dog's head, lay on the stiff clean sheet beside him. He was 67 years old and he looked 80; his mother-in-law, who walked in that moment, would outlive him.

He acknowledged his children with a slight nod of his head and stared beyond them.

'Is there anything you want?' Ana asked.

A slight shake of his head.

Salvador took one of his hands, a cluster of bones covered with loose skin, and pressed it gently. 'We are winning the war,' he said but the old man didn't care about wars. He closed his eyes, kept them shut for a few moments, then opened them. Some of his lost expression returned and there was an angle to his mouth that might have been a smile. Ana turned. The priest stood behind them. Salvador rounded on him but Ana put her finger to her lips. He stretched out one hand and the priest who had taken away his living for stealing a few expiring blossoms held it.

'May God be with you,' the priest said.

Back in the living-room the priest said, 'I think it would be a good thing if I stayed. I can administer the last rites.'

Salvador wet one finger, drew it across his own throat, and said, 'But who will administer them to you?'

Ana's sister-in-law, Antonio's wife, came to her home one late September day. She had discarded the elegant clothes that Ana associated with girls in *Estampa* and her permanent waves had spent themselves; she was pregnant, her ankles were swollen. Ana regarded her with hostility.

'Slumming, Martine Ruiz?' she demanded at the door. Not that the shanty was a slum; it might not have electric light or running water but Jesús left no dust on the photographs of stern ancestors on the walls of the living-room, and the nursery, if that's what you could call one half of a partitioned bedroom, still smelled of babies, and the marble slab of the sink was scoured clean. But it was very different from Antonio's house to the south of the Retiro which was built on three floors with two balconies.

'Please let me in,' Martine said. Ana hesitated but there was a hunted look about the French woman and, noting the swell of her belly, she opened the door wider.

Jesús was stirring a bubbling stew with a wooden ladle. Food was becoming scarcer as the Fascists advanced on Madrid but he always managed to provide. He greeted Martine without animosity and continued to stir.

Martine sat on a chair, upholstered in red brocade, that Jesús had found on a rubbish dump, the expensive leather of her shoes biting the flesh above her ankles.

Ana said, 'Take them off, if you wish.' Martine eased the shoes off, sighing. 'So what can we poor revolutionaries do for you?' Ana asked.

Martine spoke in fluent Spanish. Jesús should leave, she said. Ana shrugged. Everyone suspected everyone these days. She said to Jesús, 'I hear there are some potatoes in the market; see if you can get some.'

'Very well, *querida*. Take care of the stew.' He wiped his hands on a cloth and, smiling gently, walked into the lambent sunshine.

'He is a kind man,' Martine said. 'A gentle man.'

Born in the wrong time, Ana thought. 'You never thought much of him in the past.'

'I don't understand politics. They are not a woman's business.'

'Tell that to La Pasionaria. She is our leader, our inspiration.'

'Really? I thought Manuel Azaña was the leader.'

'He is president,' Ana said. 'That is different. He is a figurehead: Dolores is our lifeblood.' Martine leaned back in the chair. Ana noticed muddy stains beneath her eyes. 'So what is it you want?' she asked her.

Martine arranged her hands across her belly. She stared at Ana. Whatever was coming needed courage. When she finally spoke the words were a blizzard.

'The police came yesterday,' she said. 'SIM, the Secret Police. They asked many questions about Antonio. When had I last seen him? When was I going to see him? Trick questions . . . Did he give your daughter a present when you saw him? Why did my father help him to escape? Then they went to see my father. As you know, he has a weak heart.'

'I didn't know that,' Ana said. She poured Martine a glass of mineral water and handed it to her.

'He was very distressed. Another interrogation could kill him.' She sipped her mineral water and stared at the bubbles spiralling to the surface. 'The police came to my house again this morning. They asked questions about Marisa.' She blinked away tears. 'Not threats exactly but hints . . . What a pretty little girl my daughter was, intelligent . . . They hoped that no harm would befall her.'

Ana said firmly, 'The police would not harm Marisa.'

'If they took me away it would harm her. And what of her brother or sister?' pointing at her belly. 'What if I were thrown into prison? I wouldn't be the first. Then they wait, the SIM, until the husband hears that his wife is in gaol, that his child is starving. Then he gives himself up. Then he is questioned, tortured and shot in one of the execution pits.'

'Has Antonio contacted you?'

Martine looked away furtively. 'I don't know where he is,' she said, voice strumming with the lie.

'That wasn't what I asked you.'

'I had a message,' she said. 'Through a friend.'

'Is he well?'

'He is full of spirit.'

'He is a fool,' Ana said. Martine said nothing. 'So how can I help you?'

'You can move about Madrid. Meet people, talk to them.'

'And you can't?'

'None of us can.'

'Us?'

'You know what I mean.'

'I know what you mean,' Ana said. 'Fascists.'

'Anyone with any property or position. Old scores are being settled.'

'But not with pregnant women. When is the baby due?'

'I am followed wherever I go,' Martine said. 'They want Antonio badly. He knew many things. The baby is due in February,' she said.

'You were followed here?'

'Does it matter? We are sisters-in-law. But there are certain places I cannot visit . . .' She hesitated. 'Can I trust you to keep a secret?'

'It depends. The names and addresses of Mola's Fifth Column? No, you cannot trust me.'

Martine fanned herself with a black and silver fan; her hair, once so precise, was damp with sweat. She said, 'Does the man in the check jacket mean anything to you?'

Ana frowned; it meant nothing.

'He is an Englishman. And he wears a check jacket.'

'Stop playing games,' Ana said.

'I want you to swear . . .'

'I'll swear nothing. Now, please, I am hungry and Jesús will be back from the market soon.'

Martine said abruptly, 'I must escape from Spain. For Marisa's sake. For the sake of your nephew,' she said slyly, stroking her belly with one hand.

'The man in the check jacket can help you?'

'His name is Lance. He's sometimes known as Dagger. He's an attaché at the British Embassy in Calle Fernando el Santo. It's full of refugees . . .'

'From Mola's army? From Franco's army?'

'Don't joke,' Martine said. 'You know what I mean. Refugees from the militia, from the Assault Guards. Lance has been getting prisoners out of gaol. He may be able to get them out of Spain.'

'And you want me to . . .'

'I can't,' Martine said.

Ana was silent. She thought about Antonio and then she thought about Martine's daughter, Marisa, and then she thought about the unborn child and then she thought about the priest.

She said, 'Would you mind travelling with a man of God, a black crow?'

'I don't understand,' Martine said.

Ana considered telling her sister-in-law about the priest. But no, you didn't confide in women such as her brother's wife: they used secrets as others use bullets. But maybe this man Lance could take the priest off her hands. And Martine.

She thought, *Mi madre!* What am I, a daughter of revolution, doing plotting the escape of a hypocritical priest and the daughter of a Falangist?

'Where does this Englishman live?' she asked.

'Calle de Espalter. Number 11. You could go there pretending to offer your services as a cleaning woman.'

Ana laughed. 'Sometimes,' she said, 'I almost admire you.'

At that moment Jesús returned carrying a basket half filled with sprouting potatoes.

Ana went to Calle de Espalter, a short, tree-lined street adjoining the Retiro, a few days later. It was the beginning of October and the air had cooled and the trees in the park were weary of summer. Militiamen, rifles slung over their shoulders, patrolled the street because it was in a wealthy and elegant part of Madrid; a banner fluttered in the breeze: LONG LIVE THE SOVIET. Broken glass crunched under Ana's feet.

Two assault guards outside the thin block regarded her suspiciously. They wore blue uniforms and they were the Republic's answer to the *Guardia Civil* who, with their shiny black tricorns and green-grey uniforms, were always suspected of Fascist sympathies.

'What are you doing here?' one of them asked her. He was smoking a thin cigarette and smoke dribbled from his flattened nose.

'Do I have to give reasons for walking in my own city?' She folded her arms and stared at the guards whose reputation for killing was unequalled in Spain. Had they not assassinated José Calvo Sotelo and helped to spark off the war?

'You have to give *us* reasons,' the guard said but he regarded her warily because some of the women of Madrid were becoming more ferocious than their menfolk: La Pasionaria had led them from the kitchen and the bedroom on to the dangerous streets.

'Then I will give you one: because I am alive.'

The guard rubbed his dented nose and looked at his colleague for help. His companion said: 'Papers?'

'Of course.' She made no move to show them.

'If you will forgive me,' the first guard said, pointing at her cheap red skirt and white blouse, 'you do not look as though you live here. Do you, perhaps, work for a capitalist?'

Ana spat. The assault guard took a step back.

'I hope to find work. I have to feed my children and my husband who is the leader of a militia group. But not with a capitalist: with a foreigner. Now if you will excuse me.' She stepped between them, continued up the street, turned into number 11 and mounted the stairs.

The man who let her into the small apartment was thin with a strong nose and a small moustache; he laughed a lot and he wore a check jacket.

She asked if it was safe to talk. This made him laugh and she began to wonder if this was truly the man who had supposedly whisked prisoners from gaols past the guns of waiting murder squads.

She said, 'I have heard that you help people on the death lists.'

He stared at her and for a moment she glimpsed the wisdom which he was at pains to conceal.

'But you, señora,' he said in his accented Spanish, 'are not on those lists. You, surely, are a woman of the revolution.'

She told him about Martine and the children, one unborn,

and she told him about the priest. She added, 'If anyone knows I came to you for help I will be killed.'

'No one will know,' he said and this time he didn't laugh. 'But what am I to do with your sister-in-law and her daughter and your priest?'

'Hide them in your embassy?'

'Most of them are in a private hospital and it's stuffed full already.'

'Please, Señor Lance.'

'I will make inquiries.'

'*La palabra inglesa*,' she said. 'The word of an Englishman. That is all I need to know.'

'But . . .'

'You have made me very happy,' she said when, hands spread in submission, he laughed; she laughed too.

He made a note of the addresses where Martine and the priest were staying and led her to the door.

'One last thing, Señor Lance. If anyone asks, I came for a job cleaning your apartment.'

She walked into the sunlit street where, behind shuttered windows, families lived in twilight.

Madrid was doomed.

How could it be otherwise? The Government had packed its bags and on 6 November fled to Valencia, leaving behind a sense of betrayal – and an ageing general, José Miaja, who looked more like a bespectacled monk than a soldier, in charge of its defence. Radio Lisbon had broadcast a vivid description of General Francisco Franco entering the city on a white horse. And the foreign correspondents viewing the Fascist build-up to the final assault from the ninth floor of the Telefónica on the Gran Via were predicting its capitulation.

By the first weekend in the month the Fascists – Moors and crack Foreign Legionnaires mostly – stormed down the woodland parkland of the Casa de Campo crossing the bridges of the Manzanares – what was left of it after the long hot summer – and scaling the heights beside the palace. Could an ill-equipped, ill-assorted ragbag of militia, sleepless and hungry, skulls echoing with explosions, some armed with canned fruit tins stuffed with dynamite, defend itself against 105 mm artillery and the German bombers of the Condor Legion?

Some thought it could.

Among them La Pasionaria who, dressed in black and fierce of face, preached courage to dazed fighters in blue overalls.

Among them a young sailor named Coll who tossed dynamite beneath Italian tanks rumbling towards the centre of the city, disabled them, proving that tanks weren't invincible, and got himself killed.

Among them children digging trenches and old women boiling olive oil to pour on Fascist heads and younger women defending a bridge vulnerable to enemy attack and tram-drivers taking passengers to the battle front for five centimos.

And their belief given wings by the spectacle of Russian fighters, rats, shooting the bombers out of the cold skies and the soldiers, many wearing corduroys and blue berets, steel helmets on their belts, who materialized on the Sunday 8 November, singing the Internationale in a foreign tongue.

Russians, of course. Word spread through the bruised avenues and alleys: relief was at hand. Except that they weren't Russians at all; they were 1,900 recruits of the 11th International Brigade, Germans, British, French, Belgians and Poles; Communists, crooks, intellectuals, poets and peasants.

But they armed the ragbag of defenders with hope.

The Ju-52 bomber looked innocent. It had split from its formation and, with the November-grey sky temporarily free of Russian fighters, it was looking for a target with grotesque nonchalance.

Ana noticed that it was heading in the general direction of her old home but only vaguely because at the time she was preoccupied with an argument with her husband.

Jesús was writing about the war for the Communist newspaper *Mundo Obrero* and providing captions for the fine, fierce posters the Republicans were producing.

She kicked off her rope-soled shoes and said, 'So how was the housekeeping today?' Rosana, who was eating sunflower seeds in the corner of the room, spitting the husks into a basket, turned her head; she was ten years old and sensitive to atmosphere.

'I got some rice,' he said. 'A few weevils in it but we don't get enough meat as it is.'

'It's a pity,' she said, 'that you have to write for a Communist newspaper.'

'I write for the Cause. In any case, isn't La Pasionaria a Communist?'

'She is for the Cause,' said Ana who knew she was a Communist too.

'She is a great woman,' Jesús agreed.

'Fire in her belly,' said Ana who had just taken food and brandy to the high positions overlooking the Casa de Campo where, on 1 May, her brother Antonio had announced his betrayal. She had also crossed the Manzanares to the suburb of Carabanchel, and taken rifles and ammunition from dead men in the trenches to give to the living and she had taken a dispatch through the centre of Madrid, through the Gran Via, Bomb Alley, where she had seen a small boy lying dead in a pool of his own blood, and the corpse of an old man with a pipe still stuck stiffly in his mouth.

'But a Communist nonetheless,' Jesús remarked.

'So?'

'It was you who were complaining that I write for a Communist newspaper. It would be a terrible thing, would it not, if we fell out within ourselves. Communists and Anarchists and Socialists . . .'

Ana said, 'It is better to fight than to preach.'

Rosana spat the striped, black-and-white husk of a sunflower seed into the basket.

'I am no fighter,' Jesús said.

'Are you proud of it?'

'I am not proud of anything.' He went to the charcoal stove to examine the black saucepan of rice from which steam was gently rising. The ancestors on the walls looked on.

'Not even me?'

'Of you I am proud. And Rosana.' He smiled at their daughter.

Rosana said, 'When is the war going to finish, papa?' and Jesús told her, 'Soon, when the bad men have been driven away from our town.'

'By whom?' Ana asked, feeling herself driven by a terrible perversity.

'By our soldiers,' Jesús said.

Rosana said, 'Why don't you fight, papa?'

'Some people are born to be soldiers. Others . . .'

'Housekeepers,' Ana said.

'Or poets,' he said. 'Or painters or mechanics. Mechanics have to repair the tanks and the guns; they cannot fight.' He smiled but there was a sad curve to his lips.

Rosana cracked a husk between her front teeth and said, 'The father of Marta Sanchez was wounded in the stomach. He can't eat any more because there's a big hole there.'

Her hair was curly like her father's and her teeth were neat but already she is obstinate, like me, Ana thought. She wants many things and she uses guile to get them; she will be a handful, this one.

'Why are Fascists different from us?' Rosana asked and Jesús said, 'I sometimes wonder if they are.'

The ground shook as bombs exploded. Yesterday Pablo had come back with a jagged sliver of shrapnel so hot that it had burned his hand.

Ana said, 'Because they are greedy.'

'And cruel?' Rosana asked.

'But they are Spaniards,' Jesús said. 'Born in different circumstances.'

'You called them bad men just now,' Rosana said.

'Ah, you are truly your mother's daughter.' He stirred the rice adding fish broth.

And Ana thought: I should be doing that and he should be peering down the sights of a machine-gun, but since the war had begun the role of many women had changed, as though it had never been intended any other way, as though there had always been a resilience in those women that had never been recognized. And respect for women had been discovered to such an extent that, so it was said, men and women slept together at the front without sex.

She heard the sound of a plane strumming the sky; the Ju-52, perhaps, returning from its nonchalant mission. She hoped the Russian-built rats fell upon it before it landed. She wondered about the pilot and bomb-aimer, Germans presumably. She wondered about the pilots of the Capronis, Italians. Did any of them understand the war and had they even heard of the small towns they bombed? She thought the most ironic aspect of the war was the presence of the Moors: it had taken the Christians 700 years to get rid of them and here they were fighting for the Church.

Ana took the *bota* from beside the sink and poured resinous wine down her throat; it made a channel through her worries. Rosana picked up her skipping-rope and went into the yard.

Jesús settled his thin body in an upright chair beside Ana, took the *bota*, wetted his throat and said, 'Why are brothers killing brothers, Ana. Can you tell me that?'

'Because it has to be,' she said. 'Because they were bleeding us.'

'Could we not have used words instead of bullets?'

'Spaniards have always fought.' Her voice lost some of its roughness and her words became smooth pebbles in her mouth. 'But perhaps our time has come. Perhaps this war was born a long time ago and has to be settled. Perhaps we will not fight again,' she said.

'But we will always talk,' he said, smiling at her as he had once smiled in the Plaza Mayor as she drank iced coffee through a straw and thought what a wise young man he was. 'I like you when you're thoughtful,' he said.

'Is that so rare?' She drank more wine, one of those sour wines that get sweeter by the mouthful. She passed the *bota* to Jesus. 'When will the rice be ready?' she asked.

'Afterwards,' he said.

'After what?'

He bolted the door and took the combs from her hair so that it fell dark and shining across her shoulders.

The bomb had been a small one. It had removed her old home from the row of hunched houses as neatly as a dentist extracts a tooth but had scarcely damaged its neighbours, although some balconies hung precariously from their walls. Light rain was falling and the meagre possessions of her father and her grandmother were scattered across the wet mud on the street: commode, sewing basket, cotton tangled in festive patterns, rocking chair moving in the breeze as though it were occupied, Bible opened in prayer, brass bedstead on which her father had waited for death.

The bodies were laid on stretchers. She lifted the sheets from each and gazed upon the faces. Her father and grandmother, ages merging in death, Salvador now blind in both eyes, all anger spent. She did not look at their wounds, only their faces. Neighbours watched her calmly: these days death was a companion, not an intruder.

Only one occupant of the house had been saved, the priest. Blast from bombs is as fickle as it is ferocious and it had bundled him on to the street, plumply alive beneath his shredded clothes. The priest who was due to report to Lance at the British Embassy that evening said to Ana, 'It was a merciful release for your father.' She walked over to the brass bedstead. 'I prayed for their souls,' he said. She covered the bed with a sheet because it was indecent to leave it exposed.

She said: 'Why don't you go out and fight like a man?'

Jesús, glancing up from an exercise book in which he was writing a poem, looked bewildered.

So did the children, Rosana crayoning planes laying bombs like eggs, Pablo who, at the age of eight, already looked like his father, arranging his shrapnel and his brass cartridge cases and his strip of camouflage said to have been ripped from a Ju-52 by the guns of a rat.

'A little while ago . . .'

'I don't care about a little while ago. A little while ago was a long time ago. The priest was saved,' she said. 'Why the priest?'

'I don't understand.'

She told him.

'Ana, the children.'

'They have to know.'

Pablo stared hard at the piece of shrapnel lying in the palm of his hand.

'Why the priest?' she asked again.

'I don't know,' he replied, pointing at the children and shaking his head.

'I don't expect you to. What would you know about living and dying? It's written in blood, not ink.'

Jesús said to the children, 'Why don't you go out and play?'

They began to gather up their possessions.

In the distance Ana could hear gunfire, the firework splutter of rifles, the chatter of machine-guns and the bark of heavy artillery.

'This morning,' she said, 'I saw a peasant, a refugee, lie like Coll in front of a tank. The treads rolled over him, crushing him, but the tank blew up.'

'You want me to get killed. Is that it?'

'I want your children to be proud of you.'

The children remained absorbed with clearing up but Pablo's bottom lip trembled.

Jesús stood up, knocking the bottle of ink over the scrubbed table. He fetched a newspaper and soaked it up. His fingers were stained blue. The children were silent, following him with their eyes. He walked to the door.

'I hope the bottle of anis is full in the bar,' Ana said.

He stood silhouetted against the fading, rain-swept afternoon light. He looked very thin – he didn't eat as much as the children and, although he was only 32, he stooped a little, but still she let him go.

When she went to bed he had not returned.

In the morning she left the children with a neighbour and marched to the front with a platoon of women militia. They were dressed in blue, and they carried rifles on their shoulders and food for the men. They went first to University City, the model campus and suburb to the north-west of Madrid, near Tetuan, where Fascists who had crossed the Manzanares were fighting hand-to-hand with the militia and the International Brigades. They fought for faculties, libraries, laboratories, rooms. The walls of half-finished buildings swayed; the air smelled of cordite, brick-dust and distemper, and rang with foreign tongues. The Moors bayoneted the wounded; the Germans placed bombs in elevators and sent them up to explode among the Moors.

Ana shot a Moor wearing a kerchief as he raised his bayonet above a German from the Thaelmann Battalion of the 11th International Brigade who was bleeding from a chest wound. It was the first time she had killed. She took provisions to the British defending the Hall of Philosophy and Letters against the Fascists who had already taken the Institute of Hygiene and Cancer and the Santa Cristina and Clinical hospitals. Someone told her there was an English poet named Cornford among the machine-gunners. A poet!

She went about her duties coldly. She no longer thought about young men who knew nothing about each other killing each other. She thought instead about her grandmother and her father and her one-eyed brother who were dead, and she thought about the priest who was alive.

With the other women she descended the heights to a bridge across the Manzanares which the Fascists hadn't crossed. The Moors were grouped at the other side, Foreign Legionnaires with red tassels on their grey-green *gorillo* caps behind them. Assault guards and militiamen held the east neck of the bridge, another inlet to the city. The guards were armed with grenades and rifles and one of them was firing a Lewis machine-gun. When Ana and her platoon arrived the dark-skinned Moors in ragged uniforms were advancing across the bridge while the militiamen fitted another magazine on to the Lewis gun. Ana knelt behind them, aimed her rifle, a Swiss antique made in 1886, and squeezed the trigger; the rifle bucked, a Moor fell but she couldn't tell whether it was her bullet that had hit him because the other militiamen were firing, although without precision and she was dubious about the resolution of these exhausted defenders who had never wanted to be soldiers. There was no doubt about the resolution of the Moors trained by the Spaniards to fight bandits in Morocco: they ignored the bullets and stepped over the dead and wounded.

For some reason the magazine wouldn't fit on the Lewis

gun; it was probably a magazine for another gun; such things were not unknown. The assault guards and militiamen shuffled backwards. The Moors moved forward firing their rifles. A militiaman in front of Ana threw up his arms and fell backwards.

Ana shouted to the women, 'Keep firing!' But the militiamen were turning, running towards the women, blocking their view of the Moors. Ana stood up, aimed the ancient Swiss rifle at the militiamen and fired it above their heads. 'Sons of whores!' she shouted at these men who had been bakers and housepainters and garbage collectors. 'Turn back!'

They hesitated.

'*Mierda!*' shouted Ana who never swore. 'Have you no *cojones*?'

She reloaded quickly and fired between them. A Moroccan fell. And the militiamen turned away from these women who were more frightening than the Moors and the machine-gunners, fitted the magazine to the Lewis gun, and, planting it firmly on the road surface, aimed it at the Moors who were almost upon them.

Chop-chop went the gun, piling up bodies that were soon too high and disorderly for the back-up Moors to navigate. Instead they retreated. The militiamen sent them on their way with a hail of bullets. Then they looked shamefacedly at Ana.

She looked across the modest river and thought: they knocked out one of Salvador's eyes with a club then they removed the sight of the other with a bomb dropped as casually as boys drop stones over bridges. Couldn't they have left my father to die in his own time?

She said, 'Fix the next magazine.' They nodded. Then she led her women back to their *barrio* in Tetuan. Jesús was standing in the yard.

He had acquired a *gorillo* cap and a bandolier which he wore over a blue shirt she had never seen before. Slung over his shoulder was a rifle. The children, hands tight fisted, observed him wonderingly.

She smiled at him. She felt as happy to see him there as she had in the days when her whole day had been taken up with waiting to meet him.

'What game is this?' she asked.

He looked a little ridiculous. He hadn't found a jaunty angle for his cap; his ears were bigger than she remembered beneath it; the ink was still blue on his fingertips.

'The game you told me to play,' he said. 'Has it ever occurred to you that if we were all cowards there would be no wars?'

He straightened the stoop in his back and, so thin that she wanted to stretch out a hand and feel the muscles moving over his ribs, walked past her towards the killing.

CHAPTER 3

February 1937.

Chimo, philosopher, legionnaire and murderer, said, 'What are you thinking about, Amado?'

Adam Fleming, sheltering in a slit trench from rain and bullets, said, 'England.'

'More than that, Amado – you sighed.' Chimo was an authority on untruths and half-truths because they came readily to his own lips.

'Why do you call me Amado? My name is Adam. Why not Adamo?'

'You are Amado. That is you. Were you perhaps thinking about a woman?' Chimo was an authority on women, too.

'I was thinking about my sister.'

This troubled Chimo. He massaged his jagged teeth with one finger and the red tassel on his *gorillo* cap trembled with his anxiety. Finally, he said, 'But you sighed.'

'My sister is in Madrid . . .'

'She isn't a red?' Chimo, brushing raindrops from his abundant moustache, looked apprehensively at Adam through monkey-brown eyes.

'No, Chimo, she is not a red.'

'Then to be in Madrid is bad. Very bad. They are starving there. And if we cut the road to Valencia on the other side of the Jarama river then hunger will make them surrender and there will be a great killing.'

'Were you there when we attacked Madrid?' Adam asked. He had arrived in Spain last November but he had been too late to take part in the attack which Franco had called off on the 23rd, laying siege to the city instead.

'I was there,' Chimo said. 'They fought like devils, the reds. Particularly the women. Ah, those women, fiercer than the Moors. Those Madrileños, those cats . . . You have to admire them. Abandoned by their Government who ran off to Valencia, fighting with 50-year-old Swiss rifles, antique weapons taken from the museums . . . But they were good in the streets, those cats, not like our Moors who are good in open spaces, in deserts . . .'

'I heard there was a lot of killing in the city before we attacked.'

'I heard that, too. Mola and his Fifth Column! Obvious, wasn't it, that the reds would seek them out and kill them. I hear they took a thousand from the Model Prison and shot them a few miles from Barajas airport. Killing has become a pastime in Spain,' Chimo said.

'I hear that Franco could have taken Madrid if he hadn't decided to relieve Moscardó, at Toledo. I hear,' Adam said carefully, 'that Franco doesn't want to win the war too quickly. He doesn't want to rule a people who are still full of spirit.'

'You will hear many things,' Chimo told him. 'Every Spaniard is a politician.'

A shell fired from the Republican lines on the far bank of the Jarama, south of Madrid, slurred through the rain digging a crater 50 metres in front of the trench and showering their grey-green campaign tunics with mud.

'Sons of whores,' Chimo said. 'Red pigs. That was the first. The second lands behind us. The third . . .'

'I know about range-finding,' Adam said. He had acquitted himself reasonably well in the cadet corps at Epsom College at everything except rolling puttees round his calves.

'. . . lands here. With our name on it.'

Rain bounced on the lip of the trench and fell soggily onto the brown blankets covering their guns; Adam wondered if it would drown the lice; he doubted it – they were survivors.

Chimo said, 'Tell me, Amado, what are you, an Englishman, doing in this trench waiting for the third shell?'

'What are you doing, Chimo?'

'I am a *legionario*.'

'What are you fighting for, peace?'

'Peace?' The tassel on his cap quivered. 'Peace is the enemy of the soldier.'

'How old are you, Chimo?'

'Nearly 27.'

'A veteran!'

'And you, *inglés?*'

'Twenty-one,' Adam said. A confession.

'And what are *you* fighting for?'

'Ideals,' Adam said, silencing Chimo who was an authority on many things but a stranger to ideals.

Ideals, too, were self-effacing at Epsom College unless, that is, they were represented by the gods of sport, although there were outposts in that mellow-bricked academy where learning ran a close second to rugby and cricket.

Adam was sent to Epsom, close to the race-track, the home of the Derby, because his mother wished him to be a doctor and the college was renowned for its contributions to medicine.

It was at Epsom that Adam first became aware that his character was seamed with perversity. What he objected to, he subsequently decided, was the attempt to inscribe privilege on pubescent souls. To achieve this many enlightened disciplines were invoked. Games were compulsory unless a medical certificate was produced; such a document was viewed as evidence of weakness and its possessor was consigned to the company of other failures. Crimes were punished by headmaster or housemaster with a cane; misdemeanours by prefects with a slipper and they never shirked their responsibilities. Meals were passed from seniors to juniors along tables the length of the hall, any remotely digestible morsels being removed *en route* so that the smallest diners were given incentive to rise through the ranks to the heights where the food, although still largely indigestible, was at least warm. A chaplain boomed prayers at 8.40 every morning; modest homosexual practices were not severely discouraged because they were a natural adjunct of puberty and a necessary preparation for the rigours of heterosexual intercourse that lay ahead.

Adam invoked the wrath of both masters and boys not because he was one of the runts of the herd but because he seemed constructed to become one of its leaders. He wasn't tall but his muscles were long and sinuously sheathed, his expression was secretive, and his hair was black and careless and widow-peaked.

So what did he do? He refused to shove in the scrum; he played tennis, a highly suspect sport; he smoked State Express 555 in a hollow on Epsom Downs while the rest of the house made panting cross-country runs around the frost-sparkling racecourse; and, unforgivably, he read. Inevitably such transgressions brought about retribution. But again he broke the character-moulding rules that decreed that you endured cane or slipper with stoicism: he howled and yelled until the punishment was curtailed; then he rose, dry-eyed, and grinned at his tormentor.

At the end of his first year he told his mother that he had no intention of becoming a doctor. And God help the ailing population of Great Britain, he added, if any of his fellow inmates ever got a scalpel in their hands. His father, home from the City that evening and smelling slightly of whisky, was summoned but, as always, he kept his distance from family crises, regarding children as a necessary by-product of marriage. His mother accused Adam of being ungrateful but soon became accustomed to the prospect of having a barrister in the family and was heard to confide at a garden party, 'Who knows, he may become Attorney General one day.'

Towards the end of his last year, before going to Cambridge, Adam, who had no intention of becoming a lawyer, seriously endangered his reputation: he accidentally revealed that, despite his consumption of State Express, he could run and so swift was he that he was entered for the mile in the public school championships. Canings and slipperings ceased; he was extracted from the scrum and encouraged to play tennis; he was served lean meat and fresh vegetables; a maths master who reported seeing him leave the Capitol cinema in Epsom with a shopgirl was taken on one side and rebuked for voyeurism.

For Adam the mile was a triumph: he came last.

'Where did you learn your Spanish?' Chimo asked.

'At Cambridge,' Adam replied.

A rat peered over the lip of the trench. One of their own machine-guns opened up behind them. A Gatling replied; he wished the trenches were deeper but the legionnaires and Moors were used to scooping the sand of North Africa.

'Cambridge, where is that?'

'In England,' Adam told him. 'In East Anglia. It has a bridge over a river called the Cam. There are many colleges there. One of them, Trinity, was founded, refounded rather, by Henry VIII. Have you heard of him?'

'He had many wives,' Chimo said. 'He must have been a stupid king.'

'He chopped some of their heads off.'

'Not so stupid,' Chimo said. 'At Cambridge they taught you to speak with a city voice.'

'The purest in Spain. Castilian.'

'Tell that to a Basque; tell that to a Catalan,' said Chimo who spoke with a broad Andaluz accent.

The rain seeped through the blanket on to Adam's rifle, a 7 mm Spanish Mauser. He turned his head and noticed minerals, quartz probably, shining wetly in the hills.

'Catalan,' Adam said. 'Basque. Communist, Anarchist, Trotskyist . . . That's our strength, their confusion.'

'Did you know I can't read or write, Amado?'

'Does it matter? You talk enough for ten men.'

'All Spaniards talk a lot. Ask a Spaniard a question and he delivers a speech.'

A spent bullet skittered across the mud throwing up wings of spray. Chimo said, 'Tell me something, Amado, are you scared?'

'I would be a fool not to be.'

'You are a fool to be here at all: it is not your war.'

'I sometimes wonder whose war it is.'

'Clever words from one of your books?' Adam had with

him behind the lines Robert Graves's *Goodbye to All That*, the French edition of *Ulysses*, Hemingway's *A Farewell to Arms*, and an anti-war book, *Cry Havoc!* by a newspaper columnist, Beverly Nichols.

'Nothing clever. But if it had been left to the Spanish it might have been over by now.'

'Who would have won?' Chimo asked.

'Without German and Italian planes our side wouldn't have been able to land troops in Spain. Without Russian "advisers", without their tanks and planes, the Republicans would have been driven into the sea. Perhaps it is their war, Hitler's and Mussolini's and Stalin's.'

'And Britain's? You are here, *inglés*.'

'Most of my countrymen are on the other side.' Adam jerked his head towards the enemy lines across the small, thickly curved river. 'With the Americans and French and Poles . . .'

'And Germans and Italians. It isn't just Spaniards who are fighting each other.' Chimo combed his extravagant moustache with muddy fingers. 'Why are you fighting on our side, Amado? And don't confuse me with ideals.'

'Because I was looking for something to believe in,' Adam said.

A second shell exploded behind them throwing up gouts of sparkling rock.

'The third one,' Chimo said, 'is ours.'

Four of them at the dinner table to celebrate the 60th birthday of William Stoppard, Professor of Economics at Oxford. Kate, his daughter, 18 and already bored; Richard Hibbert, at Trinity, Cambridge, who would have joined the International Brigade if he hadn't been a pacifist; and Adam. Subject: non-intervention.

'It is, of course, quite disgraceful,' said Stoppard, his pointed pepper-and-salt beard agreeing with him.

'Why?' Adam asked in the pause before dessert. Two of the leaded windows in the rambling house near Lambourn were open and evening smells, chestnut and horses, reached him making him restless.

'Why?' The beard seemed suspended in disbelief. Kate, blonde with neat features, hair arranged in frozen waves, stared at him. She took a De Reszke from a slim gold case and lit it.

'I hope no one minds,' she said.

'As a matter of fact, I do,' Adam said.

'Too bad.' She blew a jet of smoke across the table at him.

'Perhaps,' Stoppard said, 'you could explain yourself, young man.'

'I'm questioning your assumption, sir,' said Adam who had drunk three whiskies before dinner. 'Am I to assume that you are referring to the possibility of intervention on the side of the Republicans?'

Was there any other kind? the silence asked.

Hibbert, who was in love with Kate Stoppard, said, 'You must have read about the atrocities perpetrated by the Fascists at Badajoz.' He turned his heavy and wrathful face to Stoppard for approval; Stoppard's beard nodded.

Adam poured himself wine and said, 'You must have read about the atrocities perpetrated by the Republicans at Madrid.'

Kate squashed her half-smoked cigarette – she didn't look as though she had enjoyed it anyway – and considered him, neat head to one side. The flames of the candles on the table wavered in a breeze summoned from the darkness outside.

Stoppard began to lecture.

'The Fascists are the insurgents. Their ostensible object: to overthrow by force the Government of the Republic elected by popular franchise. Their ulterior motive: to re-establish the privileges they enjoyed under the monarchy – in effect the dictatorship of Primo de Rivera – which were the exploitation of the poor.'

Adam said, 'With respect, sir, if you believe that you'll believe anything.' As the second silence of the evening lengthened he said to Kate, 'That's what Wellington said when some idiot said to him, "Mr Jones, I believe?" I'm a great admirer of Arthur Wellesley.'

Stoppard said, 'Perhaps, Adam, you would be good enough to elaborate on that last statement and enlighten us.'

A timorous girl in a black and white uniform served dessert, lemon soufflé.

'Certainly,' said Adam. 'Do you believe in God, sir?'

'Get on with it, man,' Hibbert said excavating fiercely with his spoon in the soufflé.

'I ask because I cannot understand how you can support a regime that condones the destruction of churches and the murder of priests.'

'Ah, the Irresponsibles; I thought we'd come to them,' Stoppard remarked indulgently. He tasted his soufflé; his beard approved.

'From February to June this year,' Adam said, concentrating, '160 churches were burned. There were also 269 assassinations, 113 general strikes and 228 half-cocked ones. Spain was in a state of anarchy, so is it small wonder that generals such as Mola, Queipo de Llano and Franco and the rest decided to bring back stability?'

'Did you do your homework on the way?' Stoppard asked. He winked at Hibbert.

'As a matter of fact I did. It was inevitable that you would talk about non-intervention. But there's nothing to stop anyone intervening. Not even you, sir.'

Hibbert said irrelevantly, 'John Cornford's fighting with the International Brigades. And Sommerfield. And Esmond Romilly, Churchill's nephew.'

'A pity they're fighting on the wrong side.'

'Are you a Fascist, Adam? A blackshirt?' Hibbert asked.

'What I am,' Adam said, watching Kate lick lemon soufflé from her upper lip and wondering about her breasts beneath her silk dress, 'is anti-Communist. We all know what's happened in Russia – a worse tyranny than before. Do we want that in Spain?'

Stoppard laid down his spoon and addressed his class. What we were witnessing in Spain, he told them, was an exercise in European Fascism. Hitler wanted to assist Spain so that he could establish bases there for the next war and help himself to the country's iron ore. Mussolini was helping because he wanted to control the Mediterranean. And both wanted to test their planes, their guns and their tanks. If they, the enemies of the future, were championing the Fascists, why should not Britain aid the Republicans?

Adam, who had learned at Cambridge never to answer a question directly, said, 'What is so different between Fascism and Communism?'

The third silence of the evening. Kate took a cigarette from her case and tapped it on one painted fingernail.

Adam said, 'Is Hitler a dictator?'

Of course.

'And Stalin?'

So it appeared.

'Are they not both anti-Semitic?'

Perhaps.

'Enemies, imagined or otherwise, purged?'

There were similarities.

'Both presiding over elitist societies in which the masses are subservient?'

'That's certainly true in Germany,' Hibbert said.

'And Russia. Ask any peasant.'

'I haven't met any recently,' Stoppard said but no one in the class smiled.

The maid served coffee; Stoppard lit a cigar. 'Adam,' he said, almost fondly, 'suggested just now that there was nothing to stop anyone intervening. On either side, you implied. Is that correct?'

'Quite correct, sir.'

'Then why, Adam, don't you volunteer to fight for the Fascists?'

'I might just do that,' Adam said.

Chimo said, 'Have you had many women, Amado?'

'Not many,' said Adam, who had made love to three girls.

'I have had many, many girls.'

'I'm sure they all remember you.'

'Oh sure, they remember Chimo. And I remember one of them. You know, she gave me a present.' He pointed to his crotch.

'You don't have to go with whores: you're too much of a man.'

'You don't know girls. How can you fuck them with a chaperone sitting on your knee?'

'Fuck the chaperone,' said Adam, old soldier with three months service behind him.

Kate took Adam to her father's cottage in the Cotswolds for a long weekend – without her father's consent – five days after the dinner party at Lambourn.

They walked through countryside where stems of smoke rose steadily from hollows in the hills and horse chestnuts lay shiny in their split, hedgehog shells and boys with concertina socks kicked flocks of fallen leaves; they drank beer that tasted of nuts in small pubs; they danced to Lew Stone records; they made love on a bed that smelled of lavender.

But throughout the interlude Adam was aware of disquiet. It visited him as he watched the sun rise mistily through the branches of a moulting apple tree, or while he felt pastoral loneliness settle in the evenings; it materialized in the wasting happiness after they had made love.

At first he blamed it on the challenge he had accepted at Lambourn: it wasn't every young man who was going to fight for the Fascists. That, surely, was enough to disturb the most swashbuckling of crusaders.

But it wasn't until the afternoon of the Sunday, when she lay in bed with her back curved into his chest and his hands were cupped round her small breasts and he was examining the freckles on her back just below the nape of her neck, where her short, golden hair was still damp from exertion, that he realized the other cause for his disquiet.

'Don't think,' she said, turning towards him, 'that you have to go and fight because of me.' Well, he didn't; but suddenly he understood that she was only there beside him because he was prepared to risk death – a refreshing change from conventional young men with normal life expectations.

And, as he considered this premise, it came to him that maybe his motives were suspect. Did he really believe in the Fascist cause or was it wilfulness asserting itself? Surely ideals were the essence of purity. How was it, then, that both he and the other Englishmen fighting on opposite sides could both possess them? Can I be wrong? he asked himself.

She said, 'What are you thinking about, Adam?' and he said, 'This and that.'

'You were in another place.' She reached for his hand and placed it on the soft hair between her thighs, and he forgot his disquiet.

Later, walking through silent woods, she held his hand. How long would the war last? she asked him. Not long, he told her: Franco was at the gates of Madrid.

'Months?'

'Weeks.'

'Everything has been so quick,' she said. 'We only met a few days ago . . .'

'What would your father say if he knew what we'd done in his cottage?'

'Cut us off without a penny,' Kate said promptly.

Us?

They sat on a log and she took a cigarette from her case, lit it and blew puffs of smoke through narrowed lips as though she found them distasteful. Ruffled pigeons settled above them.

'I'll always remember how you stood up for yourself at dinner that evening,' she said.

'They were debating in formulas. Mathematics aren't always right.'

'I hope you don't think that just because . . .'

'You're cheap?'

'Do they all say that?'

'I wouldn't know,' Adam said.

'How many?'

'None of your bloody business,' Adam said.

'You don't think I'm trying to trap you?'

'By having a baby?'

'I won't,' she said.

'Did you bring me to the cottage because I'm going to war?'

'Because you're coming back from it.'

He put his arm round her waist under her coat. He could

feel the fragile sharpness of her bones, the flatness of her stomach. He felt that he was expected to utter words of deep moment but they were elusive.

He stood up. She tossed aside her cigarette and he stamped on it, pulverizing it with the heel of his shoe. He turned her and pointed her towards the cottage. When they got back he lit a fire with pine cones and they watched the sparks chase each other up the chimney. He knew that she was waiting for the words that lay trapped in his throat so he switched off the lights and they lay down beside each other and he stared into the caverns of the fires in search of answers and justifications.

The justification was brought to Adam on a silver salver on 6 October, two days before the Michaelmas term was due to begin. He was sitting in the garden of his parents' house in East Grinstead reading a newspaper summary of recent developments in Spain. Summer hadn't quite abdicated, sunlight shining through smoke lit chrysanthemums and persistent roses, and a biplane traversed the pale sky towing a banner advertising the *News Chronicle*.

Adam read that General Francisco Franco had been appointed Commander-in-Chief of the Nationalist army *and* Head of State and that the Republicans had created a Popular Army. The Fascists seemed to be on the rampage – in September they had captured Irún, San Sebastian and Toledo – and if he didn't act soon it would be too late.

But was wilfulness enough? Do I want to be a soldier of fortune, champion of my own ego? He flung down the newspaper and paced the lawns. He was near the pond where frogs plopped in the summer when the maid found him and handed him the letter on the salver as though it were something to eat.

The envelope, which bore a new Edward VIII stamp, had been posted in London the previous day but the writing was his sister's and she was in Madrid. Fear stirred and he held the envelope for a few moments without opening it.

The letter was dated 16 August, so it must have been smuggled out of Spain – via Marseille, perhaps, on one of the British warships evacuating refugees – and posted in London.

Dear Adam,

Paco is dead. He was taken from our apartment two nights ago and driven to a village called Paracuellos del Jarama where, with two dozen other suspects, he was executed. They were forced to dig a mass grave, then machine-gunned and finished off with bullets in the backs of their necks.

I say suspects. Suspected of what I have no idea. Certainly Paco had no interests in politics, just his job and his home and his children – and me. But he was a good Catholic and an architect and relatively well off, so I suppose that was sufficient reason. Or maybe a private quarrel across the drawing board was settled in the name of the Republic; many old scores are being settled that way. All I know is that I am lost. I hear the children and I hear the maid (she is more scared than any of us) and I hear the shooting and I suppose I eat and sleep. It is supposed to be dangerous to walk in the streets but so far the Irresponsibles, as they call them, have not killed a foreign woman. Not that I care, although I should because of the children.

A part of me also knows that I must not leave Spain. For Paco's sake, for the children's sake because they are Spanish. I am writing to you because we always shared and father never much cared for Paco, did he? Well, tell him the dago is dead. He was a good man, Adam . . .

The back-sloping letters lengthened, died. The letter was signed Eve. Her name was Julia but with Adam it had always been Eve.

Adam, letter in hand, heard the plop of stones thrown by her two boys into the pond; saw the ripple of the water beneath the duckweed. They had been happy that day, Adam and Eve, sharing Eve's family, sharing a day that smelled of daffodils and hope, even sharing the hostility of their father which, now that there were children, was more a family joke than a threat.

Ah, Paco of the healthy skin and glossy hair and provident disposition who believed that Spain would be a land of opportunity as soon as the Republic had settled . . . poor, naïve Paco who was forced to dig his own grave out of the land in which he believed.

Adam threw a pebble into the pond and watched the green ripples until they lapped the bank, then strode rapidly away.

Five days later he was in the solemn city of Burgos in the north of Spain.

The third shell duly arrived in the slit trench. It came with the sound of a wave unfurling and, with an impact that shook the trench, buried itself in the mud and soft rock, resting lethally five yards from Adam.

'Shit,' said Chimo, 'we'd better get out of here.'

'It's a dud,' Adam said. It was not unknown for Spanish munition workers who didn't want to kill other Spaniards to immobilize ammunition.

'There are duds and duds. Maybe this has got a delayed fuse.'

'Why would it have that?'

'So that we all think it's a nice shiny shell. We even go up and pat it. Then, whoosh, it blows us over the countryside. That's the reds for you, those sons of whores . . .'

The legionnaire next to Chimo said, 'Those bastards . . . We came here to fight, not wait until we're blown into little pieces by one sleeping shell.'

He climbed out of the trench and made a crouching run for the concrete bunker at the base of the flat-topped hills. The others followed. Adam, taking a last look at the shell half-buried in the mud, went last. It was his misfortune that he was a good runner.

Keeping low, he passed empty trenches, a ruined farmhouse with a stork's nest on the roof, a shrike perched on a telegraph wire, shell-holes, sage and brush and leafless fig trees . . . To his left he saw the curves of the river and the rulered line of Jarama canal.

Bullets fired from across the river sang past him. But what he feared was heavy artillery or a strafing run by one of the German fighters now occupying luminous pools in the clouds.

He reached the bunker first. And found that the colonel in charge of the *bandera*, the battalion, was waiting for him. His name was Delgado, a native of Seville, and, modelling himself on General Queipo de Llano, who broadcast bloodthirsty threats to the Republicans on the radio, bore himself with exaggerated stiffness and wore his small moustache as though it were a medal; he disliked all foreigners, whether they were fighting for the Republicans or the Fascists.

He said to Adam, 'I must be losing my hearing – I didn't hear any order to retreat.'

Adam drew himself to attention. 'We're not retreating . . .'

'We?'

Adam looked behind him, spotted the last of the legionnaires who had followed him disappearing into a trench.

'I am not retreating. I've come to report an unexploded shell.'

'It's my experience that unexploded shells report themselves.'

'In our trench. If it had gone off it would have killed the lot of us.'

'Who gave the orders to abandon the trench?'

'No one, sir.'

'But you got out first?' Delgado slapped his cane against a polished boot. He looked as though he had just shaved and showered.

'I run faster,' Adam said.

'Are you implying that the rest of the men ran away too?'

'I did not run away.'

'You could hardly say you were attacking. What if other members of the company had followed your example?'

Adam didn't reply: they hadn't.

'Name?'

'Fleming, sir.'

'Ah, Fleming,' tapping his boot with his cane. 'Why do you want to fight for us, Fleming? Most of your countrymen are fighting for the reds.'

'Because I'm anti-Communist.'

'Not pro-Nationalist?'

'If I am one then surely I am the other.'

'You're beginning to talk like a diplomat.' Delgado took a step forward. 'What makes you think you can help us?'

'I can fire a rifle.'

'Where? At a fiesta, a fairground?'

Adam told him that in the cadet corps he had been a crack shot; no mention of the puttees.

'Did they teach you to run away in this cadet corps of yours?'

'I learned how to run at college.'

'In the wrong direction?'

A young captain loomed behind Delgado. Adam shrugged.

Delgado said, 'I believe this to be a Spaniard's war. I don't believe foreigners should interfere.'

Adam thought: 'What about the Moors?' but he said nothing.

'Odd that you should have chosen this time to retreat. We were going to attack in one hour from now. I should have you shot.'

'I came to warn you about the shell.'

'I don't believe in that shell. How old are you, Fleming?'

Adam told him he was 21.

'I had a son of 20. He's dead.'

'I'm sorry,' Adam said.

'He was shot in the lungs and in the stomach. He died in great pain.'

Adam remained silent.

'Do you know who shot him?'

'The reds . . . Anarchists, Communists, Trotskyists . . .'

'He was shot at Badajoz by the Legion. He was fighting for the reds.'

The rain had stopped and there were patches of blue in the sky and despite the sporadic gunfire, a bird was singing on the telegraph wire. Inside the bunker a radio crackled.

Delgado turned to the captain. 'Escort this man to his trench,' he said. 'I want to hear more about this non-exploding shell.'

The captain put on his cap and drew his pistol.

'That's not necessary,' Adam said but the captain who was young and glossy, like Paco had been, prodded the barrel of the pistol, a Luger, in the direction of the trench.

'How old are you sir?' Adam asked the captain.

'May God be with you if there isn't any shell,' the captain said.

A sparrow-hawk hovered above them.

They were ten yards from the trench when the shell blew.

The attack was delayed until dawn the following day. Then, supported by a barrage from their batteries of 155 mm artillery and a baptismal blast from the Condor Legion's 88 mm guns, they moved, legionnaires and Moors, across the wet, blasted earth where, in the summer, corn had rippled, towards the river separating them from the enemy.

Some time during the fighting, when the barrel of his rifle was hot and there was blood on the bayonet and his ears ached with gunfire and his skull was full of battle, he vaguely noticed a plane drop from the sky, gently like a broken bird; he thought it levelled out but he couldn't be sure because by then he was busy killing again.

CHAPTER 4

The smell was pungent, sickly and familiar. Tom Canfield's nostrils twitched; he opened his eyes. After a few moments he had it: locust beans. One of the maid's sons had brought some to the house on Long Island one day and they had chewed them together. His eyes focused on a dark corner of wherever he was and saw a mound of them, pods sweetly putrefying.

In front of the beans lay the broken propeller of an aeroplane. He tried to touch it but his arm was cold and heavy. He flexed his fingers; they moved well enough but there was blood between them. He lay still concentrating, then blinked slowly and deliberately. Part of the fuselage was above him, radial engine bared. So he had been flung out of the cockpit. He tested his other arm. It moved freely. So did his legs, but his chest hurt and the pain was worse when he breathed deeply.

He sat up. Easy. Except that his right arm didn't belong to him. He could pick it up with his left hand as though it were a piece of baggage. Blood dripped from his fingers. He looked for the wound and found it near the elbow. His thumb felt bone.

He stood up and, supporting himself against the walls, made an inspection of the farmhouse. It was a poor place with thin dividing walls painted with blue wash. Sagging beds were covered with straw palliasses, a jug of sour-smelling wine stood on a cane table.

The strength left his legs and he sat on a crippled chair. Where was he? Behind Fascist lines, behind the Republicans, in no-man's-land? He heard gunfire and the venomous explosions of fragmentation hand-grenades; but he couldn't tell how far away they were.

What he needed was a drink and a bandage to stop the blood seeping from the hole in his arm. He went to the kitchen and opened a cupboard painted with crusted varnish and found a half-full bottle of Magno brandy. He poured some down his throat. It burned like acid but the power returned to his legs. He ripped down a chequered curtain and tore off a strip; he eased his wounded arm from his flying jacket and bound the wound, knotting the cloth with his teeth and the fingers of his good hand.

He looked out of the window. The ground mist had returned, so it was late afternoon. Gunfire flashed in the mist.

Despite his wound he was hungry. He returned to the store-room and chewed a couple of locust pods; they made him feel sick.

He patted the fuselage of the Polikarpov. It was still warm.

He sat down and tried to visualize the battlefield as he had seen it from the air. The hills that glittered in the sun to the west, empty cornfields, vineyards, then the canal and the river and the Pindoque bridge which carried trains loaded with sugar from La Poupa factory to the railway to Andalucia. On the opposite side of the river the heights of Pingarrón where the Republicans were entrenched. But he still could not envisage where he was.

When evening had pinned the first star in the sky he opened the door and made his way towards the voice of the river.

The rabbit, one ear folded, stared at them from its hutch in the yard. It was a big problem, this rabbit. It was a pet and it was dinner. No, more – dinner, lunch and soup for supper the next day.

The rabbit, grey and soft, twitched its whiskers at Ana and the children.

'I think he's hungry,' said Pablo, thereby encapsulating the rabbit's two main faults – it was masculine and it was always hungry. What was the point in keeping a buck rabbit which could not give birth to other rabbits? What was the point of wasting food on an animal which was itself sustenance? Was there really any sense, Ana asked herself, in wasting cabbage stalks and potato peelings on a rabbit when her children were threatened by scabies and rickets?

But despite its appetite, despite its masculinity, this rabbit possessed two trump cards: it was part of the family, thumping its hind legs when the air-raid siren wailed and flattening its ears when bombs exploded, and it was available for stud to the owners of doe rabbits who would exchange a sliver of soap or a cupful of split peas for his services.

Ana regarded the rabbit with exasperation. Jesús would have known what to do.

But Jesús was at Jarama fighting the Fascists. Fighting *and* writing poetry – two of his front-line poems had been published in *Mundo Obrero* and one of them, a soldier's thoughts about his family, hung framed on the wall among the formidable ancestors.

What would Jesús have done about the rabbit? Killed it? Ana doubted that: he would have departed, and returned, a curved smile of triumph on his face, with provisions mysteriously acquired. Like a magician, he never disclosed the secrets of his bartering but Ana suspected that he exchanged poems for provender – there were still wells of compassion beneath the brutalized streets of Madrid.

He had returned once, at Three Kings, with a doll for Rosana that he had carved with his pocket-knife in the trenches, and shining cartridge cases and studded fragments of a Mills bomb for Pablo's war museum. But he had changed since Ana had sent him to war: he was still good with the children but with her, although gentle, he was wary and when they lay together in their sighing bed he seemed to be searching for the girl he had met and not the woman she now was. They hadn't made love until they were married and they didn't make love now; instead she held him until he slept and stroked his forehead when he whimpered in dreams of battle.

He was in the Popular Army, formed to bring order to the

militias and Irresponsibles, but as he walked away from the *chabola*, stooping under the weight of the carnage he had witnessed, he didn't look the least bit like a soldier. I am the warrior, Ana thought, regarding the rabbit speculatively, and he should be the provider.

Food! She turned away from the rabbit, allowing it one more reprieve, and went into the bedroom to fetch her shawl and her shabby coat and her shoes laced with string darkened with blacking. She hated the hunger that was always with her, because it was a weakness that distracted her from the Cause.

She left Pablo fashioning a whistle out of a cartridge case and Rosana painting a water colour of a harlequin in black, red and yellow, arm raised in a clench-fist salute.

As she crossed the yard the rabbit thumped its legs.

She went first to an old woman who lived on her own in a hovel that stood alone, like an ancient's tooth, in a street of rubble. Here she made wreaths with paper flowers tied with black and red ribbon; the flowers were always red and she was always busy. Sometimes she possessed extra food with which the bereaved had paid for their wreaths, but there was none on view today.

'Just a little bread,' Ana pleaded, hating herself. 'It doesn't matter if it's stale; I can toast it.' At least they had fires in the *chabola*, kindled with slats from the ceilings of collapsed houses and fuelled with furniture – a walnut writing-desk had burned for two days.

'What have you got to offer?' the crone asked. In her youth she had married a member of the CNT; when he had died she had become the mistress of a doyen of the UGT; now she believed that age was an amnesty for the past. Her face was blotched and hooked; in her youth it must have been sharp enough to cut down trees, Ana thought.

'A poem?'

'Ah, a poem. What a beautiful thought, Ana Gomez.' Beneath her arthritic fingers scarlet crêpe blossomed. 'Except that I cannot read.'

'If I read it you will remember it.'

'I would prefer jewellery,' the crone said.

'I have no jewellery, only my wedding ring.'

'I have a little bread,' the crone said. 'A little rice. Admittedly with weevils but beggars can't be choosers, can they, Ana Gomez?'

Ana twisted the gold band on her finger; she remembered Jesus placing it there.

'I have money,' she said.

'Who wants money? There is nothing to buy with it.'

'I will come back,' Ana said. With a gun! 'Tell me, do you make wreaths for Fascists?'

The crone gazed at her suspiciously. 'I make wreaths for the dead,' she said.

Perhaps one day she will make a wreath for Antonio, Ana thought as she stepped over a fallen acacia on a street scattered with broken glass. He had returned to the capital once, as furtive as a pervert, wearing a beret and filthy corduroy trousers and a pistol in his belt. He had crossed the front line, relatively quiet on the western limits of the city since the fury of November, leaving his blue Falange shirt behind him.

He had come to the *chabola* after dark while she was boiling water on the walnut desk blazing in the hearth. He brought with him cigarettes – the new currency of Republican Spain. He gave her six packs, then, sitting in Jesús's rocking chair, said, 'I went to the house; the neighbours told me that Martine and my daughter left several weeks ago . . .' Even now he smelled faintly of Cologne.

'She's with the British,' Ana said. 'Waiting to be evacuated.' She told him about Christopher Lance and his ambulance service to British warships waiting on the Mediterranean coast. 'She's well,' Ana said. 'The baby's due at the beginning of March.'

Antonio lit a cigarette, an Imperial. His curls were tight with dirt and the skin across his cheekbones was taut; he was growing old with the war.

'When will she go?'

'Soon. There were many waiting before her.'

'Is it still dangerous in Madrid for anyone who made the mistake of being successful?'

'For the Fascists who exploited the workers? Not as bad as

it was; the real pigs are all dead. As for the rest . . .' Ana tested
the water with her wrist as she had done when the children
were babies. 'They can't even buy your perfume any more.
Isn't that sad?'

'What happened to the perfume?'

'The Irresponsibles drank it.'

She lifted the pan of water from the fire and took it to the
bathroom and told the children to wash themselves, Rosana
first, then Pablo.

'I hope it poisoned them,' Antonio said. 'And how have
you been keeping, elder sister?'

'Surviving,' Ana said.

'Jesús?'

'Fighting.'

'Mother of God! He'll shoot his own foot.' Antonio inhaled
deeply and blew smoke towards the fire and watched it
wander into the chimney.

'And Salvador?'

Ana straightened her back in front of the fire. 'He's dead.'

Antonio stared at the cigarette cupped in his hand. 'Papa?'

'Dead.'

'How?'

'Killed by one of your bombs.' She placed her hands on
her hips. 'But the priest lived.'

'I don't understand.'

'It doesn't matter,' she said.

And then he had gone and she had imagined him flitting
through the blacked-out campus, and sidling through the
front lines where friend and foe called to each other, and
making his way south to the Jarama valley to resume the
fight against his own people.

In the Puerta del Sol she spoke to a lottery ticket vendor.
The lottery headquarters had moved with the faint-hearted
Government to Valencia but tickets which could make
purchasers rich beyond the dreams of working men were still
on sale in Madrid. But as the crone had said, 'Who wants
money?' If the first prize had been a kilo of sausages Ana
might have joined a syndicate and bought a fraction of a
decimo, a tenth part of a ticket.

The vendor was young and broad-shouldered with a strong waist and muscular arms but his legs were shrivelled, tucked under him like a cushion on his wheelchair.

She asked him if he knew any food resources. She had known him for three years, this robust cripple, and they admired each other.

'I know where there are candles.'

'You can't eat candles, idiot.'

'You can barter with them, *guapa*.'

'And what do I barter for the candles?'

'That rabbit of yours. He is very lucky. I wish I was that rabbit.'

'If I can't get any food today I shall eat that rabbit tonight,' Ana said.

'I wish even more that I was that rabbit.'

She frowned but she was not displeased; she liked his glow and enjoyed his vulgarity. It was rumoured that, during the frenzied days of July, he had produced a pistol from beneath the blanket covering his thighs and shot a Fascist between the eyes.

'How is business?' she asked.

'Today everyone gambles with death, not figures.'

'You get enough to eat?'

'People are good to me,' he said. 'I am, after all, at the centre of Spain.'

'Some people say the Hill of the Angels is the centre of Spain.'

'I hope not; the Fascists hold it.'

'We held it for one great day,' Ana said. 'Enrique Lister took it in January. And took 400 prisoners. We showed them what to expect.'

'Just the same, this plaza is the centre of Spain because it is in Republican hands. Kilometre 0.' He pointed across the plaza, shouldered by the red and white façade of the Ministry of the Interior, with its kiosks selling merchandise that no one wanted these days – dolls and combs and fans – and the umbrella shop with sawdust on the floor. 'Have you ever been here, *guapa*, on New Year's Eve when you must swallow twelve grapes before the clock has finished striking twelve?'

'I have been here,' she said. 'And I have been to the Retiro on a Sunday and seen the jugglers and the mummers and listened to the guitars and eaten water ices and taken a rowing boat on the lake.'

'It was beautiful to be in Madrid then,' the vendor said. 'Here, I will give you a ticket.' He tore a pink ticket from one of the strips hanging from his neck.

'But you will have to pay for it.'

'You can repay me one day when we have won this bloody war. Now perhaps you can use it to trade for a candle which you can trade for a can of beans.'

'If not, you share the rabbit with us.'

'Have you noticed that all the cats have disappeared?'

'Then there will be plenty of rats to eat. Where are these candles?'

He named a street near the Plaza Mayor where, from a height, the roofs looked like a scattered pack of mouldering playing cards.

At the stall, where a man with sunken cheeks was trading candles, Ana became inspired. Glancing at the ticket she noticed that the last three figures were 736. The seventh month of the year of '36 – the month in which the war had broken out.

'What have you to offer?' asked the trader, who was not doing good business because, after dark, Madrileños went to bed and watched the searchlights switching the sky and listening to the gunfire to the west of the city and had no need for illumination.

'I want six candles, comrade,' Ana said.

He appraised her. Ana was flattered that men still looked at her in that way; she was also aware that she carried with her a fierceness that discouraged all but the most intrepid.

'I asked you what you had to offer.' A cigarette in the corner of his mouth beat time with his words.

'This.' She held up the lottery ticket.

'You expect six candles for that?'

But Ana knew her Madrileños: they would bet on two flies crawling up the wall.

'This is a very special ticket,' Ana said. 'With this you will be able to buy a Hispano-Suiza. And an apartment on the Castellana. And a castle in the country.'

'Let me have a look at this passport to paradise.'

She handed him the ticket. He held it up to the light like a banker looking for a forgery. Cold rain began to fall from a pewter sky.

'What is so special about this ticket?' the vendor asked.

'Imbecile. Look at the last three numbers. The month of the year the war started.'

The trader hesitated. Then he said, 'Three candles.'

'*Burro!* They were looted from a church anyway.'

'Four.'

'No, it is I who am the imbecile. I have always wanted a castle in the *campo* . . . Give me back the ticket.'

He handed her six candles.

She took these to a bakery off the Calle del Arenal where they baked bread for the troops; twice a week Ana and ten other women from the *barrio* took this bread by tram to the front. Its warm smell made the saliva run painfully in her mouth but she never touched any of the loaves nestling in the tin trays on her lap.

The baker, plump with a monk's fringe, hands gloved with flour, stood at the doorway.

'You have made a mistake, Ana Gomez. Tomorrow is the day for the front.'

'No mistake, comrade. How was the electricity last night?'

'Twice the lights failed. How can a man make bread in the dark?'

'By candle-light,' Ana said handing him the six candles. 'Now give me three of those loaves.' And when he hesitated, 'You are fat with your own bread; my children are starving.'

She placed the three loaves in the bottom of her basket and covered them with a cloth. As she walked home through the rain she thought, 'Today is Friday and we will be able to eat – the bread and some of the vegetable pap that was supposed to be a substitute for meat. And on Monday there will be more rations. But what of Saturday and Sunday? We shall eat the rabbit,' she decided.

As she neared Tetuan the air-raid siren wailed. No one

took much notice: they had become used to Junkers and Heinkels laying their eggs on the city. The city, she thought, was a fine target for bombers, a fortress on a plateau.

She walked down a street of small shops guarded by two tanks. The crews wore black leather jackets, Russians probably. A bomb fell at the far end of the street; a thin block of offices collapsed taking its balconies with it and crushing the empty butcher's shop below. The air smelled of explosives and distemper.

The crews disappeared into their tanks.

Ana took shelter in a doorway beside a small church. A poster had been stuck on a shop window on the opposite side of the street, beside a bank still displaying the stock market prices for last summer. It showed a negro, an Asian and a Caucasian wearing steel helmets; beneath their crusading faces ran the caption, 'ALL THE NATIONS OF THE WORLD ARE IN THE INTERNATIONAL BRIGADES ALONGSIDE THE SPANISH NATION'.

The bombers flew lazily back to their bases at Avila or Guadalajara and the leather-jacketed crews emerged from their tanks and stood stretching in the powdery rain blowing down the street with the dust from the explosions.

Ana emerged from the doorway. She thought about the bread, still warm and soft in her bag, and thought how good it would taste tonight and then, anticipating tomorrow's hunger, she thought, 'I will kill that rabbit while the children are playing. Break its neck with a single blow with the blade of my hand. Who are you, Ana Gomez, to worry about killing a pet when you have shot Moors and Spaniards and would have shot your own kind if they had turned and run?'

She wished the rabbit wasn't so trusting.

When she got home she noticed that the faces of the children were dirty with dried tears.

'So, what have you done?'

Pablo, lips trembling, pointed into the yard, 'The rabbit escaped,' he said.

Anger leaped inside her. She went to the bedroom and shut the door behind her and sat on the edge of the bed.

When she came out the children were sitting in one corner watching her warily.

'Who let it escape?'

'I did,' they both said.

She nodded and said, 'Your hunger will be your punishment.'

Then she fetched one of the loaves from her bag and cut it in three pieces. She sliced them, then smeared them with olive oil and sprinkled them with salt.

They sat down and ate like a family.

The slaughter was cosmopolitan.

Chimo brought the details to Adam Fleming who was resting with other legionnaires in an olive grove at the foot of Pingarrón, the heights which the Fascists had just captured after crossing the Jarama.

Moors had slit the throats of Spaniards; Irish had fought Irish; Italians had checked the Fascists' advance; the French fighting for the Republicans had really shown that they had *cojones*; Balkans, many of them Greeks, had defended ferociously; the British were still fighting suicidally to hold a hill below Pingarrón; the Americans were waiting to do battle.

'Ah, those Yanks,' Chimo said. 'Soon we shall see if they shoot like Sergeant York.'

'I'm lucky to be fighting at all,' Adam said. 'Lucky to be alive. Where were you when Delgado appeared at the entrance to the bunker?'

'I was being diplomatic,' Chimo said. He tested the cutting edge of his yellow teeth on the ball of his thumb.

'And brave?'

'I know nothing of bravery: I am a soldier. They are the brave ones.' He pointed at the hills where, alongside the Popular Army, the International Brigades were fighting to stop the Fascists reaching the Madrid–Valencia road. 'They know nothing about fighting. Have you seen the British?'

'I don't want to see the British,' Adam said.

He wondered if there was anyone he knew from Cambridge fighting under Tom Wintringham, Communist military correspondent of the *Daily Worker*, and commanding officer of the 600-strong British Battalion engaged in its first battle.

Already the poet John Cornford was dead, wounded in the Battle for Madrid, killed in Andalucia the day after his 21st birthday. In that engagement half of the 145 members of the British Number 1 company had been killed or wounded.

'You should see them,' Chimo said. 'They haven't got a map between them . . .'

'How do you know?'

'You should see them wandering about . . . Their rifles haven't been greased and they blow up in their hands. And their uniforms! Berets, peaked caps, ponchos, a steel helmet or two, breeches, baggy slacks, *alpargatas* . . .'

'What are *alpargatas*?' Adam asked without interest. His body ached with exhaustion, his mind with questions.

'Canvas shoes with rope soles. Imagine wearing those in the mud. Our guns pick them off while they're still stuck in it.'

Poor, sad, would-be soldiers, Adam thought. That was true courage: even Chimo understood that. But what are you dying for? Ideals? I have those too. Haven't I? He touched his sister's letter in the pocket of his tunic.

What he feared most was coming face to face with an Englishman. Could he kill him? And in any case should it be so different from killing a German, a Frenchman, an Italian, a Spaniard? Patriotism, surely, is only an accident of birth.

No, he decided, I should not be able to kill him.

An orderly served cold rice, which they ate with their hands, and cold coffee. Rain dripped from the silver-green leaves of the olive trees. The rain in Cambridge had smelled of grass; this rain smelled of cordite.

Adam leaned against the trunk of an olive tree, shielding his Mauser rifle with his blanket. He closed his eyes and dozed on his feet, limbs jerking as he ducked bayonets. Chimo's voice reached him in snatches.

'Not saying they aren't good fighters, they are . . . but shit, how can they fight in peasants' shoes with guns that kill them instead of us?'

Delgado said, 'No unexploded shells here?' There was mud on his boots and his eyes were pouched with fatigue but his grey-green legion uniform was freshly pressed and he looked as though he had just left the barbers.

Adam pushed himself away from the olive tree. 'Not yet, sir.'

'Good. We attack in five minutes.'

Adam looked at his wrist-watch. They had been resting for 35 minutes.

Delgado said, 'A lot of your countrymen up there,' pointing at the pock-marked hill. 'You'll have to kill some.'

'If they don't kill me, sir.'

'Spaniards are fighting Spaniards . . . Now you'll find out what that feels like.'

'I know what it feels like, sir.'

'How can you?'

'Is it any different from killing a Pole or a Belgian or a Greek?'

'I didn't want foreigners in my unit,' Delgado said. 'I've been lucky: you're the only one. This is our war.' He bent his cane between his two hands.

'And the Germans' war. And Italians'. Perhaps it isn't your war any more, sir.'

'Has it ever occurred to you, *inglés*, that you're fighting on the wrong side?'

Delgado strode away, his young captain in tow.

Adam fought his fatigue. Close your eyelids for a moment and you are in the armchair of the past.

Sometimes on Epsom Downs he had played at war, storming the racecourse grandstand on one occasion while thunder flashes exploded and masters in khaki stood in the line of fire barking contradictory orders. Adam had taken the opportunity to smoke a Passing Cloud in a nest of hawthorn bushes.

A red Very light blossomed in the sky. The legionnaires moved from their oasis and advanced towards the hill which the British Battalion, intellectuals, poets, adventurers, Jews from Manchester, Leeds and London, even a few members of the IRA, was defending.

Adam, rifle bayoneting the mist gathering in the rain, advanced into battle.

Chimo said, 'Don't worry, Amado, there are Spaniards fighting with the brigade as well as British.'

How could you tell one from the other? Phantom figures in front of them. Shouts and curses in Spanish and English.

'Stay close to me.' Chimo said. 'I will kill your Englishmen for you.'

'And I will kill your Spaniards.'

And then the mist lifts and there is great confusion and it's apparent that, in their job-lot uniforms, reds are shooting reds as well as Fascists. Adam sees the scene as an old, frantically-speeded movie; when the reel spends itself the killing will stop.

He aims his Mauser and fires at nothing in particular. Finds himself on the edge of the movie screen beside a half-dug trench, cartridge cases and jagged slivers of shell-casing shining in the mud.

The Englishman stands in front of him, rifle, armed with a bayonet, clenched in white-knuckled hands. He wears a woollen Balaclava and rope-soled shoes. And spectacles, rimless and spotted with rain. An Englishman all right.

The Englishman prods his bayonet forward. The blade shines wetly but there is no blood on it. He blinks rapidly behind his spectacles, the sort you can buy in Woolworths without a prescription.

Adam holds his rifle, speared with a ten-inch blade, loosely. He does not want to kill this short-sighted Englishman. Nor does he wish to be killed. As they face each other fear pours into this pause in time, twists Adam's bowels and roughens his throat.

Before coming to Spain he has not considered death; now it is as close as life. He understands that one thrust from that wet bayonet and the half-dug trench and the shining fragments of war and Kate with her damp hair curling at the nape of her neck will be no more. What does the Englishman see through his rimless, Woolworth's spectacles?

'Come on, you Fascist bastard,' the Englishman says. 'Fight.'

But Adam can't move. He opens his mouth but his lips and tongue are frozen as they are in a nightmare that sometimes visits him.

The Englishman's bayonet stabs, nearer this time.

'Ah can't kill you just like that,' he continues, northern vowels as flat as slate. 'Not if you don't move.'

'And I can't kill you with an accent like that.'

A lozenge of silence inside the noise of battle. Then the Englishman speaks.

'Fookin' 'ell,' he says. His bayonet dips.

Unanswerable knowledge expands inside Adam. Who is the enemy?

He says, 'What are we going to do?'

The Englishman says reproachfully: 'You shouldn't be on't other side.'

'Why not? I believe in what I'm fighting for.'

'You can't.' The Englishman knows this to be true and there is nothing more to be said about it.

'I should kill you,' Adam says.

'If you don't some other bugger will.'

'And you should try and kill me.'

'An Englishman? Nay, lad.'

'Why are you fighting for the reds?'

'Because I'm Jewish.'

'Nothing else?'

'A lot more but you wouldn't understand, lad.'

'There's a lot I don't understand,' Adam says as he notices the Englishman looking beyond him, as he hears the click of a rifle bolt, as he turns deflecting the barrel of Chimo's rifle, as Chimo pulls the trigger firing a bullet into the greyness above the rain.

And now the mist embraces them again and the Englishman disappears in it, an illusionist's apparition. Adam calls out but his voice is swallowed by the mist and there is no reply.

Chimo hits him on the shoulder with the heel of his hand. 'Son of the great whore!'

'He was English.'

'So? I am killing Spaniards.'

'It's your war.'

'Then go home, *cabrón*.'

Adam tells him about his sister and what the Republicans did to Paco.

'So it's everyone's war. So try killing the enemy: if you don't they will surely kill you.'

And now they are trying to do just that. Emerging from the mist, surprising Adam and Chimo who thought they were *behind* the Englishman; but all the senses tell untruths in the gunsmoke and the noise that never ceases.

Adam fires his rifle. Once, twice. Men fall. British or Spanish? The rifle jams. He lunges with the bayonet and the blade is as red as the poppies in the field.

Chimo pulls his sleeve. 'Let's get out of here, Amado.'

And they are running along the hillside between shallow trenches, over bodies, taking cover behind a crop of boulders.

But these boulders are no one's exclusive property. These boulders are an objective within the objective of the hill which is an objective within the campaign. And suddenly the fighting is thick around them; so thick that Adam cannot always distinguish Fascists from reds.

He grabs a rifle from the tight grip of a dead soldier. Fires it. The calico-rip of machine-pistol. Men fall forward which means they have been shot in the back but no one can be blamed because the reel of the ancient movie is out of control.

A punch on the head, just below the ear; he can no longer hear. He makes his way carefully through the silent carnage. He is alone now in the mist walking with a drunkard's gait.

His head is heavy on his shoulders, his body bends with its weight; he wants to lie down and sleep. He stumbles, slides into a shell-hole, stays there, feet in a puddle, back propped against torn soil. He feels the earth shift as shells fall but he hears nothing.

The convoy skirting the Battle of Jarama at 3.30 am consisted of a black Chevrolet, an ambulance and three lorries.

At the wheel of the Chevrolet sat Christopher Lance wearing his check jacket and the pink, grey and brown tie of Lancing Old Boys. With him was a small, shy woman named Margaret Hill, matron of the British-American Hospital in Madrid and Fernanda Jacobson, head of the Scottish Ambulance Unit who often wore kilt and tartan hose and was not shy at all.

With them were 72 charges, British evacuees whom the Government allowed to leave Spain and Spanish refugees from the reds whom the Government didn't. They had gathered furtively that evening at the British Embassy at 8 pm; now they were on their way through 32 check points to Alicante to be taken by a British destroyer, HMS *Esk*, north through the Mediterranean and across the Gulf of Lions to Marseilles and freedom.

As the convoy turned on to the Madrid–Valencia road shells exploded behind them and to their right machine-guns and rifles barked and coughed.

Martine Ruiz listened to them as the baby moved impatiently within her. In the makeshift British-American Hospital in Madrid on the corner of Velazquez at Ayala before reporting to the embassy she had insisted that it had no intention of entering the hostile world for at least another week or so; but even as she had been smiling comfortably at the British women the pains had been coming regularly.

The ambulance leaped over a shell-hole; Martine moaned and placed her hands across her drum-tight belly. The priest comforted her.

'It will be soon,' an old Spanish woman beside her said. 'There is a hospital in Alicante.'

'It won't be for a long time yet,' Martine said.

'I can tell.'

'It's my baby,' Martine Ruiz said.

The convoy stopped. Martine heard voices. But she trusted this Englishman who had a pass stamped by the Ministry of Works, the War Office, the British Embassy, the syndicates and Azaña himself.

The door of the ambulance opened. A sentry looked in. He was unshaven and wore a shiny-peaked cap on his unkempt hair. He saw the hump of Martine's stomach and smiled. He would deliver a baby with one hand and shoot a Fascist with the other, this one.

'A boy or a girl?' he asked.

'A girl,' Martine said, smiling at him.

'A boy,' the old woman said.

'Twins,' the sentry said and, still smiling, shut the doors.

The convoy moved off. The gunfire grew fainter.

The baby pushed again. Not in Alicante, Martine said to the baby. There they will find out who I am and, although they may let you live, you will not have a mother. *Tranquilo*, she said. Please baby, boy or girl, *tranquilo*.

'It will be soon,' the old woman said.

The priest said nothing.

Tom Canfield, crouching, made his way along the dirt path beside the Jarama. The water idled past islands of black mud on which dark weed-like watercress grew. A stork stood alone among the bodies in a field, and its arrogance and the abandoned desolation of the field made Tom decide that the battle had passed by here, that the Fascists had crossed the river so he must be in Nationalist territory. All he could do was hold out till dusk, then try and cross the river as the Fascists had done, work his way through their lines to the Republicans and hitch a lift to the air-base at Guadalajara. Which sounded easy enough, except that the countryside with its vineyards and fallow cornfields was flat, and Fascist reconnaissance planes were flying low over the river.

Dusk began to gather with its own brand of loneliness. His wounded arm belonged to someone else; his chest hurt. A squad of Polikarpovs flew through the valley, scattering and climbing as they reached the outskirts of Madrid. One lingered. Seidler looking for him. You could bet good money on it.

Tom remembered an evening like this, a little cruel with a saline breeze coming in from the Atlantic, when he and a girl had escaped from a party at his father's mansion at Southampton and ended up of all places in the potato fields at the south fork of the island. He had taken his open Mercer with the wire wheels and white-wall tyres. She was a happy girl with golden limbs and easy ways and they had lingered in the Mercer until the spray from the ocean had cooled their ardour. When they got back to the house the party was over, his father was bust and life would never be the same again. But he would always remember the girl.

Tom smiled. A bullet hit a tree hanging over the river

gouging a finger of sappy wood from it. He dropped to the
ground, took cover behind another farmhouse with a patio
scattered with olive stones. There was some bread on a
scrubbed table and a leather wineskin. The bread was stale
but not too hard; he ate it and drank sweet dark wine from
the wineskin. The wine intoxicated him immediately.

He heard a dog barking. He opened a studded door with a
rusty key in the lock. The dog was half pointer, half hunter,
with a whiplash tail, brown and white fur, a brown nose and
yellowish eyes. It was young, starving and excited; as Tom
stroked its lean ribs it pissed with excitement. Tom gave it the
last of the bread.

A heavy machine-gun opened up; bullets thudded into the
walls of the patio. The lingering Polikarpov returned, firing a
burst in the direction of the machine-gun. Seidler without a
doubt. The machine-gun stopped firing but Tom decided to
leave the farmhouse which was a natural target. He let
himself out of the patio. The dog followed.

The river led him through the rain into mist. He came to a
broken bridge that had been blown up, coming to rest where
it had originally been built. He ran across it, the dog at his
heels.

The gunfire was louder now. No chance yet of getting
through the Fascist lines. He noticed a shell-hole partly
covered by a length of shattered fencing. He slithered down
the side, coming to rest opposite a young, dark-haired soldier
dazed with battle.

Sometimes a meeting between two people is a conceiving. A
dual life is propagated and it possesses a special lustre even
when its partners are divided by time or location. These
partners, although they may fight, are blessed because
together they may glimpse a vindication of life. All of this
passes unnoticed at the time; all, that is, except an easiness
between them.

Tom Canfield became aware of this easiness when, coming
face to face with Adam Fleming in a shell-hole in the middle
of Spain, he said, 'Hi, soldier,' and Adam replied incredulously,
'I can hear you.'

And because a sense of absurdity is companion of these relationships, Tom laughed idiotically and said, 'You can what?'

'Hear you. I was deaf until you dropped in.' And then he, too, began to laugh.

Tom watched him until the laughter was stilled. He had an argumentative face and, despite the laughter, his eyes were wide with shock. Tom was glad he was a flier: these young men from the debating forums of Europe hadn't been prepared for the brutality of a battlefield.

'Where did you learn to shoot?' he asked pointing at the Russian rifle in the young man's hands.

'At college.'

'In England? I thought you only learned cricket.'

'And tennis. I played a lot of tennis.'

'Because you were supposed to play cricket?'

'You're very perceptive. My name's Adam Fleming.' He saluted across the muddy water at the bottom of the crater.

'Tom Canfield. How's it going up there?' he asked, nodding his head at the lowering sky.

Adam shrugged.

'Fifty-fifty. I got disorientated,' he said as though an explanation was necessary. 'I didn't know who I was fighting. Maybe someone fired a rifle too close to my ear. I felt as though I had been punched.'

'I know the feeling,' Tom said.

'You're a boxer?'

'A mauler.' Tom hesitated. 'What made you come out here?' He cradled his wounded arm inside his flying jacket; the dog settled itself at his feet and closed its eyes.

'The same as you probably. It's difficult to put in words.'

'I would have guessed you were pretty neat with words.'

'I knew a great injustice was being perpetrated. I knew words weren't enough; they never are. And you have to make your stand while you're young . . . I'm not very good with words tonight,' he said.

'I guess you've been fighting too long,' Tom said.

A shell burst overhead. Hot metal hissed in the water.

Adam said, 'My father had a cartoon in his study. It was by

an artist from the Great War called Bruce Bairnsfather. It showed two old soldiers sitting in a shell-hole just like this and one soldier is saying to the other, "If you knows of a better 'ole go to it."'

'This is the best hole I know of,' Tom said.

'You're lucky, being a flier.'

'A privileged background,' Tom said. 'My old man owned a Cessna.'

Fleming, he decided, came from London; a left-wing intellectual rather than an enlightened slogger like himself.

Adam said, 'You haven't told me what you're doing here.'

'It's a weird thing to say but there was no other choice.'

'I understand that. Did you ever doubt?'

'My motives? Sure I did. I figure there's a bit of the adventurer or the martyr in any foreigner fighting here.'

'But our motives, surely, are stronger than self glory or self pity?' His voice sounded anxious.

'Oh sure. In my case anyway. I can't speak for everyone. There are a few phonies here, you know.'

'You think I'm one?'

'I think you go looking for arguments.'

'I can't stand dogma. But you're right, I'm too argumentative. It had me worried for a while. I wondered whether I was championing a cause out of perversity.'

'Not you,' Tom said. He had known this man for a long time – the frown as he interrogated himself, the dawning smile as he called his own bluff.

'Then I had a letter from my sister.'

Tom waited; there is a time for waiting and when you knew someone as well as he knew Adam Fleming you knew that this was just such a time.

'They killed her husband.'

'Bastards.'

'Then I knew I had to come here. I wish I'd come before I needed proof.'

'You would have come anyway,' Tom said.

'But you didn't need a push.'

'Try living in a company shack in a coal town,' Tom said. 'Try busting your ass in the dust bowl of Oklahoma.'

He sensed that what he had said was grotesquely wrong but he couldn't fathom why. Surely it was feasible to compare injustices in the United States with those of Spain. *I knew a great injustice was being perpetrated*. Those were Adam Fleming's very words.

But such is the spontaneity of relationships such as this that anticipation is everything. No need to tell a joke: just point the way. No need to say goodbye: there is farewell in your greeting.

And now Tom Canfield knew.

He said, 'Your sister, where was her husband killed?'

'In Madrid,' said Adam who, of course, knew by now.

'But you're holding a Russian rifle.'

'And you're wearing a German flying jacket.'

'I took my rifle from the body of a dead Republican.'

'I bought my flying jacket in a discount store in New York.'

Delgado said from the lip of the shell-hole, 'I am delighted to see, Fleming, that you have taken a prisoner.'

CHAPTER 5

Able Seaman Thomas Emlyn Jones, RN, was a man of many talents. He could sing like a chorister, pluck pennies from the ears of children visiting his ship, arm-wrestle a dockside bruiser into submission, summon delicate fevers when threatened with onerous duties and tune the Welsh lilt in his voice on to a wavelength that could cajole girls from Portsmouth to Perth into committing perilous indiscretions.

But midwifery was not one of his accomplishments. When Martine Ruiz emerged from a cabin on HMS *Esk*, swathed in a sheet, hand supporting her considerable belly, and said, 'Please help me, I'm having a baby,' he was unnerved.

He had watched her board the destroyer with the other refugees at the palm-fringed port of Alicante at dusk and she had reminded him of a galleon in full sail, so stately in her bearing that nothing untoward could possibly happen in the immediate future. Now here she was, alarm bells sounding.

His first instinct was to run on his bandy miner's legs to the sickbay to get help but the *Esk* had paused north of Alicante to pick up wounded refugees from a moonlit beach, and the ship's surgeon and his assistants were busily and bloodily engaged. In any case the woman wouldn't let go of him.

Pulling him into the cabin, she lay on the bunk and said, 'It is happening,' as indeed it seemed to be, belly convulsing, body heaving, hands white-knuckled.

Hot water and towels: those, Taffy Jones remembered, were the essentials. He had observed them being taken into the bedroom in the dark and crouching cottage in the Rhondda Valley when his exhausted mother was giving birth to one of his sisters; he had heard the doctor calling for them in the sort of movie where the heroine collapses in a snowstorm and gives birth to twins.

The woman on the bunk screamed.

He turned on the hot water in the wash-basin and grabbed the towels from the rack.

'There, there, lovey,' he said, 'everything will be all right, just you see.' He held her hand and she gripped it with a fearful strength.

What now? 'Push,' he said as the midwife, who smelled of gin, had said to his mother. 'Push, that's it, lovey, you just help her on her way,' because he had no doubt in his mind that a lady was about to be added to the passenger list.

He bathed her sweating face with a towel, not too hot, and laid another across her labouring belly. Observing her agony, hearing her cry, he determined that in future he would be more considerate towards women. No more buns in the oven for Taffy Jones.

The sheet slipped away and a head emerged from between her wide-flung thighs. 'Push,' he said gently, 'push,' although whether he was addressing mother or child he couldn't say. What did you do when the baby finally made it? All you heard in the movies was a plaintive squawk from behind closed doors.

'There, there, lovey, she's on her way.'

The fingers of Martine Ruiz gripped his hand like talons. She said, 'You will have to help.'

He stared at the baby; it seemed to have given up the struggle. Perhaps it didn't like what it saw. He placed two paws round the tiny shoulders and pulled very gently; when he got back to Cardiff he would marry the girl who worked in the newsagents and they would take out a mortgage on a £600 semi and have two kids.

The baby, creased and slippery with mucus and blood, swam forward. Taffy Jones, aware of unplumbed emotions stirring within him, sighed. 'She's almost there,' he said softly. 'Almost there.'

'In my bag,' Martine Ruiz whispered in her accented English that he found difficult to understand. 'A pair of . . . scissors.'

He opened her expensive-looking handbag and took them out. The cord had to be cut and knotted; that was it. The prospect didn't alarm him: authority had settled comfortably upon him.

He dipped the blades of the scissors into the hot water, snipped the cord with one deft cut and tied it. Then he examined the baby.

'It's a girl,' he told Martine Ruiz.

But it was making no sound. Was it breathing? He picked it up in his big hands and anxiously held it aloft. A smack followed by a squawk, he remembered.

'Come on, you little bugger,' Taffy Jones pleaded.

Still holding the baby in one paw, he ran the fingers of the other down its flimsy ribs.

And the baby laughed. Taffy Jones swore to it then and many times later in dockside bars where normally midwifery doesn't rate high in conversational priorities. Some might have mistaken that first utterance for a whimper but Taffy knew better. He was there, wasn't he? 'Made a contribution to medical science, perhaps. To mankind, maybe,' and, if it was his round, his drinking friends would nod sagely.

At the time Taffy Jones merely smiled at the baby who was now making noise that could, perhaps, be mistaken for crying and cooed, 'Oh, you little bugger you.'

He gently washed the baby and handed it to its mother.

Ana Gomez worried. Not at this moment about her husband who was fighting at Jarama but about the future he was fighting for.

In the Plaza de España in Madrid, close to the front line, she watched Pablo kicking a scuffed football near the waterless fountains and Rosana making a sketch of the statue of Don Quixote.

Pablo intended one day to play for Real Madrid; Rosana to have her pictures hung in the Prado. Or would he, perhaps, play for Moscow Dynamo while Rosana exhibited in the Pushkin Museum?

This was what worried Ana as she paused in the hesitant sunshine on her way to hear her cousin Diego, an orator if ever there was one, speak in a bombed-out church off the Gran Via.

At first the different factions within the crusade hadn't bothered her. They were all fighting for the same cause, weren't they, so what did it matter if you were FAI or CNT or UGT or a regional separatist? She herself had favoured Anarchism because the belief that 'Every man should be his own government, his own law, his own church' seemed to be the purest form of revolution.

But what she believed in even more passionately was Spain – a wide, free country where equality settled evenly with the dust in the plains and the snow in the mountains – and she now believed that this vision was endangered. By the Russians. True, they were providing planes and tanks and guns but do we have to pay with our pride? Everywhere the Communists seemed to be taking over – there was Stalin smiling at her benignly from a banner on the other side of the square. And in Barcelona, so she had heard, the Communists who took their orders from the Kremlin were poised to crush the Communists in POUM who were independent of the Kremlin.

What has it come to, Ana Gomez asked herself, when not only are we divided but the divisions themselves are split? Where was the single blade of revolution that had flashed so brightly at the beginning?

A breeze rippled the banner of Stalin making a deceit of his smile.

Ana called the children. Outside the Gran Via cinema she met Carmen Torres who was taking the children to see the Marx Brothers. She gave them five pesetas and, skirting a bomb crater, made her way through the debris and broken glass to the church.

It was open to the sky and naked and, when she arrived, Diego was about to speak from the stone pulpit. Watching him from the back of the nave, Ana felt uneasy. Although she despised the priests who had defiled religion she still believed in the God they had betrayed and she didn't like to hear politics instead of prayers in his house. But there was more to her unease than that: there was slyness abroad in the roofless church, a sulking defiance, and at the sides of the congregation stood several men with zealots' faces.

Diego offered his congregation the clenched fist salute. *'No pasarán!'* he shouted and they hurled it back at him. He spread his arms. We are one, his arms said. Then, with a plea and sally, he beckoned them into his embrace and when they were there he told them what they had to do.

Diego, with his myopic eyes peering from smoked glasses and his small, button-bursting stomach, did not have a prepossessing appearance, and this was perhaps the secret of his oratory: no one could believe that such fire could issue from such a nondescript body.

But on this disturbing day even Diego sounded suspect to Ana. First came the impassioned affirmation that they would stand together to fight the Fascist oppressors who had 'plundered their souls' – lively enough, but predictable, as were the warnings of sacrifices to be endured and the promises of the individual freedoms to be celebrated after the bourgeoisie were sent packing.

After that Diego, man of the people, faltered. And whereas normally his voice soared, hoisting collective passions with it, before diving as abruptly as an eagle on its prey, it was flat and cautious.

Ana listened. State controls, centralism . . . workers to have their say, of course . . . but while the war lasted the country must be protected against lawlessness . . . What was this?

On the sidelines the men with the zealots' faces clapped. The rest of the audience followed suit but the customary cheers remained stuck in their throats. Diego moved on to 'our good friends the Russians'.

Planes glinted si ver in the sky above the nave. The earth shook with the impact of their bombs. Anti-aircraft guns started up.

'We must never forget that the Soviet Union fought a civil war against capitalist exploitation . . .'

And look where it got them. Diego, why are you reciting to us?

'No pasarán!' she shouted and strode down the aisle towards the altar, arm raised, fist clenched. *'No pasarán!'* Ana Gomez, is this you?

Two of the men from the sidelines stood in her way. They smiled indulgently but they were snake-eyed and muscle-jawed, these men.

'Please return to your place, Ana Gomez.'

How did they know her name?

She half-turned to the audience.

'This is a woman's war as well, comrades, in case you hadn't heard. Ask La Pasionaria.'

From the body of the crowd came a man's voice: 'Let her speak. Where would we be without our women?'

'Thank you, comrade,' Ana shouted. Two years ago he would have told her to get back to the kitchen!

One of the sidesmen said, 'The meeting is over. I order you all to disperse in an orderly fashion.'

Order! That was his mistake.

'Let her speak . . . Go back to Moscow . . . This is our war . . .' The audience began to stamp and slow-handclap.

The sidesman's hand went to the long-barrelled pistol in his belt.

'Go ahead, shoot me,' Ana said.

The shouts seemed to unify into an ugly sound that reminded her of the first warning growl of a dog with bared teeth.

The sidesmen looked at each other, and shrugged.

Diego came down from the pulpit and took her arm. 'What are you trying to do to me?' He had taken off his spectacles; he was naked without them. 'Didn't you get my message?'

'Message? I received no message.'

'What are you going to do?'

'Speak to them,' Ana said pointing at the audience which was quiet now. 'The way you used to.'

She pushed past him and mounted the steps of the pulpit. She saw beneath her, as priests before her had seen, faces waiting for hope. What are you doing here, Ana Gomez, mother of two, wife of a museum guard, resident of one of the poorest *barrios* in Madrid? Who are you to talk about hope?

She laid both hands on the cold knuckle of the pulpit. She had no idea what she was going to say, no idea if any words would emerge from her lips. She noticed the scowling faces of the two men who had tried to stop her. She heard herself speaking.

'My husband is fighting at Jarama.'

A hush as silent as night settled on the people below her. She saw their poor clothes and their hungry faces and she felt their need for comfort.

'He did not want to fight.' She paused. 'None of us wanted to fight.'

Gunfire sounded distantly.

'All we wanted was enough money to live decently – decently, comrades, not grandly. All we wanted was a decent education for our children.'

A child whimpered in the congregation.

The two sidesmen seemed to relax; one leaned against a pillar.

'All we wanted was a share of this country. Not a grand estate, just a decent plot that belonged to us and not to those who paid us a *duro* for the honour of tilling their land.'

Sunlight shining through the remnants of a stained-glass window cast trembling pools of colour on the upturned faces.

'All we wanted in this city was a decent wage so that we could feed our families and give them homes and live almost as grandly as the priests.'

She stared at the sky which the bombers had vacated and whispered, 'Forgive me God.' But although she knew not where the words came from, they could not be stemmed.

'No, we did not want to fight: *they* made us, the enemy who sought to deny us our birthright. But now, at their behest, we shall win and Spain will be shared among us.'

They clapped, and then they cheered, and hope illumined their faces. The two sidesmen clapped and exchanged glances that said they need not have worried. Ana paused professionally, then held up her hands, palms flattened against her audience.

'I repeat, Spain will be shared among *us*. Not among foreigners.' A shuffling silence. The two men snapped upright and stared at her. 'We shall always be grateful for the help that has been given to us – without that we might have perished – but let us never forget that the capital of Spain is Madrid, not Moscow.'

The audience applauded but now they were more restrained. The sidesmen walked briskly out of the church.

In a bar near the church, where brandy was still available to distinguished revolutionaries, Diego said, 'Why did you do that to me?'

'Do what?'

'Attack the Communists.'

'Because I am an Anarchist like you.'

'But I'm not: I'm a Communist.'

Diego leaned forward on his stool and stared despairingly into his coffee laced with Cognac.

Ana folded her arms. 'You are what?'

'A Communist. They have even promised me a party card. That was a Communist meeting; I sent Ramón to tell you.'

'Ramón? Who is this Ramón?'

'My assistant. But he probably got drunk on his way.' He stroked his damp moustache with one nail-bitten finger. 'You were making an anti-Communist speech at a Communist meeting. *Mi madre!*' He smiled grimly.

'I was making a pro-Spanish speech.'

'The capital of Spain is Madrid, not Moscow . . . Yes, very patriotic, cousin. I congratulate you on condemning us to the firing squad.'

'Don't be ridiculous.' Ana gulped her coffee. 'How could any true Spaniard disagree?'

'It wasn't exactly diplomatic. Not when Moscow is supplying us with our arms.'

'We are paying for them in gold.'

'They have our gold: we still need their arms.'

'And so now we should give them our souls? Do you want Spain to become a colony of the Soviet Union?'

'Keep your voice down; you aren't in the pulpit now.' Diego took off his glasses and glanced around as though he could see better without them. 'We need them,' he said. 'Without them we are doomed.'

Ana said softly, 'Why did you sell your soul, Diego?'

'Because I believe that salvation lies with the Communists.'

'What about those dreams of Anarchism you once cherished? "There is only one authority and that is in the individual." Who said that, Diego?'

'Me?'

'You. What did they buy you with, Diego?'

'We are all fighting for the same cause.'

'That wasn't what I asked.'

'I have been promised a high office in the administration when the war is over.'

'And a grand house and a decent salary?'

'Commensurate with my office,' Diego said.

'Perhaps,' Ana said, 'they will pay you in roubles.'

'I tell you, we are all fighting for the same cause.'

It was then that Ana realized that one contestant had been missing from the conversation – the enemy, the Fascists.

Has it come to this? she asked herself. She strode out of the bar and down the street to the cinema where her children were watching the Marx Brothers.

On the Jarama front the fighting had stopped for the night. The combatants had retired to debate how best to kill each other in the morning and, except for the intermittent explosions of shells fired to keep the enemy awake, the battlefield was quiet.

In a concrete bunker captured from the Republicans Colonel Carlos Delgado considered the two foreigners interfering in his war. A picture of Franco hung from the wall recently vacated by Stalin; a map of the Jarama valley and its environs, crayoned with blue and red arrows, was spread across the desk.

Delgado's fingers searched his freshly-shaven cheeks for any errant bristles, tidied the greying hair above his ears where his cap had rested. His khaki-green tunic was freshly pressed and his belt shone warmly like dark amber. His voice, like Franco's, was high-pitched.

'So why,' he asked in English, 'were two mercenaries fighting on opposite sides sharing a shell-hole?'

'I guess you could call it force of circumstances,' Tom Canfield said.

'It does neither of you any credit. What is your name?' he asked Canfield.

'You've got it there in front of you. José Espinosa.'

'Your real name: non-intervention is a stale joke.'

'Okay, what the hell – Thomas Canfield.'

'Why are you fighting for the rabble, Señor Canfield?'

'Name, rank and number. Nothing more. Isn't that right, Colonel?'

The glossy captain pulled his long-barrelled pistol from its holster. 'Answer the colonel,' he said.

'You don't have a rank or number,' Delgado said.

'José Espinosa does.'

'Are you Jewish?'

'Espinosa, José, pilot, 3805.'

'This isn't a movie, Señor Canfield. Please enlighten me: I cannot understand – really I can't – why any reasonable man should want to fight for a ragged army of peasants and city hooligans whose sport is burning churches and murdering anyone industrious enough to have earned more money than them.'

'Then you don't understand very much, Colonel.'

'Anti-Hitler? Anti-Mussolini? Anti-Fascist?'

'Anti-gangster,' Tom said.

'So we have one anti-Fascist.' Delgado turned to Adam Fleming who was standing, legs apart, hands clasped behind his back, beside Canfield. 'And one anti-Communist. Do you both find Spain an agreeable location to indulge your politics?'

'*Your* politics, sir,' Adam said.

'Nice climate,' Tom said.

Delgado lit an English cigarette, a Senior Service. 'You, I presume,' he said to Canfield, 'were trying to find your way back to the Republican lines.'

'Wherever those are,' Tom said.

'And you,' to Fleming, 'were hiding from an unexploded shell?'

'I got lost,' Adam said.

'Perhaps we should provide foreign mercenaries with compasses as well as rifles.'

'Good idea,' Tom said. 'They might find the right side to fight for.'

The captain prodded him in the back with the barrel of his pistol.

Delgado blew a jet of smoke across the bunker. It billowed in the light of the hurricane lamps.

'So what shall I do with the two of you? One American fighting for the enemy, one Englishman displaying cowardice in the face of the enemy . . .'

'That's a lie,' Adam said.

'He was concussed,' Tom said.

'Your loyalty is touching. But loyalty to what, an anti-Communist?'

'I'm not a Communist,' Tom said.

'Then it is you who is serving on the wrong side.' Delgado smoked ruminatively and precisely. 'There are a lot of misguided men fighting for the Republicans. Good officers in the Fifth Regiment, like Lister and Modesto and El Campesino, of course. When he was only 16 he blew up four Civil Guards. Then he fought in Morocco – on both sides! Would you consider flying for us, Señor Canfield?'

'You've got to be kidding,' Tom said.

'I rarely joke,' Delgado said. 'I see no point to it. But I'm glad you're staying loyal to the side you mistakenly chose to fight for.' He dropped his cigarette on the floor, squashing it with the heel of one elegant boot. 'Now all that remains is to decide the method of execution.'

Spray broke over the prow of HMS *Esk* as it knifed its way through the swell on its approach to Marseilles but Martine Ruiz, standing on the deck with her five-year-old daughter, Marisa, didn't seem to notice it as it brushed her face and trickled in tears down her cheeks.

What concerned her was the future that lay ahead through the spume and the greyness for herself, Marisa and her three-day-old baby. How could she settle in England?

What would she do without Antonio? Why did he have to fight when all that had been necessary was to slip away to some Fascist-held city such as Seville or Granada in the south or Salamanca or Burgos in the north and lie low until Madrid was captured? She wished dearly that Antonio was here beside her so that she could scold him.

She stumbled across the lurching deck and went below. Her breasts hurt and her womb ached with emptiness.

The baby was as she had left it in a makeshift cot, a drawer padded with pillows; Able Seaman Thomas Emlyn Jones was also as she had left him, sitting beside the drawer on the bunk reading a copy of a magazine called *Razzle*.

He hastily folded the magazine and placed it on the bunk beneath his cap.

'Not a sound,' he said. 'Not a dicky bird.' He stared at his big, furry hands. 'I was wondering . . . How are you going to get to England?'

'Train,' she said. 'Then ferry.'

'Lumbering cattle trucks, those ferries. You mind she isn't sick,' pointing to the sleeping baby.

Martine glanced at herself in the mirror. There were shadows under her eyes and her face was drained.

'It is me who will be sick.' She spoke English slowly and with care.

'And me,' Marisa said. She lay on the bunk and closed her eyes.

'You'd be surprised how many sailors are sea-sick,' Taffy Jones said.

Martine, who was becoming queasy, stared curiously at his chapel-dark features. 'What part of England do you come from?' she asked.

'England is it?' His reaction was unexpected and, she suspected, ungrammatical.

She stared at him uncomprehendingly. 'Aren't you English?'

'Is the Pope a Protestant? I come from Wales, girl, and don't you ever forget it.'

Now she understood. He was just like a Basque, she thought. 'I'm sorry.'

'It's me that should be sorry, bloody fool that I am.' He looked at his hands, clenching them and unclenching them, and then he looked at the baby. 'I was thinking,' he said, 'when you get to England . . . Do you have anywhere to go?'

'A relative,' thinking of her brother Pierre who worked in the Credit Lyonnais in London.

'Ah, not too bad then.' He adjusted the pillow behind the baby's head. 'But just in case this relative of yours is too distant, if you're ever stuck . . . You know, if you don't have anywhere to go you could always come and see us in Wales.' He handed her a lined sheet of paper. 'There's the address, just in case.' He stood up awkwardly.

Martine took the scrap of paper. 'Thank you Monsieur Jones.'

'Taffy.'

'Monsieur Taffy. And now,' she said, as the baby stirred and prepared its face to cry, 'I must feed her.'

Taffy Jones picked up his cap and his copy of *Razzle*. 'What are you going to call her?' he said. 'I meant to ask you.'

'Isabel.'

'Can she have another name?'

'As many as she wants,' Martine said.

'My name's Thomas. I thought maybe Thomasina might be a good name. How does it sound in Spanish?'

'It sounds like Tomasina,' Martine said. 'And now if you'll excuse me.'

Isabel Tomasina began to whimper and at first the sounds were so small that to Taffy Jones they sounded like the lonely cries of the seagulls wheeling overhead.

It was dawn – the classic time for executions. Tom Canfield and Adam Fleming walked under armed guard. Behind them were Delgado and the young captain.

Mist lay in the valley but here in a field of vines the air was clean and still night-smelling. A squadron of Capronis flew high above Pingarrón.

Adam glanced at Canfield. He looked thoughtful, that was all, thoughtful and, with his fair hair and lazily dangerous face, very American, convinced that he would be welcome anywhere in the world and if not he would want to know the reason why.

Not any more, Tom Canfield, we are going to die, you and I. For what? For bringing our contradictory ideals to a foreign land?

He stumbled over a fiercely pruned vine. He looked back. The vines squatted in the wet earth like a graveyard of crosses.

There is no future. Life is an entity, not a sequence. It is mine and when it is severed there will be no life for anyone because it is I who see and hear. No life for you, Colonel Delgado, slicing the enemy bristles from your cheeks with a cut-throat razor; no promotion for you, Captain, so handy with your long-barrelled pistol, certainly no life for you, Tom Canfield, who dropped into my life just 12 hours ago.

They approached a ruined farmhouse. A whitewashed wall was still standing and there were blood stains and the pock marks of bullets on it.

Adam Fleming opened his mouth and screamed but no sound issued from his lips.

Canfield said, 'Excuse me, Colonel, may I ask you a question?'

Delgado switched irritably with his cane at a clump of nettles. 'What is it?'

'Will you grant a last request?'

'What is it?'

'Don't shoot me.'

'You have a sense of humour,' Delgado said. 'Why else would you be fighting for Republicans?'

Adam noticed that Canfield's lips were tight and a muscle was moving in the line of his jaw. They stopped in front of the wall beneath a flap of bamboo roof. Where was the firing squad?

Delgado, holding his cane between two hands, turned and faced them. 'You,' to Canfield, 'will be executed because you were found wearing civilian clothes and carrying false papers. You,' – to Adam – 'should be executed for desertion.'

Should?

'But I am willing to concede you were shell-shocked. However, you know my views on foreign mercenaries meddling in Spain's war. It seems logical, therefore, that you should carry out the execution.' The captain handed Adam the pistol. 'After all, he is the enemy.'

Adam took the gun. It had been tended with love, and he knew the mechanism would work snugly.

Delgado pointed at the blood-stained wall with his cane. 'Over there.' The blood stains were the colour of rust. 'Do you want to be blindfolded?' he asked Canfield.

'I like to look the enemy in the eye. One of the lessons you learn in boxing.' There was a catch in his voice and his body was shaking and because they had known each other a long time, 12 hours at least, Adam knew that he was thinking, 'Please, God, don't let me be a coward.'

Cowardice? Who cared about cowardice? Why did they teach children that it mattered? If I live I will teach children that cowardice is natural, the most natural thing in the world; but I shan't live because I can't shoot Tom Canfield.

'If you refuse,' Delgado was saying, 'you, too, will be executed for desertion, for refusing to obey an order, for cowardice.'

There it was again, cowardice. I wish I could pin medals on the breasts of all those who have exhibited cowardice in the face of the enemy. I wish I could tell my children that they should never be ashamed of crying.

'There.' Delgado indicated a line whitewashed on the mud. 'Get it over with quickly: we are due to attack again.'

The sound of aircraft filled the sky. Adam looked up. Russian-built Katiuska twin-engined bombers.

'Get on with it,' Delgado snapped.

Adam raised the pistol.

'I will raise my cane,' Delgado said. 'When I drop it you will fire. Empty the barrel, just in case.'

Adam stared down the barrel of the pistol, lined up Canfield's chest with the inverted V blade foresight and the V notch rearsight. Why shouldn't I shoot him? He is the enemy, a red, and I have killed many of those already.

Canfield said, 'How about that . . .' He lost his sentence, recaptured it. '. . . last request? A cigarette?'

You don't smoke, Adam thought. He stroked the trigger. Two pressures? Why do you hesitate, Adam Fleming?

Canfield chose to fight on that side, you on this. You came to Spain to kill reds, didn't you? Priest-killers, murderers of your sister's husband.

Who is the enemy?

'Permission refused.' Delgado's cane fell.

The last thing Adam Fleming remembered was the roar of a Katiuska bomber.

Tom Canfield assumed he was dead.

The crash and the pointed ache in his skull and the crepitus of fractured wall . . . Now all he could see was a khaki-coloured dustiness. Perhaps he was in the process of dying. He tested his limbs. They moved painlessly, all except the arm that had been wounded in the plane crash. His hand went to his chest searching for bullet holes. Nothing. The dust began to clear. He heard a groan. He sat up.

The flap of bamboo lay across his knees. Then he heard the drone of the Katiuska bombers.

He stood up and blundered through the settling dust. The first body he encountered was Delgado's. He was still alive but for once he did not look freshly barbered. Then the two soldiers and the captain. One of the soldiers was dead. Lastly Adam Fleming, pistol still clenched in his fist. There was a wound on the side of his head and his face was grey.

He knelt beside him. He was alive but only just. His breathing was shallow and blood flowed freely from the scalp wound. Tom took a torn cushion from a cane chair, placed it under his head and tried to staunch the bleeding with his handkerchief.

'Were you going to shoot me?' he asked the unconscious man. 'Would *I* have shot *you*?'

He heard voices. He knelt behind a heap of rubble beside a legless rubber doll. Fascist soldiers were approaching. They would look after Fleming.

He took the pistol from his hand and edged round the remnants of the farmhouse. As he ran towards an olive grove he heard a noise behind him. He flung himself to the ground and the brown and white dog with the foraging nose licked his face, then whipped his chest with its long tail.

'Another survivor,' Tom said. He patted the dog's lean ribs. 'Come on, let's find some breakfast.'

The hill where Adam Fleming had been fighting lay ahead. He began to climb towards the Republican lines on the other side.

Machine-gun fire chattered in the distance but yesterday's battlefield was deserted except for corpses. The sky was pure and pale, and the mist in the valley was rising. It was going to be a fine, spring-beckoning day.

He was near the brow of the hill now. There he would be a silhouette, a perfect target. He flattened himself on the shell-torn ground and, with the dog beside him, inched upwards.

Bodies lay stiffly around him, many of them British by the look of them, wearing berets and Balaclavas and job-lot uniforms, staring at the sky as though in search of reasons.

At the crest of the mole-shaped hill he rolled towards the Republican lines. Hit a rock and lay still. When he tried to stand up there was no strength in him. He noticed blood from his wounded arm splashing on to a slab of stone. How long had it been bleeding like that? Pain knifed his chest.

The dog whined, whip-lash tail lowered.

He continued down the hill, cannoning into ilex trees, slithering in the water draining from the top of the hill. There was a dirt road at the bottom and he had to reach it. He collapsed into a fragrant patch of sage 50 metres short of it. He stretched out one hand and felt the dog. Or is this all an illusion? Did Adam Fleming pull the trigger?

The smell of the sage and the warmth of the dog faded.

It was replaced by the smell of ether.

He opened his eyes. A middle-aged man with pugnacious features, Slavonic angles to his eyes and sparse grey hair, stood beside his bed.

The man said, 'Please, don't say Where am I.'

'Okay, I won't.' He heard his own voice; it was thin and far away.

'You're in a field hospital. A monastery, in fact. And you're extremely lucky to be alive for two reasons.'

'Which are?'

'A peasant found you bleeding to death near a dirt road. He stopped the bleeding by tying a strip of your shirt round your arm, pushing a stick underneath it and twisting it. A primitive tourniquet.'

'Secondly?'

'Then I drove by and saved your life.'

Tom closed his eyes. He was vaguely aware of something intrusive in his good arm. He tried to find it but he couldn't move his other arm. He retreated into a star-filled sky.

'Why did you come to Spain?' Tom asked Dr Norman Bethune from Montreal when he next stood at his bedside.

'I needed a war,' Bethune said. 'To see if I can save lives in the next one.'

'Which next one would that be?'

'The one we're rehearsing for,' said Bethune who was taking refrigerated blood to the front line instead of waiting for haemorrhaging casualties to reach hospitals. 'How are you feeling?'

'I wouldn't want to go three rounds with Braddock but I'm okay, I guess. Whose blood have I got inside me?' He jerked his head at the pipe protruding from his arm.

'God knows. Good blood by the look of you. Maybe you owe your life to a priest.'

'Don't tell the commissar that,' Tom said. 'Are these all your patients?' He pointed at the broken and bandaged patients lying on an assortment of beds in the stone-floored dining hall of the monastery.

'A few, those with colour in their cheeks. I gave the first transfusion at the front on 23 December last year. Remember that date: maybe it will be more important than the date the war broke out.'

Tom raised himself on his pillow, then said abruptly, 'When can I fly again?'

'When your arm's mended. You broke it a few days ago. Right?'

'I got shot down.'

'And later you must have fallen. And when you fell you turned a simple fracture into a compound fracture and a splinter of bone penetrated an artery and the haemorrhage became a deluge.'

'I can fly with my left hand.'

'When your ribs are mended.'

'Ribs?'

Bethune pointed at his chest. 'They weren't practising first-aid when they strapped you up.'

'Shit,' said Tom Canfield. 'No pain though.'

'Breathe in deeply.'

'Shit,' said Tom Canfield.

During the next five days Tom fell in love and learned how to acquire a fortune.

The girl's name was Josefina. She was 18 and stern in the fashion of nurses, although sometimes the touch of her fingers was shy. She was a student nurse, qualified by war, and she came from a small coastal town astride the provinces of Valencia and Alicante.

Her father had traded with the British in the wild days of the raisin trade, before Empire Preference in Britain and protectionism in the United States had closed down the market, and she spoke reasonable English conducting it all the while with her hands. Her hair was light brown, parted tightly in the middle, and she once showed Tom a photograph of herself in Valencian national dress and Tom, ignorant about such matters, thought she looked like a flamenco dancer. She also showed Tom a photograph of a small house with barred windows and a patio. 'How can I return there after Madrid? I would suffocate.'

At first she was studiously practical with Tom, changing his dressing, punching his pillow, taking his pulse and temperature, ordering him out of bed when the tube had been removed from his good arm; but after a while, she lingered a little longer than was clinically necessary. Or was it his imagination? At night, among the cries and entreaties of the wounded, Tom tried to usher her into his dreams, failing monotonously except on one occasion when she stripped off her national costume and stepped naked into bed with him in the mansion on Long Island.

But that dream was far removed from reality. In truth, so different were the ancient patterns of courtship in Spain to those in America that Tom, fretting between her visits, was unsure how to approach her. In the States you made your pitch and you dated and the rest was predictable which wasn't to say that it wasn't romantic and deeply felt; here there were delicacies to be observed that confounded Tom because, although he sensed them, he could not define them.

On the third day, while she dressed his arm with boracic lint and a recycled bandage, he made an approach of such gross ineptitude that, later, he groaned aloud causing the man who was dying in the bed beside him to inquire whether he was feverish. What he did was invoke the Cause, resurrect the infamies of the fascists, in particular the landowners, and suggest that the Republic could not have survived without the intervention of foreigners.

The bandage was unwound a little quicker; she didn't speak; Tom sensed withdrawal. He said quickly, 'When all this is over I should like to visit your home.'

'Why would you want to do that?' She cut the end of the bandage down the middle, reversed one strip round his forearm and tied the two ends. 'My father is a landowner.'

'Hell!' Tom Canfield closed his eyes tightly and opened them again. 'You know I didn't mean . . .'

'He treats his workers well and they respect him. He is going to organize a collective.'

'I'm sure he's a good man.'

'There, that will do for a while.' She touched the bandage with the tip of one finger. 'We don't change the dressing so often these days. It's the idea of Dr Josep Trueta; he believes the wound should be allowed to heal itself. He, too, is a good man. There are many such men in this backward country of ours.'

'I don't believe it's backward.'

'Then you are a liar. We must be backward if we can't survive without foreigners.'

'There are foreigners on both sides.'

She stood back, arms folded across the blue striped blouse

of her uniform. Usually she wore a kerchief but today she was bare-headed, hair tight-combed and polished.

'Tell me, Señor Canfield, did you come here to fight for the Spaniards or against the Fascists?'

'There's a difference?'

'For Manuel Azaña and Largo Caballero or against Hitler and Mussolini?'

'Both,' Tom said inadequately.

'How convenient,' Josefina moved to the next bed where the soldier was dying.

So Tom had to plead and on the fifth day she walked with him in the cloisters beside a cobbled quadrangle where a fountain splashed.

Tom spoke urgently. He was sorry about his clumsy words but he was nervous. Didn't she know the way he felt about her? He took her hand; it was warm and dry; she did not withdraw it. He would have to return to his unit but, from time to time, he would be able to return to the monastery. Would she, perhaps, be able to drive with him into the countryside, away from the war? Just a few hours, Tom said, wondering how many other patients had made just such an approach.

Josefina stretched out her free hand and touched a frond of salmon-pink bougainvillea, pale in the open colonnade. Had it occurred to him, she asked, that the dangers of war aroused emotions that could be confused with love? That, through circumstance, their life cycles had touched; that, after the war, he would return to America and she would stay in Spain?

'Then come with me,' Tom cried.

'We are from different worlds.'

'America is full of your ancestors.'

'There will be a new Spain to attend to when this war is finished. There will be many people to nurse.'

'Then I will stay here.'

She shook her head gently saying, 'That is the war speaking. That is a man wondering whether he will be alive tomorrow.'

'I'll take you flying,' Tom said. 'We'll fly over Madrid and then we'll fly over the orange groves by the Mediterranean. I'll show you your country,' he said.

'I can see it from the ground; that's the view that matters.'

'And I'll grow oranges,' he said. 'And we'll live in Valencia in a house where you will not be suffocated.'

'It's a beautiful city,' Josefina said, 'with fountains, not like that pygmy,' pointing at the fountain whose spray had furred the cobblestones with moss. 'And a flower market and flat beaches and mauve sunsets and pastures of water where they grow rice. You would not believe how green that rice is,' Josefina said. Her hand tightened on his.

'We will marry in Valencia,' Tom Canfield said.

She said, 'The war has given your words wings.'

'But you do feel something for me?'

She didn't answer.

'I will be very proper and I will ask your parents if I may take you out and I will not talk about Fascist landowners and when we walk among the orange groves, when the blossom is in bloom, we will take a chaperone with us.'

She said, 'I would not want a chaperone.' And then she said, 'I am betrothed.' And then she turned away from him and all Tom could hear was the splashing of the fountain.

Betrothed. How old-fashioned, he thought. And how pathetic to let a mere betrothal stand in my way. Nevertheless, he felt clumsy once more.

'Do you love him?'

'He is a good man.'

'Is it . . . an arrangement?'

'My parents approve of him,' Josefina said, raising her head a little.

'And you?'

'I told you, he is a good man.'

'Then you don't love him,' Tom said, his words brimming with relief.

She said nothing.

'Promise me one thing.'

She waited.

'That you won't marry him before the war is over.'

'I cannot promise,' she said, 'but it is unlikely.'

They turned and retraced their footsteps along the flagstones. In the windows across the quadrangle they could see the faces of wounded soldiers and the bandaged heads of children who had trusted.

'So,' he said, at the creaking door to the dining hall, 'I'll see you tomorrow. Maybe we can walk again in the cloister.'

'Maybe,' she said.

He kissed her quickly on the lips and, chest aching, made his way back to his bed.

The fortune was put his way that evening. The soldier who was dying – you could smell the gangrene in his leg – handed Tom his bowl of soup; it was made from bones and thickened with bread but it was hot and for a while it drowned the pains of hunger.

'Here, drink this,' the soldier said. 'It's no good to me.' His voice was laboured, his English jagged.

Tom held up one hand. 'You drink it.'

'I only took it for you. I have no appetite for food . . . for life.'

'Bullshit,' Tom said.

'I was in America once. On the boats. I had a girlfriend in New York. That's how to learn a language, in bed.' A laugh rattled in his lungs. 'And what words! You like my accent?'

'If I could speak Spanish as well as you speak English I'd be president of the Republic.'

'It is not so good,' the dying soldier said. 'But it is enough.' His face was taut and unshaven and his eyes were glazed. 'I am a Catalan,' he said after a while. 'We are rich in languages in Spain, not like America. Catalan, Galician, Basque – Euskera as they call it – Castilian, which foreigners think of as Spanish until they stay in Barcelona or Bilbao, and Valenciano, which when it is compared with Catalan upsets the Valencians. In the north, on the borders with France, there is even another language, Aranais. So you see, if you think of our people as languages we are a very complicated country and one war is not going to settle our problems.'

He fell back on his pillow exhausted and the smell of his wounds reached Tom Canfield strongly.

'I think,' Tom said, 'that I would like to live in your country.'

'Say that to a Catalan and he would presume you meant Catalonia.'

'Spain,' Tom said. 'I like the feel of it. It feels like a country that's peered over a mountain, seen what progress has brought to the countries beyond and withdrawn into its own values. And those values are a darned sight better than those that pass for sophistication in other countries.'

'If you believe that,' the dying soldier said, 'you'll believe anything.' He managed a fragile smile. 'Me, I like America. Budweiser and hot dogs and skyscrapers and girls who swing their asses when they walk . . . Know what I like best?'

Tom shook his head.

'The choice.'

'I guess we never think about it,' Tom said.

'And I like Americans. Know why?'

Again Tom shook his head.

'Because they're natural. You, you're natural and being nice at the same time because you know I'm a goner. Goner, a good word. I like the way Americans speak.'

'You're not a goner,' Tom said.

'Sure I am. Don't you recognize the smell of death?'

Tom, who thought that the only way to save his life was to amputate his leg, said, 'All wounds smell bad.'

'Yours too?'

'Mine too.'

'One thing you can spot when you're dying is a lie, so don't do it Yank.'

'Okay,' Tom said, 'my wound smells clean.'

'Good, because I want to give you something.'

'You don't have to give me anything.'

'You're not loaded, are you?'

'You mean rich?'

'That's what I mean. This girl in New York asked whether I was loaded and when I said I wasn't she took my wallet and I was less loaded than I was before, but she was a good girl, that one . . .'

'Have you known many girls?'

'Many,' the dying soldier said. 'And all the best were American. And now, before it's too late, I want to give you this thing.' He pointed at a canvas pack under his bed. 'Open it, Yank.'

Tom unbuckled the pack.

'There's a bag inside with a razor in it and some shaving soap as hard as a bullet and a brush, badger fur . . .'

'Got it,' Tom said.

'Throw out the shaving gear. Rip out the bottom of the bag . . .' Beneath it was an oilskin pouch. Inside the pouch was a map. 'Take the map; it's worth a fortune.'

'But you must have relatives . . .'

'Sure I have relatives. All fighting for the Fascists.'

And before he died he told Tom Canfield about the gold.

CHAPTER 6

Adam Fleming convalesced in Salamanca the university city 100 or so miles north-west of Madrid where learning now dawdled behind its once hallowed reputation. Adam sensed this decay and it aggravated his own unease.

What was he doing in this becalmed and honey-coloured city, temporarily revitalized by the arrival of Franco who had established his headquarters in the bishop's palace?

He had been slightly wounded in the head by the bomb that had landed on the farmhouse and he had been concussed, hearing echoes in his skull and, on occasions, reeling dizzily. But all that had passed swiftly, so why had his two applications to rejoin his unit been ignored?

Was he still under suspicion, even though his explanation of his presence in a shell-hole with a Republican mercenary had finally been accepted? Or did the Fascists want to keep him here in aspic because, being that rarity, an Englishman fighting for their cause, he was good publicity? One sunny February morning he settled at a table in the Plaza Mayor and brooded. The mellow façades, trimmed with balconies and crowned with balustrades, that encompassed the square were prison walls: the arcades beneath them dungeons.

He ordered a glass of red wine from a waiter and reflected that, although there were plenty of haughtily smart officers about, no city could be further removed from war than Salamanca, won by the Fascists without bloodshed.

In front of him old people, mostly men, paraded backwards and forwards. Two ancients, wearing pebble-glasses, holding each other up; a dude with a bandit face wearing a camel coat and boots; a fat promenader with a bald head and a dyed monk's fringe that shone mauve in the sunlight; three majestic matrons sharing the propulsion of a baby in a pram . . .

Adam gulped his wine and shut his eyes tightly because he knew what was coming. Sweat cold on his brow, he waited until the vision that had visited him many times since the bomb fell on the farmhouse faded, until the corpses were completely obscured by the mist. Had it really been like that?

He opened his eyes. The old people continued to promenade serenely. The sun shone thinly. Pigeons pecked at his feet. An officer strode crisply across the plaza, making a parade ground of it.

'Are you all right?'

Adam looked up. A thick-set man, with a noble nose, wearing a blue beret and fawn overcoat that stretched nearly to his feet stood beside the table.

'I thought you looked a little under the weather,' he said. 'Mind if I sit down?'

Adam gestured at an empty chair.

'You are Fleming, aren't you?'

'How did you know that?' Adam was wearing civilian clothes, black sweater, tweed jacket and grey trousers, that had been lent to him at the hospital on the Paseo de San Vicente – a dead man's, he suspected – and he did not know this man.

'Well, you're the only Englishman fighting for Franco currently in Salamanca. Have you been interviewed many times?'

'Several,' Adam said.

The waiter placed a glass of red wine in front of him and a glass of anis in front of the stranger.

'One more won't do any harm.' He sounded very English. 'Do you mind?' He produced a gold pencil and a notebook which he placed beside his beret on the table.

'Can you identify yourself?'

'Good boy.' The stranger produced a card bearing a photograph identifying him as Edmund Ross, representative of a London news agency of which Adam had never heard.

'Better than a newspaper,' he said, 'my stories go all over the world.'

There was about him a benevolent authority that contradicted his theatrical coat. His brown eyes stared at Adam as though he were composing a portrait of him.

'I don't think I'm much of a story,' Adam said.

'Nonsense. Englishman fighting against the International Brigades? Against his Cambridge chums. What could be better? Editors are sick and tired of left-wing intellectuals sacrificing their young lives for the Republic.'

'I thought newspapers had been warned to avoid anything suggesting British intervention?'

'Stuff and nonsense,' Ross said. 'Were you wounded at Jarama?' He picked up the gold pencil.

'Slightly.'

'Come on, no false modesty.' He made a note. About what Adam couldn't imagine.

'I haven't done anything to boast about.'

Ross poured water from a jug into his anis and watched it turn cloudy.

Then he leaned across the table and said, 'Not having any doubts, are we?'

'Doubts? Why should I?'

'Any intelligent person doubts. I have always considered Doubting Thomas to be a most maligned person. Personally I would canonize him.' His brown eyes gazed at Adam. 'There is a lot to be said for both sides in this war . . .'

'Is there?'

'Have you heard about Unamuno?' Adam hadn't. 'Perhaps I shouldn't be telling you . . .'

'Then don't.'

The waiter brought another anis and another glass of wine.

'He was Rector of the university here. And he made his stand on the Day of the Race, the anniversary of the day Columbus discovered America, and it's celebrated in the great hall. Anyway Millán Astray was there. You've heard of him, of course.'

'Founder of the Foreign Legion.'

'Good boy. And Unamuno was in the chair. Anyway there were a lot of gung-ho speeches – the Basque and Catalan nationalists were described as "cancers of the nation", that sort of thing. Then Unamuno got up to make the closing speech.' Ross tossed back his cloudy yellow drink and pointed at Adam's glass. 'Drink up, for tomorrow we may die.' On cue the waiter served fresh drinks. 'Know what he said?' Adam shook his head. 'He said, "All of you are hanging on my words". Just like you. Am I right?'

'So what did he say?' Adam sipped his wine.

'He said that sometimes to be silent is to lie.'

'He's right.'

Ross made a note in his notebook.

'Then he had a go at the Legion's battle cry. You must know that.'

'Long live death.'

'Well done. Well, old Unamuno – he was 72 – said that this "outlandish paradox" was repellent to him. That El Mutilado, to wit Millán Astray, was a war cripple and soon there would be many more like him "if God does not come to our aid".'

'War is hell,' Adam said. 'General Sherman.'

'Good, good. Anyway, Unamuno was far from finished. He accused the Fascists of profaning the university and told them that, although they would win, by "brute force", they would never convince.'

'Why?' Adam asked.

'Because,' he said, 'they would need what they lacked – "reason and right in the struggle". So what do you think of that, young Fleming?'

'He was a brave man. What happened to him?'

'He was sacked, of course, and he died on 31 December last year. Of a broken heart, so they say. Do you think he was justified in what he said?'

'Do you?'

'Smart thinking, I like that. So, like me, you admire the late Rector of Salamanca University.'

'I said he was brave.'

'But you admire courage, surely.'

'And cowardice,' Adam said.

Ross made his brown eyes smile. 'You should become a diplomat, Adam.'

Adam, who didn't like the premature use of his Christian name, said, 'I doubt it: diplomats don't argue.'

'Is that why you joined Franco's side, because you argued yourself into it?'

'Of course I argued. The arguments I heard in Britain were wrong.' But was Unamuno wrong?

'Did you see any of your Cambridge chums at Jarama?'

'*Chums?*' Adam tried to remember where he had heard Ross's self-conscious brand of English. 'None.'

'Supposing you had come face to face with one of them. Would you have killed him?'

'Would he have killed me?'

'I'm supposed to be asking the questions, old man.'

'I suppose we might have killed each other.'

Adam bit the inside of his lips: the ghosts were on the march again.

'You're not being entirely helpful,' Ross said. 'People want to know what motivates you.'

'And you want a story?'

'Precisely.'

How about: Englishman accused of cowardice in the face of the enemy? Caught passing military secrets to an American serving with the Republicans. Sentenced to death. Sentence commuted if he shot the American. That would be a story all right.

'How about: Englishman Barred From Returning To The Front?' Adam suggested.

'Have you been?'

'I'm sure you know all about me, Mr Ross.'

'Could it be that you're not completely fit? You didn't look a hundred per cent just now.'

Soldiers, Republican or Fascist, falling forward . . .

'I'm perfectly all right.' Adam touched the dressing on his head. 'A small scalp wound.'

Ross said, 'What were you doing when the shell or bomb exploded?'

Did he know?

'I was in a farmhouse. Standing in the patio.'

'Doing what, Adam?'

You know, Adam thought.

'Minding my own business.'

'Odd, isn't it, Englishman fighting Englishman, German fighting German, Italian fighting Italian . . .'

'Are you? English, that is.'

'Do you, perhaps, prefer the company of Americans?'

The silence descended abruptly. And while it lasted, audible like the sound of the sea in a shell, Adam hooked the exaggerated accent from its depths: an undergraduate from Kenya.

Adam said, 'When were you last in Nairobi?' – his voice projecting ripples across the silence.

Ross stood up.

'Never been there, old man. I was in Tanganyika, Dar-es-Salaam. My father was in the German army and he married an Englishwoman. He was a bloody good soldier,' Ross said.

He put on his beret and slipped the notebook into the pocket of his theatrical coat.

'Have you got everything you want from me?'

'Oh yes, I've got that all right.' He managed another tight smile. 'A word of advice, old man. Don't get too smart, you might pick your own pockets.'

As he walked across the square, parting old men in front of him, Adam called out, 'Give my regards to Colonel Delgado.'

The following day Adam once again applied to be sent back to his unit. Delgado, who must have sent Ross to entrap him, had been badly wounded and wouldn't return to active service for several months, if ever, so Jarama where his unit was still stationed seemed to Adam to be a safer place than Salamanca.

But the young medical officer with the no nonsense manner wouldn't let him go. He shook his head like a marionette, scrawled indecipherable words on Adam's medical history, and said, 'I'm recommending you for ten days' sick leave. I suggest you go south, to the sun.'

'But there's nothing wrong with me.'

The medical officer looked up sharply. 'That is for me to decide and I am very familiar with the symptoms of shell-shock. Now get out of here before I decide to report you for insubordination.'

Back in the Plaza Mayor with another glass of wine, Adam debated where to take his leave. Granada, Seville, both taken by the Fascists early in the war . . . Jerez for some medicinal sherry . . . But I am not a bloody tourist: I've come here to fight for a cause.

And then he had it. Madrid. To see his sister whose bereavement had convinced him that his instincts were right. But as a convalescent resort it had one disadvantage: it was behind the enemy lines.

From Salamanca he took a train to Medina del Campo, 50 miles away. The journey took two and a quarter hours. There he picked up a connection to Avila, and hitched a lift for the remaining 70 miles to Madrid because he didn't know the contours of the front line to the west of the capital where, last November, the Fascists had penetrated as far as the university before stalling. No one questioned him – he was, after all, a *legionario* in a freshly pressed uniform, red tassel on his cap bobbing, an Englishman who had been wounded fighting for the movement with papers authorizing him to take sick leave. In his canvas bag he carried a soiled khaki uniform, rope-soled shoes and a pistol.

He travelled in a truck taking bread, olive oil and smoked hams to the front. He sat beside the driver, a Carlist who supported the claims to the throne not of Alfonso XIII but of the Pretender, Alfonso Carlos, who had died in Vienna in September. He was from Navarre in the north where the Carlists, in their red berets, had passionately supported the Nationalists.

He drove the truck at alarming speeds through-lightly falling snow along a mountain road between the Sierra de Gredos and the Sierra de Guadarrama. Through the snow Adam glimpsed crumpled white peaks aloof from the battlefields.

The driver, stout through years at the wheel, with a happy,

polished face, told Adam how the Fascists had held Avila when it was threatened by the Republicans.

'You should have seen the reds' column. It was led by Mangada who eats no meat and sunbathes without clothes. Under him was the scum of Madrid and a bunch of whores who hand out the pox the way we hand out bullets. Then suddenly Santa Teresa appears' – holding up one hand when Adam protested and causing the truck to swerve violently – 'and tells Mangada that Avila is full of armed men which it certainly wasn't. So what does he do? Halts his advance and goes back to Madrid. So you see, *inglés*, God is with us.'

Adam said, 'Santa Teresa died in 1582.'

'Her city was occupied by a rabble, so she returned.'

The driver lit a cigarette: the truck swerved again, wheels leaving black loops in the snow.

Adam said, 'Why did you support the claims of Alfonso Carlos?'

'Because he was the rightful heir to the throne, of course.'

'You'd better explain it to me,' said Adam who thought that the only royalists in Spain were Monarchists supporting the exiled Alfonso XIII.

'It is very complicated.'

'Tell me what you know,' Adam said.

'As I understand it,' said the driver, frowning, 'there was once a law in Spain that said a woman could not succeed to the throne. Well, the Government passed a resolution repealing that law.'

'So?'

'The King, Carlos IV, never signed a decree, so the resolution never became the law of the land. The next King, Ferdinand VII, made a will leaving the Crown to his unborn child. Fine if it had been a boy.'

'He had a daughter?'

'Two,' the driver said. 'But he had a brother, you understand, so the brother was the rightful heir to the throne. And what happened?'

'The first daughter became Queen?'

'Ferdinand was a weak man but he had a strong wife, María Cristina. So her first-born, Isabella, became queen. But

María Cristina ruled for many years as Regent. Isabella became Queen at the age of 13 and later had nine children by different lovers. The last,' the driver said with relish, 'was the son of a cook and an actor. She made him Minister of State!'

'But all that was a long time ago.'

'Ferdinand died in 1833.'

'So why do you feel so strongly about it?'

'Because the monarchy was a fraud and we fought two wars over it. Because we represent the old Spain. Because we believe in the Church. What has happened in the 100 years since Ferdinand died? Marxism and Anarchism, that's what. This war,' said the driver, 'had to happen: it was written a long time ago.'

'But your candidate for the throne, Alfonso Carlos, is dead. Who do you want to become king when you've won the war?'

The driver shrugged over his wheel. 'Alfonso Carlos adopted Prince Xavier as his heir. But he is very remote. Descended from a first cousin of Carlos IV . . .'

'As remote as Siberia,' Adam said.

'Perhaps we don't stand for kings any more; perhaps we stand for traditions.'

'But surely the thirteenth Alfonso would become king again. Or his son, Don Juan.'

'Do you really want to know who will be king when this war is over?'

'Tell me,' Adam said.

'Franco,' the driver said.

Adam left the Fascists' forward positions in the university at 11 pm. The moon shone fitfully. Rifles and machine-guns sounded occasionally, and soldiers from both sides called out to each other across the sandbags and barbed wire.

Keeping low, Adam made his way along the base of a gaunt wall. Bricks grated, powdered rain blew through the sockets of glassless windows as he changed out of his Fascist uniform. His feet found puddles and rubble and, once, a body. Had he crossed the demarcation line? Was he still Adam Fleming, *legionario*? Or was he by now Fleming, Adam, *Date de naissance*: 10-10-1918. *Lieu de naissance:* London. *Nationalité:* English. *Pays:* England. *Ville:* East Grinstead. *Parti Politique;* Anti-Fascist. *Date d'entrée:* 16-11-1936. *Profession*: Student. Chimo had found the blank International Brigade passport on a corpse at Jarama and given it to Adam. On the top left hand was a passport photograph of Adam squinting at the cameraman.

A rifle-bolt clicked. A voice as Andaluz as Chimo's said, 'Advance and identify yourself.' One hand on the pistol in his belt, Adam stepped forward and handed the passport to the soldier standing in the shadows, eyes shining in the moon-light.

'*Inglés?* What the hell are you doing here? You're supposed to be at Jarama.'

Adam, roughening up his accent, said, 'I was wounded.' He tapped his head. 'Shell-shock. They brought me back here for treatment. He pointed at the Santa Cristina Hospital. 'No one told me the Fascists had taken it.'

'What unit, comrade?'

'Fifteenth International.'

'Where did you learn Spanish?'

'The Polytechnic.'

'Where's that?'

'London,' Adam said.

'I'd like to go there some day,' the soldier said and handed the passport back to Adam. 'Pass, comrade, and keep going east.'

Adam picked his way through the rubble towards the centre of the city. He had memorized the route to his sister's house near the Retiro. He reached the Plaza de España, almost deserted, the few pedestrians deathly pale in the light from the blue-painted street lamps, and struck south-east down the Gran Via. In one cinema they were showing *The Festival of the Dove.*

He was stopped once by a militiaman brandishing an ancient musket. The militiaman examined the passport upside down and, after taking two cigarettes, allowed him to proceed. Still following his memory, he crossed the broad reaches of the Salón del Prado and the Paseo de Recoletos at the Plaza de la Cibeles, where the Greek goddess Cybele sat in the rain in a chariot pulled by two lions, and made his way down the Calle de Alcalá towards the park.

The house stood on the corner of a tall terrace adorned with balconies enclosed with glass which had somehow survived the bombs. It had about it a distinguished and inviolate air, and the unshaven militiaman in the vestibule beside the old-fashioned, out-of-order cage lift carried himself awkwardly.

He examined Adam's passport with exaggerated interest; he said that most occupants of the terrace were members of the Fifth Column and he thought that all such residences should be occupied by the workers. Wasn't that what the revolution was all about, equality?

'But my sister's English.'

'Then why doesn't she go back to England?'

'Because she married a Spaniard.'

'But he's dead.'

'His boys aren't.'

The mention of children had its customary effect. The militiaman was no longer an urban warrior: he was a porter with a gun and he wished fervently that the war hadn't penetrated the nursery. They were nice kids, he said, and 'between you and me I don't think their father was a Fascist but when men smell blood what can you do?'

'The boys are Spanish,' Adam said. 'That's why Eve has got to stay.'

'Eve?' The militiaman stared at him suspiciously.

'Julia. I call her Eve because my name is Adam.'

'In Spain,' the militiaman said, 'everyone has a nickname.' He paused as a dark imperious-looking woman came down the marble stairs. '*Adios*, Ana Gomez.'

The woman stared at Adam as though she was peering through the sights of a rifle. Then she was gone.

'That one hasn't got a nickname,' the militiaman said.

'Who is she?'

'A fighter. Her brother and his wife lived in a flat here but her brother . . . Now he *was* a Fascist. He fought with the Falange.'

'What was she doing here?'

'Making sure there's nothing there worth stealing. She's very loyal, that one.' He rasped the bristles on his chin with his hand. 'I like your Eve. She gives me carrots,' he said mysteriously.

Adam walked up the stairs to the first floor and rang the bell. He sensed someone examining him through the Judas Eye. Then the door was flung open and her arms were round his neck and she was crying.

In the elegant drawing-room, unused behind wooden shutters, he said, 'What's all this about carrots?' – because he could think of nothing else to say and then they were laughing as they always had done.

'A great discovery,' she said. 'Carrots keep in moist earth. I've got three boxes of them and I give some to the militiaman. He's rather sweet, really, although he wouldn't thank me for saying that. Would you like some carrots, Adam? Grated, boiled, diced – I've even made carrot marmalade. It's revolting,' she said.

'And the boys?'

'They're fine, but it's difficult. I try to teach them because their lives would be a misery at school, even if I could find one, but I was never any good at college.'

'You were good at playing truant,' Adam said. 'That's what you were good at.'

He smiled and examined her. She had been content and loved for so long that the worry pulling at her eyes was an awkward visitor. Her body had lean angles to it and her pale hair was combed severely. But if she hoped this made her a member of the proletariat she was sadly mistaken.

Paco regarded them glossily from a photograph on the top of a black Steinway.

Adam took packets from the pockets of his soiled tunic. Slices of ham, Manchego cheese, milk chocolate, two bars of Pears soap, a tube of Pepsodent toothpaste, four envelopes of tea.

'No carrots?'

'I couldn't bring any more – I would have been shot if I had been caught.'

She picked up a brown, translucent bar of soap and smelled it. 'Home,' she said. And then, 'No, this is home.' She sat on the piano stool still holding the soap and with her free hand picked out a few notes; they hung in the room beneath the chandelier.

'I never could play,' she said. 'How can you learn when you're in love with your music master?' She looked at Paco's picture; there was a patina of dust on the piano but the photograph was spotless. 'How on earth did you get here?' And when he had told her she said, 'Then why don't you stay?'

'Because I have to fight for what I chose.'

'And was your choice the right one?'

'I suspect that everyone made the right choice.'

'Did you know they stone women here if they wear hats?'

'Some of the hats you wore should have been stoned.'

'What's so sad,' Julia said, smelling the soap again, 'is that the people here are fighting for equality and all they've got is hardship the like of which they've never known before.'

'You can still talk like that after what they did to Paco?'

'I shall love Paco for as long as I live,' Julia said, 'but *they* didn't do it. Not the people of Spain, not the people of Madrid. A few madmen did it; but, of course, madness is infectious.'

'You amaze me,' Adam said. 'They murder your husband and you become a Communist.'

'I was never very bright, but in many ways I am wiser than you, Adam.'

'You know what you're doing to me? I came here to fight the people who murdered Paco and now you're robbing me of my purpose.'

'You would have come anyway,' Julia said. 'This war has to be fought and there have to be two sides.' She rippled a cascade of notes on the piano. 'I'm going to indulge in a platitude. Do you mind?'

Depression settled bleakly on Adam. 'Be my guest.'

'I don't want to think that Paco died in vain. There, how's that for a cliché?' She picked up his photograph and held it in her lap. 'He was a Republican, too.' Tears fell on the photograph and she wiped them away with a small handkerchief.

Adam became aware of unspoken appraisal when he took Julia's two boys, Manolo and Juan, for a walk in the Retiro. They didn't ask, 'Why did papa have to die?' but, silently, 'Why are you alive when he is dead?'

He took them on a rowing boat on the mossy waters of the lake, and bought two liquorice roots and a bottle of fizzy water at a stall. They watched girls flirting with gun-toting soldiers of the Popular Army, they played tag among the Lebanon cedars and rose gardens. The boys displayed some interest in the statue of the Fallen Angel, a little more in two monarchs with eroded noses, but for most of the time they conducted themselves dutifully and reproachfully. They made Adam feel like a stage uncle.

They ate meat-tasting vegetable pancakes and carrots for lunch; they drank a bottle of Rioja which Julia had saved and the boys ate the chocolate for dessert.

'Isn't it good of Uncle Adam?' Julia demanded and, staring at their empty plates, they said that indeed it was. As dusk settled smokily and casual gunfire made a Guy Fawkes night of it Adam saw them as they might one day become.

When they were alone Julia said, 'Can't you stay?' and Adam said, 'You wouldn't want me to become a turncoat, would you?'

'Ideals come in different garbs.'

He kissed her on the forehead. 'You really have become very wise.'

'And very lost.'

'I will never be far away,' he said, picking up his bag and walking towards the door.

She handed him a box dressed with Christmas wrapping and pink bows. 'A present. Don't open it now.'

He unwrapped the box in the street. Inside it was a carrot.

Tom Canfield's convalescence was occupied by ambitious visions in which he and Josefina shared a life of great contentment funded by gold. The gold, according to the

Catalan soldier who had died in the bed beside him, was part of Spain's gold reserves which, in the spring of 1936, had been the fourth largest in the world. In September, the soldier had told him, the Cabinet had decided to ship the bulk of this to Russia – to remove it from the clutches of the Fascists should Madrid fall and to open a bullion account in Moscow to pay for Soviet aid. But it had to be done secretly because, if the Anarchists learned that gold worth $500 million had been given to the Communists, there would be a civil war within a civil war. The gold, stored in the vaults of the Bank of Spain on the Plaza de la Cibeles, had been loaded into ammunition boxes and carried by 50 soldiers of the Popular Army to waiting trucks.

'Such gold,' the Catalan had said to Tom who was sitting in a cane chair next to his bed. 'Not just ingots – although there were 13 boxes of those – but coins from all over the world. Sovereigns, dollars, pesetas . . .'

'How do you know all this?' Tom had asked.

'Guess who was one of those 50 soldiers.'

The first consignment had been driven to Atocha railway station half an hour before midnight on 15 September and put on a train bound for the Mediterranean port of Cartagena in the south-east. At Cartagena this and the shipments that followed had been stored behind steel doors in three caves. Then, superintended by Alexander Orlov, an officer in the NKVD, the Russian secret police, and adviser in intelligence to the Republic, it had been driven in trucks by Russians stationed nearby to the harbour and loaded by Spanish sailors on to four Soviet ships, the *Volgores, Jruso, Kim* and *Neva*.

According to Spanish records 7,800 boxes had been loaded on to the ships. According to the Russians 7,900. And the Russians, according to the Catalan, had been correct because that night, with the unsolicited help of the Germans who bombed the harbour, 100 boxes had been off-loaded from one of the ships.

'You mean hijacked?'

'An American expression? It is good.'

'Who organized this hijack?'

'Guess who was one of the soldiers on that first train.' The

Catalan smiled. 'It wasn't very difficult. Not with the help of two officers on the ship. Orlov reckoned that 50 boxes were enough for one truck but we got 100 on board. That truck, it was like riding a pregnant elephant.'

'You were still there?'

'Guess who was one of the soldiers guarding the gold in the caves.'

'How many of you?'

'Eight, including the two Russian officers and two members of the crew. They got paid. In gold, of course. They were going to smuggle it ashore at Odessa.'

'But the gold was going to pay for arms for the Cause.'

'The Cause? Communism? Did you come to Spain to fight for Communism, Señor Tom?'

'I came to fight Fascism.'

'Which is very different.' His voice was growing weak and Tom had to lean forward in the cane chair to hear him. 'There is only one thing wrong with Communism: it doesn't work. So why shouldn't a few Spaniards who don't think a Republican victory is a dead cert – American again – take out a little insurance for the future?'

'A hundred crates of bullion? Some insurance.'

'For one man, certainly.'

Tom frowned. The Catalan pointed at his rotting leg. 'Where do you think I got that?'

'Jarama?'

'On the Córdoba front. My friends, my very close friends, all died there.'

Tom began to understand. 'The other hijackers?'

'All the gold is mine. Yours any minute now.'

'You're not dying,' Tom said, although he knew the Catalan spoke the truth.

'I am already making the acquaintance of death. In Spain these days he is a frequent visitor and there are times when you welcome him into your house.'

'I can't take all that gold,' Tom said.

'That is for me to say, Señor Canfield. It is my gold and I don't want my Fascist relatives to have it.'

'They are all Fascists, your relatives?'

'They think I am a traitor. There are many such families in Spain. It is the saddest thing about this war. Much sadder than death.'

Tom, thinking of Josefina, said, 'Where is this gold?'

'Ah, so you're an adventurer at heart. An American adventurer. I am glad the gold is going to an *americano*.'

'Where is this gold?'

'In the mountains to the north, close to the border with France. It is marked on the map. Take good care of that map, Señor Tom.' He held out his hand and Tom held it. 'Promise me one thing. That you will find that gold and you will keep it and you will do what you think best with it. For yourself and Josefina.'

'How do you know about Josefina?'

'I am a Spaniard,' he said, and those were his last words.

When they had taken away his body Tom sat for a long time in the cane chair thinking about the gold. Didn't it represent everything he had come to fight? But what was that? He wasn't sure any longer that he knew. He worried for many days and nights until he dreamed an almost perfect dream in which he and Josefina, parents of three children, two boys and one girl, owned a whole province of oranges spun from gold.

Then a new nurse came to his bedside and told him that Josefina had gone.

Tom wrote:

> *Dearest Josefina, I love you very much. Do not marry anyone else. I will find a way to reach you. Then we will fly over the orange groves together.*
> *Tom.*

He addressed it merely to Señorita Josefina Ronda, in the small town in Valencia where she lived because she had told him that was sufficient and the matron who said she had been granted leave because of 'bad news' had no further details. And wouldn't part with them if you were General Miaja himself, her tone implied.

'I disapprove of relationships between nurses and patients,' she told him in English.

'Did she leave a message?'

'Not that I am aware of,' said the matron, and Tom knew she was lying.

'Why is it wrong, ma'am, for a patient to fall in love with a nurse?'

'It isn't wrong for the patient: it is wrong for the nurse. The patients die – or return to distant places where they swear they will never forget and most probably never do, not even when they're married to the girl next door and have four children. America, Señor Canfield, is a very great distance from Spain.'

Tom said, 'I'm going to marry Josefina Ronda, ma'am,' and it wasn't until later that it occurred to him that the matron might once have been in love with a patient.

He asked a nurse to post the letter in Madrid.

Soon afterwards Tom was discharged. The dog with the whip-lash tail was waiting for him outside the monastery. It rode with him in a five-ton truck to Guadalajara. Seidler stood outside the hut. He said, 'What kept you?'

In March Ana got a job as a chambermaid at the Hotel Florida on the Plaza de Callao. The pay was pathetic but the foreign correspondents who stayed there brought her scraps of food from the Gran Via Hotel where they ate in the basement restaurant; she would have preferred to work at Gaylords, where the Russian advisers stayed, because they ate better but there was a long waiting list for jobs there and in any case, since her speech in the ruined church, it was safer for her to stay well clear of Communists.

The correspondents divided their time between the front line, Chicote's bar and the Telefónica. They complained a lot about censorship; they remembered other campaigns and other hotels, they took whores through the darkened lobby to their rooms and they drank a lot. But Ana liked them because, unlike reporters in the movies, they also laughed a lot and they were kind.

From the Florida, while Rosana and Pablo were at school,

she walked to the front line at the university, above the Manzanares, where she met other women from her *barrio*. There they handed out bread, olive oil, salt and cigarettes. Once she asked if she could sight the enemy from a trench and the men, remembering her ferocity when Madrid held four months earlier, let her occupy a water-logged slit and shoot Fascists.

In the homeward-bound, bell-clanging tram Ana thought about Jesús and his gentle ways. Where was he? Jarama was over, stalemate, waste. Guadalajara, where the Fascists had been sent packing? She hadn't heard from him for weeks but that wasn't uncommon when you were married to a soldier. Jesús a soldier? She smiled sadly as the tram swayed past heaps of rubble.

In the yard behind the *chabola* Pablo was kicking his scuffed football around with the same intensity that other slum kids, hoping to become a Joselito or a Belmonte, practised bullfighting as they waited to become *espontaneos* and jump over the barrier to confront a bull before being hustled off to gaol. Pablo's ambitions were less dangerous: he wanted to play for Real Madrid. Ana knew that even now, as he took the ball round the drying puddles, he could hear the roar of the crowd as the ball flew from his foot into the net at Chamartín.

Rosana was sitting beside the door painting on a canvas made from starched sacking. She still painted planes and bombs and guns but the planes had lost their inquisitive faces, the bombs their egg-like fragility, the guns their bullets chasing each other like broken pencil-leads. Her war had marched out of the nursery: her bombs were wickedly snouted, her planes had sharks' faces.

Ana held aloft a package containing chick-peas, fish and three oranges saved for her by the correspondents and said, 'A feast tonight.'

'Do we have to share them?' Rosana nodded inside the *chabola*.

Diego was standing in front of the cold grate, hands behind his back. He greeted her cordially, raising himself up and down on his toes like a Hollywood Englishman in front of a blazing fire.

She sat down, kicked off her shoes and stared at him without speaking.

'I came to warn you,' he said releasing one of his hands and searching for his small, wet moustache with it.

'I don't need warnings.'

'You're a hard bitch.'

'Most women are these days.'

'And stubborn.' She rubbed her bare feet together, arch against instep. 'Your speech the other day upset a lot of people.'

'Then it must have been a good speech.'

'It was discussed at a committee meeting of the Party.'

'Where? At Gaylords? I'm told the food is very good there. Perhaps you could get us some caviar, Diego.'

'I wasn't there. You have done me a lot of harm, Ana.'

'I weep for you,' Ana said.

'You are stupid as well as stubborn. Don't you realize that without the Communists we cannot win this war? That they supply our guns, our tanks, our planes, our ammunition? We're fighting the Fascists, Ana, not the Communists.'

'Would you like a box to stand on?'

'*Mierda!* It's the Communists who are organizing our army. What was it like before? A rabble, that's what.'

'A brave rabble,' Ana said.

'But a rabble just the same. You don't win wars with courageous, suicidal mobs.'

'How do you win them, Diego? Become a colony of the Soviet Union?'

'You compromise.'

'Grovel?'

'We have to co-operate with the Kremlin. Surely even you can see that.' He made a prayer of his hands over his tight little stomach.

'So that you can have a cosy job in the Comintern?'

'So that we can win the war.'

The football bounced into the room. Pablo retrieved it, shaking his head as though he had missed an open goal.

'Who would think,' Diego said, 'that I came to do you a favour?'

'And do yourself one at the same time?'

'And your children.' He paused with an orator's timing. 'Life could become very hard for you, Ana.'

'Harder than it is now?' She laughed harshly.

'It is always harder in prison.'

Ana stood up, hands on hips. 'Let them try, cousin. Let them try. If the Communists throw me in jail then the women of this *barrio* will march to Gaylords and the women of Madrid will march with them and then God help the Communists because no one else will.'

Diego spread his hands to an invisible audience. 'Very well,' he said. 'I tried.' He walked slowly to the door.

'Diego.' He turned. 'Do you remember how it was in the beginning?'

He looked at her. He opened his lips but his tongue found no words. He walked into the flimsy sunshine.

The message was brought by a dusty young soldier on a motorcycle. He had fine golden hair on his forearms and nail-bitten fingers; Ana remembered the hair and the nails quite clearly.

She opened the envelope carefully with a kitchen knife so that it could be used again. She read the brief note inside, then replaced it in the slitted envelope. She placed the envelope on the pillow of her bed.

Then she served the children breakfast. Bran-mash and what was left of yesterday's oranges and goat's milk brought by a friend from the country. The children were noisy that morning. But she didn't admonish them: she sought details that confused the shape of truth. When they left for school she stood at the door and waved as they opened the gate that swung on homemade, wire hinges, and walked down the mud road beginning to harden in the sun. Pablo's football lay in the middle of the yard.

She cleared the table, replacing the bowl of dried flowers and grasses in the middle; Jesús had picked those with the children when they had spent a week in Catalonia with one of her uncles. As they gathered the rustling bouquet he had been overcome by a fit of sneezing; he even sneezed in the house when he was close to the bowl; Ana smiled – poets should never sneeze.

Keeping her distance from the bedroom where the envelope lay on the pillow, she walked to the door. A plane flew high in the blue sky. One of theirs or one of ours? The children always knew . . .

The details were beginning to lose their power. She twisted the gold ring on her finger; it was warm with promises kept. She waved to a neighbour; the neighbour who must have seen the motorcyclist waved back uncertainly. She went into the bedroom, stared at the envelope, then picked it up, feeling it between thumb and forefinger in the way of lonely people who received little mail. She took out the officially-phrased letter. The words hadn't changed: . . . *at Jarama during the month of February.*

'I killed him,' she thought.

She stared through the window at the football lying in the middle of the yard.

CHAPTER 7

When Tom Canfield left the monastery he escaped, like an eagle freed from a cage, into the skies.

There he fought ferociously – some said suicidally – against the new Messerschmitt 109s which were superior to any fighter the Republicans possessed, shooting down four of them.

He was in the north when Fascist bombers razed the town of Guernica, killing more than 1,000 of its inhabitants and destroying the 600-year-old oak tree that was the sword of the Basque people. He was there, too, when their capital Bilbao, fell.

He was flying with Seidler from an airfield near Tarragona when, on 15 April 1938, the Fascists reached Vinaroz on the Mediterranean coast, cutting the Republican forces in two.

All the time he kept a diary.

5 May 1937. Now we're fighting each other. Communists v. POUM in Barcelona, POUM being Marxists who want to be independent from Moscow. There's a lot of shooting and the Communists are putting it about that POUM are in the pay of the Fascists. Is this what I came to Spain to fight for?

29 October 1937. The Republican Government has moved north from Valencia to Barcelona.

30 November 1937. Recovering from a fever, so plenty of time to write. I think about J. most of the time when

I'm not chewing the rag with Seidler or shooting down Messerschmitts or getting shot down. All those girls Stateside and yet here I am obsessed, *obsessed*, with one señorita. If I could I'd fly south to Valencia and try and find her but I've been warned that if I tried anything like that I'd be charged with desertion and shot and after what happened at Jarama who am I to argue? What happened to Fleming, I wonder? Would he have shot me? I have a hunch that pretty soon we Internationals are going to be shipped home. I shall stay put, until I find J., that is. Could she have married that guy? Did she even get my letter?

12 December 1937. Read in a newspaper about the visit to Madrid by members of the British Labour Party, with their leader Clement Attlee who, in the photograph, looks like an undertaker at a wedding. What good can they do, other than smoke their pipes and shake hands with lice-covered soldiers who haven't seen a bar of soap since last Christmas? At least we can do better than that. Paul Robeson has been wowing them in the International Brigade Hospital at Benicasim, especially the Abraham Lincoln Battalion. I met a guy from Cleveland who was there when he was singing. He reckoned everyone was crying buckets with 'Old Man River'. I wish I'd been there, it might have restored some of my faith. I *think* I still believe in the *Causa* but, Jesus, I wish there wasn't so much in-fighting, so much bitterness.

Christmas Day 1937. Not much of a celebration. What is there to celebrate? In any case Spaniards, so I'm told, celebrate Three Kings or Epiphany more.

12 March 1938. Just heard that the Lincoln's leader Merriman was killed when the Fascists swarmed into the province of Aragon. The retreat is fast becoming a rout. Rumours of executions for cowardice, desertion and incompetence. International Brigades still fighting heroically but said to be on the point of breaking up.

And, as usual, a lot of blame lies in the skies – the Heinkel 111s and the Italian Savoia bombers, backed up by Messerschmitts and Fiats, dominate. But we do our best with our little rats.

13 March 1938. Tailplane shot to bits by a 109. Seidler brought down too. So off we go to the fleshpots of Barcelona for a couple of days.

15 March 1938. Fleshpots? Well, we did find a kind of nightclub where they sold diluted Vermouth and a sort of band played jazz and there were a few available girls, but I guess fleshpots don't thrive on a ration of 150 grammes of bread, 100 grammes of chick-peas and 50 grammes of ordinary dried peas, no meat for the past month. Seidler and I walked down the Ramblas and tried to imagine it as it was before the barricades went up, before it went into mourning for Barcelona's dead. It wasn't difficult. Kiosks at one end – I bought two Nick Carters, would you believe – and then the bird market and the flower market and more kiosks where you used to be able to buy sodas and finally the waterfront. And the buildings! Spires, domes, turrets, balconies, tiles hemmed with blue ceramic flowers . . .

I'm writing this in the Majestic Hotel near the Plaza de Cataluña where you can get a sort of a meal for 50 pesetas. Seidler is asleep in the bed beside me. He snores but without his glasses he looks almost childlike. My first impressions of Barcelona: a vibrant, independent city which has managed to keep its graces in its salons and its factories in the backyard. You get the impression here that Madrid doesn't exist; or, if it does, it's the capital of a foreign country, another Paris or Rome. If Franco wins this war, as indeed he must, he's going to have as much trouble with the people of Catalonia as he will with the Basques.

16 March 1938. One of the biggest air-raids the virtually defenceless city of Barcelona has experienced. Eight raids, in fact, in four hours. Full moon, natch. During the day we wandered round the city, drinking beer we'd brought from the base and handing out our cigarettes. Gold-dust! Seidler gave a girl a whole pack and disappeared with her for half an hour. This was in the Barrio Chino. This district between the Ramblas and the Paralelo, is a concentrate of squalor and vitality. Gangsters, pick-pockets, whores, beggars, cripples and old men and women picking their way back into the past. Once you've been in it you no longer wonder why men and women become revolutionaries.

We got back to the hotel early, just in time, in fact, for the first air-raid at 10.15. By sea-planes (Hydro-Heinkels), of all things, based at Majorca. These were followed by Savoias. God, if I'd been in my little rat I'd have got my whiskers into that lot. If you can forget what's happening on the ground – the concentrated carnage, say, in the Fifth District where there is no escape (perhaps never was) – there is a terrible beauty about an air-raid. Searchlights sweeping the sky, sometimes snaring a plane like a silver fish, red tracer bullets chasing each other towards the stars, the sparkling flash of anti-aircraft guns which never seem to hit anything, the spouting red roar of bombs exploding . . .

17 March 1938. Whole streets squashed by a giant hand . . . apartment blocks sliced in half, privacy exposed (even a bicycle hanging from a beam), street cars mangled . . . bodies laid out in the Ramblas . . . blood congealing on the sidewalks . . . a boy cradled in a policeman's arms, lifted lifeless from the rubble that had been his home . . . What had he ever done to upset the Fascists?

19 March 1938. Back at base, the tail on my rat mended. I escape into the sky. Shake off the memories in the blue space and the valleys between the mountains of cloud. But the visions return when I touch down.

They say Franco is furious at the terror bombing of Barcelona and has given orders that it must stop. A little late for some. I wish that what I saw reaffirmed my decision to come here. But I didn't volunteer to fight for the Communists, or the Anarchists for that matter, or for the enemies of religion. I came here because it was the only thing to do. I wish sometimes that I could stay up there in the blue sky.

In London, 700 miles from Barcelona, Adam Fleming made his way along Fleet Street towards the City for an interview for a job he suspected he didn't want.

Indeed, since his enforced return from Spain 17 months earlier in April 1937, there had been little he did want. He had revisited Cambridge but its lazy indulgences had made him restless and when he had contemplated the waters of the Cam he had heard gunfire over the Jarama. He had spent a weekend with Kate Stoppard at the cottage in the Cotswolds but her insistence on treating him as a martyred hero irritated him and he had departed prematurely. He had worked for three separate companies – tea, oil and Baltic amber – but their ledgers had been prison bars.

What had intrigued him about the job prospect ahead was the letter from the managing director '. . . I understand that we may have a lot in common.' How could he possibly know? The company, according to the letterhead, was concerned with import/export; well, that could cover a multitude of sins and that was another small incentive to make the journey to the City from his lodgings in Marylebone.

He hesitated in front of a news-stand on the corner of Ludgate Circus. These days he bought newspapers with reluctance because every day they questioned what he had indirectly fought for. The German occupation of Austria, the proposed acquisition of the Sudetenland, the persecution of the Jews . . . Had he really been so innocent that he hadn't recognized Fascism for what it was? And today the Prime Minister, Neville Chamberlain, had flown to Munich to meet Daladier, Mussolini and Hitler.

Adam bought an evening newspaper but there was no

hard news about the outcome, merely speculation.

He walked up Ludgate Hill. Buildings were being buttressed with sandbags in case of war. When he had visited his parents, who still didn't understand why he had left home, trenches were being dug, gas-masks issued.

Adam skirted St Paul's Cathedral and walked down Cannon Street towards Mansion House. Despite the threat of war the impression was one of post-lunch lassitude – slow red buses and upright taxis and pecking pigeons and clerks returning to their offices. Adam wanted to shout, 'I was ordered to shoot my best friend.'

He turned down a side street.

The offices were in an atrophied and sooty building, decorated with three brass plates, squeezed between corporation granite. Adam was greeted by a grey-haired, camphor-smelling woman. Mr Trepper, she said, was expecting him.

Trepper, despite his mid-European name, looked as English as could be. Balding, with a rear-admiral's features, he was one of those men about whom women said, 'He must have been handsome in his day,' and still thought he was. He exuded rectitude and was wearily courteous.

'Tea?' He waved Adam to a seat across a desk scattered with papers weighted with brass shell-cases.

'No thanks.'

Trepper raised his eyebrows. 'Something stronger?'

Adam shook his head; he felt as though he had passed a test.

'Cigarette?' Trepper offered a dented gold case.

'I don't smoke.'

'Secret vices?'

'I read *The Well of Loneliness*.'

'And why not?' Trepper selected a cigarette and lit it with a Swan Vesta match. Adam felt he should be smoking a bulldog pipe and doubted whether he was the author of the letter he had received '. . . I understand that we might have a lot in common.'

'A momentous day,' Trepper said, blowing smoke towards a window as grey as fog. 'What way do you think it will go?'

'Poor Czechoslovakia,' Adam said.

'Not in favour of appeasement?'

'Nor non-intervention.'

'But you were fighting for the Fascists, weren't you?'

'I'm not in favour of weakness. Strength generates peace,' Adam said. 'How did you know I fought with the Fascists?'

Trepper pointed with his cigarette at a tinted photograph of George VI on the peeling wallpaper behind him. 'Are you a royalist at heart?'

'Up to a point,' Adam said. 'I was entirely in favour of the abdication.'

'Because of Mrs Simpson?'

'Because he was weak,' Adam said. 'And you still haven't answered my question.'

'I make it my business to find out everything I can about applicants for jobs.'

'You applied to me,' Adam pointed out.

'Because I liked what I had found out about you.'

'Why me?'

'You practise what you preach: you're strong. Although sometimes you cloud the issue by being argumentative. That's not strength, you know.'

'Stoppard?'

'I beg your pardon?'

'Was it Stoppard who told you about me?'

'I don't believe I know anyone called Stoppard.' Trepper poked at the white silk handkerchief in the breast pocket of his pearl-grey suit. The suit was out of character: it was a cad's suit. 'Where were you injured?'

'What part of my body or what part of Spain?' Trepper smiled indulgently. 'At Jarama. Does that mean anything to you?'

'If the Fascists had cut the Madrid–Valencia road the war would have been over a damn sight quicker. But I never got the impression that Franco wanted it to end quickly. He wants his enemy to be defeated and exhausted.'

'In any case I wasn't badly wounded; I was shell-shocked.'

'They invalided you out for that?'

Adam, who suspected that he knew anyway, told him about the unexploded shell, the meeting in the bomb crater with Canfield and his efforts in Salamanca to avoid repatriation. He added, 'I don't have to answer any of these questions, you know. This isn't an interrogation. What do you import-export anyway?'

'Somebody,' Trepper said, 'must have had it in for you.'

'The commanding officer of my unit didn't like foreign interference.'

'Not even 40,000 Italian troops?'

'He thought the Spaniards should sort out their differences among themselves. I appealed to Franco,' Adam said.

'And?'

'I'm here.'

'What do you think of Franco?'

'A survivor.'

'Frankly, I think it's all up with the Republicans. Their last fling was the Ebro; now the Fascists have recrossed it. Why did you fight for the Fascists, Adam?'

'I like to be on the winning side.'

'But you're a Fascist at heart . . . As a matter of fact I'm a member of the British Union of Fascists.'

'Mosley's gang?' Adam stared at him incredulously.

'They're patriots,' Trepper said. 'More than you can say for the Communists.'

'They're Jew baiters.'

He remembered Shoreditch in the East End where one hot, tar-smelling July day, he had watched Sir Oswald Mosley's black-shirted troops campaigning from their headquarters in Mintern Street. He heard again the beating of their drums and the clashing of cymbals and the breaking of shop windows and he saw Jewish shopkeepers looking on with forlorn resignation.

'How would you feel,' Trepper asked lighting another cigarette, 'if you were just making ends meet in the rag trade and a Jew who had fled from the Germans bringing the family jewels with him opened up beside you and put you out of business?'

'I'd open a sweet shop,' Adam said. 'Who wants a gown shop next to a sweet shop? All those sticky fingers . . .' He stood up. 'That letter of yours, you were wrong.'

'Wrong?'

'We haven't got a damn thing in common.'

'If you say so.' Trepper leaned back in his chair, unabashed.

Adam pushed at the door. 'By the way, what do you import?'

'This and that.'

'And export?'

'Guns,' Trepper said. 'Interested?'

Adam closed the door firmly behind him. The camphor-smelling secretary smiled at him as he made for the sun-light.

That day Chamberlain bought a little respite using Czechoslovak territory as coinage and announced on his return to England from Munich that he had secured 'peace in our time'.

While Britain rearmed, Adam joined the Territorial Army and sold advertising space for magazines to pay for his room in Marylebone, bed-sitter, bathroom and kitchen, which cost 30 shillings a week. He was bored and broke most of the time, eating frugally at Lyons or ABC tea-rooms, drinking the occasional half pint of bitter in the Volunteer, and sheltering from the rain in public libraries.

In the libraries he read the newspapers and learned one day that the International Brigades had left Spain. He related their long-ago enthusiasms to his own and felt desolate.

Why had they left? Because, according to an editorial, the veterans were mostly dead or departed anyway and Juan Negrin, Largo Caballero's successor as the Republic's prime minister, had gained a moral victory by proposing their withdrawal to the League of Nations.

There was, Adam realized, another reason: the Republicans had lost and in the final reckoning the foreigners would merely be a nuisance.

Adam, 20-year-old war veteran, adjourned to the Volunteer and got unambitiously drunk on the proceeds of space he had sold in *Everybody's* and *John Bull*. Standing at the bar, he could hear himself being boring and repetitive and, at closing time, allowed himself to be guided home by a middle-aged man carrying a purposeful rolled umbrella and wearing a decently crumpled blue suit and a Crombie.

Adam opened the door of his rooms in Nottingham Street with a classic fumble and his companion, saluting with his umbrella, disappeared into the rainy night. Adam went to bed half clothed and wept dramatically for Spain into his pillow.

His companion presented himself at 11.30 the following morning. This time he was wearing a charcoal-grey suit and a Brigade of Guards tie. He sat on the only easy chair in the room beside the broken teeth of the gas-fire, crossed his legs and, placing clasped hands on the handle of the umbrella, surveyed the bachelor debris of the room.

Adam said, 'Would you like some tea?' It was the last thing he wanted; a beer might have helped but emphatically not tea. He wondered what the middle-aged man whose name he couldn't remember wanted; if his mouth had been a little less dry, his skull less resonant, he would have asked him.

'Coffee?'

'I'll have a look.' Adam, tightening the belt of his dressing-gown went into the disgraceful kitchen. He found a bottle of Camp Coffee and heated a saucepan of milk.

'Feeling a little delicate, are we?' The stranger's voice reached him from the bed-sitting room. 'Hardly surprising. We quaffed a few. *Arriba España*.'

Had they made some arrangement for this morning? Adam watched wrinkled skin forming on top of the milk. He felt a little sick. 'Did I carry on a lot about Spain?'

'You spoke of little else. Understandable. It was a traumatic experience for all you youngsters. Whichever side you fought for.'

Adam said casually, 'Did I talk a lot about the actual fighting?' He was always afraid that when drunk, he would step into the recurring dream in which with bullet and bayonet he killed friend and foe indiscriminately; that, in company, he would freeze, mouth open, and cry out soundlessly.

'You were more concerned with the return of the International Brigades.'

'Poor bastards,' Adam said. 'They went out as crusaders and came back refugees.'

'Better to lose your dignity than your life.'

'I suppose you're right.' Adam mixed the milk and liquid coffee in two cracked mugs and handed one to the stranger. 'I came back in disgrace.'

The stranger sipped his pale brew. 'You made that point last night. Frequently. You do remember my name?'

'Waugh?' Adam frowned.

'Huxley. As in Aldous.'

'Did we arrange to meet this morning?'

'I didn't see a great deal of point in making an appointment.'

Adam wondered abruptly if he was queer. He was apologetically elegant with wings of grey hair combed above his ears but there was about him the restrained muscularity of a retired athlete still in condition. He certainly didn't look queer, but they wore many guises.

Huxley placed his mug on the mantelpiece beside a Westminster chiming clock and said, 'I think that's just about enough of that. And now I think you should know that you came through with flying colours.'

'Came through what?'

'Trepper is one of the best we've got,' Huxley said.

Astounded, Adam said, 'Best what?'

'Assessors,' Huxley said. 'Of character, that is.'

'Guns?'

'Forget it,' Huxley said.

'Mosley?'

'Doesn't even know his first name is Oswald.'

'For Christ's sake,' Adam exploded, 'what the hell is this all about?'

'Takes quite a long time to explain. You see,' Huxley said, attending to the wings of hair above his ears with the tips of his fingers, 'we've had our eyes on you for some time.'

'We?'

'From the moment you went to Spain. Maybe a little before. Not many British fighting for the Fascists, were there?'

'Plenty of Germans and Italians. The enemies of the future.'

Huxley subsided in his chair with evident satisfaction. 'That's just what I want to speak to you about,' he said.

Adam sat on the dishevelled bed. Huxley made the room look even more untidy than it was.

'It must be apparent to you,' Huxley said in his careful voice, 'that sooner rather than later we shall be at war with Germany and, presumably, Italy.'

Adam said the possibility had not escaped his notice even if it had escaped Baldwin's and subsequently Chamberlain's.

'And Spain will play a vital part in that war. If Franco throws in his lot with Hitler then the Germans will be able to sweep right through the Iberian peninsular to Gibraltar. If we lose Gib we've lost the Mediterranean.'

'Well,' Adam said, shivering, 'he certainly won't throw in his lot with the Russians.' He struck a match, leaned forward and lit the gas fire; its broken fangs glowed and small blue flames plopped at their roots.

'We don't think' – Huxley favoured the first person plural – 'that Franco will want to go to war. On the other hand he must favour the Axis powers. Without them he couldn't have won the civil war.'

'He hasn't won it yet,' Adam said.

'Just a matter of time.' Huxley sniffed the gas escaping from the rubber pipe leading to the valiant little fire. 'Fancy a stroll?'

'Why not?' Adam retired to the bathroom, washed, brushed his teeth and grimaced at the face in the mirror; the dark features of a seeker of truth stared back muzzily. He put on flannels, black polo neck and a Harris tweed jacket with the obligatory leather at the elbows.

Regent's Park, jewelled with frost and smelling of fallen leaves, helped to revive him.

Huxley, prodding at leaves with the spike of his umbrella, said; 'You're a curious case, Adam.'

'I didn't realize I was a case at all.'

'I mean fighting for the Fascists. Under normal circumstances we wouldn't have considered you at all.'

'Considered me for what?' Adam watched two pretty nursemaids pushing prams with aristocratic coachwork; he smiled at them and one smiled back.

'Why did you fight for the Fascists?'

'Would you have "considered me" if I had fought for the Republicans?'

'Most young men who went to Spain did.'

'What you don't understand is that none of us was pro anything. We were all anti. They were against the Fascists, I was against the Communists. Have you been following what's been happening in Russia this year? The purges, the staged trials, the executions? Or have you been too busy concentrating on German aggression?'

'I hope,' Huxley said, spearing a leaf as they skirted the boating lake, 'that you're not pro-Hitler.'

'I told you, I'm not pro anything. Obviously we'll have to fight the Germans' – Huxley looked relieved – 'but I don't think we should lose sight of the fact that the Communists are our enemies too.'

'You sound a little paranoid.'

Perhaps I am, Adam thought as he fired his rifle into the confusion of bodies and heard the shots and the screams.

'Are you all right?'

'I need a beer.'

'Hair of the dog? Good idea.' Huxley sign-posted the Hanover Gate exit with his umbrella. 'But I'd better have my say before we get to the pub. You see you are in a unique position. Epsom, Cambridge . . .'

'. . . dropped out.'

'Spanish, fought for Franco . . .'

'. . . checked out.'

'Invalided out. A bloody hero. The Fascists will welcome you back.'

'Who says I want to go back?'

'We do.'

'Who's we, for Christ's sake?'

'You see,' Huxley said as they walked in the general direction of Lord's cricket ground, 'the average Englishman in Madrid will be treated very circumspectly when war breaks out. If Franco supports Hitler then we're the enemy. But not you: you were one of them. Ever thought of joining the Diplomatic Corps, Adam?'

'Diplomats don't argue.'

'Then you will be a refreshing change on the Madrid scene.'

'What exactly do you want me to do?'

'We want you to work for us.'

'To become a spy?'

'A word we don't encourage.'

'Against the Fascists for whom I fought?'

The umbrella pointed at the high walls of Lord's. 'Red Indians camped on the pitch in 1844 and gave archery displays. My,' Huxley said, 'how times change.'

Towards the end of 1937 when, in between the victories at Belchite and Teruel, optimists still believed that there was hope for the Republic, Ana Gomez did something that she had never believed possible: she left Madrid.

She did it for the children because the Communists' threats now had the edge of a butcher's knife and she did it for herself because there was no longer any place for her in an atrophied city. She told the children that they were going to live on the great plain of La Mancha.

'Where Don Quixote tilted at windmills,' she reminded Rosana.

Did they detect the change in her, indifference? She wasn't even sure how deeply the bereavement had affected them; death was as common as toothache these days. They had seemed embarrassed but later in their bedroom, their voices had sounded lonely. But it wasn't loneliness that afflicted Ana; nor, for that matter, predictable grief; she was detached from her widowhood and saw herself as a stranger.

Meanwhile she packed their meagre possessions into battered suitcases and cardboard boxes, concocted ingenious meals and exchanged trench gossip with the foreign correspondents at the Florida.

On the evening before she put the children on the train to Ciudad Real, 110 miles south of Madrid, she was visited by a member of the Communist Party wearing a black leather jacket with a red star pinned to the lapel. He was a well-rehearsed man with pale hair and eyes who seemed a little ashamed of himself.

'It has come to our notice, Ana Gomez,' he began, 'that you are making plans to move.'

Who had told them? The old bitch who now made wreaths solely of red instead of Anarchist black and red?

She didn't invite him indoors where the suitcases and the boxes strapped with rope would give him all the answers he needed, even the address in black marking ink.

'What if I am?'

'You have done the Cause a lot of damage in Madrid, señora.'

'Your cause, perhaps.'

'The common cause. Could we perhaps go inside?' His breath smoked on the cold air and the chilblains on his fingers, a common complaint in Madrid these days, were raw.

'I like to take the air at this time in the evening,' Ana lied.

Shrugging, he tucked his hands inside the leather jacket. 'Where are you going, Ana Gomez?'

'My business, comrade.'

'Our business, comrade.'

'We're not in Russia,' Ana said.

'I'm not a Russian.'

'But you were trained in Moscow?'

'I'm a Madrileño,' he said with a spark of pride.

Ana, assuming he was a member of SIM, the secret police, said, 'Then as a Madrileño, as a cat, you will know that although we are an extrovert people we enjoy our privacy.'

'You have a way with words, señora. Now, please, where are you going?' He took his hands from inside his jacket and rubbed them together; flakes of skin fluttered to the ground.

'If I don't choose to tell you?'

'We shall find out.'

'If I have made so much trouble aren't you pleased that I'm leaving Madrid?'

'Delighted. We want to make sure you don't make any more where you're going.'

Ana gazed at him reflectively. He was a man who was not proud of himself.

'If I tell you will you leave the children alone?'

'As if we would harm them.'

'Your word?'

He stuck his hand out and she took it feeling its shiny bumps and its roughness.

She said, 'Where is the fiercest fighting just now?'

He ran his fingers through his pale hair. 'Teruel probably.'

'Then that's where I shall be,' Ana said.

When he had gone she went indoors and sat at the head of the scrubbed table. Then she went into her bedroom, took the newspaper cuttings of Jesús's poems from an old wallet beneath her pillow and gazed at them for a long time, mouthing the gentle words.

The following morning she put the children on the train to Ciudad Real where they were being met by another cousin, Diego's elder brother. Not that they wanted to go – hunger and danger were part of growing up in the city of Madrid – but they accepted adult wisdom because there was no other. Except for one moment on the platform: Rosana flung herself at Ana and clung to her. Then Pablo took his sister's arm and escorted her on to the train and Ana piled the disreputable luggage in behind them.

They didn't wave as the train, its engine billowing smoke and steam and smuts, moved off but they pressed their faces against the grimy window and for a moment Ana felt a parting of the flesh. Then the flatness settled once more and she returned to her empty home.

There she sat for a few moments beside her own luggage and drank some gruel for she was determined to keep fit for what lay ahead. My husband is dead, she thought, my children have gone, my cousin is filled with hatred for me, by brother is the enemy. This is truly a family war.

She put on thick underclothes, black dress and *gorillo* forage cap, took a last look at the ancestors on the wall and locked the front door; not that it would deter an intruder but one of the advantages of being poor was that you had little to offer a robber.

From the *chabola* she walked, carrying her cardboard suitcase, to the highway to Valencia; there she hitched a ride on a lorry taking ammunition to Teruel, one of the coldest cities in Spain, 150 miles or so due east of Madrid and 3,000 feet high. At Tarancón the driver, a jovial and unshaven brigand, branched left, stopping for lunch at Cuenca where houses hang over a sheer rock face. He bought bread and olives and a jug of rough wine and claimed payment 30 miles outside Teruel. Ana removed his hand from her waist, pulling the little finger so that it was in danger of breaking; then she took a pistol which she had acquired in the fighting at the university from her belt and stuck it in his ribs. 'Keep your hands off me, *cabrón*.'

He shrugged, laughed, started the engine and drove into the snow falling steadily around Teruel.

It was 17 December and Enrique Lister's 11th Divison of the 22nd Corps of the Army of the Levante had encircled the walled city.

Ana stowed her suitcase in a cottage and made her way to a hill overlooking the River Turia where the dead still lay in the snow. She eased a rifle from the frozen grasp of a steel-helmeted Fascist and buckled on his belt and ammunition pouches. Then she went to do battle.

At first they wouldn't let her. This bleak and bloody fortress was no place for a woman, they said. Then she found an officer in the 18th Army Corps whom she had known during the defence of Madrid in November 1936. He told his superior officer that nothing short of a shell, and an armour-piercing one at that, would stop Ana Gomez.

'You should have seen her at a bridge over the Manzanares,' the officer told his superior sheltering behind a tumulus of boulders from the snow which, at dusk, swept down from the mountains like buckshot. 'She was shooting Fascists, okay, but she was just as willing to shoot any Republicans who wanted to retreat.' The superior officer wearily waved Ana into battle.

And she fought remorselessly, firing her rifle from behind brown rocks, lying flat as mortar shells kicked up dirt and the snow, sleeping between the warm bodies of exhausted men, dipping hard bread into pans of scalding goat-meat stew, creeping up, corpse by corpse, to the walls of the city.

On the 21st the dynamiters from the coal mines of Asturias arrived and bombed their way towards the Moorish towers beyond the walls where El Cid had once fought the Moors. Within a few days the defenders of Teruel were cornered in the Bank of Spain, the convent of Santa Clara and the governor's office.

On Christmas Eve, while frost-bitten, exultant soldiers paused to sing the Internationale, defiant voices turning to crystals on the night air, Ana stood back in her black skirt and her officer's fleece-lined jacket and her *gorillo* cap, going about her calculating business.

Had anyone here fought at Jarama? Had they known a tall, gentle-faced soldier who wrote poetry for *Mundo Obrero*? No matter, there would be other battles, other gatherings of veterans, and one day someone would remember the manner of his death.

But never forget, Ana, that although you did not shoot him in the back it was you who sent him to his death. But with vengeance there comes a little peace; that is the way it is.

So Ana, now known as *La Viuda Negra*, The Black Widow, fought with the troops who, on 8 January 1938, won a famous victory when the commander of the garrison surrendered with the Bishop of Teruel at his side, and fought a rearguard action the following month as the Fascists recaptured the city.

She took part in the crossing of the River Ebro in July 1938; she took part in the retreat across the same river the following November. She was in Catalonia as the haemorrhage of refugees, bewildered elders and limbless children among them, bled through the snow-covered peaks of the Pyrenees to France; she was there when Tarragona and the capital, Barcelona, fell. When the end came she was in Alicante where thousands of refugees waited for ships to evacuate them.

She heard about the struggle between the Prime Minister, Juan Negrin, and Colonel Segismundo Casado who had assumed power in Madrid. Negrin wanted resistance to continue, Casado wanted an end to the blood letting, a negotiated peace – and good riddance to the Communists. She heard that in Madrid, Republicans were fighting Republicans, just as they had fought Fascists in that brave, long-ago summer of 1936. She heard that La Pasionaria had left Spain by air from Elda, a few miles from Alicante; she heard that Negrin had flown to France from the same airport. She heard that at midday on 27 March Fascist troops had taken Madrid. On 1 April she heard Franco's victory communiqué that concluded, 'The war is finished.'

But not for her.

She remembered a guest at the hotel near the Puerta del Sol telling her that, in Britain, 1 April was known as All Fools' Day. This war, she thought, should have ended on the equivalent day in Spain, 28 December, the Day of the Innocents.

Jesús had been an innocent.

PART II
1940–1945

CHAPTER 8

What war?

At least half a million Spaniards had died and there hadn't been one.

Ask any peasant who had slaughtered a landowner's prize bull and now feared his own executioner's knock on the door.

Ask the Fascist mayor who, anticipating the vengeance of his parishioners, had hastily organized a farming commune and sung the Internationale on the steps of the town hall.

Ask the lazy and piqued younger son who had denounced his industrious elder brother as a member of the Falange.

Ask the privileged of Madrid or Barcelona or Valencia who had parleyed with Communist commissars.

Ask the solidiery, Fascist or Republican, who had put their countrymen to the sword.

Ask the parents of young cripples, *mutilados de guerra*, who wore boots on their hands because they had no feet.

Ask and polite smiles assumed slippery angles. Eyes focused on distant horizons. Important appointments were remembered. Doors closed firmly.

What war?

The amnesia about the conflict that had left scars deep in his own soul was one of the greatest challenges to Adam Fleming's newly acquired diplomatic skills.

In the early days in Madrid he occasionally blundered. At a dinner party given by a Spanish diplomat at the Restaurant

Botin he engaged a suave official from the Foreign Ministry in conversation about the civil war.

'What civil war was that, Señor Fleming?' the diplomat asked. 'The American or the English?' And when Adam stumbled on he said: 'There was a crusade not a civil war. A crusade against those who wished Spain ill.'

And at a party thrown by a German newspaper editor in the Ritz, rendezvous of spies, mostly Nazis, he drank too much schnapps and questioned a Berlin columnist about the destruction of Guernica by the Condor Legion. But the name didn't seem to register. All the columnist said was, 'I must remind you, Herr Fleming, that the Condor Legion was made up of volunteers, just like the International Brigades.'

Adam's indiscretions, however, were largely forgiven because he had fought for the Fascists in the war that never was. Ironic, he reflected, that he should now be intriguing against them.

But, although the dark moods and visions that visited Adam remained, espionage did provide some sense of fulfilment. Not only were the Germans winning World War II on all fronts – they had occupied most of Europe and were setting their sights on beleaguered Britain – but in these late summer days of 1940 they acted as though they ruled Spain from Berlin. They censored Spanish newspapers, campaigned against Britain in publications such as *Arriba*, filled the best hotels with their delegations, impeded the escape of British prisoners-of-war from France and peered belligerently across Spain from the peaks of the French Pyrenees.

Adam's old obstinacy resurfaced, foundering occasionally on the smooth rocks of diplomacy which, as a second secretary at the British Embassy, he was obliged to observe. How could an undergraduate renowned for perverse debate at the Cambridge Union learn to compromise?

His attitude, which he did not always manage to conceal at the embassy on Fernando el Santo where Sir Samuel Hoare was ambassador, did not endear him to his colleagues, and he sometimes wondered if they suspected his true calling. He was, after all, an unlikely candidate for one of the most sensitive missions on the diplomatic circuit.

He was relieved of routine and conciliatory duties by the intervention of an unlikely benefactor, a German spy.

It was 11 am on 16 September, a dry and expectant morning. He was sitting in his suit of diplomatic grey on the corner of Serrano and Ayala, at a bar furnished with fumed oak and silver-painted columns and decorated with prints of racehorses, drinking coffee and ruminating about the briefing he had received from Huxley on their last stroll round Regent's Park.

'Broadly speaking,' spearing an empty packet of Players with the spike of his umbrella, 'what we want to know is whether Franco intends to throw in his lot with Hitler. Stands to reason, doesn't it? More specifically we need to know about Herr Hitler's intention irrespective of whether the Caudillo co-operates with him. In other words, does he aim to march through Spain and go for the jugular – Gibraltar?' Huxley removed the blue wartime cigarette packet from his umbrella. 'What would you do, Adam, if Hitler did try and pinch Gibraltar?'

'Blow it up?'

'A thought. Although it might be cutting off your Rock to spite your face. Know what I'd do if I were Churchill? I'd promise Franco that, when we'd won the war, he could have Gib, provided he didn't do a deal with Hitler.' He glanced at his watch. 'Time for a pint?'

Adam scanned his morning newspaper in the bar in Madrid. According to the BBC earlier that morning the Luftwaffe had yesterday suffered an overwhelming defeat as RAF Spitfires and Hurricanes had shot its bombers and fighters out of the skies over Britain. The brief dispatch in the Spanish paper merely recorded the bombing in England of 'strategic targets'.

The stranger said, 'You won't read anything about it there.'

Adam looked up. He was shortish with brown hair so precise that it looked like a wig and smiles glued at the corners of his eyes. Ill-advisedly, he wore a Prince of Wales check and brogues.

'Won't read what?'

'About the air-raid. According to the British newspapers the RAF shot down 175 Huns.'

'Are you with the embassy?' He reminded Adam of an actor over-playing the part of an Englishman. He had trouble with his sibilants, too.

'In a manner of speaking.' The assumption seemed to please him. 'They managed to haul a time-bomb out of St Paul's too.' He smoothed a non-existent moustache. 'Fancy a stroll?'

'Why should I?'

'I have a proposition to put to you. And no I'm not a bloody queer.' His voice cracked with suppressed laughter; the adhesive smiles moved in unison. 'Could be to your advantage; but whatever you do don't make a scene here.'

'As if I would – I'm an Englishman too!' Adam left some change on the table and followed the stranger on to the pavement beneath the acacia trees.

'You really do think I'm English?' the stranger said when Adam caught him up. He adjusted a tongue of yellow silk handkerchief lolling from the breast pocket of his jacket.

'As English as frankfurters and sauerkraut.'

The stranger's laugh was like cracking ice.

They walked south. The streets were elegantly crowded but even now, 18 months after the end of the Civil War, they looked as if they had just emerged from moth-balls. Adam wondered what it was like in the poor suburbs where hunger still sat at the head of the table.

Finally the stranger came out with it. 'Austrian, in fact.'

'So is Hitler,' Adam said.

'And yes I'm at the embassy. The German embassy. Didn't I fool you for one minute?'

'Before you spoke. It's your s's,' Adam said. 'You hiss them.'

'I'll have to work on that. By the way, Moser's the name.' He stuck out his hand and Adam thought, 'I've never seen anyone shake hands while walking,' but he took the Austrian's hand just the same. 'Moser . . . Did I hiss that, too?'

'Spot on with your Moser,' Adam said. What if anyone from the British Embassy saw him consorting with an Austrian from the German Embassy? They would report him and he would be cleared by his undercover superior in Chancery and everyone would whisper, 'Told you so', but the game would go on.

Adam said, 'So, what's the proposition?'

'We've been studying your form, old man.'

'I'm not a racehorse.'

'Your pro-Fascist stance in Britain in 1936. Your enlistment in the Nationalist army during the Civil War. You speak fluent Spanish too, I believe. No hissing.' He laughed loudly.

'I speak German, too. Would you prefer it if we spoke your language?'

'No,' Moser said, 'let's stick to English, old man. After all we look like two Englishmen.' He glanced anxiously at Adam.

'What do you want?'

'You weren't too happy in London. One job after another. Soldiers who fought for Franco not appreciated, eh?'

They passed a one-legged man begging. A blue beret lay on the pavement in front of him; beside it a piece of cardboard bearing the information that he was a war veteran with a wife and children to support. His cheeks were hollow with hunger. Adam dropped 25 pesetas into the beret.

'Hey, steady on, old man,' Moser protested.

'He must have fought for the Fascists,' Adam said, 'otherwise he wouldn't be there. Now about this proposition . . .'

'You were anti-Commy, I believe.'

'Which is why I fought for the Fascists.'

'Germany is still anti-Commy,' Moser said.

'Is that why Hitler signed a non-aggression pact with Stalin?'

'Just biding his time, old man,' lowering his voice. 'Don't forget what Ribbentrop said six months earlier.' He paused, moving his lips silently. Then: '"Towards the Soviets we will remain adamant. We never will come to an understanding with Bolshevist Russia".'

'Didn't take him long to change his mind,' Adam said. 'Anyway, Stalin only signed the pact because Britain and France refused to sign one with him.'

'Biding his time, too. When will the English realize that the final struggle will be with the Communists?'

'The proposition, Herr Moser.' Adam, who had an appointment with his sister, glanced at his watch.

'It is obvious, I think. We want you to help us fight Communism.'

Adam stopped and faced the Austrian, who stroked his invisible moustache with the tips of his fingers. 'I have always thought,' he said slowly, 'that I should like to live beyond my means.'

Moser's cheeks bunched the smiles at the corners of his eyes. 'That can be arranged, old man.' He stretched out his hand. 'I think everything is going to be very satisfactory,' he said, contentedly hissing the s of satisfactory.

Adam told Atherton, his MI6 superior in Chancery, about Moser's approach as they sat on a park bench near the rose gardens in the Retiro, watching a boy in a sailor-suit and a girl wearing a bottle-green coat and bonnet bowling a hoop.

'Ah, our friend Moser.' Atherton was a well-nourished man fitted tightly into chalk-stripe suits. 'Department Six of the RSHA. Implacable enemies of the Abwehr. Thank God German intelligence is as divided as the Republicans were in the Civil War. Well, you're doing well, young Fleming.' He patted Adam's knee. 'Now's your chance to become a double agent and feed the buggers a lot of bull.'

The boy in the sailor suit gave the hoop a whack. The girl clapped her hands. The hoop raced down the path past the neglected blooms of the roses.

Adam said tentatively: 'I think it would help if I appeared to be intensely patriotic and anti-Nazi. Moser's cronies would like that. The perfect front for someone spying for them inside the British Embassy.'

'Good thinking.' Atherton, who always gave the impression that he had just emerged from a long sojourn in a bath, examined his little pink fingernails. 'Anything in mind?'

'How about helping to spring escaped British POWs from Spanish gaols?'

'Excellent. That's one of Sam Hoare's crusades.' He stood up, chalk stripes on his suit tightening. 'I'll see what I can do.'

The boy hit the hoop towards Atherton. He watched it,

then stepped aside with surprising agility. '*Ole,*' he said, as the hoop hit the bench and subsided lazily on the path.

Three weeks later, in the second week of October, Adam drove through Aragon and Catalonia to Figueras in the north-east of Spain, close to the border with France. Many British prisoners-of-war escaping from France into Spain were imprisoned there, and the journey gave him his first opportunity to observe the deprivations of victory.

Whenever the embassy's black saloon with the Union Jack fluttering on the bonnet stopped in a village it was besieged by children with stomachs swollen with hunger. Adam handed out money and cigarettes but it was food they wanted.

He saw old people foraging in the ruins of houses. They had lost the war, these old people and these children, and their homes had not yet been rebuilt. He saw peasants, hands tied behind their backs, being led at gun-point down dusty roads to oblivion.

He took a wrong turning and came to a concentration camp – 250,000 Republicans were still said to be locked up – and heard gunfire, the volley followed by intermittent shots that characterize an execution carried out with rifles and concluded with pistols. He tried to speak to some of the emaciated prisoners on the other side of the wire but two Civil Guards, sunlight glinting on their black tricorn hats, waved him on with machine-pistols.

By the time he reached Figueras it was time once more for his familiar spectres to pay a visit. They had grown bold on the long journey and in the winter-smelling wind blowing from the Pyrenees they loomed menacingly in the blizzard of his thoughts.

The prisoner Adam wished to see was Second Lieutenant Peter Charlesworth of the 6th Battalion Durham Light Infantry who had been captured in France during the Battle of Arras on 21 May, five days before the evacuation at Dunkirk. He had escaped from a temporary POW camp, fled south through Paris, Dijon, Lyon and Nîmes and crossed the

border into Spain at Le Perthus. Charlesworth had been
arrested by Spanish border police and taken to Figueras gaol
where he had remained for three months.

Adam didn't expect the Spanish to be co-operative: they had
only just admitted Charlesworth's existence. Now they would
claim that under the Hague Convention of 1907 they
would need proof that he was an escaped POW and point out,
under German pressure, that even if he was, he had entered
Spain illegally, without a passport or visa. 'How do we know he
isn't a Republican spy?' they would ask.

Charlesworth, wearing a blue fisherman's jersey and
crumpled grey trousers, certainly didn't look like a spy. He
was a thin, sandy individual, with a lugubrious moustache
and reproachful brown eyes. Nor did he seem incensed about
his imprisonment; if it hadn't been for the war, he implied,
he would never have travelled further south than Scar-
borough, let alone taken part in a memorable battle and seen
the inside of a Spanish gaol.

The Spaniards, he assured Adam, were treating him 'pretty
decently' which was more than could be said for some of the
reds sharing the prison with him. There *was* one thing Adam
could do for him: get word to his wife in Bishop Auckland
that he was well.

Adam said, 'You do want to get out, don't you?' They
faced each other across a table furrowed with cigarette burns.

'Of course I do,' although Adam got the impression that he
wasn't in a hurry to return to Mrs Charlesworth.

'Well, I'm bloody well going to get you out,' Adam said.
'You're a test case. If we spring you then there's a chance for
the rest of the poor sods who thought they'd got away to
freedom.'

'The Germans took my papers,' Charlesworth said. 'But I
only gave them name, rank and number.'

'Well, we've got duplicates of your army records, and your
birth certificate and a photograph and your dental records . . .'

'So there's not much chance.'

'Of what?'

'Of being left here.'

'None,' Adam said. 'Does that upset you?'

'Of course it doesn't. I wonder where my next posting will be.'

'First you'll get some leave,' Adam said. 'To be with your wife.'

'That will be nice,' Charlesworth said.

'We'll get you out through Gibraltar.'

Charlesworth brightened. 'I'll spend a few days there?'

'I except so,' Adam said. 'What were you in civvy street, Mr Charlesworth?'

'I was a travel agent,' Charlesworth said.

In the office of the prison governor Adam handed over Charlesworth's papers and photograph. 'I don't think there can be any doubt,' he said.

The governor, pale and plump with a creased bald head, regarded the documents warily. 'I regret that I don't have the authority –' he began.

'Yes you do, you're the boss.'

'Authority has to come from –'

'The Ministry of Foreign Affairs, the Ministry of War and the Ministry of the Interior. I happen to know you have authority from all three,' said Adam, who knew he had authority from everyone except the Ministry of the Interior.

'I'll have to make a couple of telephone calls.'

'Please do. I have no intention of leaving here without Lieutenant Charlesworth. It would create quite a stir if it became known that a British diplomat was detained in Figueras gaol.'

'But you won't be.'

'I shall report otherwise.'

'Where did you learn your Spanish?' the governor asked.

'Madrid. Where else?'

'If you'll excuse me.' The governor got up from his desk in the sparsely furnished carbolic-smelling office where José Antonio Primo de Rivera and Franco ruled from picture frames and went out of the door. When he came back he said, 'Everything seems to be in order.'

'You have been very helfpul,' said Adam who, despite himself, was learning the rudiments of diplomacy.

He spoke to Charlesworth in his cell which he shared with

a failed bullfighter who had knifed his wife, a pickpocket and two Republican soldiers caught hiding in the Pyrenees.

'I'm taking you with me tomorrow,' he said.

'To Gibraltar?'

'Unless you prefer to fly to Lisbon.'

Charlesworth thought about it. Then he said, 'No, I think I prefer Gib. But don't bother to contact Mrs Charlesworth now. We don't want to worry her, do we?'

Adam deposited Charlesworth at the embassy the following day and turned his attention to the Puente de Vallecas stadium where a British soldier was said to be imprisoned with thousands of Republican sympathizers.

Armed with his diplomatic papers and his impeccable accent, Adam found the soldier, head shaved and dressed, like Charlesworth, in a fisherman's jersey and grey trousers, sitting on a tiered bench, staring across the churned-up ground where the prisoners were camped. It had rained overnight and the clothes covering their thin bodies steamed in the wan sunshine.

The soldier, whose name was Thompson, greeted Adam without surprise. 'Thought you'd never get here,' he said, Scouse accent as thick as black pudding. He patted the bench. 'Anyway I got a good seat; always did. Saw Liverpool's last game day before war broke out. Whacked Chelsea one nowt.'

Adam looked round the stadium. The prisoners in transit to concentration çamps or firing squads huddled listlessly together for warmth. From time to time a name was announced over a loudspeaker and a prisoner stood up and slouched over to a table where his captors decided his fate.

Thompson pointed at the tiers high above him that were empty. 'They cleared lads away from those. Too easy to commit suicide by diving off head first. Got a fag?'

Adam handed him a packet of Rhodian. Thompson took two and gave the rest to the prisoners hunched around him. They lit them with shaking hands, inhaling hungrily, holding them in cupped hands.

Thompson said, 'You'll have to hurry up, lad, Gestapo is said to be on't way to take me back to France. Fuck knows why they think I'm so important.'

'Because you used a new escape route,' Adam told him. 'And you got to Madrid. They want the details. And as you're in civilian clothes they might not be too polite about it.'

'Let's get on our bikes then,' Thompson said.

As they left the stadium, a Mercedes from the German Embassy stopped outside the gates and two men wearing dark overcoats got out.

On the way back to the British Embassy, Adam noticed teams of labourers repairing bomb damage and rebuilding houses that had been removed like pulled teeth from terraces. Prisoners working on reconstruction had their sentences reduced, but it took a lot of sweat to make much impact on a 20-year stretch. Anything, Adam supposed, was better than waiting for the executioner's summons or slow death from malnutrition. In one year nearly 200,000 were said to have died. The figure had appalled Adam but, such is the numbing effect of statistics, the shock had been filed away. Now, suddenly, the figures were flesh and blood. How many were in the stadium purely because of geographical accident? Because they had been born in Republican territory?

Thompson lit a Rhodian, saying, 'Gone quiet, haven't you, lad?'

'I was thinking about another war,' Adam said.

'Well you enjoy this bastard,' Thompson said. He rubbed his shaven scalp. 'Must be great to have a cushy job like yours.'

Atherton was waiting for Adam in his office. He held up a sheet of notepaper bearing the letterhead of the Spanish Ministry of the Interior. 'What's this about trying to speak to prisoners in a concentration camp?' he demanded.

'I took the wrong road,' Adam said.

'You're supposed to be anti-German not anti-Fascist. After all, you fought for the buggers.'

'I *was* going to rescue a British POW. And I *have* rescued another today. And the Germans *did* see me as I left Vallecas stadium. Moser thinks I've got the perfect front. In the Embassy. So bloody patriotic that I must be able to gain access to secret documents.'

Atherton, who smelled faintly of Pear's soap, handed

Adam another sheet of paper. 'Try this for size,' he said. 'Nothing spectacular, but it's a start. Softly, softly, catchee monkey.'

It was a carbon copy of a letter dated 12 October 1940 from the ambassador to Winston Churchill, who had become Prime Minister after the resignation of Neville Chamberlain five months earlier.

> I fully agree that steps should be taken urgently to prevent, as you put it, the consummation of the honeymoon between Franco and Hitler. The situation is, of course, logical because without the help of Hitler it is problematical whether Franco would have won the civil war. Nevertheless, despite his apparent procrastination when decisions are required, Franco is one of the most able leaders in Europe today and an admirable foil for Hitler's bluster. (I heard him described the other day as a pouter pigeon with the wisdom of an owl and the claws of an eagle.) We shall naturally pursue every avenue in our efforts to cause disunity between the Führer and the Caudillo, *although Hitler, with his designs on Gibraltar which I mentioned in my previous communication, may create more discord than we can ever hope to manufacture.*

'What designs on Gibraltar?' Adam asked.

'Your guess is as good as mine.'

'Didn't you see the previous communication?'

'There wasn't one,' Atherton said, clasping his hands behind his head and endangering the buttons on his waistcoat.

'This is a fake?'

'Absolutely.'

'Who underlined the last bit?'

'You did,' Atherton said.

'Who wrote the letter?'

'I did. Rather good, I thought. Especially that bit about pouter pigeons and eagles.'

'How was the letter supposed to have been sent?'

'In the bag, of course.'

'How can you pursue an avenue?'

'Don't be impudent.'

'What's the point of it?'

Atherton sighed, unlocked his hands from behind his head and wagged one small finger at Adam.

'One – and most importantly – we establish your credentials with Moser. You're his protégé and he'll do his damnedest to extol your virtues with Department Six. One over the Abwehr, that sort of thing. Secondly the *designs on Gibraltar* bit will throw them into a panic. What do we know?'

'Well,' Adam said, 'what do we know?'

'Sweet Fanny Adams as a matter of fact. But they're bound to have some designs on Gib, aren't they? And guess what they'll ask you to find out?'

'The contents of the previous communication?'

'Spot on,' Atherton said. 'Which is when you can start fishing for us. You see we really would like to know what their designs on Gib are. Then we can tell Franco and the shit, as they say, will really hit the fan.'

'Don't you think they'll see through all this?'

'My dear Adam,' Atherton said, 'never make the mistake of thinking that those who work for intelligence are necessarily intelligent.'

Adam met Moser on a Sunday night on a bench beneath the crisping leaves of the chestnut trees in the Plaza de Santa Ana. Moser wore a peaked cap, tweeds, and was smoking a cigar that smelled of Boxing Days in East Grinstead.

'Hallo, old man,' Moser said. 'Take a pew.' He drew on his cigar; its glow made claws of the smiles at the corners of his eyes. 'Anything for me?'

'As a matter of fact I have. Something from the bag.'

'Keep your voice down, old man,' a rasp of clandestine excitement in his voice. 'Something hot?'

'Warm,' Adam said. 'It's here, inside this copy of *ABC*.' He passed the newspaper to Moser.

'How warm?'

'Gibraltar,' Adam whispered.

'What about it?'

'The German plan,' Adam said.

The leaves of the chestnut trees rustled. Old men in berets shuffled past. Moser's cigar glowed and faded.

'Are you sure?'

'Of course I'm sure.'

'Christ Almighty, that's dynamite.'

Confirmation, Adam thought.

Moser said, 'I'd better be on my way.'

'Haven't we forgotten something?'

Moser reached into the inside pocket of his tweed jacket and handed Adam an envelope. 'Twenty-five quid. In pesetas. All right, old man?'

Adam said it was all right.

The following day Adam went with his sister, who knew where to shop, to a store with bare shelves: from under the counter he bought cigarettes, wine, Manchego cheese, olives, tins of anchovies and dried tuna fish. He took these to the Puente de Vallecas, showing the guards his diplomatic papers and handing the brown paper bags to the prisoners who had been sitting around Thompson.

They each smoked a cigarette first, then fell on the food and drink. Before he left, one of them – bow-legged with a mouthful of broken teeth – handed him a locket and asked him to deliver it. Adam opened the locket. Inside was a photograph of a young man with a handsome, bandit's face.

'You?'

'A rifle butt in the mouth does wonders for your teeth. Every dentist should have one.'

'Who shall I give it to?'

'A young girl in La Mancha. Here's the address.' He handed Adam a scrap of paper. 'Just tell her that her uncle sent it.'

'Can't she visit you?'

'Not where I'm going.' He smiled his broken-toothed smile. 'Will you do it?'

'It's a long way,' Adam said, looking at the address scrawled with indelible pencil.

The prisoner stuck out his hand. 'The word of an Englishman?'

Adam took his hand; his grip was strong. 'What's the girl's name?'

'Rosana Gomez. A good kid. Tell her brother that he'll play for Madrid one day.'

A voice issued through the loudspeaker. A man's name. The prisoner took another cigarette, lit it and stuck it in the corner of his mouth at a jaunty angle. 'That's me,' he said. Half-way to the judgement tables he turned. 'Don't forget, *hombre*. Otherwise, when we meet up there,' pointing at the sky, 'or down there,' pointing at the ground 'this . . .' He slashed at his throat with one finger.

The cigarette wagged in the corner of his mouth and he grinned and he was the young man with the bandit's face in the locket.

CHAPTER 9

It is one of the small tragedies of life that swashbuckling and romantic notions are often caged inside bodies that were never fashioned to put them to good use.

Sol Seidler was the possessor of just such a self-defeating combination. He was romantically and audaciously inclined but he was also squat, double-chinned and myopic.

It was Tom Canfield who, with his warm blond hair and his aviator's face and his long, not-quite-awkward limbs, had been constructed for the sort of exploits that Seidler had kept in harness since his schooldays. Seidler gladly helped out with his unrequited feelings one hot August day in 1939 in Paris.

'You are truly crazy about her?' he asked Tom in the café where they had first met.

'Dumb question.' Tom made patterns with the moisture from his glass of Pernod on the marble top of the table.

'Okay, okay. So what we're talking about is a passage back to Spain.'

'I shouldn't have left.'

'If you had stayed you would have been shot. Flying for the reds, shooting down goddamn Heinkels and Junkers, Jesus! As it was we only just got out in time.'

'In a DC-2 mailplane to Oran. Couldn't we have flown direct to France?'

'We ran out of gas as we landed. Try being realistic.'

'I'm sorry,' Tom said. 'How do I get back to Spain?' He ordered two more Pernods and watched the yellow liquid turn milky as the waiter added water.

'First you need a passport,' Seidler said.

The waiter mopped the table with a cloth. At another table an old man with a gooseberry chin sat reading an article in a newspaper bearing the headline, EINSTEIN WARNS USA ABOUT ATOMIC BOMB EXPERIMENTS.

'A forgery?'

Seidler shook his head. 'As you know, when we arrived at Albacete some of the guys handed over their passports. "Supposing you lose them at the front . . . What will happen if the Fascists take them? Isn't America supposed to be neutral?" Et cetera, et cetera?' So where do you think those passports went?'

'Moscow?'

'Damn right. Handed over to the secret police and kept in cold storage. Wait till their owners are confirmed good and dead, then doctor them for Soviet agents infiltrating the United States. Well, not all those passports reached Moscow because not all the commissars were as loyal to Joe Stalin as they appeared to be.'

'They're in Paris?'

'Some of them. But you couldn't afford one. Okay, you got some of your salary paid into an account in Paris; but you can forget the balance paid into the account in Spain.'

'How much?'

'Anyone who steals passports from the NKVD has to be a gambler . . .'

'How much?'

'Cut him in on the gold and you've got yourself a new identity. Double-cross him and you've got no identity.'

'But the guys who owned these passports . . . They must have fought for the Republicans. Isn't one of those passports a death warrant in Spain?'

'Nope.' Seidler raised his glass to a girl sitting at the next table. 'Those passports were processed by the Russians for their own purposes. There's no way they can be traced back to their rightful owners in Spain.'

'How the hell do you know all this?'

Seidler tapped the side of his nose. 'I just happen to know the commissar in question. So do you as it happens.'

'Oh, Jesus,' said Tom, as the Russian he had knocked down in the café three years earlier walked through the door.

The Russian's eyes were still lustrously dark but his potato belly had shrunk and his fighting spirit with it. 'Shit,' he said. 'You of all people.' Like many Russians he spoke English with a slight American accent. 'Here, let's go in a dark corner.'

He ordered two beers. Seidler, departing with the girl, waved from the door.

'So,' the Russian said, 'we lost.'

'Who lost, the Communists?'

'Spain lost.' He drank some beer and licked the froth from his lips. 'My name's Belov. We weren't introduced last time we met . . . I always remember asking you if you were a spy. Do you know what you answered?'

Tom shook his head.

'You said you were an idealist. Weren't we all,' Belov said, staring into the street. It was raining as it had been three years ago and, when the door opened, wet, city smells crept into the café. 'I was a Communist and you were . . . anti-Fascist?'

'The Communists didn't do a hell of a lot for ideals.'

'Who did?' His sad eyes stared at Tom from his bruiser's face. 'What are ideals anyway? An escape from reality? A pious luxury?'

Tom tried to remember what he had once felt. He said, 'Maybe ideals are innocence.'

'Then thank God I've learned cynicism. If I had returned to the Soviet Union I would have been shot. Tainted by the West, working for American intelligence . . . some sort of crap like that. They say that the only important military adviser who has survived is Malinovsky.'

'The trouble with ideals,' Tom said speaking slowly, 'is that they can be stolen.'

'And used. My God, how they were used in Spain.'

'Where did you learn to speak English?'

'In Moscow. Pretty good, huh? I think they were going to send me to the States to spread the word.'

'Pretty damn good,' Tom said.

'So what have we got left when our ideals have been spent?'

'Survival,' Tom said.

'Tell me about the gold,' Belov said.

And when Tom had told him: 'Okay, you can have your passport, but it will cost you one quarter of whatever you sell the gold for.'

'So who wants a passport?'

'Twenty per cent?'

'Ten.'

'Okay, fifteen.' Belov stretched out his hand and Tom took it.

'Good luck, Jack,' Belov said.

'Jack?'

Belov took a passport from the inside of his shabby jacket and handed it to Tom. Jack Raymond Palmer from San Diego.

'What was I?' Tom asked, closing the passport.

'A lecturer. A Communist. An idealist.' Belov smiled crookedly. 'Most Communists are, you know. Trouble is they're colonists, too.'

'Age?'

'Twenty-nine. About right?'

'Near enough.'

'A kid,' Belov said.

Tom gulped some beer. 'Here's to survival,' holding up his glass and draining it.

'I'll drink to that.'

'And to hell with ideals.'

Belov lowered his glass. 'I can't drink to that.'

'But you said —'

'We've got to survive. Really put our minds to it. But maybe the ideals will survive, too. Like poppies on a battlefield.'

'Blood red,' Tom said.

'Here's to survival.'

'And love.'

'And ideals.'

'And innocence.'

In the bedroom of his small, soup-smelling hotel, Tom Canfield, drunk, lies on the brass bedstead and asks Jack Palmer many questions.

'Are you a Socialist, Jack?'

'I guess so.'

'Socialists are against rearmament, right?'

'Makes sense.'

'Then why the hell did people like you take up arms in Spain?'

'Because we were anti-Fascist.'

'You can't have your cake and eat it, Jack.'

Traffic pulses outside. Throbs in the ears and becomes the waters of the Seine.

'Now concentrate, Jack. Cast your mind back. It is 1936 and your father's gone bust and you're bumming a living in the dust bowl. Why Spain?'

'Okay, here goes. I saw a whole lot of inequality in the States. And suddenly there was the whole rotten situation crystallized in Spain. But in Spain they were doing something about it.'

'Which was?'

'The underprivileged were rising against the privileged. And boy, were they ever underprivileged. A whole history of oppression. Then what happens? The privileged hit back. The army, the Church, the Falange . . . I had to go, Tom. I had to go.'

'Tell me one thing, Jack, now that you know what you know, would you still have volunteered?'

'Yep, I would. You see all that mattered was that I believed.'

'Thank God you said that.'

He stretches out his arms and, as one, they sink in the beckoning depths of the Seine.

The driver of the old Citroën taxi taking Tom to Le Bourget to catch an Air France flight to Madrid held up his hand and tapped his wrist-watch.

'Okay,' Seidler said. 'Don't hang around.' He stuck out his hand. 'Take good care.'

'What are you going to do in New York?'

'Open a discount bookstore. Not much of a profit margin, but just think of all those novels. Romance, adventure . . . I'll live them second-hand until the future Mrs Seidler walks into the store and asks for a book about the Spanish Civil War and I'll say, "You don't want to read about it, lady, you want to hear about it."'

The taxi driver revved the engine of the Citroën.

Seidler said, 'So what are your priorities?'

'First a girl in Valencia.'

'Me, I'd go for the gold.'

'Then the gold. Then a dog with a tail that can beat you to death. Then . . .'

Seidler looked at him curiously. 'There's more?'

'The guy who was ordered to shoot me. He fought on the winning side. Chances are he's still there. I'd like to know if he would have pulled the trigger. That,' Tom said, 'would clear up a lot of doubts in my mind.'

He climbed into the taxi. As it accelerated down the street he glanced out of the rear window. Seidler was standing on the pavement polishing his glasses vigorously.

Odd that, although he had flown for the Republic for more than two years, he had never visited Madrid. In a way Tom had come to regard Barcelona as the capital of Spain: the Republican government had abandoned Madrid, first for Valencia and then Barcelona.

It was said that you could always recognize a citizen of Barcelona because he walks quicker than a Madrileño, but this gentle September morning everyone walked at the same wary pace, as though they still distrusted the peace that had settled over the land scarcely five months earlier. Indeed, if your sympathies had been Republican there was a great deal to distrust.

Tom strolled round the Puerto del Sol, past the depleted kiosks selling newspapers and magazines promoting the Fascist and Nazi causes. He bought a newspaper and a copy of the German armed forces magazine, *Signal*, translated into Spanish. The magazine, printed before Britain and France had declared war on Germany on 3 September, was full of parade-ground soldiers and aviators gazing victoriously into an infinity of summer skies; there was even a photograph of an Italian model wearing a diaphanous nightdress revealing legs up to her hips, crotch coyly hidden by the garment's hanging belt, which the censor must have passed because of the magazine's Teutonic origins. Tom had that morning seen a priest admonish a couple for walking arm in arm, had read a leaflet advising women to wear long-sleeved dresses in the interests of decency.

He strolled down a side-street, ordered a coffee in a café papered with pictures of pre-war bullfighters and football players and read the newspaper. Spain had declared its neutrality and the announcement was accompanied by avuncular photographs of Hitler and Franco. The German army was smashing its way through Poland, and Russia was poised on the eastern border to grab the slice it had been promised in the non-aggression pact with Germany, signed the previous month. Who would have thought, during the Civil War, that the sworn enemies, Hitler and Stalin, both flexing their muscles in Spain, would one day, through the emissaries Ribbentrop and Molotov, stare deep into each other's calculating eyes and shake hands? What did Franco, sworn enemy of Russia, think of that?

The stranger who joined Tom at the table beneath a photograph of the matador, Belmonte, wore a black leather coat despite the warmth of the day; his hair was sleek and black, his face thin and older, somehow, than his hair. He drank coffee with bird sips and held a cigarette in his left hand.

He pushed a pack of Ideales across the table. 'Smoke?' His voice was high-pitched, not unlike Franco's.

'No thanks, I don't smoke.'

'American?'

Tom, disappointed because since he had met Josefina he had been working on his Spanish, confessed.

'So, how do you think the war's progressing?' changing to English.

'Early days,' Tom said.

'Do you think America will interfere?'

'You mean intervene?'

'My English is not good.' He stubbed out his cigarette and stretched out a fragile hand. 'My name is Ignacio. Nacho for short. As you can see I am a sinistral, left-handed. Sinister, an appropriate adjective for my profession. You see Mr –'

'Palmer.'

'I am a member of the *Cuerpo de Vigilancia*. In other words a policeman, a cop. I normally keep this to myself because it affects the way people talk.' He lit another cigarette; his fingernails were polished but two of his fingers were so stained with tobacco tar that they reminded Tom of ancient piano keys. 'It is quite a handicap, Mr Hunter' – he smiled wistfully at his joke – 'to be left-handed. At school my teacher tried to make me write with my right hand and when I failed cracked me on the left hand with a ruler for being obstinate. I think it had a profound effect upon me. Perhaps that's why I became a policeman.' He offered Tom another apologetic smile.

'Who do you want to win the war, Nacho?'

'It is not a question of who I *want* to win. It is obvious to me who is *going* to win.'

'The Nazis?'

'Chamberlain and Daladier have only once choice – to come to terms with Hitler.'

'And his buddy, Stalin?'

Ignacio was silent.

Tom said, 'I wouldn't underestimate the British, Ignacio. *Perfidious Albion*. Trisky bastards,' wondering again if Adam Fleming would have shot him.

'They would only stand a chance if America interfered. I asked you before, Mr Palmer . . . Do you think they will?'

'Roosevelt has proclaimed a state of "limited national emergency".'

'We have learned in Spain that words can swiftly become bullets. He has also authorized increases in the armed forces, has he not?'

'He didn't intervene in Spain,' Tom said.

'Did you, Mr Palmer?'

'I was in Paris at the time.'

'So were a lot of people. They had a habit of coming to Spain. Can I see your passport, Mr Palmer?' He stretched out his left hand. 'You do know it's an offence not to carry identification?'

Tom handed him his passport. Ignacio flipped the pages like a bored immigration officer.

'What did you lecture in, Mr Palmer?'

'Economics.'

'What were you doing in Paris?'

'I opted out. I wanted to see the world.'

'Paris, Madrid? A very small world . . .'

'I loved Paris. I'm sure I'm going to love Madrid.'

Ignacio made some notes in a blue notebook. 'Do you have plenty of money?'

'Enough.'

'It costs a lot of money to live well in Madrid these days.'

Tom said, 'Can I see your identification, Ignacio?'

Ignacio lit another cigarette. The smile took longer this time; finally he handed Tom his ID. A younger Ignacio with a well-fed face stared threateningly at Tom. Tom handed back the ID.

'Satisfied, Mr Palmer?'

'You can't trust anyone these days.'

'Tell me, what are your first impressions of Madrid?'

'It's punch-drunk,' Tom said.

'It will take time. The reds behaved like pigs.'

Careful, Thomas Canfield, he's putting you on, boy.

'I heard what they did to the priests.'

'Not just the priests. Anyone who had made anything of themselves. Anyone with any pride. Did you hear about the shooting pits where they made them dig their graves before they shot them?'

'No,' Tom said, 'I didn't hear about those.'

'Pigs,' Ignacio said.

'Spaniards just the same.' Careful, boy.

'There has been a great cleansing,' Ignacio said. 'Perhaps every country has to have one. Now we are going to rebuild Spain and there is going to be respect for old and established virtues. God and family, ambition and honour. Not a lot wrong with any of these, Mr Palmer?'

'Hell, no,' Tom said.

'They're very precious. They have to be protected – and anyone who threatens them has to be disciplined. We cannot allow dissent. Maybe one day but not now. You see, Mr Palmer, we have to build both an altar and a foundation.' He stood abruptly. 'Enjoy Spain. And don't forget that Leonardo da Vinci was a sinistral.'

So was Jack the Ripper, Tom thought.

From beneath another photograph, this time a footballer who played for Real Madrid, Tom telephoned the British Embassy and asked if anyone could help him trace a Mr Adam Fleming who lived in Spain. The operator hesitated, then told Tom that all such inquiries were dealt with by a Mr Atherton.

Atherton's voice issued tinnily from the receiver of the wall telephone. Fleming? It rang a bell but he couldn't quite place it. Could the caller please explain why he wanted to see Mr Fleming? Ah, wartime comrades; nothing like the conviviality of remembered hardship. You also fought for the victorious army? The Republicans, ah . . . another hesitation – they seemed to lodge in the embassy switchboard like biscuit crumbs in the throat. But didn't you say you were old comrades? A long story, ah . . . a rustling of paper. Atherton had just remembered; *his* Fleming was a Charles Wintour Fleming and he imported razor-blades – there was an acute shortage – into Spain.

Tom replaced the receiver. Well, it had been a long shot. Adam Fleming was probably an officer in the British Expeditionary Force in France waiting to fight the very Germans who had been his allies in Spain. He paid for his coffee and walked into the street. That left Josefina, the dog and the gold. He went to his room in the Hotel Paris on the Calle de Alcalá, packed a bag, caught a tramcar to the railway station and a train south-east to the province of Valencia. Across the valley of the Jarama where he had nearly died, through Aranjuez, past the bleak and empty sheep pastures and stunted windmills of La Mancha, past salt lakes and castles and vineyards to Albacete where Seidler and he had alighted to fight for the Cause.

He changed trains at La Encina, spent the night at Carcagente nestling among orange and mulberry trees. The following morning he boarded the narrow-gauge train to Gandia and Denia.

As the little train approached Josefina's home town, Tom felt a lightness in his chest. Had she ever received the letter he had written? *I love you very much. Do not marry anyone else* . . . If she hadn't received it then she probably had married the Spaniard to whom she was 'betrothed'. If she *had* received the letter she might still have married him: the Spanish were very strict about such arrangements. And what was the bad news that had summoned her home? And had she then returned to the monastery near the Jarama? Supposing she isn't here? She hadn't replied to any of the subsequent letters he had written. Or had she? He had moved base so often . . . Or were the letters a source of amusement in the town? Tom massaged his hands together and bit the inside of his lip so fiercely that the old woman in Bible-black sitting opposite him asked if he was ill.

He tried to relax. The oranges in the groves between the sea and the spiny, lizard-grey mountains to the west were green and heavy on the branches; stems of smoke rose stiffly into a placid sky; villages stirred beneath autumn-leaf roof-tops gathered around churches that had survived the recent blasphemy.

By the time the train pulled into the station he was in such a state of agitation that the old woman had moved to the other side of the carriage. He smiled at her wildly and, picking up his bag, stepped on to the platform. He was the only passenger to disembark; the only other occupant of the platform was an emaciated alley cat.

He walked on to a dirt road followed, at a distance, by the cat. A woman wearing a blue headscarf was mopping the doorstep of her home set in a terrace of ochre houses; two small girls were hopping in squares drawn in the dust; a heavy-headed dog stared morosely at the cat. Somewhere in the gathering heat a man sang a lament from Andalucia. Tom put down his bag. Was this the homely Mediterranean paradise of which Josefina had spoken? Could I live here?

He heard the throb of engines and, picking up his bag, made his way across the railway line, past the low shed of the station, to another unmade road. Now he could see the polished sea and the harbour trapped between two drystone claws. The throb emanated from two fishing boats pushing lazy arrows in the harbour; a cargo boat listed brokenly at the quayside; a railway engine stood immobilized by rust on its track.

He walked past a line of palms to a bar in a terrace of houses with balconies like brooches. He ordered a beer and, watched by a brooding barman, sat on a stool guarding his bag. Behind him men of indeterminate age played cards, slapping them down as though they were well pleased to be rid of them. Franco and Marlene Dietrich, separated by a bottle of herbal aperitif, stared benignly across the harbour from behind the bar. Flies droned in decreasing circles.

Tom said to the barman in careful Castilian, 'Could you please help me?'

The barman, hair centre-parted like a gangster's barber, continued to polish a glass.

Tom said, 'I am looking for someone.'

The barman polished.

One of the card players glanced up. 'He only speaks Valenciano.'

'Only sometimes,' said another and they laughed secretly.

Tom turned to the card players. 'I'm trying to find someone named Josefina Ronda.'

The silence stiffened.

'Does anyone know her?'

The first card player said, 'Ronda is a very common name here. There are three Rondas in this bar at this moment.'

'Then you must be able to help me.'

A church bell began to toll.

The barman poured himself a measure of mud-coloured drink from an unlabelled bottle and tossed it down his throat, licking the residue from his lips with the tip of his tongue.

'Surely someone knows Josefina Ronda?'

The silence extended. Slap, slap from the cards. Throb, throb from the fishing boats wading through the abandoned harbour.

Tom said to the barman, 'Give me a drink of that,' pointing at the bottle of mud-coloured drink. The barman picked up another glass and began to polish it. Tom leaned across the bar and slapped him off his stool with the flat of his hand.

The barman stood up slowly. He said in Castilian, 'I shit in your mother's milk,' but he poured the drink just the same.

'Where can I find Josefina Ronda?'

Red weals appeared on the barman's pendulous cheek.

'I don't know any Josefina Ronda,' he said.

The first card player said, 'Are you American?'

'No,' Tom said, 'Chinese.'

'Take my advice, don't ask too many questions.'

'You have something to hide?'

The card player slapped down a card and picked up the coins in a beret in the middle of the table. 'Perhaps everyone has something to hide.'

'No one can help me?'

The church bells stopped pealing; the engines on the fishing boats had been cut and the silence lingered.

'I will find her,' Tom said.

They watched him out of the door.

He walked down the main street past a grocer's shop selling chick-peas and olive oil; past a yeast-smelling bakery and a sour-smelling bodega; past a knife-grinder and a crippled lottery-ticket seller and a funeral. In a small square wreathed in mauve bougainvillaea old men lingered in the past while no-longer-young men waited to occupy the vacancies on the wooden benches.

He walked along a street beneath a thin strip of blue sky. He felt vaguely as though he were being followed. He glanced behind. Two children disappeared into doorways beneath geranium-filled balconies.

He came to a smaller square. Crimson hibiscus bloomed on straggling bushes in a sandy garden enclosed by a low wall. Tom sat on the wall. A little girl with polished hair and gypsy-brown skin sat on the wall opposite him and began to eat *pipas*, sunflower seeds, cracking them with her front teeth and spitting out the husks. Tom smiled at her; she stared at him incuriously.

A woman entered the square and spoke to the child. She was sturdily built, this woman, but she held herself with galleon grace. She wore a rust-coloured dress that had been washed many times and her black hair, streaked delicately with the years, was held with a tortoiseshell comb. She was shielded by a gauze of shyness but Tom, student of Spain, knew that when the gauze dropped this woman could fill an evening with words.

She approached him by a circuitous route. She said, 'I understand you are looking for Josefina Ronda.' Her arms were folded, hands trapped beneath her elbows.

'Do you know where she is?'

The woman said, 'Perhaps we could walk a little.'

They reached a cemetery hedged with pencil-point cypress. She nodded towards it. 'The war placed many people in its walls. And now this town is dead.'

She opened a door set in a whitewashed wall opposite the cemetery. The patio had recently been watered and the geraniums in earthenware pots dripped beneath a fig tree with wandering branches. The woman went indoors and Tom sat beside a cane table; over the top of the wall he could see the ramparts of a ruined castle that had seen many wars. She returned with a jug of homemade lemonade and a plate of small biscuits that tasted of honey.

She sat opposite him. A yellow leaf fell from the fig tree on to the table. She brushed it aside. Tom smiled and held up a half-bitten biscuit. 'Delicious,' he said.

'Yes,' she admitted. 'I make good biscuits. Right through the war I made them. It was hard here but not as hard as other places. We had oranges and vegetables and we had fish which we exchanged for bread in other villages.'

It would take a long time to reach the subject of Josefina: Tom knew this; he harnessed his impatience. 'Not many people talk about the war,' he said, in his terrible but improving Spanish.

'That is true. The war, just a little misunderstanding.' She laughed without humour. 'But what I have to tell you concerns the war and it is a relief to talk about it. In many ways it was a private war here because our cities, Valencia and Alicante, were among the last to fall to the Fascists.'

She sipped her lemonade. Tom thought, 'What does she have to tell me that concerns the war?' Fear moved inside him.

She said, 'Many houses were visited, many men were taken for a little *paseo*, a little walk. They never returned. Many people fled; it was not wise to stay if you were rich. I had no such problem.' She smiled and was transformed.

'Did they return?'

'Oh yes, they returned when the war was over and then it was the turn of the poor people to hide or flee. They are scattered all over Europe, all over the world. Just as it once was with the Jews. What was that called?'

'The Diaspora,' Tom told her. 'But thousands of Republican refugees ended up in the French camps. The French didn't want them and they say conditions in those camps are as bad as the concentration camps.'

She shook her head vehemently. 'Nothing is as bad as the concentration camps. There is one south of Alicante, in between Elche and Orihuela, in a grove of palm trees. The palm trees are dying with what they have seen.'

Tom said gently, 'You mentioned Josefina Ronda . . .'

'One of the old men in the bar on the port told me you were looking for her.'

'And you can help me?'

She bit into a small biscuit. Swallows perched on a telegraph wire above the patio like notes of music.

'So you see,' she said, 'small towns like ours suffered twice. First from one side, then the other.'

'But you believed in what happened when the Republicans rose against the Fascists?' Tom asked, because clearly the time had not yet struck for Josefina to be discussed.

'Oh yes, I believed. The landowners and the priests . . . They were hard men. But even when the churches were being burned I prayed every day.'

'For what?' Tom asked.

'For my daughter, Josefina.'

The swallows took off from the the telegraph wire and flew south. When they had departed, Tom said, 'Your prayers were answered: she helped to heal many wounded men.'

'You were one of them?'

'I think you know that.'

'Señor Canfield?'

'She spoke of me?'

'She received letters from you from Barcelona.'

'Not from Madrid?'

Josefina's mother shook her head.

'I gave one to a nurse . . .'

'The mail was very bad in those days . . . She said she left a message for you at the monastery.'

When I return, Tom thought, I will strangle that matron. His knuckles shone white on his fists.

'And by the time your letters arrived from Barcelona it was too late.'

'For what?' The fear caged in his body beat its wings.

'You know why she returned here?'

'Bad news; that's all I knew.'

'My husband died,' Josefina's mother said.

'I am truly sorry.' *Too late for what?*

'It was nothing to do with the war. He had a fragile heart. Josefina was our only child . . .'

Was?

'And before he died he said that he wanted to see her married well. To her *novio*. He was a clever young man and he had good prospects in the bank.'

'Josefina is married?'

'The ceremony was held in the church here. Her *novio* was one of those who tried to burn it but God blew out the flames. I don't think God was happy that he was married in the church he tried to destroy.'

Tom waited.

'They came for him three days after the wedding,' Josefina's mother said.

'Who came?'

'The Fascists. It was his turn for a little walk. Mostly they took the reds to the cliffs. There they had two choices – to be shot or walk over the cliffs on to the rocks far below.'

'And Josefina's husband?'

'He was lucky. He must have had good friends among the Fascists. He was taken to a camp.'

'Where?'

Josefina's mother shrugged. 'There are many. He isn't at Orihuela – we checked.'

'His name?'

'Garcia. There can't be a much more common name than that.'

'And Josefina?'

'She is in Madrid. That's all I know. She writes but there is no address on her letters.'

'Is she nursing?'

'She says she is happy. That's all. I know that is not true.'

Tom leaned across the table and touched her hand. 'I will find her,' he said.

It was the second time that day that he had used those four words.

That afternoon he caught a train to Valencia to pick up the dog that he had left with a Spanish aviator. But it had disappeared taking its punishing tail with it.

He began his search for Josefina in Madrid the following day. He visited every hospital, every clinic, every nursing home in the city. No one had heard of Josefina Ronda.

He spread his net wider. It reached Toledo to the south and Salamanca to the west and Segovia to the north and Cuenca to the east. It did not reach Josefina Ronda.

He tried to check the camps for a prisoner named Garcia, but the authorities laughed at him.

No Josefina. No Adam Fleming. No dog. That left the gold. But first, he thought, I will try once more to find Adam Fleming. Would he have shot me?

CHAPTER 10

The windowless room was the length of two tall men and the width of one and a half; Diego, Ana's cousin, had lived in it for six months, two weeks, three days and 48 minutes.

He knew the hills and valleys of the whitewashed walls, the constellations and nebulae of the curly-grained beams, the plains and river-beds of the brick floor.

He fed dead flies to a spider hanging on its trembling web angled between beam and ceiling; he waited anxiously for the chafing of the insects inside the beams; he tried in vain to make friends with a gecko which lived somewhere behind his books. The room was his bedroom, living-room, library, study and bathroom.

He had emerged into the village only once – three weeks after he had arrived in the village in La Mancha, south of Ciudad Real – but an informer had spotted him. Half an hour later the *Guardia Civil* had called at the house at the end of the dusty street.

But it was deceptively large this terrace house, with its courtyard and its byre for two donkeys and its dark living-room where, in the doorway, the grandmother sat with two cronies weaving baskets, and its creaking bedrooms; and it had been easy enough to build a false wall and install Diego behind it.

Not that they searched too diligently. Ally or enemy according to the fortunes of war, they had become impervious to loyalties and perceived in this *pueblo* only the need to survive in the hungry years that lay ahead. If the denunciations were spurred by fear of conspiracy – for the villagers, like most Spaniards, were sick to their souls of bloodshed – then the policemen picked up their carbines and went looking for the conspirators; if they were seeded by feud or jealousy then they searched with heavy-lidded eyes.

And indeed the denunciation of Diego was just such an affair, aimed at the owner of the house who had been a jovial Anarchist during the war, rather than his cousin, who, wet moustache shaved off, button-tight belly sagging like a deflated balloon, lurked fearfully behind the false wall. A few glasses of rich, raw wine in the courtyard among the pecking chickens, a few cursory taps on walls that had manifestly been in existence since the Moorish occupation and the policemen had departed sweating amiably beneath their sinister black hats.

Their visit had fascinated Rosana Gomez, almost 14, and her brother Pablo, 12, contributing a significant chapter to the Great Intrigue – the presence of the fat pale man in the secret room. Other children, if they could read, had to steal their excitement from story books: theirs was a sitting tenant.

But what really sustained the intrigue which might otherwise have withered and died, as children's enthusiasms are wont to do, were their vows of secrecy. Lying on the straw mattress above the living-room, they debated the identity of the stranger, rejecting overheard allusions to Communism because it had a dull ring to it, short-listing at Pablo's instigation José Antonio Primo de Rivera, the leader of the Falange who, according to authorities less informed than Pablo, had been executed at Alicante in 1936.

'But why would he hide in a Republican's house?' asked Rosana still working with her paint brushes.

'Because it wasn't just the Fascists who admired him,' said Pablo, whose intuition might one day serve him well on the football field. 'Everyone did.'

'But he doesn't even look like José Antonio. José Antonio was handsome; he looks like a slug.'

'Surgery,' said Pablo mysteriously, turning over on the mattress where once they had found a dead mouse and feigning instant sleep.

So Rosana decided to tackle Uncle Kiko, not really an uncle at all but a distant relative of her mother's.

The opening came one afternoon when he sat among the chickens in the courtyard watching her paint while his wife took a siesta. A fractured cheroot protruded from his happy, rebel's face and his head was tilted at an inquisitive angle.

He pointed the cheroot at her painting. 'What is that?'

'The battlefield where papa died,' she told him.

'And that cross in the sky?'

'For all those who died with him.'

'On both sides?' His head tilted more steeply.

'I don't know,' Rosana said. 'I don't want to think about it. Because, you see, if that cross is for both sides then none of them need have died.'

He nodded; his movements were normally snappy but these few nods were slow and thoughtful. 'I understand,' he said. He took the cheroot, bandaged with tissue paper, from his mouth and stared at the smoke dribbling from it. 'Your father was a good man,' he said eventually.

Uncle Kiko was a good man, too, but she didn't tell him so; that would have been a disloyalty to her father. Kiko was good in the way of uncles, not fathers. She loved him but only because her father had died on the battlefield beneath the cross in the sky. Whereas her father had reached her with words, sometimes unspoken, Kiko reached her with jokes. Sometimes, she suspected, grown-ups who joked all the time were ashamed of their true thoughts.

She applied white paint to the cross rising from storm clouds and led Diego into the war.

'Did he fight on the same side as you, Uncle Kiko?'

'He didn't fight,' Kiko said. He replaced the cheroot in his mouth and drew on it noisily; he rolled these gnarled cylinders himself and they smelled like the smoke that rose from the rubbish when it was burned on the waste land at the end of the street.

'Then why does he hide?'

'Everyone is hiding from something.'

This seemed an unsatisfactory reply.

She tried again. 'So what does Uncle Diego hide from?'

'Do you regard him as an uncle?'

'No,' replied Rosana, realizing that Kiko was once again avoiding the issue. 'But he is a relative of yours, isn't he?'

'I don't like to think of him as such.'

'If you don't like him why do you hide him?'

'He is family. In Spain families are clans. That is why so many women wear black: there is always someone to mourn.'

'Were you a Communist?' trying to shock him into an indiscretion.

He rekindled his cheroot using a flint lighter with a long wick. Then he said, 'I fought for what I believed in.'

'Was Diego a Communist?'

'Don't you fret any more about Diego,' Kiko said, his voice sterner than she had ever heard it.

She made one last attempt. 'Is he José Antonio?'

Then Kiko laughed, an uncle again, and the laughter was squeezed into tears at the corners of his eyes.

Pablo tackled their mother when she made one of her intense, fleeting visits from the north. He kicked his football into the corner of the courtyard by the donkeys' byre and made a slanting approach.

'Mama, why can't you stay here with us?'

'Perhaps one day I will,' said Ana, swaying gently in a rocking chair.

Pablo retrieved the football. 'Why do you have to stay in the north?'

'There are still many things to be done.'

'What sort of things?' asked Pablo, who knew they were connected with his father.

'Making a future.'

He dummied the ball, dribbled it past two bewildered players of Atlético Aviación and steadied himself to shoot for the goal framed by the entrance to the dusty street.

'Are you on the run like Uncle Diego?'

He had heard the phrase when Kiko had taken them to the cinema at Ciudad Real and he liked it although Diego wasn't exactly running because he was a slug.

'Diego isn't your uncle.'

'Why is he hiding here?'

His mother, dressed as usual in black, rocked a little quicker in the rattan chair. 'A lot of bad things happened during the war.'

Pablo knew this – there had been a hole in his life ever since his father had died. He nodded impatiently.

'There were injustices,' his mother went on. 'That always happens in wars. And they linger afterwards. Diego has to escape from those injustices.'

'Like you?'

'In a way.' She reached out and touched his cheek but there was a distance between them, an invisible wall that had been there for a long time now. 'But it won't always be like that. One day we'll all be together.'

'What I can't understand,' Pablo said carefully, 'is why you should be on the run if you fought for your country.'

'We wanted a different country,' his mother said. 'One day you will understand,' but he didn't think he would.

He kicked the ball hard and watched it fly into the top left-hand corner of the net and heard the roar of the crowd.

The village which had remained in Republican hands throughout the war, was an afterthought. A parched dormitory – even drinking water cost 50 centimos a flagon in the summer – deposited there some time in the sun-faded past for the men who worked the wheatfields, or the olive groves or the vineyards on the great plain of La Mancha where all the sheep paths of Spain converge and the horizons are infinite.

The streets – one main thoroughfare and a few blind turnings – were thick with dust in the summer, deep with sucking, toffee-coloured mud after a storm. They contained a kneeling church which had lost its spire to a stray Fascist bomb; a store that sold pygmy rations of food and long white candles and wooden clothes pegs carved by gypsies; a schoolroom where a priest who had survived the revolution taught; and a communal laundry where housewives pounded and scrubbed clothes with furious application.

If the village possessed one virtue it was cleanliness: the houses, clustered against the brazen heat of summer and the unforgiving winds of winter, were as white as a baby's teeth, doorsteps undefiled by footprints.

To the north lay the untrammelled mountains of Toledo, to the south the lazy waters of the Giudiana river, to the east the modest town of Ciudad Real, to the west the quicksilver mines of Almadén. When Ana journeyed south to visit her children she took them walking in the wheatfields, which were beginning to recover from the enthusiastic attentions of the liberated peasants, and where poppies bloomed as blood-red as war.

She described the castles of La Mancha while Rosana painted them in her mind and Pablo attacked them with subtle dispositions of troops but she wished, as the breeze stroked the ripening wheat, that she could tell them about the Pyrenees where she now lived, where mountain peaks snared captive clouds and eagles ruled the sky. About the indomitable men and women with whom she still fought in silent pine forests, above giddy precipices, across boulder-combed rivers, blowing bridges, rescuing hostages and killing Fascists who were still the enemy.

About her meeting with a man known as *El Sentido* – the cunning of a bull which knows that its true adversary is not the cape but the man behind it – who had made all this possible.

The refugee camp, one of 15 where the French accommodated their guests from Spain, was delightfully situated on a beach lapped by the blue Mediterranean at Argelès near Perpignan in the south-east corner of France.

Accommodation was limited – a few tents and shanties built from driftwood – and residents were encouraged to take advantage of the natural amenities: in the summer they could lie with the sandflies beneath the stars, in the winter they could sleep and at the same time be cleansed by rain sweeping down from the Pyrenees.

The curriculum was, in fact, survival orientated because it was recognized that refugees, often frost-bitten, sometimes limbless, who had trekked through mountain blizzards to avail themselves of their neighbour's hospitality, would only succumb if they were over-indulged.

Food was therefore strictly rationed, sanitation minimal.

Medical treatment was provided in cases of direst need: those who failed to survive the regimen were buried decently. Anyone trying to escape this benificence was shot by a Senegalese guard.

Ana had been in the camp for two months when she was approached by *El Sentido*. He was a Basque, in his mid-thirties with a wrestler's crouch and a predatory walk, black hair abundant everywhere except upon his scalp, grey eyes perched on a smile that had frozen when Bilbao had fallen to the Nationalists.

It was May, perfect weather for a vacation if you weren't suffering from dysentery or gangrene, and she was standing beside the high wire fence gazing across the sea.

He joined her, leaning with his back against the fence, hands deep in the pockets of his patched blue trousers and said: 'We are leaving tonight. Do you want to come with us?'

'We?' She had watched this man for a long time because it was difficult to ignore him and she had observed him commit deeds of great brutality and acts of deep compassion.

'Twenty of us. We are returning to continue the fight.'

'Against what?' because she knew that *El Sentido*, as he was known in Castilian, didn't grieve for Spain – he mourned for *Euskadi*, the Basque republic which had been created early in the war by the Republicans and nullified by Franco.

'Against the enemy, the Fascists.'

'It was people like you who destroyed the Cause.'

'I was told you were argumentative. Tough as a *toro bravo*, a fighting bull, too.' His voice was hoarse and he spoke Castilian badly; reluctantly, she felt.

'You divided us. You and the Catalans and the Communists and all the rest . . .'

'We were divided too. You would be surprised how many Basques wanted to fight for Franco. You musn't despise people because they have personal loyalties – they are born with them. What matters is the greater injustice. Do you know who was sitting on the first Fascist tank to enter Barcelona?'

'Franco?'

'A German Jewess saluting like a good Fascist. Now what

do you think all the Jews who fought for the Republicans would have made of that?'

'If we had been united,' Ana said, 'she wouldn't have been on that tank.'

'But we have learned our lessons, *guapa*.' It was a long time since anyone had called her that. 'First the Fascists, then our own grievances. For instance we are close in spirit to the Catalans. They were a Republic, too. No longer. The Fascists have cut out the Catalan tongue and banned its dances but they will never destroy its soul. Nor ours.'

'What is your real name?' Ana asked.

'Sabino,' he told her. 'I was named after a Basque hero, Sabino de Arana Goiri. He called our dream *Euskadi*.' He paused. 'Will you come with us?'

'Why do you want me, a woman?'

'Your reputation crossed the Pyrenees before you. But I'm puzzled why such a woman is still here, a prisoner.'

'I'm puzzled that *El Sentido* is still here.'

'I'm recruiting. To do that I have to bide my time.'

'I, too, was biding my time.'

'Then we have a deal.' He kissed her on both cheeks.

'You spoke just now of personal grievances. I, too, have one,' said Ana.

'Then one day you must settle it. But first the great injustice.'

Eight hours later, in fitful moonlight, Sabino slipped a knife between the ribs of a guard who had entered the camp to investigate a fire, grabbed his machine-pistol and shot his two back-up companions.

Silently the 20 refugees made their way towards the land from whence they had come on the other side of the Pyrenees. As they approached the foothills they struck west to avoid the posts where border police and *Guardia Civil* would be waiting for them and began to climb.

Ana wished she could tell the children about the night journeys through dark-grassed valleys where cow-bells rang as cattle moved in their grazing dreams.

About stars that fell from the skies on to crumpled peaks

where the snow never melts. About the smell of wild herbs crushed underfoot and the frost-taste of mountain streams.

About her fall down a precipice into a clump of oleander in a dry river-bed. About the ambush by border police on a mountain pass stage-managed by Sabino so that they fell upon each other.

About the caves where they made their headquarters – sanctums deep in the rock, connected by dripping passages, teethed with stalactites and stalagmites, decorated with prehistoric murals of horse, chamois and bison.

But how can you tell children as they search among the stubble for ears of wheat, rubbing them between their hands, blowing away the chaff and nibbling the hard grain, that you are a guerrilla, a bandit, a wanted woman with a price on your head?

She turned and led them back to the village waiting defenceless for winter. On the outskirts they met one of the *Guardia Civil*, a stout and muscular man who might have become a butcher if circumstance had not made a policeman of him. He was smart, this *cabo*, despite his girth, pistol handy in its holster, tricorn shining in the fading sunlight, but his features were angled with conflict.

'Señora, a word in your ear.' He guided her towards the square where, at dawn, the *encargado* selected the men lucky enough to work in the fields or the olive groves for five pesetas a day. 'Perhaps the children could play a little on their own?'

She told them to go home but he said: 'No, señora, not just yet. Let them play over there by the palm tree.'

'We have a problem,' he told her when the children were on the other side of the square. 'A stranger has arrived in the village. He wears sharp suits and he asks many questions.'

'One of your men?'

'I'm afraid so. We hope he will not stay long.'

'So there must be a special reason for his visit.'

'It concerns your cousin,' the corporal said.

'Diego?' and put her hand to her mouth to erase the name.

The *cabo* said gently, 'No, not Diego. Your other cousin, Kiko.'

'He is a good man,' Ana said. 'He is full of laughter. The children love him.' She stared fearfully at the stout corporal.

He placed two hands on his belt and lifted it a little. 'He has been denounced,' he said.

'For what?'

'I think you know.'

'For what he did during the war?'

'He was a Republican, an Anarchist. He was very active in the village.'

'So were a million others in other villages.'

'And many have been denounced. Many are in prison. Many are in camps. Many are dead. Your cousin Kiko has been lucky so far.' He examined the hard, shiny palms of his hands carefully. 'But it isn't Kiko that I want to speak to you about.'

'Me?'

The stout corporal nodded apologetically.

'Then arrest me.'

'That is not why I have brought you to this square.'

'I don't understand.'

'I don't have to be a Fascist because I am in this uniform.' He smiled his friendly, butcher's smile. 'I have a great admiration for you, Ana Gomez; I don't want to see you come to any harm. So you must hide until this man in the sharp suit leaves the village. Then say goodbye to your children and return to wherever you came from.'

'And Kiko?'

'They have already taken him. His wife will look after your children. I will take them back now and tell the man in the sharp suit that you have gone. You will have to trust me, Ana Gomez: you have no other choice. And you don't have much time . . .'

She crossed the square and told Pablo and Rosana to go home with the corporal. She told them to say that she had left the village and they nodded wisely in the way of children who have grown up too quickly and she turned her head away because she knew Pablo would not want her to see his bottom lip trembling.

She told the corporal that she would hide in the stable

beside the church and watched him lead the children across the square. He looked, she thought, as though he were taking them to school.

Later, when the stranger had left the village, she went back to the house. It was dark and the sky glittered with inquisitive stars. Kiko's wife was sitting alone in the living-room, her pretty, heart-shaped face still slapped with shock.

Ana held out her arms and she came to her. She wanted to say, 'Don't worry, he'll come back,' but lies had never come easily to her.

She said goodbye to the children who were lying awake on their mattress. She told them she would be back and she said this easily because it was the truth.

But who had denounced Kiko and herself? She spoke about it to Kiko's wife before she left.

'The police never tell you,' Kiko's wife said. 'It is one of the promises they give to informers.'

'But why would anyone wish Kiko any harm?'

'It happened before. But this time it was more important. Because you were here,' she said. 'The informer must have made a telephone call to Ciudad Real. Offer information that leads to the capture of Ana Gomez, the Black Widow, and your own crimes may be forgiven.'

They stared down the corridor at the partition behind which Diego lurked.

Another village. In the foothills of the Pyrenees, on the Spanish side of the border, 350 miles north of the village in La Mancha where Ana had been betrayed. It was grey and cosy with alpine roofs that were bonneted with snow in winter, two bars dispensing a hot-breathed spirit made from mountain berries, a general store that stocked *chorizo* resembling sticks of red marble, a pharmacy and a Romanesque church that, with the help of God and the stonemasons of old, had resisted the designs of the Anarchist fire-raisers.

It had been Republican and, after the war, a few deterrent sentences had been imposed – an execution, a couple of gaol sentences. Then it had settled back into its inviolate, valley existence, threatened only by rumours of guerrillas in the mountains.

On this crisp day towards the end of October 1940, one of the biggest landowners in the area and, in his own estimation, the most important man in the village, sat in one of the two bars sipping a glass of firewater.

His name was Don Federico and he was the living contradiction of that argument which contends that our physical appearance does not necessarily reflect our character. He possessed a thin, questing nose, cash-register eyes and rodent ears. When war broke out he fled across the border to France taking his money bags with him; when it was won he returned to extract from his workers in field and forest a maximum of work for a minimum of payment.

He finished his potion and, feeling warmth beginning to creep into his lean nose, ordered another. He liked this bar because it was austerely furnished – schoolroom tables and chairs and a wall-clock with a hypnotic pendulum – and an all-embracing heat issued from the wood-burning stove in the corner.

He was half-way through his second drink when he was joined at the table by a bearded stranger wearing hunting apparel, tall boots, corduroy trousers and jungle-green jacket, and carrying a double-barrelled shotgun. Momentarily this took Don Federico aback because he was not accustomed to company here or anywhere else; but, of course, this man was a foreigner and had not been poisoned by the villagers' ingratitude.

The stranger invited him to have a drink and Don Federico was courteous enough to accept. They talked about the weather – a hard winter lay ahead because the berries were thick on the bushes – and the soil in the valley that had been atrophied by amateur tilling. The landlord thrust fresh logs into the mouth of the stove, the pendulum of the clock swung rhythmically and Don Federico, accepting another drink, was overcome by a pleasant lassitude, so much so that, when the stranger confided that he, like Don Federico, had taken his money to France at the outbreak of the war, Don Federico said, 'It was the wise course to take,' without questioning how the stranger knew that he had acted with such acumen.

'And like me you brought it back?'

'Of course.'

The stranger stroked the barrels of his shotgun lying on the table. 'I have a favour to ask,' he said, speaking more softly.

'Speak your mind,' urged Don Federico who understood the currency of favours.

'I am a red.'

'Of course.' Don Federico favoured him with a razored smile.

'And a guerrilla.'

The smile lodged in Don Federico's thin features.

'And I need 50,000 pesetas.'

Don Federico erased the smile with the tips of his fingers. 'I have enjoyed your hospitality,' he said, beginning to rise. 'There is a bank in the next town and I am sure they will accommodate you.'

'Sit down you money-grabbing, granite-hearted son of a whore,' the stranger said. He moved the shotgun so that its barrels pointed at Don Federico's belly. 'I want the money tomorrow at ten in the morning. Here. Tell anyone and I'll hang you in my ice-house beside the boar I shot today.'

The stranger smiled, picked up his gun and, at a leisurely pace, made his way out of the bar.

Don Federico waited a while before driving his Fiat 500 to his big cold house. From there he telephoned the border and the municipal police and the *Guardia Civil*. The *guardia* advised him to take the money with him because if he didn't the stranger might shoot him on the spot.

The following morning the street in which the bar stood was stiff with concealed police. Don Federico sat at a table near the stove. The stove was unlit and an October breeze full of winter threats breathed through the half-open door. The money, all in used notes, rested in a gunny bag between his feet. He drank his firewater with delicate sips. He was not afraid because cowardice had long ago been ousted by avarice. And, truth to tell, he enjoyed the situation because it invested a life of miserly application with audacity.

Five minutes past ten and the stranger had not been sighted. Ten minutes.

What Don Federico now feared was humiliation.

Fifteen minutes.

You son of the great whore, where are you?

He imagined he could hear the snigger of the police peering through the sights of their rifles behind chimney tops, in attics, behind boulders on the slopes above the village.

A black Citroën with a low belly drew up outside the bar. A captain of the *Guardia Civil* wearing a beautifully tailored uniform, hat projecting barbs of sunlight, stepped out.

He said to Don Federico, 'We think we have apprehended your man.'

Apprehended. Don Federico liked the parade-ground snap of the word.

'Perhaps,' the captain said, 'you would care to come with me to identify this bandit.'

Don Federico, carrying the gunny bag, stepped into the Citroën beside the captain. Eight miles outside the village the Citroën stopped and the captain, pistol in hand, said, 'I have to tell you, Don Federico, that I, too, am a red, and I must ask you to hand over the bag containing the money.'

The cave beside a gallery of stalactites and stalagmites was relatively dry and a blackened hole in the roof served as a chimney. When Sabino entered Ana was trying to coax flames from a disorderly pile of pine-wood and cones. Smoke rose thickly making her eyes water.

Sabino placed the uniform of a captain in the *Guardia Civil* and the gunny bag containing the money in one corner of the cave and knelt beside her. He separated the cones into a pile, lit them with a burning brand, waited until they were blazing, then angled the sticks of pine around them.

'A fire must have a heart,' he said in his hoarse voice. He lay on the straw mattress, hands behind his head. He reminded Ana of a bear that has eaten well.

'And do you have a heart?'

'It is a soul that I am missing.' He drew on a cigarette. 'That died in Bilbao.'

'You lost someone?'

'My wife.'

Silence, punctuated by the crackling of the fire, filled the cave.

'I'm sorry,' Ana said after a while, because there was nothing else to say.

'At least you understand.'

'I sent my husband to his death.'

'The war was to blame. You were merely its instrument.'

'I killed him,' she said.

He patted the mattress. 'Come, sit here.'

She hesitated, then joined him.

'We will avenge your husband, you and I.'

'And your wife?'

'I don't seek vengeance for her. I'll settle for what she and I wanted.'

'Euskadi?'

'It is a very pure vision. I'm sorry you don't understand it.'

'Spain first,' she said. 'Then *Euskadi*. I will settle for that.'

He drew on his cigarette. His face glowed in its light.

He said, 'Would you like to hear about the Basques?'

'I will listen,' she said.

'Our language is very old. One of the oldest in the world. And we have been in *our* country since time began. They say we are the only survivors of the original population of Europe. You Spaniards, you Madrileños, are new tenants.'

'Who wants to be the oldest resident?'

'Our land was protected from the outside world by mountains and forests; that's why we kept our character. You remind me of a Basque: you are as obstinate as a bull that does not know when to die.' The sticks of pine fell forward into the heart of the fire and blazed. 'I won't torment you with our history; it's sufficient to say that we've always been more independent than anyone else. And we respect our womenfolk.'

Ana was about to say that she hadn't noticed but that wouldn't have been true: chivalry could wear rough armour.

'And now we eat and drink! You must try our fresh wine, our cider. Do you like sport?'

'My son makes sure I like football.'

'I was a great *pelota* player. And a wood-cutter.'

'You look like a wrestler,' Ana said.

'That should be a compliment, but you make an insult out of it.' He shifted his heavy body and the straw rustled beneath him. 'We are great gamblers too.'

'Any Spaniard would bet on two flies walking up a wall.'

'We want our own country. Can't you understand that?'

'I understand people who are sincere,' she said.

'You don't understand me?'

Blue smoke from the fire coiled and uncoiled and sped up the chimney taking sparks with it.

'I didn't say that.'

He stretched out one hand and drew her down on to the mattress beside him.

She thought of Jesús and she wondered if he had found poetry in his dying.

She said, 'Wait.'

She went outside the cave to a corner of the gallery where she poured a jug of ice-cold water over herself and lathered herself with soap made from the residue of a wine press and caustic soda. She remembered undressing long ago in a small and ordinary hotel in Madrid that had been blessed that night. She thought how good Jesús had been with the children and how useful he had been around the house and how innocent he had looked as he went to war.

Then she went back to the warm, smoke-smelling cave. Sabino, too, was naked. He stretched out his arms and they shared what war had taken from them. But when the sharing was over Jesús returned and she knew that he would never leave her. And that as she grew older his presence would become stronger until one day she would stand beside him.

She visited the children once more that year and then again in January 1941.

It was on the second occasion that the children told her about the Englishman who had come to the village in a black car with a Union Jack fluttering on the bonnet.

'What was he like, this Englishman?' Ana asked.

'Dark,' said Rosana. 'Full of deep thoughts.'

'Kind,' Pablo said. 'He brought us chocolate and ham and fruit.'

'And this,' Rosana said, showing Ana the locket containing the photograph of Kiko.

Then Ana knew. Why else does one send a locket?

'Where did this Englishman meet Uncle Kiko?'

Pablo said quickly: 'In a stadium. Not Chamartín,' he added regretfully.

'He was going to be judged,' Rosana said. 'Do you think he's dead, mama?'

'Not Uncle Kiko,' Pablo said. 'He sent a message. He said I'd play for Madrid one day.'

'And so you will,' Ana said. 'Was he from the British Embassy, this Englishman?'

And when they nodded, 'Then I shall have to go and see him.'

'He supports a team called Arsenal,' Pablo said.

'I should like to paint him one day,' Rosana said.

CHAPTER 11

He was known as *El Pistola*. He possessed, of course, other names, but they were merely labels which he retained to satisfy the bureaucrats. To the postman, to the grocer, to his clients, to himself, he was *El Pistola*.

The name echoed back through the years to his first explosion. A modest endeavour in which he detonated a mixture of charcoal, sulphur and saltpetre, the results reverberating in his skull less than the crack round the ear he received from his father. The second explosion, the climax of an experiment with guncotton destabilized by a long hot summer, broke windows for a distance of two blocks, but he was not prosecuted because of the damage it did to his body; instead he was authorized to sell lottery tickets and, as he sat in his wheelchair, tickets cascading in ribbons from his shoulders, his head sometimes jerked as crackers and cannon boomed inside his cranium.

It was from *El Pistola* that Adam Fleming bought his lottery tickets. He had, since his arrival in Madrid, become an enthusiastic gambler – a trend that worried Atherton, finding in the caprices of luck an escape from the fates that had led him to Jarama. Could it have been bad luck rather than his own murderous intent that had led to the deaths of the soldiers he had killed?

On this January day in 1941, Adam stopped beside *El Pistola*, who was sitting in his wheelchair in the Plaza Colon opposite the statue of Christopher Columbus, to buy a ticket for the lottery. He had invested in several tickets for the Christmas draw, *El Gordo*, the Fat One, but he had been unlucky; he had subsequently invested twice the amount in *El Niño*, the Child, in January, and been unlucky; by the law of averages he had to get lucky soon.

He dug his hand into the pocket of his Crombie but *El Pistola*, snugly wrapped in a tartan blanket, snow dusting his shoulders, shook one finger. 'Not today, Señor Fleming.' His face which had become plump and childlike since the gun-cotton affair shone with knowledge that he was impatient to impart.

'Why not?'

'Have you forgotten the date?'

'The thirteenth? But it's not Friday . . .'

'Indeed it isn't: it's Tuesday and in Spain Tuesday the thirteenth is unlucky. I should know – that was the date when I experimented with the guncotton. Buy tomorrow, Señor Fleming, then perhaps you will be lucky.'

But should I choose a number today? Adam wondered. Or would that be unlucky too? He tried not to look at the numbers on the tickets. But one leaped at him. 31939. The third day of a month in 1939. The third of September, the day Britain and France declared war on Germany? Hardly propitious but irresistible. Adam determined to buy that number the following day.

As if coincidence counted! His brain was becoming as addled as that of *El Pistola*. Nevertheless, there was always a chance, and that was what helped to keep hope alive all over Spain. To be rich beyond the dreams of working men . . .

Adam walked briskly down the broad *paseo* and turned into Fernando el Santo. The receptionist at the embassy, a Great War veteran wounded at Ypres who always looked as though he was about to spring to attention, said, 'Visitor for you, Mr Fleming.' He nodded a warning towards the woman sitting in the lobby beneath a photograph of Winston Churchill.

She was dressed all in black, dark hair swept severely back, a hawkish set to her finely-boned features. Adam thought, 'I have met you somewhere before.'

He sat on the opposite side of a glass-topped table bearing dog-eared copies of *Picture Post* and *John Bull* and said, 'I understand you want to see me, señora . . .'

'To look at you,' she said.

The receptionist coughed behind his desk. All that was needed, the cough said, was a signal from Adam to implement the normal ejection procedure when a trouble-maker or a lunatic called at the embassy.

'Well, you're looking,' Adam said. Her dark eyes stared at him from the foot of the marble stairs in the block where his sister lived.

'So it's true,' she said.

'That we've met before?'

'That you're a Fascist.'

'The war's over, Señora Gomez.' A fighter, the militiaman in the block had said.

'Not for me.'

'You have two fine children,' Adam said. 'They must be allowed to forget the war.'

'Their lives have been founded on the war. The Spain of the future has been founded on it.'

'Your daughter will be a fine painter. Pablo will one day play football for Madrid.'

But she didn't smile. Her hands rested, unmoving, in her lap; her brown eyes regarded him steadily.

He undid his overcoat and crossed his legs. Churchill gazed invincibly upon them.

She said, 'Thank you for the chocolate and the ham. And for the locket. How was Kiko?'

'Resigned,' Adam told her. 'Like everyone in that stadium.' He didn't tell her about the broken teeth.

'He is dead?'

'It is possible.'

She stared at her hands. Then said, 'He looked after my children.'

'And you cannot?'

'I think you understand. As a good Fascist you should.'

'The war is over,' he said again.

'I knew you were a Fascist when the children said you were from the British Embassy. They said you spoke perfect Castilian; they said you knew Spain . . . It wouldn't do for the British to employ a Republican in their embassy, would it, Señor Fleming?'

'A lot of people in the embassy speak good Spanish.'

'But they didn't sneak into blocks of apartments in which Fascists lived during the war . . .'

Adam leaned forward. 'What were you doing there, Ana Gomez?'

'Did you fight with the Fascists, Señor Fleming?'

'I think you know the answer, Señora Gomez.'

'At Jarama?'

'That was the only place I fought.'

Her hands moved in her lap. 'Then hear me well. Never call upon my children again. Leave us all well alone. Do you understand?'

'I am not a deaf and dumb mute,' Adam said. He stood up. 'I hope the children enjoyed the chocolate and the ham and the fruit.'

'If I had been there and known who you were they wouldn't have eaten it.'

She, too, stood up. The receptionist watched her warily.

Adam said, 'I wish I could talk with you. There are many things I would like to discuss.'

'The only thing I would care to hear from you, Señor Fleming, is your confession on your deathbed.'

She walked briskly out of the lobby into the falling snow.

The contempt with which Ana Gomez viewed him was so ferocious that Adam, sitting in his small office studying the Spanish newspapers, found it difficult to concentrate. What was the source of such hatred?

He glanced at a copy of a Falangist paper. Predictably it contained little about the British successes in North Africa – the Australian 6th Division had just captured Bardiyah in Libya – but did carry a lengthy article about the brilliance of the German Ambassador in Madrid, Baron Eberhardt von Stohrer.

Sir Samuel Hoare also held the tall, sophisticated German in much esteem – just as well, because they were next-door neighbours. Hoare reserved his spleen for the Nazi propagandist in Madrid, a Turk named Lazar who was reputed to sleep on an altar in his bedroom, and the Spanish Foreign Minister, Ramón Serrano Suñer, Franco's brother-in-law.

Adam didn't altogether share Hoare's indignation about the pro-Nazi stance of Franco and Serrano Suñer. Germany and Italy had helped Franco to win the Civil War: Britain had done nothing. In fact Adam believed that, by professing undying friendship with Hitler and simultaneously denying him access through Spain to Gibraltar, Franco was doing Britain a great service.

At a meeting with Admiral Wilhelm Canaris last July the Caudillo had been less than enthusiastic about an attack on the Rock through Spain. After a meeting with the Caudillo at Hendaye on the French border in October, Hitler had supposedly said he would 'rather have four teeth pulled out' than ever meet him again.

In Adam's view Franco, the cautious and shrewd Galician, thin-voiced and diminutive, who had never totally committed himself to the Nazis, was a consummate negotiator. What he wanted before total commitment was grain. Why not? People were collapsing on the streets of Madrid from starvation. Give him the grain and he would seek more concessions – a slice of the French colonies in Africa for instance.

What Hitler failed to understand was the obstinate pride on which the Spanish character is founded. He bullied and was therefore outwitted. Adam hoped the British did not make the same mistake. If they deferred to Spanish dignity then historians might one day acknowledge that the *Generalisimo* had saved Gibraltar for Britain, kept the Mediterranean open for her ships and helped her win the war.

The phone rang. Moser. 'I must see you,' he said. 'Now. It's very urgent.' His voice had a nervous breaking quality about it.

'Where?'

'In the Casa de Campo. On a slope just north of Morán Hill. There's an old fortification from the Civil War there. Don't let anyone follow you.'

'Where are you now?'

The line went dead.

Adam took a taxi to the edge of the big natural park and walked across winter-pale grass. Snow fell hesitantly, birds rose testily from umbrella pines. What was left of the fortification consisted of three low walls in the shape of a U. Moser was leaning against one of them. He was wearing a Burberry raincoat and peaked tweed cap.

He stuck out one gloved hand. 'Good of you to come, old man.' A twitch had developed beneath his right eye.

'What's the trouble?' Adam raised the collar of his Crombie and plunged his hands deep into its pockets. Snow fell lightly on his cheeks.

Moser stared furtively into the pine trees. 'You weren't followed?'

'Not as far as I know.'

Moser, brown hair protruding from the cap above his ears, said, 'Bad news,' with a hiss of the final s.

'I've been blown?'

'Nothing like that. If anything it's me who has been blown. You see I once committed the unforgivable crime and now I have been exposed.'

'What was the crime?'

'I was born a Jew,' Moser said.

A breeze sighed in the pines.

'The RHSA knows?'

'Himmler knows,' Moser said, a catch in his voice. 'Someone must have ratted when he was in Madrid.'

'But that was last October.' Adam remembered the draped swastikas shivering in the breeze.

'They must have been investigating me ever since.'

'They've taken their time,' Adam said.

'German intelligence is very bureaucratic. You wouldn't think so, would you, with a man like Himmler in charge.'

'Who denounced you?'

'A friend, I think.' Moser brushed his eyes with gloved fingers.

'A very dear friend?'

'I have never disguised my inclinations,' Moser said, and suddenly Adam felt sorry for him. 'I admire you very much, you know.'

'So what do you want me to do?'

'A deal,' Moser said. 'Shall we walk?'

They passed a courting couple lying entwined on the grass, insulated against the cold by passion, and a lonely man who looked as though he were searching for a body on a battlefield.

'What sort of a deal?'

'Have you ever heard about Operation Felix?'

'Gibraltar?' Adam asked intuitively.

'I have the details here.' Moser patted the front of his raincoat.

Adam clenched his fists inside his pockets. 'What do you want in return?'

'Asylum,' Moser said.

'In Madrid? You'd be gunned down before you even reached our embassy. There are more Gestapo agents in Madrid than traffic policemen.'

'No,' Moser said. 'Not in Madrid, old man. England,' and Adam was visited briefly by a preposterous vision of Moser in hunting pink riding to hounds.

'How do you propose we do that?'

'It's simple,' Moser hissed softly. 'A night flight from Barajas airport to Lisbon.'

'The Germans check every flight; you know that.'

'A special flight. One passenger.' Moser touched Adam's arm. 'I think your people would be very interested to know about Hitler's plans to capture the Rock.'

'I would have to see the plans first.'

'Of course.'

'You realize I could take them from you now.'

'I don't think so, old man,' Moser said, producing a Walther 7.65 mm pistol from the pocket of the raincoat.

Adam said, 'You never cease to surprise me. Would you shoot me?'

'Much as I admire you, I'm afraid I would. But there's no need, is there?' He looked earnestly at Adam.

'Put that cannon away and let me have a look at Operation Felix.'

'Your word?'

'You have it,' Adam said. 'When is Operation Felix planned for?'

'10 January,' Moser said, replacing the Walther in the pocket of his raincoat.

'That's in two days.'

'I can count, old man.'

'And when do you want to fly to England?'

'Tonight,' Moser said, straightening his cap.

The date of the proposed invasion of Gibraltar supplied by Moser was not, strictly speaking, accurate, but the postscript considerably enlivened the normally ponderous Atherton. As indeed did the whole battle plan.

He pinned each page on a green baize notice-board on the wall of his office and flattened the maps and diagrams on his desk with ink-wells, paper-weights and fossils.

He pointed at the row of houses facing Gibraltar on the mainland between La Linea and Algeciras – Villa Leon, San Luis, Villa Isabel and Haus Keller. 'Well, we know about those,' he said massaging his soft hands together. 'Observation posts, known as *Spy Row* on the Rock.'

He read aloud from a report compiled by the Abwehr, German military intelligence. '*Surprise attack impossible. Sheer rock faces and treacherous wind currents make glider and paratroop landings out of the question. Conventional advance across the neutral isthmus linking the Rock with Spain would be vulnerable to heavy and accurate gunfire.*'

Adam pointed at the minutely detailed map of the Rock. 'And they know where the gunfire will come from.' With his forefinger he prodded some of the gun batteries – Princess Caroline, Glacis, Montague, Breakneck, Napier, Devil's Gap . . .

Atherton read on, '*Troops required, 65,383* . . .' Atherton whistled soundlessly. 'Why the odd three I wonder? *Plus 1,094 horses, 13,179 tons of ammunition, 136 tons of food a day and a total of 9,000 tons of fuel. With bases in transit at Burgos, Salamanca, Merida and Seville.* I wonder how Franco would take to that?'

'There's a good hospital in Salamanca,' Adam said, 'if they rupture themselves lifting all that ammunition.'

'Ah, and the Totenkopf Division of the SS, the Death's Head, as back-up *if the British attempt a landing in Spain behind the attack*. As if we would,' Atherton said, displaying a keyboard of square teeth.

'*Estimated garrison strength on Gibraltar: 10,000. Siege potential: 18 months*. Not far off,' he commented admiringly. 'And listen to this: *Duplicates of Gibraltar's defences have been built for training near Besançon because the limestone formations in the Jura mountains in France closely resemble the Rock*. Bit of a jape to blow them up, eh, Adam?'

'It would give the game away,' Adam said.

'*In charge of the attack: Feldmarschall Walter von Reichenau, Commander of the Sixth Army*. Wonderful detail, Adam. They'll give you an invisible gong for this. So, if they can't take it with a surprise attack how the devil are they going to manage it?' He ran one finger down the contingency plan. 'Ah, here we have it in Adolf's own fair hand . . . Two gongs, Adam, and a knighthood for unspecified services rendered.'

'What about Moser?'

'Don't worry about your chum,' Atherton said. 'We'll fly him to Lisbon tonight. Now let's see what the Führer has got to suggest. *Directive No 18, 12 November 1940* . . . A Blitzkrieg: Luftwaffe planes taking off from France, bombing the Navy and a landing in Spain . . . special units sealing off the peninsula . . . then the main attack from the Spanish mainland . . . *The Germans would consolidate their positions and close the Straits*. Dire straits for us . . . if, that is, the Italians hadn't attacked Greece and cocked it up so badly that the Germans had to go to their rescue and abandon Gibraltar for a while.'

'But the Germans still want Gibraltar,' Adam said.

'If Franco lets them through Spain,' reading from the plan, 'then the Germans intend to fire 100 shells at each pertinent gun emplacement on the Rock. A total of 210 German heavy guns against 98 artillery and 50 anti-aircraft guns on the Rock. They've got good intelligence,' Atherton said. 'Spy Row – and Spanish workers crossing the border every day into Gib.'

'But Franco's torpedoed the plan?'

'In a manner of speaking,' Atherton said. 'He hummed and hawed so much that Hitler decided to postpone Felix.'

'So 10 January isn't accurate?'

'That was the last firm date. The launching of the operation through Spain followed by a direct attack on Gib on 4 or 5 February.'

'And now?'

'Very interesting,' Atherton said. 'Hitler is still bringing pressure against Franco but it reads as though it's a mite half-hearted. Until – now this postscript is interesting.'

Adam waited.

'All of a sudden the operation becomes Felix-Heinrich. And the date set for it is 15 October. Now that's a hell of a leap ahead. I wonder if Franco knows . . .'

'I think we should tell him,' Adam said. 'Because it sounds as though Hitler intends to march through Spain whether the Caudillo likes it or not.'

'We'll do that, of course,' Atherton said. 'Stir things up with a sodding great wooden spoon. But what intrigues me is why Hitler has postponed Felix for nine months. What's he planning to do in the meantime?'

Eve's apartment had shed its dust and gloom. Anemones bloomed in ceramic pots; dyspeptic ancestors in oils had fled from the walls; the tall rooms had shrunk; Eve played Chopin on the Steinway.

Adam, who had moved into a room with an adjoining bathroom in the apartment, patrolled the resuscitated rooms restlessly. Atherton had promised to telephone with news about Moser before the 9 o'clock news on the day after his flight from Madrid to London via Lisbon, and it was now 8.54.

To his surprise Adam had become concerned about the fate of the strutting little Austrian whose mannerisms, his attempts to compensate for his sense of inadequacy had, in his absence, become endearing.

He went into the living-room where Eve was sitting with a resourceful-looking American girl named Irene Hadfield who was not unlike Norma Shearer in appearance. They were drinking coffee and eating rugged sandwiches made with *serrano* ham and *chorizo*.

Eve said, 'Relax, you look like one of those husbands in the movies waiting to hear if he's the proud father of a baby girl or boy.'

Adam spun the hand on the dial of the radio until he picked up the BBC. The reassuring voice of Alvar Liddell.

Roosevelt had asked Congress to appropriate $10,811,000,000 for defence in 1942 . . .

'The hell he has,' Irene Hadfield exclaimed.

Adam held up one finger.

. . . an air-raid on Cardiff . . . further advances by British and Australian troops in Libya . . .

The dependable voice made Adam even more restless. Why hadn't Atherton called?

Irene said, 'That Roosevelt, consistent he is not.'

'Because he refused to send arms to Spain during the Civil War?'

'Because when the war was almost over he said he wished he had. You fought for the Fascists, right?'

'You know damn well I did.'

'Proud of it?'

'What do you think?' Irene Hadfield was beginning to get under his skin. 'You would have fought for the reds?'

'I'm a pacifist.'

'One of the great don't-knows . . . What are you doing in Madrid, Irene?'

Eve smiled and her smile now had a warmth in it that had been frozen during the war; her figure had filled out, too, and her hair was softly waved. 'She's working with me for the Red Cross.'

How did his sister live the way she did? Adam wondered. Funds must have been salted away. Maybe her husband *had* been a member of the Falange.

Irene said, 'I'm a rich bitch. Well, daughter of a rich sonofabitch.'

'In Madrid?'

'In business.'

'Comfortable berth, Madrid.'

'You should know.'

'If you work for the Red Cross shouldn't you be carrying stretchers in North Africa?'

'That's your war not ours.'

'The Civil War was your war?'

'It should have been everyone's war,' Irene said. 'And don't let me stop you purging your complexes about it.'

'Accept my apologies,' Adam said, 'for not fighting for the losing side.'

The phone rang in the hallway. Adam strode to it.

Atherton said: 'They're over the moon.'

'Who's over the moon?'

'You know who,' Atherton said. 'Three gongs and a knighthood.'

'You were going to tell me about . . .'

'Our friend.' A pause. 'He wouldn't have settled down in Britain, Adam.'

Adam gripped the receiver. 'What the hell are you talking about?'

'An accident. On the way to the airport.'

Adam stared at the receiver. 'What sort of an accident?'

'Frosty night . . . slippery surface . . . bloody great Hispano-Suiza coming the other way.'

'Dead?'

''Fraid so, Adam. Casualty of war . . .'

'The driver?'

'Thrown clear.'

'You killed him,' Adam said.

'Steady on, old man.'

'Don't call me old man.' Adam replaced the receiver.

'Moser,' he said softly, 'hunting pink would have suited you.'

He walked into his room and closed the door behind him.

The lottery ticket didn't win any of the big prizes, nor, for that matter, any of the lesser ones; nor were any of the tickets that Adam bought in increasing numbers from *El Pistola* during the ensuing months any more successful. Like a man who no longer expects any good news in his mail-box, Adam was philosophical about these disappointments: he had persuaded himself that his life and his gambling were following parallel courses and that when the first changed for the better then so would the second. But at the moment his life showed no signs of turning the wheel of fortune whose revolutions now included poker and *pelota*, the Spanish ball-game that provides an easily available service for those wishing to lose their life savings without tiresome application. The spectres of the Civil War had been joined by Moser and Spain was settling into *Los Años de Hambre*, the Years of Hunger.

Wherever he went he saw queues for coal and food. He saw prostitutes bargaining on the streets for the money to buy their children a meal. He saw the privileged who had cowered in their homes for nearly three years parading the easy graces of wealth in smart restaurants. He bought cakes made from lupin flour from women whose eyes were glazed by despair. He listened to deals being struck on the black market, that ubiquitous companion of human suffering.

Now that his contact at the German embassy was dead, murdered, Adam's humanitarian duties had, despite exhortations from Atherton, replaced his intelligence activities. 'Moser must have a successor,' Atherton said. 'The RHSA must know you were Moser's contact here. Get in there, Adam, and make yourself available.'

Adam contrived to give the impression that he was doing just that, but when he left the embassy for a clandestine meeting he either wandered alone round the Retiro or went to a café in the old quarter behind the Plaza Mayor and looked for answers in cups of dark coffee laced with brandy. The pretence enabled him to continue visiting prisoners and refugee camps and in one month he freed 14 POWs who were repatriated to Britain via Gibraltar.

On his visits to the camps teeming with French, Dutch, Belgians, Poles, Czechs and Jews fleeing from the Nazis, Adam was occasionally joined by Irene Hadfield mediating for the Red Cross. Together they picked their way past huddled families, girls with shaven heads, pet dogs who hauled themselves upright on spindly legs to protect their masters, old ladies whose rings had long ago slid from their bone-thin fingers.

It seemed to Adam that Europe was populated by the homeless in flight. First the Spaniards who had sought asylum in France – many of them sent back by the Vichy government, puppets of the Germans – and now these pitiful hordes.

It was Irene who pointed out that the Spanish Government,

hard pushed to feed its own subjects, was doing its best for the outcasts.

'You should see some of their travel documents,' she said. 'Before the war they would have been laughed back across the frontier. The trouble with you British, is that you think you're the only country that matters in Europe.'

'At the moment we are,' Adam said. 'We're the only one fighting.'

They were sitting in a bar in the valley of the Ebro near Zaragoza, drinking red wine and eating olives and hard bread, waiting for the storm that had materialized over the hills of Torrero to pass. Lightning fizzed, thunder rolled and rain bouncing high in the dilapidated courtyard released scents of dust and hibernating summer.

'Waiting for the Americans to help you out again?'

Adam pushed the bread across the faded oilcloth. 'Never argue on an empty stomach, it reflects the condition of your head.'

'Ha, bloody, ha. Are all the British as sniffy as you?'

Adam didn't reply. He was pleased that the wine hadn't affected his judgement. He ate some olives, refilled his glass, drank half of it, held it up to the light and drained it; it was innocuous enough, not like the wine from Rioja he drank in Madrid.

A sad-faced young barman polishing a glass stared through the rain in search of lost love. Old men sitting beneath a poster advertising a bullfight that had taken place six months earlier venomously slapped dominoes on their table. Lightning split the sky; thunder cracked above the bar.

Irene, whose brown curls had been straightened a little during the dash through the rain, said, 'Well, we helped you out of a mess once. I guess we'll have to do it again.'

'Maybe we won't ask you,' aware as he spoke that he had blundered.

Irene sat back in her chair, arms folded. 'Do I hear someone saying, "Give us the tools and we will finish the job"?' Have you forgotten that the day before Churchill broadcast his appeal for arms the House of Representatives approved the Lease-Lend Bill?'

Adam said, '*We* will finish the job, not you.'

Irene nibbled an olive. Adam drank more wine.

Irene said: 'Are you a spy, Adam?'

'Of course.'

'Julia –'

'Eve.'

'– says she doesn't know what you do in the embassy.'

'Apart from rescuing servicemen.'

'That's what makes me wonder. Chancery is political not humanitarian.'

'I speak Spanish, I know the country.'

'Of course, you were a good Fascist.'

Adam bit on an olive stone. 'Everyone in an embassy is a spy. Even the ambassador.' He drank some more wine and gnawed a piece of the bullet-hard bread. The rain assaulted the windows, cascading in zigzag torrents to the sill. He glanced at his watch. Four o'clock. It was a long way to Madrid in the dark on a narrow road running with flood water.

He said, 'I think we should finish our drinks, drive into Zaragoza and put up for the night.'

'You're the driver,' Irene said, leaving him with a lingering inference that she would have made it to Madrid.

The rain fled across the fields and the sky shone wih silver light.

'Let's go,' Adam said.

As he went to the bar to pay the phone rang somewhere in the living quarters, startling the sad barman in his reverie. When he returned he said: 'You cannot leave, señor, the road has been washed away.'

'To Zaragoza?'

'In both directions.' He sighed.

'When will it be repaired?'

The barman spread his hands.

Adam told Irene.

She said, 'Bullshit, there must be a way round.'

'He should know.'

'Phooey. Do you want me to drive?'

'Not in your condition.'

'What the hell's that supposed to mean?'

'That wine's stronger than you think,' Adam said choosing his words carefully.

'Listen, smart ass, I could drink you under the table any time you want.'

He took her arm and, leaning a little to one side, led her out of the bar, across the cracked concrete to the embassy car. Small waterways of brown water rippled across the road; the tyres hissed through them, throwing up wings of spray.

'What did I tell you?' she said, unbuttoning her coat and combing her wet hair with the tips of her fingers.

'What *did* you tell me?' The words were slippery on his tongue.

The road ahead ended in a small ravine; what looked like a tributary of the Ebro gushed through it. On either side of the torrent lay fields of water. Dusk was thickening. Another instalment of the storm was making its appearance over the Torrero hills. Lightning blinked, thunder grumbled.

Adam made a five-point turn and drove back to the bar.

'So what do you want to do?' he asked. 'Try the other direction?'

'I know when I'm beat,' said Irene.

They walked across the courtyard. In the flickering light, smelling mud and, faintly, electricity, glimpsing ahead the containment of the bar, Adam experienced emotions that must have been gestating in him for a long time.

They were greeted by the slap of dominoes and the gentle smile of the young barman. Adam asked him if there were rooms available. The barman wrenched his gaze from the blurred horizon. He would find out, he said.

The rain returned and machine-gunned the window. Lightning slashed the sky, staying in your brain even when you shut your eyes.

The barman returned. There was one room. He favoured them with a smile that was at the same time apologetic, romantic and conspiratorial.

Irene said, 'I don't believe it.'

'My father,' the barman said, 'wants to know if you have got passports.'

Adam handed him his diplomatic passport.

The barman, unimpressed, took it. 'That will be 50 pesetas,' he said.

'I still don't believe it,' Irene said, as they climbed the stairs. There was a straw mattress in one corner of the room. Nothing else.

'Let's dine first,' Adam said. 'A bottle of Bollinger. *Pâté de foie gras* – they say it's very good in this area. Trout with almonds . . .'

They ate rashers of bloodless meat, diminutive potatoes in their skins, bread smeared with olive oil and salt and they drank another jug of wine. They lay fully-clothed on opposite sides of the mattress listening to the storm.

When Adam awoke the storm had passed. Water dripped from evergreen leaves and the sunlight fashioned jewels in their clasps and birds sang. Lying on the mattress, head buzzing from the wine, he remembered the emotions he had experienced crossing the courtyard the night before. Now he understood what they had meant: he was a Spaniard.

He stretched out one hand and touched Irene Hadfield's face. Then he rolled clear.

Three days later Adam was sitting in his office in the embassy thinking about Irene Hadfield when the house phone rang and the receptionist, voice to attention, said, 'There's a Mr Jack Palmer from San Diego to see you, Mr Fleming.'

'What's he want?'

'He won't say, except that it's something to your advantage.'

'Tell him I'll be down,' Adam said irritably.

As he walked into the lobby, Tom Canfield held up his arms and said, 'Don't shoot.'

CHAPTER 12

And now the gold.

Tom, sitting in a carriage of a labouring train, stared at some of the Spaniards parading past the window. Wheatfields and vineyards, scrub and spine-backed mountains cutting the blue sky. America seemed part of someone else's adolescence.

Just the same, before leaving Madrid, he had registered at the United States Embassy – as Thomas Canfield rather than Jack Palmer – following the move the previous September to conscript all American males between 21 and 35 for a year's military training.

Thirty-five. Jesus, he was only seven years short of the limit. Academic in any case – he had reported to the embassy doctor who had listened to his lungs and announced that he would only be required to fight if pensioners were called upon to man the last-ditch defences around the White House.

After that he had gone to the British Embassy and, by the basic ruse of substituting Palmer for Canfield, met Adam Fleming who had probably been there all the time. Why had they been so cagey?

Gazing at peasants working like forlorn black crows in the fields, Tom recalled the dark bar behind the Plaza Mayor where he had sipped *fino* while the ancient barman tipped brandy into Fleming's black coffee. They were two old campaigners, Adam in a pin-stripe, Tom in his flying jacket, invisible medals jingling on their breasts.

'That shell-hole,' Canfield said. 'I still dream about it; hear the rats paddling in the water.'

'I hear the guns,' Adam said. 'And I see the bayonets.' His

eyes had a distant gaze to them and his hand holding the cup shook a little.

'That bastard Delgado.'

'He was a bastard all right.'

'Let's hope he got his just deserts.'

'I often wonder what happened to Chimo,' Adam said.

'Chimo who?'

'A legionnaire I fought with. I tried to trace him but no one wants to know about the war.'

'You went back to England?'

'For a while.'

Adam was less communicative than Tom remembered him. It was, he supposed, embarrassing to meet the man you were once poised to kill. Nonetheless there was between them the same easiness he remembered in the shell-hole. A brotherhood.

'Unfit for active service like me? Weird, isn't it, that we were fit to fight another country's war but not our own.'

'I was diplomatically unfit.'

'What's that supposed to mean?'

'They thought I would be more use as a diplomat than a soldier. My Spanish, my knowledge of Spain . . .'

Adam beckoned the barman who poured more thin sherry into Tom's glass and a brandy for Adam. Tom thought he was drinking it a little too thirstily. The barman replaced the bottles on a shelf in front of a mottled mirror, gave them salted almonds and olives and retired to his armoury of barrels in the fumed darkness at the end of the bar.

Adam said, 'Did you go back to the States?'

'To Paris. But that's a long story.'

'Señor Palmer?'

Tom put his finger to his lips. The dark bar made a conspirator of him.

'Who would have thought six years ago that it would have come to this,' Adam said. 'We're foreigners now in our own countries.'

'How was England?'

'Blinkered,' Adam said.

'They must have known war was going to break out any moment.'

'They knew that all right. But they didn't know what war was like. Not like us.'

'Some did,' Tom said. 'Those who fought in the last war to end all wars.'

'The young people didn't. To them it was gas-masks and sandbags and training with the territorials.'

'Do you often wonder why we did what we did, you and I?'

'All the time,' Adam said. He bit crisply into a salted almond. 'Especially as we fought on opposite sides.'

A group of well-dressed businessmen came in from the light and isolated themselves at the end of the bar. The barman made his way arthritically to serve them. Somewhere outside a child cried without enthusiasm.

'In this war they're told to kill each other: we volunteered. Why?'

'The sad thing,' Adam said, 'is that it's difficult to remember why.' He glanced at his watch. 'I have to get back.'

They walked across the Plaza Mayor. Rain was beginning to fall, polishing the lonely statue of Philip III. Half-way across, Tom stopped. 'There's something I have to know.'

'Would I have pulled the trigger?' Adam's face was rain-wet and there were smudges like fading bruises beneath his eyes.

'Well, would you?'

Adam stared at him for a moment. Then he said, 'No, I don't think I would,' and in a perverse way Tom was disappointed.

As the train taking Tom towards his pot of gold nosed its way through the snow-dusted foothills of the Pyrenees, a spoilt small girl bounced under sufferance on the knee of her godfather in an apartment 800 miles away in Kensington, London. Isabel Tomasina Ruiz wasn't sure why she had to endure this routine every time Uncle Tom paid one of his visits, but she hoped profoundly that the gallop on his knee would end soon. 'This is the way the gentleman goes. Trit, trot, trit, trot . . .'

Martine Ruiz, sitting on a Regency-stripe sofa in the staidly comfortable flat behind the Albert Hall lacquering her nails, was inclined to agree with her daughter's views about Thomas Emlyn Jones but he had, after all, brought her into this world and helped her before Antonio's new prosperity had begun. She merely wished that he would stay at sea a little longer, guarding the Atlantic convoys perhaps.

'This is the way the farmer goes . . .'

'Careful Tom,' Martine said, holding out one hand to dry its pink nails.

She picked up an old newspaper and read on the front page about the death of Alfonso XIII of Spain in Rome on 28 February. She had been very young and living in Paris when the king, with his quizzical features and theatrical moustache, had fled from Spain in 1931 just before the advent of the Second Republic, but his passing made her pine for her adopted country. His son, Don Juan, Count of Barcelona, was now King-in-exile. Perhaps one day his son, Juan Carlos, might reign in Madrid; he was only three.

And perhaps now, at long last, they could return home, leaving Marisa behind to complete her education in England. Martine didn't delve deeply into Antonio's business affairs because they bored her, but she knew that, although perfume necessitated frequent visits to Grasse and Geneva, it was now subordinate to wolfram. She knew that wolfram, also known as tungsten, was supplied by Spain to the Germans who needed it to toughen steel for their weapons and she knew that it would soon be fetching £7,000 a ton. She also knew that the Allies had to outbid the Germans and that the middle-man, Antonio, stood to make a fortune out of such negotiations. I will tackle Antonio tonight, she thought. After he has eaten and before we have made love.

Martine flexed her fingers; the nails were quite dry. She was lucky to get the lacquer in wartime Britain, just as she had been lucky to get perfume in Madrid. And Antonio was lucky to marry me. Where was that peasant of a sister of his, Ana? She had always been an embarrassment and now, according to reports from Madrid, she was some sort of guerrilla leader in the Pyrenees.

'Come on Tom,' she said, 'that's enough – you'll wear yourself out. No girls chasing you tonight?'

'Queuing up outside,' he told her.

As he swayed towards the door, Isabel switched on the radio.

Antonio got home at seven. He wore an overcoat with velvet lapels and a grey, tight-waisted suit. His hair was tightly curled and she noticed how grey it was at the temples. His face looked hungry but then it always had; his eyes were lustrous, pupils dilated. He ate listlessly and drank only a few mouthfuls of wine, and she wondered illogically if he had found another woman.

Later, he undressed discreetly and lay in bed beside her. As usual he smelled faintly of perfume. Hands behind his head, he talked vaguely about negotiating Britain's aid to Spain, mentioning, in passing, wolfram.

God, she thought, has it come to this? She felt the bones of her own body and their unyielding angles, with the tips of her fingers, and lay stiffly beside him.

He said, 'By the way, we return to Madrid next week.'

Then he turned to her and entered her with surprising ease.

Tom, rucksack on his back, alighted from the train at Jaca, 2,700 feet up on a plateau in the Pyrenees, 30 miles from the French border. The railway ahead was blocked by snow and so, presumably, was the route to Baños de Panticosa.

He stood undecidedly outside the station of the garrison town, breathing the bright air and feeling it cold in his lungs. He hadn't bargained for so much snow, not in March.

Two *Guardia Civil* wearing capes came out of the station, a portly prisoner in leg-irons between them. They, too, looked uncertainly around them as though the night's snow had interrupted the journey to death or incarceration. Then they set off for some unscheduled destination, police station presumably, the prisoner's leg-irons ringing briskly.

Tom wandered through the narrow streets above the river. They were muffled with snow and the citizens had hibernated inside their lidded houses, the soldiers in their barracks. Eventually he retreated into the cathedral. It was as cold as a tomb inside but comforting in its sepulchral way. Old women knelt in prayer; candles burned beneath unwavering halos.

He sat in the penultimate pew and took the sketch-map that the dying patient in the monastery had given him. It was probably blasphemous to make mercenary calculations in a palace of God, but God would surely understand because he had made it so damn cold outside.

The map was crude. Black ink on white cartridge paper. Brown half-moon from a coffee cup in one corner. Scale, expansive. Focal points, two crosses like gun-sights at Baños de Panticosa, a spa 40 miles from Jaca. What lay at the intersections of each cross was not revealed.

A small unshaven man with a white forehead above walnut features sat down close to Tom, and leaned forward in prayer. His prayers reached Tom in breaths of garlic and stale wine, then took a corporeal turn.

'Señor, I saw you get off the train.'

Tom folded the map and slid it into one of the pouches on the rucksack; later he would hide it inside the binding of his diary. 'What of it?' His Spanish was becoming instinctive – well, almost – and he was proud of it.

'You want somewhere to stay?'

'I want to get to Baños de Panticosa.'

'The road is closed, señor.'

'I know,' Tom said, voice devout in the incense gloom.

'It is also dangerous.'

'Why dangerous?'

'Because of the guerrillas. They kill *Guardia Civil* and Fascists but sometimes they make mistakes. It could cost you plenty,' the man said in a burst of pickled words.

'What could cost me?'

'A mule. It is the only way. I can let you have two very cheap.'

'How cheap?'

'Twenty-five pesetas a day.'

'Ten,' said Tom averting his gaze from the altar.

'Twenty.'

'Fifteen.'

They settled for 17 pesetas 50 centimos.

On his way out of the cathedral Tom dropped 2 pesetas 50 centimos in the offertory box which had a neglected air about it. Tom's new companion confided that he was known as the Beggar, which wasn't strictly true because he was a Provider, begging for that which he provided.

'Did you beg for the mules?'

'The mules are mine: we have lived together for many years.'

The Beggar took Tom to a stable near the Convent of the Benedictines where the mules waited stoically. In the stable, out of reach of the mules' hooves, stood a collection of merchandise begged to provide. China dog, ear trumpet, cat's whisker wireless, scrubbing board, castanets, one football boot, Bible . . .

The Beggar poured wine from an earthenware jug. Tom sipped some: it tasted of herbs and he drained his glass.

'Do you live here?'

'Live here, sleep here, hide here.'

'Who do you hide from?'

'Anyone, everyone. You see I have begged many secrets. The mountains are dangerous places these days. The guerrillas are fighting for a lost cause and no one else wants another war – they have suffered too much. So they betray the guerrillas and then the guerrillas seek vengeance in the villages.'

'Do you betray them?'

'Shit, what a question.' He rubbed the knuckle of one hand across his white forehead. 'But I don't blame the informers: for once they have right on their side.'

'Jaca was red, of course?'

'Jaca,' said the Beggar raising his glass in a toast, 'was the cradle of the war. The Republic began here on 13 December 1930. The beginning and end of the kings.'

'The king died the other day,' Tom told him.

'I will drink to that.'

'How long will it take us?' Tom asked, sitting on a wooden box beside a degutted Ultra wireless.

'Two days, maybe three.'

'With two mules?'

'There will be other mules along the way. I will beg and I will provide.'

'And if the snow melts?'

'Then we will drown.'

By nightfall they had reached a village 15 miles from Jaca. The Beggar begged a stable for the two of them and in the kitchen of an inn they ate stew and drank wine from a *bota* and slept on straw close to the exhausted mules. Frost patterns of fern and palm froze on the inside of the window and through them Tom could see the teeth of the mountains, the stars pinned above them, and he could smell the snow.

The Beggar passed the *bota* and, as Tom poured wine down his throat, said, 'Tell me, señor, why do you want to visit the baths at a time like this?'

'They're warm, aren't they?'

'There are many strange tales about the baths,' the Beggar said.

'Such as?'

'A stranger who came to Jaca said the rainbow ended there.'

'What did he mean by that?'

'Your guess is as good as mine – he was very drunk.'

'How long ago was this?' Tom asked, nipping the interest out of his voice.

'During the war. There was no real time during the war. Only the time of the reds and the time of the Fascists. You were killed by one or the other. It didn't matter which.'

The Beggar burrowed into the straw. 'What do you think he meant, Señor Tom, about the rainbow?'

'It's a line of poetry,' Tom said.

'Shit, is that all? I thought it meant there was gold there.'

The Beggar moved lazily in the straw and began to snore.

They set off again at dawn after breakfasting on bread and olive oil and ice-cold water from a well. Ice-dust hung in the dawn air and the emerging mountains looked down upon them with disdain. Pines grew as sharply as pencil points on distant flanks of snow and eagles rested predatorily in the winter-blue sky. The mules, moving doggedly, had just rounded a bend beneath an overhanging crag when the shooting started.

'Shit,' said the Beggar.

He jumped from his mule and threw himself behind a boulder. Tom joined him. The mules stopped and looked at them.

Guardia Civil in capes and tricorn hats were running for cover in the gorge as bullets chipped the boulders. One was kneeling, shooting with a rifle at the source of the gunfire high among the teeth of the mountain. On the track stood a snow-plough, concave blade poised above a wedge of snow. Behind it a khaki truck, windscreen smashed, driver lolling over the steering wheel.

'An ambush,' the Beggar said. 'That's the truck bringing the pay to the garrison at Jaca. It must have been delayed while they fetched the snow-plough. A sitting duck,' the Beggar said. 'The guerrillas must have waited all night.'

A bullet struck the boulder sheltering them.

'Sons of whores,' shouted the Beggar.

The *guardia* were fanning out but there were only a few of them, half a dozen maybe. One of them spun in front of Tom and the Beggar, dropping his rifle and falling forward, hands groping in the snow for it. His blood was very bright on the snow.

A pause. Then shooting from lower down the ravine. Tom saw smoke puff from a line of pines. Bullets clanged on the blade of the snow-plough.

'Don't worry,' the Beggar said. 'Unless . . .'

'Unless what?'

'It doesn't matter,' the Beggar said. 'They're friendly.'

A *guardia* let loose with a machine-pistol, but the pines were far beyond its effective range. More puffs of smoke, rifle-cracks following. Snowflakes fluttering from a darkening sky. Shouts from among the boulders as round as cabbage hearts.

A cry of pain. A *guardia* staggers and falls, rolls slowly towards the track, picking up snow as he rolls, and Tom is reminded of a snowball he made once in Vermont and rolled until it seemed to be as big as the Michelin man. He feels he is in a cinema watching a movie. For some inexplicable reason the Beggar takes off his beret and his forehead above his walnut features is as white as a corpse's.

Bullets sing. One hits a mule and it falls to its knees like a bull in a *corrida* and stares uncomprehendingly at Tom. Smoke puffs from lower down the flank of the mountain.

The Beggar says, 'I must get that,' pointing at the rifle dropped by the dead *guardia*. 'Rifles fetch a good price.'

'I will fire it at your funeral.'

'Don't waste a bullet; they, too, are valuable.'

He inches forward and is flattened into the snow by a bullet.

Tom worms through the snow but this beggar will provide

no more. His bargain-hunting eyes stare into the snow. An eagle hovers. Is eclipsed by snow falling prettily from an inexorable sky.

Tom takes cover behind the warm, stable-smelling body of the mule. A bullet hits the beast's chest and Tom feels it as though it has embedded itself in his own flesh.

The *guardia* in their spectacular hats confer in shouts and contradictory orders. They don't, as far as Tom can make out, stand a chance.

Another bullet thuds into the warm, mule-meat in front of him. Another *guardia* opens his arms to the bruised sky and falls back into the snow.

The *guardia* are withdrawing towards the snow-plough and the truck, their strategy unclear.

A machine-gun rips open the morning. But it is firing from the other side of the track. Another *guardia* falls. Machine-gun bullets clank against the snow-plough's shovel. Is it not time that these brave policemen called it a day?

A black egg tumbles through the air.

A pause.

White smoke and sparks and a crack that sounds, puny among the mountains as the grenade explodes.

A white flag, waving on the barrel of a *guardia*'s rifle.

'And who might you be?'

The Spaniard wore a hunting jacket, laced boots and a Balaclava. He was tall with a starved face and feverish eyes and spoke Castilian like a professor. He pointed a long-barrelled pistol at Tom's head.

'I could ask you the same.'

The Spaniard held out his hand. 'Papers.'

Tom picked up his rucksack.

'Give it to me.'

Tom handed it to him.

He glanced at the diary containing the map inside the binding, perused the passport. Jack Raymond Palmer from San Diego. 'What are you doing here, Señor Palmer?'

'I'm a tourist,' Tom said. 'Didn't you know Franco has arranged tours of the old battlefields?'

'This,' the Spaniard said, 'is a new battlefield.' He replaced the diary and the passport in the rucksack. 'I think we should talk English, Mr Palmer; I suspect you are better at it. Now please tell me what you are really doing here.'

'Sightseeing.'

'With that?' pointing the barrel of the pistol at the Beggar's body.

'He was a good guide.'

'He was an informer. He has betrayed many of my men. We were going to execute him.'

'He was a beggar,' Tom said. 'A provider.'

'A provider of men's lives. Why were you keeping company with garbage like that?' He jabbed the barrel of the pistol in Tom's chest.

'He said he was a guide.'

'To where?'

'To the French border.'

'That isn't difficult to find.'

'In the snow?'

'If you don't tell me the truth, Mr Palmer, I shall shoot you. Tell me, are you as brave as you sound?'

Suddenly Tom was not brave at all and his skull was packed with ice. *But if he shoots me now he will think I died bravely.*

The Spaniard said, 'Give me one good reason why I shouldn't kill you.'

'Because you're the second bastard to try.'

'The first?'

'A Fascist.'

'Are you trying to tell me you fought for us?'

'Oh yes,' Tom said, 'I fought for you all right.'

'Can you prove it?'

'Read the diary,' Tom said.

Then he knelt beside the dead mule and stroked the fur between its eyes.

The log cabin was on a ledge on a mountain overlooking a sleeping valley and it was guarded by four guerrillas.

Inside the hut a stove glowed incandescently, the heat running along a pipe in the ceiling and filling the room. The

Spaniard sat with his feet on a scrubbed pine table, pistol resting in his lap. He looked to Tom like a man who had grown into toughness.

He said in English, 'So why did you fight for us, Mr Palmer?'

'Who is us?'

'The proletariat. Ordinary people.'

'I fought against injustice,' Tom said. He sat on a stiff-backed chair opposite the Spaniard; a little steam rose from his disgraceful flying jacket.

'Difficult to fight against a generalization. Especially when you are no longer very young. You must have been 25 when the war broke out . . .'

'There was plenty of injustice in America and it wasn't a generalization.'

'Odd that you didn't put your name in your diary.'

Tom shrugged. 'Supposing it had fallen into Fascist hands.'

'You don't strike me as a man who is bothered by such details.' The Spaniard lit a cigarette, inhaled deeply and coughed billows of smoke. He tapped his chest. 'Tuberculosis. The doctors say the mountain air should be good for it.'

'I, too, have bad lungs.'

'Please don't try and make a friend of me.'

'What are you trying to achieve, Señor –?'

'My name's Andrés,' the Spaniard said. He inhaled again as though he were angry with the healing mountain air. 'The fight doesn't end just because the Germans and the Italians gave more help than the Russians.'

'You are beaten,' Tom said. 'Everyone in Spain knows you are beaten. You were beaten because you fought among yourselves. In the end,' Tom said, 'it made me sick to the stomach.'

'That is very sad because the fight, the true fight, will never end. You fought the Fascists, the Germans. Even now we are fighting them. For the Resistance, the *Maquis*, in France. That way we keep our spirit alive; that way we win guns and ammunition and explosives to continue the fight here.'

'The fight for what?' Tom found he was shouting. 'For Christ's sake, what are you fighting for?'

'Mankind?'

'Bullshit.'

'If everyone thought that way then it would be. Happily not everyone does.'

'What made you fight in the first place?'

'Because there was no alternative. The Fascists hated us worst of all, you know.'

'Us?'

'The intellectuals. We frightened the shit out of them.'

'You have a way with the English language.'

'I taught it,' Andrés said. 'At Madrid University. Before the Fascists blew it to bits.'

'Intellectuals!' Tom kicked the table, dislodging the Spaniard's feet. 'Bandits with brains!'

'I'm sorry you feel that way. You see it means you have to die even though you fought for us.'

The sun had strengthened and a finger of snow slid down the window.

'I'm tired of people threatening to kill me.'

'It might not be necessary if you fought for us again.'

'I told you, I don't give a shit for the Cause any more. The only cause I care about now is Tom Canfield.'

The Spaniard took his time. Picked a shred of black tobacco from his lower lip. Examined it, discarded it, said, 'Really? And who is Tom Canfield?'

Tom walked to the window. The forest silence of the pine trees was punctured by the sound of gunfire. A volley of shots. *Guardia Civil*, he supposed, being executed.

'You know damn well who Tom Canfield is.'

'I know damn well you're not Jack Palmer. My speciality was accents. New York, Mr Canfield?'

'I had to do it to fool the Fascists,' Tom said. 'Tom Canfield fought against them. He was a dead man if he came back to Spain.'

'So what brought you back if you didn't give a shit for the Cause any more?'

'A girl,' Tom said.

'Then I am sorry for her.' The Spaniard lit another cigarette, grimacing as though the smoke had burned his lungs. 'You do see that we have to kill you, don't you? You know our

faces, this place,' putting his feet back on the table, 'our
weapons, our methods . . .'

'How much money was there in the truck?'

'Not so much. Spanish soldiers are not well paid. But the
money is life or death to us.'

'Supposing I could multiply your loot a hundred, a
thousand, a million times –'

'I would say you were out of your mind.'

'You are out of your mind if you don't listen to me.'

'I am listening,' Andrés said.

Then Tom told him about the gold. When he had finished
he said, 'If I lead you to that gold I can return to Madrid?'

'You have my word.'

'In Spain they say the word of an Englishman.'

Andrés smiled through the cigarette smoke wreathing his
face. 'I can do better than that,' he said. 'The word of an
American.'

Tom approached the sulphurous waters of the spa at Panticosa
with a surefooted intent that he didn't feel. No map? Andrés
had asked and Tom had said no, he had memorized it and
destroyed it as they did in all the best espionage movies.
Andrés walked behind him, pistol inside his hunting jacket;
three of his men waited at the edge of the spa in a cirque high
in the mountains. The spa was deserted. Who wants to come
for a cure and be felled by a stray bullet?

The sulphurous smell grew stronger. They stopped on the
shore of the lake which had once teemed with trout before
the famished guerrillas had blown them out with grenades.

'Over there.' Tom pointed at a clump of pines and drew a
line with a stick from one tall tree to a smaller one dying from
over-crowding, then crossed it with another line from one
stump to another. He pointed at the intersection. 'Tell your
men to dig there.'

He sat on a stump and watched as two guards thrust the
blades of their shovels into the wet earth. The pine needles
looked as though they had remained undisturbed since the
trees were seeds in cones. Pistol in his hand, Andrés leaned
against a tree and waited.

Twenty minutes later the blade of a shovel struck what sounded like wood. The two guerrillas dug faster. Tom and Andrés joined them. There, three feet or so below them, was the rotting, green-painted wood of an ammunition box that had once contained Russian-made 7.62 mm Mosin-Nagant bullets.

It took them another 20 minutes to excavate the box, pour the gold coins spilling from the smouldering wood into gunny sacks and load them on to the truck they had ambushed.

On the way back to the log cabin Andrés, words as shiny as ingots, said: 'Do you know what we're going to do with all this?' and when Tom shook his head, 'We're going to invade Spain, that's what.'

It was three months before Tom returned to the spa, on the day in June, as it happened, that Germany invaded Russia, restoring some of Franco's wavering regard for Hitler who had at last taken up arms against the enemies of Mankind, the Communists.

He drove there by night, at the wheel of a truck he had bought in Huesca. At the spa he consulted the sketch-map by flashlight, then began to dig at the point indicated by the second cross, in the middle of a crescent of boulders, six metres due east of a stone bench beside the lake.

It took him two hours to find the second box and bury the gold bars beneath the builder's rubble in the back of the truck.

Then he drove back to Madrid.

CHAPTER 13

Rosana Gomez decided to leave home on her 16th birthday, 28 November 1943. She couldn't precisely explain why, not even to herself. Of obvious reasons there was an abundance. The confines of the village on the plains of La Mancha. The self-conscious ribaldry of the young men swaggering round the square on summer evenings. The hostility that her painting aroused. The atmosphere in the house where Diego still lurked obscenely and Kiko's widow mourned.

But all these could have been endured. No, there were whispers within her more insistent than facts. As subtle as spring and obdurate as winter, they told her that she had to journey north to the place of her birth.

She tried to tell Pablo on the eve of her birthday. They were walking beside a ploughed field: silver tracks of snails shone on the path; split pomegranates grinned from a leafless tree; Pablo kicked stones and hurled pebbles across the wet waves of the field.

'I think,' she said, 'that there are stations in our lives. When we reach one we have to change.'

'You're leaving?' He hurled a stone into the pale sky.

Disconcerted, she said, 'How did you guess that?'

'The way you've been acting.'

'And how have I been acting?'

'With your mind somewhere else. Planning, saving . . .'

'Clever, aren't we?'

'I just felt it.'

Feeling tears beginning to gather, she said, 'It might interest you to know that I only made up my mind today.'

'No,' he said. He shook his head, listening to the echo of the half-truth she had uttered. 'No, I think you knew some time ago.'

'I'm not in the habit of lying.'

'No,' Pablo said hopelessly, 'I know that.'

'Then what do you mean?'

'Maybe you lied to yourself.'

She stared at the grinning pomegranate. 'I just know I have to go,' she said. 'I know the time has come.'

He kicked a stone with such ferocity that it must have hurt his foot, but he didn't flinch.

He said, 'I'll come with you. I'm almost as old as you.'

He was 13, but even if he had been 16 he would still have been too young. Girls grew older more quickly than boys; she had always known this.

'No,' she said gently. 'I will go first. I don't want to go.' Nor did she: the future yawned with fear. 'But I have to.'

'Of course.'

He kicked wildly and a stone flew past Rosana's head.

'I have reached a station,' she said.

'Of course.'

'These things happen.'

'Yes,' he said.

'As we get older.'

He nodded vigorously.

'So you stay here –'

'While you go to Madrid.' He picked up a pebble, examined it and dropped it.

'I'll come back.' She stared across the fields towards the village. She felt that she was embarking upon adult untruths for which there were so many excuses that they appeared preferable to the truth.

'I don't want to leave you,' she said.

'So why are you?'

'I've tried to tell you.'

'It doesn't matter because I don't care.'

'I'm glad.'

'One day you'll be proud you're my sister.'

'Top goal scorer?'

'Someone has to score them.'

'You'll score them,' she said.

'I wish –'

'I know,' she said.

'See that goal?' He pointed at two silver-birch saplings.

'I see it.'

'Goal?'

'Goal,' she said.

Pablo placed the stone on top of a pyramid of soil. Then he walked back like a player taking a penalty.

She said, 'What was the free kick for?'

'A foul,' he said.

She felt the impact of the stone on the bones of his small foot beneath the imitation leather of his shoe. The stone skidded between the two saplings. Pablo turned, spread his hands.

'Well played,' she said, and wanted to weep.

That night he burrowed deep in the straw of their mattress.

'Your bed tomorrow,' she said.

No reply from the spiky mattress where the mouse had once nested.

'It happens to everyone, parting.'

No reply.

'I must do whatever mama would have wanted.'

'She didn't have to leave us.'

'She couldn't stay with us: they would have killed her.'

'Like they killed papa?'

'Yes,' Rosana said. 'Like they killed papa.'

'Why us?'

'Why us what?'

'It wasn't like this with other children.'

'It's different for everyone,' Rosana said. She stretched out one hand and touched Pablo's back. 'We'll be together again. But first I have to go to Madrid and prepare things for us. Madrid is where we belong,' she said.

She stared out of the window into the sky where an autumn moon hung high and bright in the sky. Pablo moved on the mattress. They had burrowed into sleep many times together, taking their hunger with them.

'I wish I didn't have to go,' she said.

'Liar.'

'But I have to.'

'Then take me with you.'

'You know I can't.'

'Don't want to.'

'You know that isn't true.'

He was quiet. She heard the patter of rodent feet on the roof, the distant barking of a dog. It seemed to her that the moonlight had its own sound too, a soft and lingering chime. How could you paint moonlight? Downstairs someone snored. Kiko's widow or Diego in his cell. According to the priest there were many men such as Diego hiding from retribution.

She listened for Pablo's breathing. Nothing. It was an old trick of his to hold his breath so that she feared for him. But it always worked.

'Pablo, are you all right?' Could he have suffocated? 'I know you're pretending,' she said.

She held her breath and listened. Nothing. She reached out her arms. Turned him. And when he began to breathe again held him.

In the morning she dressed quietly. Washed in ice-cold water and slid tortoiseshell combs into her fine black hair. Then she reached under the bed for the old suitcase tied with rope she had packed the previous evening. Pablo lay quietly, hair dishevelled, truculence dissipated in sleep; he looked vulnerable and innocent. She bent and kissed him on the forehead. He didn't stir.

When she reached the door she turned. His eyes were open and he was looking at her, lips pressed so tightly that they looked bloodless, but they trembled just the same. Then she was gone, leaving behind part of her life.

The priest – who was driving to Ciudad Real to pick up a soldier wounded while fighting with the Blue Division in Russia – was a grey and comfortable man who smelled of soap and sanctity. As the car bounced along the dirt road he questioned her about her visit to Madrid. She told him that she was staying with her uncle, Antonio, and that she would be back in three weeks, but the lies sounded so loud in the small white car that she diverted the conversation and was surprised at her resourcefulness.

'Why should our soldiers fight in Russia?' she asked the priest.

'To help the Germans conquer the Communists.'

'The Germans are Fascists?'

'That's right, my child.'

'The Fascists killed my father.'

'It was a terrible thing, the war,' he said. He was a kind man but his beliefs had become confused and he prayed alone. 'Take my advice, don't dwell upon it. And don't talk about it . . .'

'Why should we fight other people's wars? Wasn't three years fighting our own war enough?'

'We have a debt to the Germans. They helped us win the war.'

'*Us*, father?'

'Spain,' the priest said. 'Is your uncle meeting you in Madrid?'

'My mother fought with Russians.'

'Your mother is a good woman,' the priest said. He smoothed his soutane over his thighs.

'Everyone in Spain is hungry,' Rosana said. 'Shouldn't the soldiers be helping to provide food instead of fighting for the Germans?'

'Fewer mouths to feed. There are 18,000 of them.'

A bird of prey swooped from the cold sky and rose gripping a small, struggling animal in its talons. In the fields beneath a range of rounded hills men and women worked with forlorn rhythms.

'Why is it, father,' Rosana asked, 'that whatever happens, ordinary people always suffer?'

The priest sighed. 'I shouldn't like to be interrogated by you, Rosana Gomez.'

'Why, father?'

'We are all in transit, my child.'

'But the journey is better for some than others.'

'Indeed it is. But worldly goods are not important.'

Rosana gazed at the stooping figures in the fields. Would

they sacrifice worldly goods? Food, for instance? Blankets, fuel for their stoves, for the winter which was already biting?

The soldier was waiting outside the station. He wore a khaki uniform, blue shirt protruding from the neck, and a red beret; a rolled blanket was slung round his shoulder; aluminium plates and ammunition pouches were attached to his leather belt. One arm was in a blood-stained sling. The priest pointed to a badge above a tunic pocket. 'The Sacred Heart of Jesus,' the priest said. He was, according to the priest, a sapper in the 2nd Battalion of the 269th Regiment. He had been wounded during the siege of Leningrad, where 3 million starving Russians had capriciously declined to surrender.

The soldier's hair was cropped, brutalizing his thin face, but his mouth was sensitive. A girl's mouth, she thought. His hand shook as he took a yellow cigarette from his mouth; he inhaled deeply, coughing smoke.

The priest took them to the station restaurant to wait for Rosana's train. The station was bleak, like the town. They drank coffee reputed to be made from acorns picked from prickly oak.

'So,' the priest asked, grimacing as he tasted the coffee, 'what's it like to be back on Spanish soil?'

'The same as when I left it,' the soldier said. He lit another cigarette and stared at the track gleaming in the midday sun.

'But good to be back?' the priest said hopefully.

'Perhaps.' The soldier shrugged. Flies settled on the blood on his sling.

Rosana said shyly, 'What was Russia like?'

'Cold,' the soldier said.

'Just cold?'

'And dark. It was always night,' he said. 'From two in the afternoon until ten in the morning it was night.'

The priest said, 'Will the Communists be beaten?'

'You mean the Russians?'

The priest spread his hands.

'Don't you read the papers?'

'The papers, alas, are not always accurate. I read that the Germans had lost the Battle of Stalingrad. A strategic withdrawal . . .' He smiled to show that even a priest can appreciate such interpretations; his hands came slowly together in supplication.

The soldier said, 'The Russians, sorry, Communists, are winning the war.' The flies moved busily on his sling but he made no move to remove them. 'And that means that the Americans and the British and their empire will win the war. The Generalisimo will have to change allies.'

'Not change,' said the priest, looking nervously around him. 'Franco has been very clever managing to remain neutral. After all, he could have let the Germans march through Spain to Gibraltar.'

The soldier lit another cigarette, sucked smoke into his lungs.

'Let me get this straight,' he said in a raw voice. 'If Franco managed to stay neutral then I can't have been fighting for the Germans. It was all a mirage? Is that what you're saying?'

The priest opened the prayer of his hands a little and searched inside.

Rosana said to the soldier, 'But you *did* volunteer.'

He turned to her. 'How old are you?'

'Sixteen. Why?'

He looked at her in a male way, but not in the crude way the boys in the village did before averting their eyes and punching each other on the shoulder.

'You sound very wise for sixteen. Have you grown up too quickly too?'

She became aware of her breasts beneath her blue frock. She drew the old black coat across her.

The priest said: 'You will meet Rosana often when she comes back to the village.'

'And when will that be?' The soldier's brown eyes searched her face. Don't lie to me, they said.

The priest, thank God, answered for her. 'In a few weeks. We shall miss her. She helps in the church.'

'It seems to me,' the soldier said, 'that the Church needs all the help it can get now. I was with some Spanish soldiers on the banks of the Oshora. They were singing a hymn when they were crushed by a T-34. God moves in mysterious ways, eh, father?'

'Jesus died for us,' the priest said closing his hands once more.

'I remember you telling us kids that life was a journey.'
'Indeed it is. Rosana and I were just talking about that.'
'To heaven?'
'To heaven, my son.'
'I think you're right, father.'
The priest smiled hesitantly. 'I'm glad you believe that.'
'It can't be to hell.'
'Why's that, my son?'
'Because I've just been there,' the soldier said.

Madrid assaulted her. Its pace and its indifference; its wide boulevards and baronial mansions; its inexorable buses, ancient cabs and trucks delivering cans of milk; its street vendors offering black market cigarettes and its pedlars selling fountain pens made in Barcelona.

She walked to the centre of the city and paused in front of the Prado to get her bearings. According to her mother on one of her visits, long after Kiko had been denounced and taken away, the street where Antonio and Martine lived was north of the Prado, in the Salamanca district, where the wealthy resided. Rosana was no longer intimidated by schoolmasters or doctors or priests, but she wasn't sure how she would react to the rich because she had never met any.

She counted her money, saved from what she had earned from the priest. Thirty-two pesetas 50 centimos. She walked along the wide *paseos* that divide the city, turning right along Goya. The house certainly intimidated her. Tall and thin, one of a terrace, but as elegant as an old lady with a lorgnette. The railings guarding it from the pavement were speared with gold and there were balconies on two levels; the brass knocker defied anyone to leave a fingerprint on it.

A maid wearing a black dress and white cap answered the door. Could this really be the home of Antonio, her mother's brother? Yes, said the maid, Señora Ruiz was at home but not Señor Ruiz; he was travelling abroad. Abroad! For a moment Rosana wanted to flee; instead she pushed past the maid into the hall where miniature rainbows, reflected from a chandelier, danced on the walls.

'Who shall I say is calling?'

'Her niece,' Rosana said.

She placed the shabby suitcase beside the stairway, then took off her moulting black coat and placed it over it. She smoothed the blue dress where the soldier's eyes had pried and looked at herself in a mirror where the rainbows moved tremulously like butterflies in the autumn. Her hair had escaped from the combs and her face, so grave always, was smudged; her thick brown stockings were twisted, sensible shoes scuffed. She looked as though she had escaped from an orphanage through a hedge.

'My dear, what a surprise.'

Rosana turned. She scarcely recognized Martine. Some people grew younger as they grew older; Kiko, for instance. Not Martine. She had retired prematurely into middle-age. Chic enough in an autumn-coloured costume with wide shoulders, but remote.

Rosana felt that she should curtsey but Martine cupped her face in her hands and planted feathery kisses on her cheeks. 'How you've grown,' she said. 'But not too old for tea and cakes?'

She led the way up the staircase into a living-room where no one, surely, had ever laughed. Museum furniture stood to attention on spindly legs; shafts of fading sunlight made avenues of refined dust.

'Not there,' said Martine, as Rosana went to sit on a chair with bandy legs. 'What would Antonio say if he came back and found that broken?' She patted the lime-green sofa. 'Here, sit beside me and let's have a look at you,' not bothering to look. 'So, how's your mother?'

'We don't see much of her,' Rosana said.

'I'm not surprised. But when things have settled down . . .' Martine vaguely waved a hand heavy with gold.

'It will be a long time,' Rosana said.

'Yes, I suppose so. But your mother was, well, a little foolhardy.'

'She fought for what she believed to be right.'

'I'm sure she did . . . Ah, here we are,' as the maid wheeled in a trolley bearing a silver tea-pot, sugar and milk and lemon and a plate of cakes. Such cakes, honey, marzipan, crystallized cherries, oranges boiled in syrup . . .

'Milk?'

Rosana, who had never drunk tea, said milk would be fine. And sugar. Just one spoonful.

'Help yourself to cakes.'

Rosana took a sponge with a cherry on top of it like a nipple. Her mouth ached with saliva; her stomach whined. Martine was already eating, popping pastry between cupid lips, licking the crumbs off her fingers with her tongue.

'So what brings you to Madrid?' she asked, nibbling a chocolate Swiss roll.

'You didn't get my letter?'

Martine paused in between bites. 'Letter? What letter?'

'I wrote asking if I could stay with you for a while.'

Martine sipped lemon tea from a fragile cup decorated with cornflowers and yellow roses. 'Are you sure you posted it?'

'I'm sure,' Rosana answered. 'Three weeks ago. When I didn't get any reply . . . Well, I didn't think it mattered anyway. You know, this big house . . .'

'Not so big. Not when Antonio's here. Not when Isabel's in residence.' She glanced at her wrist-watch. 'She'll be home from school soon. What a lovely surprise for her.'

'Will it be all right if I stay?' Rosana asked. The cake was dry in her mouth.

'Of course it will. Family is family. That's what Antonio always says and I agree with him.'

The saliva flowed again. Rosana sipped some tea. It tasted insipid compared with coffee even when it was made from acorns. 'I'm very grateful,' she said.

The doorbell rang and they heard the maid open it. Footsteps pattered up the stairs.

'Isabel,' her mother said, 'I want you to meet Rosana, your cousin.'

They kissed warily.

'You're Aunt Ana's daughter?'

'Your Uncle Jesús was my father,' Rosana said, not answering directly because Isabel's tone would have made a confession of it.

Isabel turned to her mother. 'But you said –'

'It doesn't matter what I said.'

'– that Ana –'

'I said it doesn't matter.'

At the age of 8 or thereabouts Isabel, with her dark, discerning eyes and unquenchable belief in her wisdom, did not seem lovable. Rosana hoped that her first impression was flawed.

'I believe you live in the country,' Isabel said – anywhere outside Madrid was a wasteland.

'Near Ciudad Real.'

'The Royal City? Is there anything royal about it?'

'The people,' Rosana said.

'Oh, the people.' Isabel lost interest in Ciudad Real. 'Do you have a tutor as well as going to school?'

'Tutors aren't necessary: the schools are very good in the country.'

Steady, Rosana warned herself.

'Do they teach pig-farming?'

'Now,' Martine said, smiling at Rosana, 'that will be enough. I want you two to become friends. Rosana is staying here,' she told Isabel.

'For how long?'

'A couple of days,' Martine said. 'Maybe three if she hasn't found anywhere to stay by then.'

The cake was sawdust in Rosana's mouth. 'But I thought –'

'But I expect you'll find somewhere tomorrow,' Martine said. 'Where you used to live, perhaps.'

'My mother says they've pulled it down.'

'Where is your mother?'

'I don't know,' Rosana said.

'Why don't you know?' Isabel asked.

'Don't ask so many questions,' Martine admonished her. 'I'm sure Rosana has a good reason for not knowing.'

Rosana took an orange boiled in syrup. Juice spurted in her mouth. Her taste-buds prickled with it.

'Do you want to play with my dolls?' Isabel asked Rosana.

'She's got some beautiful toys,' Martine said. 'Her father brings them from Switzerland. Soldiers that beat their drums and dogs that walk along and wag their tails.'

Rosana selected a chocolate éclair, bit into it squeezing out tongues of cream and said: 'Any pigs?'

'Pigs? Why should there be pigs?'

'To keep her company at school.'

Holding the éclair in one hand, Rosana crossed a shaft of sunlight and walked regally down the stairs. At the bottom she put on her black coat and picked up her suitcase, wishing she had never hidden it.

'Goodbye, Aunt Martine,' she called up the stairs. 'Don't bother to ring for the maid.' She opened the door and marched into the cruel evening.

She paused when she reached Goya. Homeward crowds swept past her. Lights shone cosily from apartment windows. Everyone had somewhere to go. Except me.

Don't feel sorry for yourself. Don't ever do that.

She walked towards the central boulevard. The air smelled of winter and loneliness. She sat on a bench. It had seemed more friendly, this city, when bombers were flying overhead and shells were picking out homes from terraces of houses.

What was Pablo doing now? Stupid. Kicking a football in the patio. What else? She brushed her cheek with her fingertips and found to her surprise that it was wet. She located a morsel of cake in her mouth. Éclair, she fancied. When had she last tasted pastries like that? Never, stupid. In fact the only really good food she had tasted recently had been brought to the village by the Englishman.

The Englishman!

She picked up her suitcase, found a policeman and asked him the way to the British Embassy.

That evening Adam Fleming sat alone in the small apartment he had rented close to the Plaza de España, drinking whisky and commiserating with himself about the remote and furtive war he waged in Madrid. Not that it had been unsuccessful. Through Moser's successor, a chubby homosexual in the Ernst Röhm mould, presumably the 'friend' who had betrayed Moser, he had been able to keep Atherton informed about Hitler's designs on Spain. Operation Ilona for instance. Its aim was the occupation of Spain to pre-empt any similar notions by the Allies and to establish the Wehrmacht on Gibraltar's doorstep. To implement Ilona, Hitler dispatched troops to Bordeaux and aircraft to Bayonne. But instead of a friendly paw stretched across the Pyrenees he discovered new Spanish fortifications.

'I wonder who tipped him off,' Atherton had said, smiling a feline smile when he heard that Franco had created five military regions in the Pyrenees to repel any attack.

But Ilona hadn't been abandoned, although, because of a security leak – Moser's successor must have sweated on that one – it had been renamed Gisela. Gisela's commander was a general with a daunting name, Freiherr Leo von Geyr von Schweppenburg, and its objective was the occupation of the whole Iberian peninsula.

'You see,' Moser's successor had said, 'if the Allies invaded we would lose all that iron ore and wolfram and we would be finished. Kaput!' He slipped the 5,000 pesetas Adam had given him into a pocket in his bulging waistcoat – bribery reversed these days – and went away to look for penniless young men.

According to Adam's latest information Gisela, née Ilona, had now been abandoned.

He picked up an old British newspaper. A headline above advertisements for Lux and Sunlight soaps announced the recapture of Kiev by the Russians.

Clearly the enemy – I fought *against* the Russians, Adam remembered – was on the run. An inexorable process that had begun in December 1941 when the United States had entered the war.

'Not before time,' he had said to Irene. 'Did you have to wait until the Japanese bombed Pearl Harbor?'

'Timing is everything,' she had said. 'That's how we won the First World War for you.'

He turned the page of the thin newspaper. British patrols in Italy had reached the Sangro River. Well, they wouldn't be in Italy if the Allies hadn't been able to land in Algeria and Morocco and they wouldn't have been able to do that if the Germans had reached the gateway to the Mediterranean, Gibraltar.

So, Moser, you and I made our contribution. Adam poured himself another whisky. He didn't particularly want it but what was the difference between three and four drinks? You should be proud of yourself, he lectured himself, sitting in cafés and bars and squares dictating the course of a corner of the war.

But that wasn't why I came to Spain.

He drank some more whisky. He wished Irene, who had gone with Eve to a concert to raise funds for the Red Cross, would drop by. Or Tom Canfield. But Tom moved mysteriously these days.

Adam paced the small room adorned with memories of Cambridge, thin, war-starved novels and paintings including an original Norman Rockwell that Irene had given him. The walls squeezed him. What would he do when the war was over? For the end was surely in sight – the US 2nd Division Marines had landed on the Solomon Islands, a stepping stone to Japan, and it was only a matter of time before the Allies invaded mainland Europe. Could anything be more confusing than emerging from an era in which you had campaigned for *and* against the Fascists?

Perhaps he should stroll across the Plaza de España, where Cervantes and Don Quixote and Sancho Panza ruled, and visit a bar that stood like a solitary tooth in a side-street demolished six years ago by Fascist shells. The plaza in those days hadn't been far from the front line . . . The familiar spectres joined Adam in the cramped room.

The phone rang. The duty officer at the embassy. A girl to see him. Most persistent. A looker, too, if you disregarded the shabby and old-fashioned clothes, the duty officer drooled. Name: Rosana Gomez. 'Oh Jesus,' Adam said, causing the duty officer to ask rhetorically: 'Anything wrong, sir?' No, there was nothing wrong, Adam said. Not much!

'What shall I do, sir?'

'Is she . . . distressed?'

'On the contrary, sir, she seems very self-possessed.'

With a mother like Ana Gomez what did you expect?

'Tell her I'll meet her in half an hour.'

'Where, sir?'

'Outside the lottery office, *La Hermana de Doña Manolita*, in the Puerta del Sol,' Adam told him.

He wasn't quite as she remembered him; perhaps people never were. A little darker, more intent, almost theatrical with his black coat undone, collar raised. He bent – but only just, because he wasn't tall – and kissed her on both cheeks.

He smiled. 'Orphan Annie,' he said in English. His breath smelled of liquor. 'Shall we go and get something to eat?'

Eat what? Ice-cream and a fizzy drink? She was sixteen now. Aware of his masculinity even if he was old; twenty-five or so, a quarter of a century. He needed a shave, she noticed.

He took her arm.

'We're supposed to walk apart,' she said.

'Don't worry about the priests: they're all tucked up in their cassocks by now.'

His Spanish was perfect, too perfect. Perhaps when he relaxed – or when he hadn't had so much to drink – it would become more familiar.

He led her down a side-street to a smoky café where a young man with a hungry face was playing a guitar.

'What would you like?'

'Not an ice-cream.'

'I doubt if they serve them.'

How could she tell him that less than two hours ago she had devoured five cakes, one of them an orange boiled in syrup? How was that for sophistication! She said, 'Just a coffee, please.'

'So what brings you to Madrid?' he asked.

'It was time to come.'

'You're a Madrileña, of course. I had forgotten.'

'Don't you ever want to go back to London?'

'I'm a Spaniard,' he said. He poured brandy into his coffee. Odd how people who knew they had drunk too much – they must surely know – drank more.

'My mother says you fought in the war.'

'On the opposite side,' he said, staring into his coffee.

'That's all over now. There are no sides.'

'I wish that were so, Rosana.'

'I know there are many prisoners. I know people are still executed. But the ordinary people, they don't fight any more.

I don't think they ever will. Spain has had enough fighting,'
she said.

'You are very wise . . .'

'For my age?'

'I wasn't going to say that.'

The guitarist smiled at her but she looked away.

'A lot of people do.'

'That's very patronizing. I was very wise at –'

'Sixteen.'

'Wiser than I am now.' He drank his fortified coffee in one
swift gulp. 'Did your mother warn you against me?'

'She said I must never see you again. Because you fought
for the Fascists and they killed my father.'

'You don't agree with her?'

'I told you, all that is in the past. The war has been over more
than four years. I was a child then.' She studied his features for
any hint of amusement but the remark seemed to make him
sad. 'I know you fought for what you thought was right.'

He looked up from his empty cup. 'Do you, Rosana? Do
you really?'

'Why else would you have fought?'

'We all thought we were right,' he said. 'Some of us must
have been wrong.'

'No,' she said, 'you were all right. I know that sounds
stupid and I can't explain it but I know it's true. You all
believed in something and therefore you were right. Because
something didn't turn out as you hoped it would doesn't
mean you were wrong.'

'But I fought on the winning side.'

'The stronger side,' she said.

And the wrong side, she thought, but she didn't add this
because it was sufficient that he believed he had been right.
Her measured reasoning sometimes disconcerted her but she
proceeded with it just the same: it was a legacy of her childhood, an inheritance from her mother.

He beckoned the waiter and while he waited for yet
another brandy she said: 'The trouble was that we were
taught at school that war was glorious. Well, Spaniards know
differently now. Especially the young ones.'

He tossed the brandy down his throat.

'You didn't look as though you enjoyed it,' she said.

'I sense a lecture coming on. Why did you want to see me?'

'I haven't got anywhere to live. Although I could sleep in a bombed-out ruin with the other vagrants.'

'Where do you think I can put you up?'

'You must have a home.'

'Do you really think we could live in the same apartment in a city where couples aren't even permitted to walk arm in arm?'

'You could say I was your daughter.'

He sighed. 'Do I look that old?'

She considered him critically. In his present condition he could pass for 35. 'No,' she said charitably, 'you're too young. Uncle?'

'They'd love that at the embassy. Uncle Adam living with his niece.'

'I don't understand . . .'

The guitarist brushed past her, whispering in her ear.

'I'll find somewhere,' she said.

He said, 'Rosana, whatever happens in the future, never take me for a complete idiot. Come on, we'll make a phone call.' He paid the bill and they walked into the night.

Irene Hadfield said to Tom Canfield, 'That was Adam. He wants me to give some girl a bed for the night. Maybe more than one night . . .'

'Who's the girl?'

'Damned if I know. Her name's Rosana.'

'A little girl?'

'Sixteen,' Irene said, stepping into her skirt and buckling it at the waist.

'Some girls are pretty big at sixteen.'

'You would know, I guess.'

'Rosana what?'

'Gomez, I think he said. She's turned up in Madrid without a roof over her head.'

'And she went straight to Adam . . . I wonder why.'

'Anyway,' Irene said, buttoning a yellow blouse, 'you'll have to get out.'

'Maybe now's the time to tell Adam.'

'It's long past time. Why didn't you tell him before? After all, we met through him.'

'Guilt.'

'No need to be guilty. We weren't in love.'

'But you were lovers.'

'When the mood took us,' Irene said. 'Most of the time we fought.'

'There's fighting and fighting.'

'And loving and loving.' She stroked his face as he knotted his tie.

'I'm a coward. I guess. We're pretty close.'

'Don't worry. Adam will understand. I promise you. I know Adam in a different way to you.'

'Okay, I'll tell him,' Tom said, as she moved away from him and began to make up the bed in the spare room of the apartment.

'He'll understand,' she called out from the thin, lavender-washed room. 'There's just one thing . . . When you tell him, duck.'

Adam made the phone call to Irene from a small hotel near the Puerta del Sol. Her mother, Rosana remembered, had once worked in a hotel in this area. The same one? It reminded her of an old clock ticking away untouched by the time it recorded. A couple of palms grew dustily, footsteps on the marble floor lingered forlornly.

What would her mother have done if she had seen her waiting at the reception desk with the man she had banned from her life?

CHAPTER 14

The Arán valley is a green finger of Catalonia that tentatively probes France to the north of the Pyrenees and, like most of Spain, bears little resemblance to the country that strangers determinedly envisage. Even those who have learned to distinguish Catalan from Castilian will discover that yet another tongue, Aranais, is spoken.

In spring and summer the valley is embroidered with wild flowers – poppies and scabious and, on the flanks of the guardian mountains, gentians. In winter it is fleeced with snow. Dark woods of pine and beech grow in its folds; 36 villages of slate-roofed cottages kneel at the feet of Romanesque churches.

Until 1925, when a road of sorts was built, it was isolated in the silence of the mountains: even by the late summer of 1944 it had not seriously been violated by explorers. Church bells tolling their Sunday chimes in the lowlands were answered by cowbells in the highlands; donkeys laboured beside the scurrying waters of the River Garona; and men fished in lakes with tranquil blue and white reflections.

In short, it was the ideal terrain in which to mount an invasion of Spain. And when Ana Gomez realized why she had been dispatched to Arties, a village bisected by the Garona near the valley's diminutive capital, Viella, she at first agreed with all the arguments for such a campaign.

The Allies had captured Paris, the Russians had crossed the Danube into Romania . . . the war against the Fascists who had supported Franco was almost won. Wasn't it logical, therefore, to suppose that if the guerrillas – the Republicans, that is, in adjacent exile – invaded their own country the Allies would swarm to their aid to overthrow the Fascists in Spain? And wasn't the valley a mere 50 miles or so from Toulouse where the guerrillas who had fought for the French Resistance had established their headquarters?

It wasn't until Sabino joined her in the wooden house hanging perilously over the waters of the Garona that Ana began to doubt.

They were strolling through the village towards the somnolent church of Santa María, columns in the nave leaning outwards instead of inwards, and as they strolled they observed; for that was why Ana was here, to reconnoitre. A site for a machine-gun post on a moss-green hill overlooking the village? A sniper behind the blue shutters of Number 3 Placa Ortau?

Sabino, walking with his bow-legged, wrestler's gait, pointed to a legend daubed on a wall sprouting with mauve stonecrop. ARAN NON EI PAS CATAUNHA. She sighed. So even within Catalonia separatism flourished.

Who, she asked Sabino, were the leaders in Toulouse who had decided to mount the invasion at the end of September? When he answered evasively, 'A junta, you know that,' the doubts took root.

'Communists?'

'Republicans.'

They walked up a cobbled street, past a garden jungled with seeding onions and fading marguerites.

'There are Republicans and Republicans. Name a few.'

'I told you, the *Junta Suprema de Unión Nacional*.'

'Names, Sabino.'

'Andrés, of course.'

'By kind permission of the Kremlin.' She remembered the hungry face of the guerrilla leader. His eyes that glowed deep in their sockets with a fanatical light, the beam of which swept the world in search of inequality. But it was only Spain that interested Ana – even the victories and defeats of the world war reached her from a distance as though she were learning them from history books.

Sabino pointed at the comfortable church standing on

high ground behind a tower of the Knights Templar and a cluster of lime trees in which late summer bees still worried the dead blossom. 'We could put a machine-gun there.'

'Names?'

'My God, you're a relentless woman.'

'I have to be.' *If I am to find the man who shot Jesús, whom I dispatched to his death.*

A cool breeze found its way through the mountains and lingered in Arties. Sticky leaves fell from the lime trees, dust swirled restlessly. Sabino gave Ana a couple more names.

'Both Communists,' she said.

'*Mierda*, woman, what's so wrong with Communism? The Russians fought a revolution just like us. The only difference is that they won. Let them show us how they did it.'

'They don't care about Spain in Toulouse,' she said.

'How can you say that?'

'They're all Communists, aren't they? In the pay of Moscow?'

'Not all. I'm not a Communist.'

'You're a Basque. You have your own reason for carrying on the fight.'

'Let's win it first, then look for directions.'

But the doubts flourished. How did these Communists who had divided the Cause during the Civil War know the Allies would come to their aid? Why should they? The Americans and the British were surely as sick of war as most Spaniards. And those Spaniards who were truly sickened by conflict could betray the insurgents. It wouldn't be the first time they had reported the guerrillas to the *guardia*.

Do we have sufficient weapons? Is the end of the world war really so close?

The breeze rounded a corner of the church and chilled her. She became aware that she was observed. Children hid; dogs pressed themselves close to the ground. The Black Widow is among us . . . Send word to the *guardia*.

Sabino took her arm. 'You wouldn't be strong if you didn't doubt. Only fools are born without questions in their brains.'

He led her back to the wooden house drooping over the river and after they had made love she shed some of the doubts. When she emerged on the balcony the breeze had returned to the mountains and the river was scurrying exuberantly along the bed of the chosen battlefield.

She went to Toulouse because Sabino persuaded her to and because she knew that he was proud of her, that he wanted to display her, he who was the lover of the Black Widow. The visit was probably a mistake, but at least it armed her with vision.

They booked into a small hotel on the fringe of the pink-brick city. Ana looked around for Germans but they had been summoned to reinforce their beleaguered armies in the north and that was another good reason, the Communists argued, to attack Spain from this area. But Ana didn't like the way some of them discussed Spain as though it were a foreign land. Another kingdom to be nailed, like a red pennant, to the revised Soviet map of Europe.

At the councils of war held in a nearby hall she kept her views to herself for the sake of Sabino, *El Sentido*, and from one end of the long table spread with thick pads of paper and flasks of water he smiled his gratitude, massaging his bald scalp with one hairy paw.

In the dining-room she allowed her disquiet to cut loose. Andrés listened, drinking red wine copiously as though it were beer; the wine floated red blotches on his cheekbones but didn't affect his speech or, it seemed, his reasoning. Beside him a barrel-chested Russian in black trousers and white shirt, who looked naked without a uniform, chain-smoked, nodding as he made notes inside his skull.

Ana's sentiments were much the same as those she had delivered in the roofless church in Madrid. Spiked now with pertinent comments about the imminent invasion. 'How can you hope to co-ordinate guerrilla groups in the Asturias, Galicia, Andalucia?' or 'Spain is a big country, you know,' as though Russia were not.

When she had finished the Russian said, 'I take it you know that a provisional Republican government with Juan Negrin as president is to be set up in the occupied territory?'

'I hadn't heard,' Ana said. She suspected that the Russian

was unused to opposition from a woman; few men who hadn't fought in the Civil War were.

Andrés said: 'You make it sound as though we are not organized. In fact we've created the 204 Guerrilla Division and 5,000 troops are standing by.'

'No,' Ana said, 'I do think you're organized. Too organized. From a long way off. But I don't think you realize how organized the Fascists are in Spain.'

'I should,' Andrés said. 'I fought against them.'

'They haven't changed overnight.'

The red patches on Andrés's cheeks glowed like birthmarks. 'Do I take it you don't want to fight?'

Ana studied her fingertips. Blunt-nailed. Unfeminine. She felt Sabino looking at her intently. He had told her that morning that she was a handsome woman. Handsome? Well that was something.

'Well?'

'Of course I want to fight.'

'Even though it's a foolhardy venture?' the Russian asked.

She gave an eloquent Spanish shrug.

Andrés said, 'If it hadn't been for the Communists we would have lost the war within the first six months.'

'But we paid for their help. In gold,' Ana said, repeating a rumour she had heard. She caught a glance between Andrés and Sabino. 'How was that gold spent? On world Communism?'

'What gold?' The Russian stuck his thumbs in the waistband of his black, waiter's trousers.

'You *gave* us all those tanks and guns?'

'History will tell,' the Russian said.

'One more thing.' Andrés rubbed the red patches on his cheeks. 'Can you tell me,' to Ana, 'just what the hell you're doing here anyway? You're supposed to be in the Valle de Arán.'

'I wanted her here,' Sabino said.

The beads of the chandelier tinkled in the silence.

'And why was that, comrade?'

'Because we go together.'

The silence settled – it was not advisable to argue with *El Sentido* even if you outranked him.

'You will be returning soon?' The Russian looked first at

Ana, then at Sabino. 'We need as much intelligence as we can get.'

'Tomorrow,' Sabino said.

'And you will stay there? We need your help in the mountain passes. We need your help to kill Fascists guarding the frontier. I'm told you're good at that.'

Sabino said abruptly, 'Why aren't you fighting Germans? You've lost millions of men. Aren't you needed on the eastern front?'

'The fight goes on everywhere,' the Russian said.

'But this fight,' Ana said, 'is for Spain.'

'The long-term fight is against Fascism.'

'What will happen,' Ana asked, 'when you've beaten the Germans? Will you make pacts with America and Britain?'

'Bourgeois countries,' Sabino said.

Sometimes she loved this bald, bow-legged fighter and she thought how different life might have been if she hadn't met Jesús first. But life was booby-trapped with ifs.

'First we have to beat the Germans,' the Russian said.

'Nothing can stop you now.'

'Then we will share the spoils of war.'

'So you'll give the Allies some of that gold?' Sabino asked, and when the Russian said, 'That was a different war,' the flesh on his forehead rose pushing a smile across the bald expanse of his scalp.

The Russian, realizing he had been trapped, snapped, 'Piss on the gold. What we're talking about is a grand design.'

'Piss on your grand design,' Sabino said. 'All we are concerned with is Spain.' *You with Euskadi*, Ana thought.

Smiling at him she said, 'I'll be waiting for you in the Valle de Arán.'

In the room upstairs fitted with a peach-tinted mirror on the ceiling, Sabino said, 'Why did you do it?' He tore off his clothes and dropped them on the carpet.

'Do what?'

'Antagonize them.'

'You didn't do such a bad job yourself.'

'In a support role.' He threw himself on the bed, naked and hirsute. 'You realize they will want to kill you now?'

'Fascists *and* Communists. I must be a very dangerous woman.'

She took off her clothes and, lying beside him, gazed at herself on the ceiling.

Ana returned to the Valle de Arán from France at night through a gorge near the border post at Pont de Roi. She wore a russet dress and a brown shawl over her hair and carried papers identifying her as Angela Boya from Viella.

For a week she toured the valley, starting with the hamlet of Pontaut, then following the road and river through the small towns of Lés and Viella, culminating at Puerta de la Bonaigua, 6,900 feet high. Whenever a track branched into the mountains she explored it, choosing vantage points for guns seized from the Germans in France, meeting Republican sympathizers.

The *guardia* and border police, fearing trouble as Fascism faced defeat elsewhere in Europe, were vigilant and trigger-happy; but she was co-operative and after they had scrutinized her papers they bowed stiffly and saluted. It wasn't until she reached the hillside village of Vilac where, in the church tower, there was a perfect platform for a heavy machine-gun to cut up anything that moved in the valley, that she first sensed danger.

Nothing that she could identify but she had been in the mountains for five years and she anticipated danger as other people anticipate rain. Curtains ruffling as she approached, footsteps slithering down cobblestone alleys, a breathing silence in the church . . .

Her contact in Vilac, where the wooden houses were steaming in the sun after a shower, was a carpenter, a monkish man with sawdust in his fringe of hair, who smelled of resin and glue. His eyes were as bright and true as his tools and yet the angles of his face as they walked in the dripping woods were out of line with them.

'How many will fight with us in Vilac?' Ana asked him. There were wild boar and wolves in the woods and he carried a shotgun with him.

'A few.' He seemed more vague than she remembered him

on her previous visit, this dusty warrior who had fought with the 46th Division in the Battle of the Ebro.

'It's your village; you must know how many.'

'Maybe six.'

'No more?'

'People are sick of war.'

'They prefer servitude?' she asked, although she knew what he said was true. Had he tipped off the *guardia*? Others had before him.

'They prefer peace. They are trying to mend their families.'

'You don't believe in the invasion?'

'Do you?'

'I believe in the Cause,' Ana said.

'What sort of answer is that?'

She glanced at him but he was staring at the ground, kicking beech leaves, and she decided that she was being offered a last chance of redemption.

They turned and began to walk back to the village. Through the trees she could see the valley. She imagined guerrillas in corduroy trousers and bandoliers marching beside the banks of the small, galloping river.

She said, 'I know what you mean. This shouldn't be political.'

'All wars are political. We die for politicians, you and I.'

'What are your politics?'

'My own business.'

'Communist?'

'They gave us guns; without them we would have been nothing.'

'But you don't want to fight any more, do you?'

'Don't put words in my mouth.'

'I don't blame you.'

'I have a wife and three children. If you don't have family you don't understand these things.'

'Widows have children.'

'Why don't you drop this Communist thing? Communists, Anarchists, Separatists . . . What does it matter?'

And then she understood and the smell of danger was as sharp as frost.

The carpenter dawdled behind her. A wood-pigeon took

off from the treetops, wings rippling the silence. Ahead Ana could make out the bell-tower of the church through the trees. The church was built on a broad terrace and at its haunches sat a small and wasted garden like a graveyard of children. The carpenter fired the shot when they were about 100 metres from it. It echoed in the valley as pellets dropped among the trees; they reminded Ana of the first raindrops of a summer storm.

'Missed,' the carpenter said. He lowered his shotgun.

'Missed what?'

'A hare.'

'In the forest?'

She walked more quickly, veering to one side. The shot had been a signal. To whom? *Guardia*? Border police? If she could reach the sanctuary of the church . . .

'Hey,' the carpenter called, 'not so fast.'

She increased her stride. Ahead lay the terrace on which the church stood and the faded garden. She heard an aircraft strumming the skies, heard the beat of her heart. She saw the faces of her children among the trees and she saw Jesús going to war.

Another shot. Farther away this time. An instant echo. Except, of course, that it wasn't an echo at all, it was another shot, the two of them almost synchronized.

She tripped and fell, cheek against a cushion of moss. From that position of inelegant comfort she watched the body fall from the balcony of the bell-tower. Watched Sabino standing on the terrace lower the rifle from his shoulder. Heard the body, after it had half-turned in mid-air, thump into the garden.

Sabino led her away from the village, down the hill to the bank of the river. There he laid down his gun, spread his jacket and from his rucksack produced grainy bread and goat's cheese and a bottle of pacheran, the red Basque fire-water made from berries.

He said: 'I warned you, they wanted to kill you.'

'Past tense?'

'They still do, but I have spoken to Toulouse. I have influence . . . They want us Basques to fight with them. But you must stop this anti-Communist talk. They see you as a threat. And that is what you are, a threat to unity.'

'Unity! The unity they want in the Kremlin?'

'The unity we want,' he said.

'The Basques?'

'Everyone who is against the Fascists.'

She tore some bread from the loaf, wrapped it round a piece of cheese, chewed it and washed it down with the sweet, strong liquor of *Euskadi*.

She said, 'What happened? How did you find me?' and he told her, 'It wasn't difficult: I knew they wanted you dead so I followed you to the valley. I have never been far away,' he said, tilting the bottle into the back of his mouth. 'But I needed to know whether they were serious. I know the people of Vilac,' he said. 'I have been here before you.'

'How did you know he wouldn't shoot me in the forest?'

'He isn't the killing sort. He was told to take you into the woods. To fire a signal so that the marksman in the bell-tower could pick you off.'

'And the marksman's dead?'

Sabino nodded. 'But the people of Vilac are very close, they won't talk. No one is dead, the marksman is hunting in the mountains . . .'

'And the invasion . . . Will it succeed?'

'If we believe,' he said. 'All of us.'

In what? she asked herself.

The capture of the valley wasn't a glorious military feat because there were 5,000 guerrillas and relatively few *guardia* and police. But the *guardia* – whose bravery had never been doubted, even though, silhouetted in their capes and tricorns, they had become symbols of repression – fought stubbornly, and for a day gunfire put the church bells and cow bells to flight.

Sabino and Ana led an attack on a hillside gunpost dominating the main road near Arties. Her group, co-ordinating with the 204th division which had taken Viella, comprised guerrillas who were more patriotic than political and, as they made their way through a copse of skinny pines, she thought, 'Those Communists in Toulouse aren't so stupid.'

From the fringe of the pines she looked down at the *guardia*, who had a heavy machine-gun trained on the village and the road. I don't want to kill those men, she thought, take them from their wives and families; then she remembered the children who had died as bombs were dropped at random on Madrid and her finger crept to the trigger of her rifle.

Sabino took grenades from the gunny bag hanging from his belt and handed them to the other two guerrillas. 'Give me one of those,' Ana said and when he asked if she had ever thrown one before she said no but you didn't have to be an Einstein to throw a grenade. He gave her one and showed her how to remove the pin. 'And lob it high so those sons of whores don't have time to throw it back.'

The grenades sailed through the air as innocently as toys but the *guardia* saw them coming and threw themselves to the ground. She heard three explosions but there had been four grenades. She heard cursing and screaming, then the fourth grenade came sailing back to them; it landed on a ledge just below and lay quietly there. Hers?

The machine-gun swivelled, its barrel pointing at the pines. It coughed. Bullets hit the thin trunks of the trees and the boulders spat splinters of stone. Ana, lying flat, smelled the dry scent of pine-needles, felt bullets wounding the earth. She inched forward towards the grenade. *A woman's throw.* That's what they would say, even if they didn't say it to her face. Her fingers crawled crab-like across the pine-needles.

'No!' Sabino reared up but, even as he shouted, her fingers had found the warm cubes of the grenade and she was throwing it, raising herself from the ground to do so, watching the black egg rise against the pale sky, watching it explode as harmlessly as a firework at a fiesta, hearing the cough of the machine-gun, feeling the bullet tear into her flesh.

A doctor came from Viella to the wooden house above the river and bathed the wound and, with a pair of forceps, removed the bullet from the abdomen just below the ribs.

'It must have been the uphill climb,' he said. He was a stooping man who pretended to find humour in his work.

'What uphill climb?' Sabino asked.

'The bullet. Heavy machine-gun? It should have gone right through her and knocked down the man behind her.'

'That man is in my debt,' Ana said. The wound was hurting more now and she could feel the blood flowing where the bullet had been plugging the blood-vessels.

'You be quiet, señora,' the doctor said, working with swabs and probes. 'Why in God's name were you throwing grenades anyway?' He looked at Sabino for answers.

'You haven't tried arguing with her. Shouldn't she go to hospital?'

'It's not advisable.' The doctor lit a cigarette and went on working, pausing once to blow a flake of ash from the blood-stained sheet. 'When the government troops come any patients who fought with you will be taken prisoner.'

'And when will that be?'

The doctor shrugged. 'It is only a matter of time; you must know that.'

'We can hold out here,' Sabino said. 'Until the British and Americans come to our aid.'

'And the Russians,' Ana said.

'You be quiet,' the doctor said.

She heard their voices faintly, swimming on the tide of the river below.

A snip as the doctor cut away flesh.

'I listened to the BBC today,' the doctor said. 'A recording of Churchill addressing the House of Commons on 24 May this year.'

'So?'

'Churchill said that "internal political problems in Spain were a matter for the Spaniards."'

'He was telling the world the Allies won't come to our help?' asked Sabino.

Silence. Ana looked up. The doctor had spread wide his hands. 'Churchill is very pro-Franco. He believes he did Britain a great service by not letting Hitler march through Spain. By making the landings in North Africa possible. And now Franco has closed down the German consulate in Tangier and expelled all the German spies in Spain.'

Ana said, 'What about the Russians? Won't they help us?'

'All the way from Czechoslovakia? From Estonia?'

Gunfire chasing itself through the valley. The throb of an aircraft. The wound throbbing in time with its pulse.

The doctor, after a pause: 'That radio in Toulouse is making some broadcasts. Franco shipping arms to the Germans . . . rioting in Barcelona . . . fighting in Seville and Bilbao . . . Was that the sort of rubbish that made you invade?'

Silence except for the call of the river.

Ana: 'We'll go on fighting.'

'Well, I have to go now,' the doctor said. 'There are many others to treat . . . How we love death, we Spaniards. If you want to make money in Spain, become a pharmacist or a doctor or a mortician.'

'Or a priest,' Ana said.

'Now, now,' the doctor said.

That night as she lay above the river, imagining that its waters were cooling the burning wound, she heard heavy traffic on the road following the bed of the valley from Bonaigua. Sabino heard it, too.

He whispered in her ear, 'I think this is the end.'

'Fascists?'

'The doctor was right.'

'I think we were all right; I think we all knew.'

The noise of the river was loud in her ears.

There were said to be 45,000 troops. They entered the valley at the Bonaigua extremity and they went about their business with method and, when necessary, ferocity.

They took the villages one by one: Tredos, Salardú, Casarill, Betren . . . and they turned their big guns and heavy machine-guns and mortars on to the pockets of resistance and removed them. But it was the position the troops established on a hill above Viella that devastated the guerrillas: because the capital stands at the apex of the valley, they could turn their guns north or east.

More than 1,000 insurgents were taken prisoner; an uncounted number killed. And as the soldiers fanned out across the valley the guerrillas shrank back into the mountains, escaping north into France or south into Spain, some even reaching the Guadarrama mountains near Madrid.

Within a few days it was commonly agreed that the invasion, the last of an historical progression of incursions into Spain – the invaders could number themselves alongside the Vandals and the Visigoths, the Moors and the French – was an error of judgement and those who had claimed that the Allies would rally behind the insurgents deserved to be put up against the wall of Radio Toulouse and shot.

Meanwhile the house over the river in Arties was visited by two members of the punitive soldiery, one of them a sergeant. When Sabino heard them mounting the steps he laid a pillow on Ana's belly, pulled the bed-clothes up to her neck, scattered water on her face and told her to groan.

The sergeant, flat-faced and weary-eyed, regarded Ana gently, the way Spaniards do when they look upon the very young or the women who are about to give birth. He looks at me as if I were his own wife, Ana thought.

'When is it due?' the sergeant asked.

'Any time,' Sabino said.

'Shouldn't the doctor be here?'

'He's on his way.'

'Do you want any help?'

'We can manage,' Sabino said.

The sergeant bowed stiffly and self-consciously and saluted. When they had gone Ana remembered she had forgotten to groan.

Ten days later she left by night with Sabino. They travelled for three days and as they climbed towards the starved peaks of the Pyrenees the pain from the wound increased and it bled a little.

On the fourth day they arrived at the caves. My home, she thought bleakly. Before entering them she paused outside. Snow was falling and the high crags were coated majestically with it. She turned and faced Spain and, as the snow made a white shawl on her shoulders, as the wind played distant music in the heights, she felt her exile strongly. 'One day I must return,' she said, her words as silent as the snowflakes.

CHAPTER 15

One day, Tom Canfield decided, he would be a man of property. His mansions would hug the shores of the Mediterranean and his estates would be planted with orange, grapefruit and lemon. He could smell the twilight scent of the blossom and see the fruit hanging heavily on the branches.

But he couldn't do that without first making his contribution to the war effort because if he didn't the dead of Guam and Wake Island would always be with him in his citrus groves. And as he was unfit to fight the only help he could give was financial; gold, that was, to outbid the Germans for Spain's wolfram. But to become a respectable financier – not a freebooter who had robbed Russia of its gold in transit from Spain – he had to have a wife and a family.

Before proposing marriage to Irene Hadfield, the ideal bride for a man of property, he mounted a last search for Josefina, whose husband, according to her mother, was now dead. Threw his net wider until it fell, empty, on the shores of the Mediterranean and the Atlantic and the borders with Portugal and France. He checked out the Balearic Islands, Majorca, Minorca and Ibiza, and the Canaries and the Spanish possessions in North Africa. But no one knew of her and in the small town in the province of Valencia where she had been born friends talked only of Madrid postmarks. Had Josefina, perhaps, confided in her mother? In the patio beneath the winter-bare fig tree she shook her head, a little vaguely, perhaps, but stubbornly too.

'But why doesn't she want to see me?' he asked.

'Who says she doesn't?'

'She loved me,' Tom said.

'But she married another.'

'And he's dead so she needs me.'

'She is content,' Josefina's mother said.

'How do you know?'

'I can feel it in her letters.'

'Have you told her I want to see her?'

'What I write in my letters is my business, Señor Canfield.'

'Does she ever mention me?'

'You must stop this, Señor Canfield.'

'There's something you're hiding from me, isn't there?'

She rose, turning her back on him. At the door leading from the patio into the whitewashed cottage she turned. 'Please don't come back, Señor Canfield,' she said and closed the door behind her.

Three months later he married Irene Hadfield, discovering to his relief that Adam Fleming did not object. What if he had? Tom wasn't sure: there was between them an understanding as strong as an oath, and he wondered whether such rapport was not more important than the conventions of marriage.

Why hadn't Adam been more antagonistic? He had, after all, been Irene's lover. 'I think,' Irene had said, 'that all the time he was with me he was searching for someone else. Maybe he's found her,' and Tom had thought, 'Lucky guy, because for each of us there's only one.' Irene wasn't that one, but their marriage would be warm and it would contain laughter.

They spent a brief honeymoon in Granada, wandering round the dreaming gardens of the Alhambra, then they returned to Madrid where the reflections of the world war shifted and shimmered conspiratorially. Their focus was now wolfram and Tom Canfield went after it as obsessively as an old-time gold prospector in the Klondyke.

Wolfram, he knew, was a metallic element found in wolframite and scheelite. In 1939, when it was used principally in the manufacture of filaments for light bulbs and radio valves, it sold for a song; by 1943 it was worth £7,500 a ton.

The reason for this was that it made ordinary steel diamond-hard and the warring nations of the world needed it for their new and sophisticated weapons.

The main sources were America, Australia, the Far East and the Iberian peninsula. With the Far East effectively blockaded by the Allies the Germans looked to Iberia for their supplies. As Spain was neutral it could sell to the most generous bidder and Madrid soon became the capital of speculation, manipulation, fraud and associated crimes, on a scale as ambitious as anything engendered by diamonds, guns or gold.

Tom made his first approach to a diplomat at the United States Embassy, where the astute Carlton Hayes presided. The diplomat, a cadaverous Bostonian named Hooper who was obviously working for American intelligence, listened with patience and a measure of distaste to Tom's proposition. Assets, gold in particular, seemed to offend him.

'I'm doing this for us for Christ's sake,' said Tom, subsiding angrily into an easy chair in the apartment he had bought in the centre of Madrid.

'Of course you are. But you won't lose out on our account?' Hooper poured beer frothing into his glass and stared into it disapprovingly.

'Look,' Tom said, reining his anger, 'what we're talking about is buying futures, right? Pre-empting the Germans. In 1941 the Allies didn't buy a dime of wolfram but the Germans bought 300 tons. Which was clever. Squirrel away wolfram while no one even realizes what's going on. In 1942, however, we buy 760 tons while Hitler purchases 900 tons. Still nice going for the Germans but we're beginning to get wise.'

'And now, Mr Canfield?' Hooper pinched the bridge of his thin nose.

'The price is going to rocket. There will be an auction between the Allies and the Germans and at the price per ton it's going to reach I wonder if we have sufficient peseta funds.'

'But you have gold?'

'Sure. And the Spaniards want gold.' After all it was theirs, he remembered.

'May I ask where you obtained this gold?'

'No,' Tom said, 'you may not.'

Hooper stared through the long windows. His fingers strayed to the fragile hollows at his temples. No one had told him that intelligence entailed mixing with bullion robbers. He sipped his beer, leaving froth on his mauve and puckered lips.

'How will you make your approach?' he asked, searching for the froth with the tip of his tongue. 'You, an entrepreneur, can hardly approach the Spanish Government directly. That's a matter for the embassy. And we can hardly offer gold . . .'

'The usual way,' Tom said. 'A middleman.'

'Any idea who?'

Tom, who had no idea, said, 'A Spaniard.'

'We wouldn't want to jeopardize relations between our two countries.'

'Jeopardize shit,' Tom said. 'What do you think diplomats do every day of the week? If it hadn't been for Chamberlain there wouldn't have been a second world war.'

'You fought for the Republicans, I believe.'

'You don't believe, you *know*.'

'And came back here on a false passport?'

'A long time ago,' Tom said. 'Now I'm Thomas Edward Canfield. With gold that glisters so brightly it dazzles immigration officials. But you know that too.'

Hooper squeezed his lips together, then gave two bird-like nods with his bony head. He advised Tom that nothing too adventurous should be contemplated. No apple-carts toppled, no cats among the pigeons. 'We mustn't forget oil,' he said.

'Oil?'

'Ah.' Hooper smiled enigmatically.

'So you want me to go ahead?'

'Don't worry if you make a little on the side.' Hooper said.

It was Adam who gave Tom his first lead.

They were standing in a small square the colour of old teeth during a fiesta in a *barrio* in Madrid, wincing as fireworks exploded in rips of machine-gun fire and booms of artillery. Smoke drifted through the mauve blossom of bougainvillaea, and the square with its impotent fountains smelled of gunpowder.

Tom's ears ached with the fusillades. He glanced sideways at Adam. His face was pale and he blinked rapidly as the fireworks exploded and Tom knew that he was at Jarama. Tom was worried by his appearance; it was as if a transient mood had settled upon him and failed to rise; his hair was dull, the skin at his cheekbones tight.

'Takes us back, huh?' Tom gave him a small punch, Spanish style, on the meat of his arm. They sat on a bench peeling with wings of green paint beside two ruminative old men in berets who didn't appear to hear the battle. How old they were Tom could not imagine: the war and the hungry years which still stretched into infinity had melded middle and old age. Plump children bounced and squealed in front of them: if locusts stripped the peninsula the children of Spain would still be fed. In his wheelchair *El Pistola* clapped his hands.

Tom suspected that Adam had brought him to this cordite-reeking place to confide. To seek advice, perhaps, although Tom knew that people didn't really want practical wisdom: confirmation of what they were hell-bent upon doing anyway was what they wanted.

It was probably connected with Rosana Gomez who was now living in a studio apartment and taking art lessons, both funded by Adam. Tom thought that Rosana was a schemer but perhaps none the worse for that because the war and its aftermath had bred resourcefulness. What he did not comprehend was Adam's feelings for the girl. He was what, 28? And she was 16, 17, a child. But when he was, say, 33, she would be 21, and then traditional wisdom would pronounce the age difference perfect. But what of the present?

Tom waited.

'In England,' Adam said, 'we let off fireworks on 5 November, Guy Fawkes' day.' The sulphurous memories led him to Cambridge in other seasons. 'They used to jump off Magdalene Bridge into the Cam shouting "Geronimo!" Are they as crazy as that at American universities?'

'I guess so,' admitted Tom.

The firework foreman, wizened and nimble, attended to

the long fuse from which the fireworks hung which had snapped, and Adam eased Rosana into the conversation. She looked older than her years, he asserted, and Tom had to agree, but thought 'Not by much, though.'

'Almost a woman.'

'They grow up quicker than English and American girls.'

'She has great talent. Have you seen her paintings?'

Tom had not, but considered the moment had arrived for plain speaking. 'What you're doing, is it wise?'

'Helping her?'

'Don't act dumb. You know what I mean. You're a foreigner, an old man, 28 if you're a day, and Rosana is a kid. This is Spain where chaperones are required, no holding hands in public, nothing outrageous like that, and her mother has forbidden you to see her daughter and she has relatives who would cut your balls off for less.'

An old Citroën, powered by burning almond shells, made a slow circuit of the plaza. Birds dispatched from trees by the explosions settled once more, chattering angrily.

'For looking after her?'

'Don't be naïve. She's an attractive kid' – not woman, deliberately – 'and you're a red-blooded Anglo-Saxon. Don't kid me, Adam Fleming, you've got the hots for her.' Thereby, he conceded later, effectively sabotaging any confidences that might have been coming his way.

'In any case,' said Adam, 'there's only one brother. Antonio. A wheeler-dealer. Making a fortune out of wolfram.'

The fireworks, fuse mended, zipped round the square until two fearsome rockets parted the clouds, concluding the display.

Tom strode through the swing doors of high finance with a zest that at first dismayed him. What had happened to the youth who had once fought police in Kempton, West Virginia, when they tried to arrest a pregnant woman for stealing a loaf of bread? Where was the young man who had fought for the oppressed in the Spanish skies?

It took a victory – outbidding the Germans for wolfram so comprehensively that by August 1943 they had stopped buying – to blunt his doubt. Was he not still fighting Fascism by drawing the teeth of the Nazi weaponry? Such was the headiness of his triumph that he began to understand public misconceptions about commerce: what the layman mistook for dishonesty was in fact business practice.

He was abetted in this conclusion by the discovery that politicians and diplomats involved in the wolfram war were more devious than any financier. They were also bunglers and much of Tom's time was taken up with repairing statesmanlike balls-ups.

His tutor in these matters was Antonio Ruiz, who had learned his profession in London and Zurich. Tom learned that a bribe was a misnomer for a judicious gift, that blackmail was the art of persuading the unworthy to change their stance. 'When will people begin to realize that it is the subject of the blackmail who is the criminal?' Antonio demanded in his accented English which, with its speed and manual accomplishments, seemed more fluent than the measured vowels of Oxford and Broadcasting House.

Antonio was outwardly flamboyant – greying hair tightly curled, suits made in Berne instead of London where austerity reigned – but contained in his shell was a deep and well-guarded reticence.

Two months after the wolfram coup he summoned Tom to his office in the Calle Alcalá. The coup he said, winding and unwinding one tight curl with his fingers, had not been a coup at all. The Germans had merely withdrawn from the market because they could not muster eight million pesetas in Spanish currency to pay the export tax on the wolfram. 'So?' Tom sipped his dark sweet coffee and stared through the steam at Antonio sitting on the other side of a desk as elaborately carved as an altar.

'They're back in business. They've billed the Spaniards for everything they gave them during the Civil War which means they're now in credit. *And* they've promised to give Spain guns and machinery and wheat, 20,000 tons of it. I calculate,' said Antonio, counting on his slender fingers, 'that the Germans are in credit to the tune of 400 million pesetas: that's a hell of a lot of wolfram.'

The news did not depress Tom, it inspired him. A rush of his father's blood in his veins. How to counter the Nazis' guile? But first he must find out what stratagems lay stored in the dark cellars of Antonio's mind.

Antonio stretched backwards, fingers touching the portrait on the wall of José Antonio Primo de Rivera, the Falange leader executed by the Republicans in Alicante in 1936. His remains had been ceremonially transferred in November 1939 to El Escorial outside Madrid, where nearby a vast monument to the dead in the war, the Valley of the Fallen, was being excavated inside a rocky hillside. Antonio breathed deeply as he touched the picture, as though finding reassurance for whatever he had done during the Civil War. Finally he said, 'Can you match any offer the Germans make?'

'Four hundred million?' Tom shook his head. 'How much wolfram can Spain produce in the next year?'

'About 4,000 tons.'

'What can you raise?'

'Me? I'm merely the middleman, the broker. I carry your offers to the vendor.'

'And the German offers?'

'Of course.' Antonio tipped forward again and began to toy with the bloodstone fob hanging from a gold chain on his waistcoat. 'What you need is a little diplomatic intervention.' Which was when Tom first became acquainted with diplomatic insensitivity.

The first overture was reasonable enough. It was made to the Spanish Foreign Minister, Count Gómez Jordana, by the American Ambassador, Carlton Hayes, and it suggested that Spain should reduce all its exports to Germany. After all, the Allies were winning the war and the Americans needed oil to finish the job so why should they continue giving it to Spain, if Spain continued to trade with the enemy? The Spaniards, it seemed to Tom, appreciated this argument.

Then someone in the Spanish Foreign Office committed the first blunder – they sent a cable to a man named José Laurel. Laurel had been made President of the Philippines by the Japanese who had captured the islands from the

Americans. And the cable congratulated him on his appointment!

The next blunders were the copyright of the US State Department. Incensed by the cable which was interpreted as a slight – in fact, Tom gathered, it had been a mistake and Franco didn't intend to recognize Laurel – America *demanded* a total embargo on exports of wolfram to Germany.

Tom sighed deeply within himself. You do not demand anything from a Spaniard: it is the surest way of ensuring that you do not receive what you seek. In particular you did not demand anything from Franco: Hitler had learned that.

By the end of the year the Americans were still demanding an embargo, Franco was still contemplating his pending tray and Germany was still buying wolfram.

In February 1944, Franco consented to cut deliveries of wolfram to Germany for that year to 720 tons; the American and British emissaries in Madrid thought this was a reasonable concession and so did Tom. Washington did not and when the total embargo was refused they stopped supplying Spain with oil.

Result: the petrol ration was cut in Spain, the Americans were vilified and Germany went on getting its wolfram.

'How,' Tom asked Irene over breakfast, 'can we be so stupid?'

'What are you going to do about it?' She dipped her spoon into a bowl of canned grapefruit segments; she looked very sexy in a pink silk robe.

'Go to war again, I guess.'

She looked up from her grapefruit. 'Don't be mysterious: you're not the type.'

'Know what I found out? Antonio has been smuggling wolfram to the Germans.'

'Figures: he's a Fascist.'

'Phoney lading bills. Trucking it across the French border at night, bribing border guards. Giving them judicious gifts . . .' He smiled secretly.

'And you're going to stop him?'

'Something like that.'

'For God's sake stop being inscrutable. You're a bold aviator not Fu Manchu.'

He walked round the table and undid the belt of her robe, smiling inscrutably.

Franco was often described as a typical Galician, a wary and canny native, that is, of that misty land in the north-west of Spain where they speak their own language in three dialects, play the bagpipes or *gaita*, a legacy from their Celtic forebears, breed troupes of poets and musicians, keep a weather eye open for werewolves and, spurred by poverty, travel so extensively that there are parts of South America where a Gallego, or Galician, is presumed to mean Spaniard.

Their guile was one of the reasons that Tom chose Galicia as his headquarters: he needed resourceful men and women as his mercenaries. There were two other reasons. Although Santiago de Compostela, the ancient capital of the region, is the shrine of Spain's patron saint, St James, the Galicians had only been deprived of home rule by the outbreak of the Civil War – and there were many rebellious spirits abroad in its green pastures.

The third reason was just as practical. Wolfram was mined in the north-west of Spain and in the north of Portugal, which abuts Galicia, so why not begin operations there? And why not at the same time sabotage some of the Portuguese wolfram en route to the Germans to toughen their secret weapons – rockets, according to rumours reaching Madrid – which could still win the war for them?

Tom went first to the small and sanctified city of Santiago de Compostela, and booked into a modest hotel near the towering cathedral. Walking round the great square Tom was reminded of Venice and reminded that he had never been there. Where had he been? Long Island, New York, a few depressed states of America, Paris, Spain . . . When all this is over, he thought, I will travel.

He turned up the collar of his raincoat – when it wasn't raining in Galicia, it was said, the water was dripping off the trees – and made his way along the Calle del Franco to a rendezvous with his campaign adviser, the boss of a trucking company transporting wolfram and a member of the *Partido Galleguista* which had championed home rule before the Civil War.

He was a big man with coarse grey hair and startling dark eyebrows; his face was seamed with dark thoughts but he possessed a grin as startling as his eyebrows. He was waiting for Tom outside the university college of Fonseca. He took Tom's arm and led him away to a crouching café where he plied him with cider which he poured down his own throat from a *porrón*. 'Makes you drunker this way,' he confided in Castilian. 'Something to do with oxygen getting into it.'

Tom drank his cider from a tankard and looked around the smoky café which had been moulded for conspiracy. Yellow candles burned on the tables, building stalagmites of grease; men bent low over the tables; a fire laid with damp logs puffed smoke towards a ceiling as dark as treacle.

'You sounded very mysterious on the telephone,' said the Gallego whose name was Julio.

'Are you a rich man, Julio?'

'Richer than I was. Everyone who touches wolfram is richer than they were.'

'But you'd like to become richer?'

'Is the Pope a Catholic?'

Tom leaned back while a waiter with a hunched back served bowls of *Caldo Gallego*, the life-blood of Galicia, white beans, salt pork and ham, new potatoes, greens and leeks. Then he placed an unlabelled bottle of red wine and two white porcelain drinking bowls on the table. Julio poured the wine into the bowls, no bigger than glasses, and it lay there dark and still.

They ate the peppery stew and they drank the wine and Tom felt a flush burning his cheeks, sweat beading his brow.

He said, 'I thought food was supposed to be scarce.'

'Depends on your wallet. Now, why the mystery?'

Tom told him about the Allies' failure to stop the flow of wolfram to the Nazis and he told him how it could be stopped and he told him about his own stock of gold – but not all of it.

'And why should I help the Allies defeat Germany?'

'You were anti-Fascist, weren't you?'

'We were beaten very soon.' An historic sadness settled upon the Gallego and he watched mournfully as the waiter placed a golden-skinned pork pie between them. He cut it with the air of a surgeon performing a hopeless operation. 'They were too strong for us. What did you expect? Franco was born in El Ferrol.'

Tom, who hadn't expected anything, stared with consternation at the slice of pie steaming on his plate. Then he attacked it boldly, suggesting, between courageous bites, that Julio's rebellious spirit had surely not been quelled over the years.

Perhaps, perhaps not. The startling eyebrows rose and fell. Then Tom who had, perhaps, Gallego blood in him, performed a sleight of hand. He agreed with a defeatist shake of his head that any such adventure was out of the question.

Not necessarily so. Anything was possible. There were still guerrilla bands in Galicia.

If only, Tom thought, the State Department had realized that the surest way to persuade a Spaniard to help you is to suggest that such assistance is impossible.

What was it that Tom wanted and how much gold was he prepared to pay? The remnants of the pork pie were removed and the witches' brew, *Queimada*, over which all Galician plots are hatched was produced.

Tom knew all about *Queimada* and its ferocious heathen associations. How sugar and slices of apple are tipped into an earthenware pot of the local firewater, *orujo*, which is like the Italian *grappa*. How a flame is applied to the brew while it is stirred. He also knew that when the *Queimada* is produced the first hurdle of negotiation has been cleared.

The waiter lit the brew in a bowl and quickly extinguished the flames: the longer they burned the weaker the potion. They drank it from earthenware mugs. Heat swelled Tom's reason, the sweat dried on his forehead, his ordered plans took audacious turns. And the Gallego said, 'Now, let's get down to business.'

The trucks left north-west Spain and Portugal in the morning so that they could cross the border into France at night. On 6 March when rain was falling in the lowlands, thickening to sleet and snow in the highlands, three trucks set out for the border, two from Ponferrada and one from Portugal.

The driver of the Portuguese truck was thick-set with a boxer's fists. Despite his years behind the wheel he was a carefree man who sang to the hum of the tyres and observed the seasons changing on either side of the treacherous roads he travelled. Hanging from the dashboard were miniatures of his wife and two boys and a medallion of St Christopher; without St Christopher he was convinced that long ago he would have toppled off a precipice or been swept from the highway by a snow-swelled torrent.

Normally this sanguine Portuguese drove north, picking his way through the verdant hills of Galicia or negotiating the coal fields of Asturias or pointing the nose of the truck up the Pyrenees. On this day, lodged uncertainly between winter and spring, he crossed the border between Portugal and Spain at Portelo in the normal way and then turned south towards Zamora, but as he drove he didn't sing.

Instead he pursed his lips and whistled soundlessly and from time to time fingered the upholstery of the driving seat where the money was hidden. When he pulled up to rest he examined the papers lodged behind the sun visor authorizing him to make the trip. Perfectly admissible, according to the big Gallego from Santiago. Forgeries just the same.

'Don't worry,' the Gallego had said, switching a smile on his melancholy features. 'Spain and Portugal are neutral. They can trade with whoever they like.'

Then why had the bills of lading for the wolfram been changed?

From Zamora the Portuguese continued south through Salamanca. At Béjar he was stopped by *Guardia Civil*. They examined his cargo cursorily, his papers intently. They consulted each other, shrugged eloquently beneath their capes and then nodded him through the check-point.

On the approaches to Caceres they were more inquisitive. Why hadn't he driven south through his own country before bearing east? *Because there were Germans at the point of departure to make sure I went north.* He said, 'I have a sister in Zamora and she has just had a baby.'

The *guardia* unstiffened. One produced a cracked photograph of his last-born. He showed it to the Portuguese who smiled. 'Just like his father,' he said.

'His mother, too – she is a wonderful woman.'

And now as he drove the Portuguese began to sing a little because, apparently, St Christopher wasn't adverse to a little deceit and with the money in the upholstery he would buy a truck for himself, and then another, and the devil take the sour-faced Gallego.

He slept in his truck with his money at the impoverished village of Santiponce, near Seville. The following morning he struck south again, round the tip of the peninsula until he reached the border with Gibraltar. There he stopped singing.

Formalities on the Spanish side of the border were minimal. He edged his truck towards Gibraltar. There they were more interested. He produced an envelope addressed to the Governor. It was received with suspicion as though it were explosive. He was told to go and wait. He gazed speculatively at St Christopher who stared sternly back. An hour passed. Then he was ushered into the British colony as though he had arrived with news of the second coming. Which, he reflected later, was understandable, as he had delivered large quantities of wolfram destined for Germany into the hands of her enemies.

The second truck-load that day was driven by a citizen of León named Alfonso who was renowned for his devil-may-care attitude to the serpentine bends of the roads climbing through the mountains towards the French border.

Today he drove even more extravagantly than usual, as befits a man who knows he has money in his pocket to bribe and corrupt and a surplus with which to reward himself.

He reached Pamplona at 9 pm and presented himself at the border with France 30 miles further north at 11.10. According to his papers he was carrying a load of gravel, although why it should be necessary to ship such a commodity across the Pyrenees was far from clear.

The border guards examined his papers. A flashlight

winked and another answered on the French side of the frontier.

Alfonso said, 'Do you know what I am carrying?'

'Of course we know,' the uniformed guard said. 'On your way.'

'You have been advised?'

'On your way, idiot.'

'I am carrying wolfram,' Alfonso said.

'I know. Get moving.'

Alfonso stuck his fist out of the window of the cab of the truck; its contents rustled faintly. 'I don't think you should let me through.'

The guard stared at Alfonso. 'Are you crazy?'

Alfonso opened his fist a little; the paper money was balled inside. The ball disappeared.

The guard said, 'I must ask you to pull over.'

'And take the wolfram back from where it came?'

'If I must,' the guard said.

The third truck left Ponferrada at dawn. At the wheel was a thin and bitter driver whose ears looked as though they had been bitten by rats. He had made the wolfram run many times and he cared little that he was taking it to the Germans: the civil war had taught him that allegiances were treacherous currency.

By dusk he was in the foothills of the Pyrenees. So bad was the visibility that he almost missed the sign, DIVERSION. He swung the wheel, mounting a dirt track to the left of the road.

After five minutes he became uneasy. Pine trees loomed to one side of the track, stones spat from beneath the tyres but he never heard them fall on the other side. He fancied he saw leonine eyes peering at him from the darkness of the forest. Moths of snow flew at the windshield becoming bolder by the moment.

He saw the boulders across the track just in time. Braked. Skidded. Stopped.

A voice said, 'Get out,' and he did so with relief because there was no reason to shoot a mere carrier of disputed merchandise. Was there?

Figures emerged from the pines. They carried rifles. One of them said, 'Get away from the truck, towards the trees.'

'Okay,' the driver said. 'I don't care what you do with the truck. Just don't shoot me. Okay?'

'Why would we shoot you?'

Because it had become a habit during the civil war and afterwards, the driver thought, but he shouted back, 'No reason. Do what the hell you like with the truck.'

'Do you know where we are?'

'You don't want me to know?'

'Forget where we are.'

'I've forgotten,' the driver said. 'I don't give a shit who you are or what you're going to do with the wolfram. I'm just a driver,' he said.

Bullets from a machine-pistol hammered the side of the truck, throwing sparks into the night.

'Why the hell did you do that?' another voice demanded.

'For the hell of it.'

The guerrilla who had ordered the driver out of the truck said, 'Okay, now get back in the cab.'

'I just climbed out.'

'We wanted to see you. Make sure you were a genuine Fascist.'

'Fascist? *Mi madre!* I'm just a driver.'

'In the truck,' the voice said.

A rifle shot. Bullet whining from the mudguard of the truck.

The driver climbed into the still-warm, oil-smelling cab of the truck. He felt the wheel with his hands and the worn, familiar pedals with his feet.

'Start the engine.'

He started it.

'Now drive.'

Into the boulders? He switched on the headlights. They had been removed. He depressed the clutch, engaged first gear, let out the clutch and drove, screaming, into space.

The driver was the only casualty during Tom Canfield's private war which lasted until the end of April 1944, when

Churchill persuaded Roosevelt to drop his oil embargo. Almost immediately Franco cut wolfram exports to Germany to a mere 40 tons a month.

Tom warned Antonio to stop smuggling it to the Germans – if he didn't he would denounce him to the Francoists who were now more benevolent towards the Allies. He reverted to more conventional commodity dealing and congratulated himself that, even if he hadn't taken to the skies against the Germans or the Japanese, he had fought and won his own battle.

He frequently reminded himself about this as, in Madrid, he followed the last victorious strides of the Allies. The conquest of France and the Low Countries as the Russians swept through East Europe to Berlin; the defeat of Japan as the Americans erased the cities of Hiroshima and Nagasaki with atomic bombs.

After the war Spain subsided even more hopelessly into the Years of Hunger. And, stigmatized by her associations with the vanquished Fascists, drifted into the Years of Isolation.

CHAPTER 16

An *espontáneo* is a spectator, often a boy, who jumps into a bullring and, brandishing a rag or perhaps his mother's shawl, tries to make a few passes at a bull before he is grabbed by the *cuadrilla*, the matador's assistant. A few display enough skill to embark on the path to recognition; the majority end up humiliated or gored or both.

If stripling bullfighters could do it, Pablo Gomez reasoned, why not apprentice footballers? And, lying alone on the straw mattress in the village in La Mancha, he raced each night into a goal-mouth mêleé. Wearing the white strip of Real Madrid, he took the ball from the feet of a defender, slipped two tackles, fooled the advancing goalkeeper and thumped the ball into the corner of the net.

He felt the ball spring from his boot. Heard the roar of the crowd. And so fast did his blood race that he lost many hours sleep and the priest who was teaching him when he wasn't working in the fields worried about his health, so pale and glittering-eyed did he become.

Of course he would be escorted from the ground, thrown out of the stadium and possibly locked up in the police station. But his skills would have been noticed, and his audacity – the hallmark of an opportunist centre-forward such as César who, half-way through the 1948 season, was maximum goal-scorer in Division 1.

By day while he was closeted with the priest or sawing olive branches or ploughing the reluctant earth Pablo, aged 16, planned. Timing, that was the essence. A game at a small ground where the barriers were puny, security suspect.

In the evenings he practised football with the boys in the
village but he was too good for them and, humiliated, they
hacked him down. But he didn't care: although his shins
were bruised and bloodied he was learning how to evade the
tackles of thwarted defenders.

At weekends he took the bus to Ciudad Real and was
picked one bitter December to play for the reserves. He scored
the winning goal and was taken aside by the trainer, an old
professional who had once played the occasional game for
Mestalla.

'You have a future,' he told Pablo. 'Soon you'll be playing
for the first team,' and Pablo, whose sights were set far
beyond the capital of La Mancha, thanked him and went on
training and slipping the tackles of the village boys.

But what worried him most was his physique. Like his
father he was finely muscled, but he was skinny, too, with
washboard ribs and sharp elbows and, as there wasn't enough
food to fatten him up, he took to scavenging from garbage
cans and stealing crops. He even boiled grass and ate the
mash because, if grass fattened cows, it would surely put
flesh on his bones.

Sometimes, staring at his naked body in the splintered
mirror in his room, it seemed to Pablo that a little padding
had grown around his ribs; at other times it still looked as
though you could play a tune on them. It was after one such
disappointing appraisal that he volunteered to take Diego's
evening meals to him – chick-peas or rice or watery soup on
which cubes of toast floated. By the time Pablo reached the
cubicle where Diego was still incarcerated nine years after
the end of the Civil War, the tray was lighter. Diego, grey
flesh hanging from his jaws, was surely overweight and he
was doing him a service. Pablo, nibbling chick-peas or biting
crisply into a cube of toast, shook his head at the contradictions
of life.

Food at the table of Kiko's widow was scarcely appetizing.
Since her husband's death she had grown old beyond her
years and she could muster none of the inventiveness that
other women of the village displayed in presenting their
meagre fare. At the age of 18 her son, Francisco, took off for

a reopened quicksilver mine at Almadén where he worked in a gallery 200 metres below the surface, returning at weekends with 20 pesetas housekeeping for his mother.

So how could Pablo leave Kiko's widow alone during the week? He consulted Diego one evening after he had removed two spoonfuls of rice from his bowl.

'How are you today, Uncle Diego?' He sat on the edge of the unmade bed in Diego's 'cell' which smelled of rotting geraniums.

'The same as always. Why do you ask?' Diego began to eat with measured appetite.

'I thought some fresh air might do you good.'

'You've taken a long time to reach that conclusion.' Diego picked some grains of sodden rice spilled on the expanse of his belly, drum-tight beneath his shirt.

'Don't you want to see what the world is like, Uncle Diego?'

'Much the same as it was in 1939 I imagine.'

'There's a new bakery in the village,' Pablo said. 'You can buy bread the day after it's been baked for 50 centimos.'

'I know,' Diego said. 'I've tasted it.'

'María Fernandez is grown up now. She's very pretty. And Don Miguel has got a car, a Citroën. And a bull got into the church the other day. There's a cinema in the next village. It's called the Ritz.'

'What's showing?' Diego asked.

'*Siempre Vuelven de Madrugada*. A slice of palpitating life, according to the poster. Just what you've been missing, Uncle Diego.'

'I can't leave here. You know that. They'd shoot me. There are thousands like me, hiding from the executioner. We're biding our time,' Diego said mysteriously.

'For what?'

'For the revolution, of course. Already we have a Government in exile in Mexico led by José Giral.'

'But Mexico is thousands of miles away.'

'The whole world is against Franco. Spain is isolated, thrown out of the United Nations. I know the resolution by heart,' Diego said proudly. '"Incontrovertible documentary

evidence establishes that Franco was a guilty party with
Hitler and Mussolini in the conspiracy to wage war against
those countries which eventually in the course of the World
War became banded together as the United Nations."'

'It wasn't very well written, was it, Uncle Diego.'

Diego ignored him. 'We have people everywhere. Argen-
tina, Uruguay, Venezuela, Mexico, the United States, Britain,
France, Russia . . .'

'Shouldn't they be here?'

'Not even Pablo Picasso will stay here.'

'Do you know what the Caudillo was doing on the day the
United Nations passed the resolution?'

'I don't care what he was doing.'

'Painting,' Pablo said. 'He paints very good pictures. Almost
as good as Picasso.'

'No one paints as well as Picasso.' Diego found a grain of
rice on his lip and captured it with the tip of his tongue.

'Why doesn't he come back to Spain? A painter hasn't got
anything to fear, has he?'

'Because he is an idealist,' Diego said sonorously.

'How do you know all these things, Uncle Diego?'

Diego pointed at his ancient wireless. 'The BBC. And
certain publications reach me. I was a fairly important
member of the movement, Pablo.'

Pablo struck. 'You don't look very important locked up in
this room.'

Diego hit the table with his podgy hand. 'You would prefer
me dead?'

'There haven't been any house raids in the village for more
than three years. And the *guardia* is a decent fellow. He plays
football. And the house is cosy these days. Pictures which
Rosana painted on the walls, vine roots burning in the
fireplace . . .'

'You are very sly,' Diego said, pushing aside his empty
bowl. 'I wonder where you get it from. Not from your mother:
she's as subtle as a Miura bull.'

'They're not so stupid,' Pablo said. 'It was a Miura bull that
killed Manolete last year. Its name was Islero.'

'Sly and perceptive,' Diego said, but the combat had left

his voice and Pablo sensed restlessness stirring within his hulk.

'I'll take the tray back,' Pablo said. 'I want to sit beside the fire. It's got a fine smell, vine root burning. It reminds me of candles.'

He took the tray and went through the secret door into the parlour where Kiko's widow sat beside the empty grate weaving a basket. She had been weaving it for a long time and it never seemed to get any bigger.

A week later the door opened cautiously.

Diego's voice entered the parlour first. 'Is there anyone there?'

'Only me,' Pablo said.

Diego's bulk followed his voice. He stood in the doorway for a moment like a man alighting from a train in a strange country. He blinked and, head lowered, looked around.

'It is as I remember it,' he said. 'And yet it isn't. It smells different . . .'

'The smell of hunger,' Pablo said.

'Kiko used to sit over there,' pointing at an upright chair with a cracked leather back beside the hearth.

'Dinner will be ready soon,' Pablo said. He laid three places at the table and when Kiko's widow came in from the kitchen she placed three bowls of transparent soup on the mats. She showed no surprise that Diego was there. They dined as silently as one can with soup.

The following morning, when the street was rimed with frost, Pablo lit a fire and fanned smoke beneath the secret door. After 20 minutes Diego materialized once more and Pablo knew that Kiko's widow would not be alone when he went away.

He left three days before Christmas when the countryside was hushed with cold and the praying houses were filled with the voices of orphans in Madrid chanting the winning numbers of the lottery, *El Gordo*, on the radio: a few of those homes scattered over Spain would suddenly become warm that day.

He struck south and on the way met up with a gang of *maletillas* foraging the land for a living, many of them scarred by forays into small-town bullrings. From them Pablo learned that until now he had lived a life of luxury; their roofs were flaking bamboo or the branches of carob trees.

He rode the roofs of trains with them, thieved with them and took a savage beating from a landowner who caught him stealing oranges from a grove in Andalucia, but he was never troubled by guilt.

He saved his money – he had 150 pesetas sewn into the lining of his old grey jacket – and his brain became as fit as his body. As he lay in a barn listening to the scutter of rats he planned shots and swerves and tackles. He would poach goals just as he poached oranges.

After he had reached the Moorish city of Córdoba, after he had gazed through the pillars in the mosque within the cathedral, listened to the lament of flamenco trapped in whitewashed alleys, he struck west along the banks of the Guadalquivir towards Seville. Eighth in Division One! And as he walked and hitched and robbed he became aware that he was in another land. The bare skies picked up the glare of faraway deserts and the white cottages wore their geraniums with a gypsy flourish.

In Seville he spent the first five pesetas of his capital on his board in a little house in the potters' suburb of Triana on the west bank of the Guadalquivir which he shared with a street-cleaner and his wife and two children, a shy boy of 10 and a girl of 14 who, when she walked was already aware of herself, lowering her gaze elaborately when she caught Pablo looking at her.

The street-cleaner's mother had worked in the tobacco factory on the Calle de San Fernando and he talked wistfully about the days when she came home after packing eight bundles of 50 cigars in one day wearing her starched cotton gown and a flower in her hair. Pablo wandered past the old factory and loitered in white patios encircling fountains and chattering women, and the old Jewish quarter of Santa Cruz where the secrets of the silent houses were imprisoned behind wrought iron grilles.

One January day two nights before Three Kings, Pablo found himself alone in the house with the street-cleaner's daughter, Encarna. A fire built with orange boxes and damp sawdust burned in the grate; the intimacy that had once lodged years ago in the poor house in Madrid reached out a finger and touched him.

He felt a little embarrassed. That they had been left alone together was surely an error in these suspicious days when the *guardia* visited cinemas to make sure that no young men had taken advantage of the darkness to slip their arms round their girlfriends' waists. She too, was uneasy and yet there was a challenge about her disquiet. Her eyes were dark brown, almost black with the pupils dilated, and he could see the flames of the fire reflected in them.

'So what brings you to Seville?' she asked, lady of the house for a few minutes.

'To make my fortune, what else?'

'Seville is poor,' she said. 'It wears riches over its rags.'

Pablo thought about the phrase. He warmed his hands in front of the lazy fire; he noticed that they were grubby and clenched them so that she could not see his nails. 'Did you make that up?'

'I wish I had.' Her hands went to her polished hair. 'No, they are my mother's words. She was very beautiful.'

Alarmed, Pablo felt his lips forming words he didn't want to utter. *So are you.* And so she was but he didn't want to tell her because she would invest the words with another meaning. He felt as though he were on the threshold of great and subtle discoveries. He heard castanets and a man singing sadly.

He said, 'My mother was very beautiful, too.'

'Was?'

'I haven't seen her for a long time.'

Encarna didn't ask why and Pablo admired her for it. She said, 'Are you going to stay long?'

'Long enough,' Pablo told her.

'I may go away soon,' she said, and he knew she was lying. 'I'm going to Madrid one day.'

'Don't you like Seville?'

'It's beautiful,' he said.

'You should be here in Holy Week. See the processions,

the statues garlanded with flowers carried on the men's shoulders, the penitents in their hoods, the dancing . . . You should be here for the April Fair – horses and fine carriages and bullfights and dancing.'

'My sister would like it,' Pablo said. 'She would paint it.'

'Where is your sister?'

'In Madrid.'

'And that's why you want to go there?' her voice subtly different.

'We are all from Madrid. We are cats.' Pablo smiled at her and watched flames break through the sawdust and settle like butterflies flexing their wings in sunlight.

'What is your sister like?'

'Tougher than me. Funny, isn't it, she paints and yet she's tough. She gets the painting from her father – he painted in words – and the toughness from her mother. You would think it would be the other way round.'

'Why do you say she's tough?'

'Because she left me,' said Pablo, who had never forgiven her.

'And you? What do you get from your parents?'

Pablo considered this. 'Determination,' he said after a while.

'Isn't that the same as toughness?'

'I don't think so.' He thought about it again. 'No, I have ambition; that doesn't necessarily make me tough.' It was surprising how easy it was to talk to Encarna.

'Ah, ambition . . .'

'My mother said a lot of people lost their ambition after the Civil War. All they wanted was peace.'

'Isn't that a sort of ambition?'

'I suppose so,' Pablo said, surprised at the small revelations that were being unfolded in front of this reluctant fire.

'What is your ambition, Pablo?' She pulled her long red skirt tightly across her knees.

'Would you like to come to a football match one day?'

'I don't like football.'

'Have you ever been to a game?'

She shook her head. 'Who would come with us?'

'Your father?'

'He only goes to bullfights.'

'Supposing I paid for his ticket.' One hand wandered to the lining of his jacket.

'He might, I suppose. But he would think it very odd.'

Pablo wanted to say, 'What if I were playing?' but he had discovered in the village that the best way to broadcast a secret is to confide it. 'I'll talk to him,' he said. 'We'll go to a big game. Madrid.'

At that moment her father, pinched and bowed from a lifetime of sweeping, came into the room.

The following day Pablo went to see Seville's reserve team play before a sparse crowd and picked the spot where he would vault the barrier. The afternoon sun was mild – the city seemed to lure the winter warmth from Extremadura to the north – and the white strip of the Seville players shone brightly in it.

White! He had bought a white shirt and shorts because that was Madrid's strip. But here against another team wearing white they would appear in their mauve away colours. Idiot!

But how in Seville could he obtain Madrid's away strip? As he promenaded that evening with Encarna's family beside the river in the Parque María Luisa he manoeuvred so that he walked with Encarna behind her parents and her brother. And he told her about the Grand Stratagem.

Her hand flew to her mouth. 'But they'll throw you in prison.'

'They only do that at bullfights because an *espontáneo* is dangerous: he's so amateurish that he can make the bull realize that he should be charging the matador not the cape.'

'Aren't you amateurish?'

'I am. But I have the instinct.'

'But you're so . . .'

'Skinny? Why is it that boys are skinny and girls slender?'

'Perhaps because we're built differently.' She turned her head away from him and the fragile sunshine shone on the tortoiseshell combs in her hair.

'Can you sew?' he asked.

'Of course.'

'So if I get the materials you could make the shorts and shirt for me?'

'I might.' She regarded him speculatively. 'If you promise to score a goal.'

'Then make them for me,' he said, as her brother bore down upon them.

'Secrets time?'

'There are things,' Encarna said with dignity, 'that you do not discuss with your brother.'

'But you do with the lodger?'

'With friends.' She lengthened her stride so that she caught up with her parents and, as she did so, the sun made a halo of the fine hairs that had escaped from the combs.

Pablo arrived at the ground early to make sure he got a place by the barrier. But it was Madrid playing and crowds were already converging from all over the city. Outside vendors sold sunflower seeds, liquorice roots, badges, rosettes, banners, scarves; inside the terraces were filling. Scratchy martial music blared from loudspeakers; an old biplane towing a streamer advertising Bisonte cigarettes flew across the winter-blue sky.

Pablo, wearing a long black coat over his strip and carrying his football boots in a shoe box, pushed his way to the barrier close to one of the goals. When the crowds had thickened around him he knelt and put on the boots, cleaned and greased, new studs hammered into the soles, tying them tightly, laces underneath to make them part of his legs.

The Seville players trotted on to the pitch to exercise and practise. The young lords from Madrid stayed in their dressing room. Anticipation as the spectators began to identify with their team tightened around Pablo. He began to tremble as though in a fever.

The players departed; then both teams ran on to the pitch from the cave in the grandstand. A roar rose from the terraces.

The referee consulted his watch, blew his whistle. But Pablo was near the Madrid goal so he would have to wait until the second half. Would his determination survive that long? He studied the terraces but he couldn't see Encarna and her father. He concentrated on the game. Play flowed back and forth, honours shared. A tumult of outrage, vicarious pain, when a Seville player was fouled, and the referee was a *burro*, a donkey, a son of a whore, if he didn't award a free kick. A gathering cheer as the ball soared towards the Madrid goal, a sigh as the keeper got his hands to it.

At half-time the score was one-all.

No, he couldn't do it. What sort of fool are you, Pablo Gomez? You'll be pulled down before you even reach the pitch. Humiliated, beaten up . . . Wait for the talent scouts to find you like any other kid foot-juggling a ball in a *barrio*. When did you last see a scout, imbecile?

The Madrid left-winger, leg muscles leaping, slips two tackles, and races towards the Seville goal. Centres the ball. Up go the heads. And Pablo, coat discarded, is over the barrier and running towards the goal-mouth. Players shout and point but the referee has his back to him and in any case he pays little heed to indignation.

Pablo knows his advantage: such will be the concentration of the Seville players that they will only see a player in mauve and will respond to him. And, momentarily, continue to do so even after the referee has blown his whistle.

Pablo sees only the ball and the goal. Intercepts a short pass. Legs lunge at him but he is over them, rounding the scramble of players. Dummies, evades another tackle. Sees the goal, the keeper crouching, hands hanging loose.

He hears the whistle but it only occupies a sliver of his consciousness. All he sees is the top right hand corner of the net. Arms are grabbing for him now but he slips them. His foot is raised. The ball is spinning in front of him. He kicks it with his instep and the keeper is rising, arms reaching classically. The ball billows the net. The moment is frozen.

Then he hears the roar and the whistles of the crowd; sees the referee marching towards him, finger prodding. He is frog-marched from the pitch by two Seville players but the crowd is cheering him. Clapping as two policemen drag him up the aisle.

He leaves the stadium precipitately, propelled by a

policeman's foot. He lies for a moment in the dust. He thinks, 'We're winning two-one,' and then thinks, 'But what am I going to do now?'

Ernesto Villar was a fat sports writer. The combination is not unknown; nevertheless, early in his career, it did detract from his credibility. Recognizing this, Villar, reasoning that it was better to be conspicuous rather than nondescript in journalism, cultivated his bulk; besides, he liked eating.

Despite his size Villar, who recognized a story when he saw one, was also nimble on his feet. Sitting with his camera behind the Seville goal, he decided at once that the *espontáneo* that he had just photographed would merit more space in newspapers and magazines than any orthodox action that might lie ahead. Thrusting his way through the crowd, he made his way towards the exit through which the young gladiator had vanished.

He found him, leaning despondently against a fence to which the tatters of Seville's previous games still adhered, and his belly wobbled busily as he made his way towards the skinny youth with the razored features.

'Hold it right there.' He raised his camera, focused and photographed him slouched beside the torn posters. If the picture was bigger than the story then Villar, a freelance, was a cameraman; if the story was bigger he was a writer.

'*Hombre!*' he said. 'Some goal.'

'It won't count.'

'So what? A cannon-ball, first-time shot. Just one more . . .' aiming his camera again.

'Why do you want all these photographs?'

'Because you're going to be famous,' Villar said. 'What's your name?' And when he told him, 'Well, from now on your name is *El Flaco*, the Skinny One.'

'I don't think I like it.'

'Trust me,' Villar said. 'Why did you do it?'

'Because I want to play for Madrid.'

'And you will,' Villar said. 'One day.'

He patted Pablo on the shoulder, made a note of his address and returned to the stadium as the crowds were streaming on to the streets. No further score, he gathered; a one-all draw.

He found the scout for Madrid, whose career had been laid waste by the Civil War, still sitting staring at the empty pitch.

'So what do you think?' Villar sat beside him.

'About the *chaval*, the kid?'

'He was good,' Villar said.

'There are thousands just as good.'

'Then why don't you find them?'

'I help to build a team: I don't want 50 promising centre-forwards on my books. They all want to be centre-forwards, did you know that? Or wingers.'

'He's got star quality,' Villar said. 'You must know that. Put him in your junior squad and in a couple of years he'll be slotting them past the keepers of Atlético, Barca, Valencia . . .'

'You mean he's a good story?'

'That too.'

The scout shook his head. 'Can't be done, Ernesto. If he makes it then they'll all want to make it and there'll be kids leaping the barriers at every game.'

Villar said gently, 'How did you start?'

'I got a break. A scout spotted me playing for my *pueblo*.'

'*El Flaco* doesn't play for a team so he can't be spotted.'

'Who?'

'The kid.'

'So he's got a nickname already. Quick work, Ernesto. Why doesn't he play for a team?'

'Because he's got no home,' Villar said, moving easily into the realms of fiction.

'How do you know all this? It only happened half an hour ago.'

'I am a trained journalist,' Villar said with dignity.

'Why does he want to play for Madrid?'

'He said, "Because it's the only team." Do you know who he reminds me of?'

'Me?' the scout asked wearily.

'A poacher of goals like you. An opportunist.'

'He's that all right,' the scout said. 'But if he doesn't play for a team then he has no idea of teamwork. Am I right?'

'Your trainer will teach him that.'

Villar consulted his watch anxiously: he had to write his reports, telephone them, develop and print his pictures and wire them to Madrid from the post office on the Calle de San Acasio.

'He took his chance well, that *chaval*,' the scout said. 'He has the instinct; that's what counts.'

'You too had the instinct,' Villar said.

'Instinct is everything. Animal instinct. But it has to be schooled.'

'If *El Flaco* becomes a star then you will be known as his mentor.'

'Not you?'

'My photograph will live.'

The scout felt his thigh where a Republican bullet had lodged for three days before a field surgeon had removed it. 'I wish you hadn't come to me,' he said.

'It took courage to do what he did.'

'Into the corner of the net.'

'Slipping so many tackles.'

'How old is he?' the scout asked.

'Sixteen,' said Villar who had no idea how old Pablo Gomez was.

'Such an age. Neither man nor boy. Very conscious of himself and the changes that are taking place within him'.

'He is only interested in football. In Madrid.'

'He is from Madrid?'

'Of course,' said Villar wondering where he came from.

'Why has he no home?'

'The war,' Villar said, lowering his head.

The terraces were almost empty now and the pitch was darkening in the late afternoon light. A cool breeze blew across it from the river.

'I wish you hadn't come to me,' the scout said again.

Villar waited to find out why this was so.

Again the scout's hand strayed to his thigh.

Then the scout said, 'If you had not come to me I would have found this boy myself.'

Pablo, confused, sat before the smoking fire. Encarna sat opposite him. She hadn't been to the match, she said – her father didn't think the terraces were the place for a 14-year-old girl – but she had heard the commentary on the radio. Had heard the excitement in the voice of the commentator as Pablo scored.

'It didn't count,' he said.

'I know that. I'm not a fool.'

'I'm sorry.' He poked the crust of the sawdust fire with a stick allowing a small flame to escape. 'What else did the commentator say?'

'That you showed promise.'

Pablo heard the sharing in her voice and was disturbed by it. 'Is that all?'

'He said it was a good goal . . . well taken, I think he said. Then he described the players leading you off and the police . . . I heard the spectators cheering you,' Encarna said.

He could hear that she was proud of him and he smiled shyly at the flame spreading its wings across the sawdust.

'Will you play for Madrid?' she asked.

'I made a fool of myself.'

'No,' she said, 'not you.'

'An idiot,' said her brother coming through the door with their father. And her father said, 'Where is my coat?'

CHAPTER 17

Ana didn't hear about her son's escapade until the spring when the snow on the lower slopes of the Pyrenees was melting and the streams were brimming and dark woods were lit with birdsong.

She was wandering through the rooms of a brooding house that the dwindling band of guerrillas had raided when she found an old copy of *Triunfo*. She thumbed the sepia pages guiltily because the lives of movie stars intrigued her and this was surely a weakness. There was Danny Kaye with his wife – she liked the stars to be faithful, Alan Ladd, Joan Caulfield, Virginia Mayo ... She flipped the pages, and turned to the centre-pages devoted to football.

ESTE 'ESPONTANEO'. She glanced at a photograph of a skinny youth in shirt and shorts being hustled from a football pitch. She contined to stare at the picture; the magazine shook in her hands. Seville! What was he doing there? She read the story underneath. *Pablo Gomez*, El Flaco, *has been signed for Madrid junior squad* ... She folded the magazine and placed it in her string bag.

She spent a splintered night dreaming fitfully about her children when they were young and in the morning she knew that a time for change had dawned. Rosana, supported by Antonio and his wife, was in Madrid studying art and now Pablo was there too. I have to return, she thought, sitting in a chair outside the cave darning one of Sabino's shirts.

The air was wet with the thaw, the blue sky ragged with clouds. A time for decisions. But how could she get back? The road-blocks were more sophisticated, the ambushes more educated. On the last two occasions that she had tried to reach Madrid to see Rosana she had been chased into the foothills by the *guardia*.

Being a woman was an advantage. But not if you were the Black Widow. She felt the skin on her face and, with her fingertips, found a few lines. How old was she? Nearly 40. And what had she achieved in all those years? A home in a cave in the range of mountains that had, since time began, severed Spain from the rest of Europe.

She gazed in the direction of Madrid. What would Sabino say? He believed he loved her but he was driven by his own cause. He was a Basque.

So I shall have to go alone through the mountain passes, bluff my way past the caped *guardia*, sleep with cattle and rats . . . And then what? A wanted woman in Madrid where informers are waiting with their fingers on their purses? A reward or pardon for every successful denunciation, identity kept secret.

I will have to get papers, she thought. And change my appearance. She stroked her hair, tight-combed at the temples, and pushed at the lines on her forehead. And wear different clothes. Blues and reds and russets.

She stared at the white peaks, as arrogant as the stars, overlooking the cirque.

'You look as though you've lost a peseta and found a centimo.' Sabino stood in the mouth of the cave, stretching and inhaling the fresh, wet air.

'We have been together a long time, you and me.' Ana pulled the cotton taut on his shirt and examined her handiwork.

'Eight years. A little more, perhaps.'

'A full chapter,' she said, looking fondly at his squat, wrestler's body.

'There could be more.'

She hesitated, then said, 'It is spring and it is time to go our separate ways.'

'You don't hold any surprises for me – you talk in your sleep. Both your children are in Madrid but . . .' He stepped into the sunshine. 'They're old enough to look after themselves, aren't they?'

'They have grown up without parents; they have missed something along the way. Perhaps I can still give it to them.'

'Rosana is a woman.'

'A young woman; there is much a mother can tell her daughter at that age.'

'Do you think she doesn't know already?'

'It's more than a year since I saw her,' Ana said. 'Eighteen months since I saw Pablo. Did I talk about football in my sleep?'

'I read about it,' Sabino said.

'You should have told me.'

'I didn't want you to go.'

Such words, she knew, did not come easily to him.

'You have your cause, I have mine. This fighting in the mountains is almost over. Perhaps when Franco is dead . . .'

'He will live for ever,' Sabino said. 'He will outlive me. They are tough, these Gallegos.'

'As tough as the Basques?'

'No one is as tough as a Basque.'

'Tell that to any Spaniard.'

'We are not Spaniards,' Sabino said.

'But I am.'

'You are a Madrileña.'

'Isn't Madrid the capital of Spain?'

'By accident. Because there was once a fortress there on a mound on the plain. Toledo was the capital, Córdoba before that. If there is a true capital it should be Barcelona.'

And she laughed because this was the way it had always been with them and it was the way she would remember it.

'Can you help me?' she asked.

'To leave me?'

'You would leave me soon. Let us end it now.'

'Eight years,' he said. 'More than a chapter.'

'A lifetime?'

'For some a lifetime. I will help you,' he said.

'Perhaps the words we don't utter are the most eloquent.'

'Then I shall remain silent.'

'We would look like two big fools if we stayed here speaking without words.'

He moved further into the sunlight and laid his hands on her shoulders. 'I will help you,' he said again.

'And follow your beliefs?'

'What else is there?'

He began to massage the muscles at the base of her neck with his thumbs.

They left on horseback, he on a chestnut mare, she on a grey, striking southwest to a small town lodged on a mountainside where a forger who had operated in Lerida during the Civil War was still in hiding.

He greeted them without enthusiasm in a cottage situated, audaciously, next to the gaol where locals conversed with prisoners through a street-level grille. From the bars there arose an odour of stables.

The forger led them through a bead curtain to a parlour where he lived in twilight. The walls were blue-washed, the floor tiled; in one corner lay a chandelier wrapped in old newspapers.

The forger, fragile and stooped, showed them his hands, knuckles balled with arthritis. 'I cannot help you,' he said.

'You were the best once upon a time,' Sabino said.

'I don't think about those days any more: it was a fever that has passed.' The forger spread his misshapen hands. 'A glass of wine?'

Sabino said, 'You need ink not wine.'

'Can't you see my hands?'

'I can see this.' Sabino held up a letter lying on the table. The words were an aristocrat's, a sign-writer's script, and the signature was as elaborate as any lawyer's.

'It caused me a lot of pain, that letter.'

'It is almost as well written as this.' Sabino produced a 500 peseta note from the pocket of his hunting jacket.

'What do you want?'

'Papers for María Fernandez from the Carabanchel district of Madrid. She has been attending the funeral of a dear relative in Pamplona and lost them at the graveside.'

'It will take time.'

'How long?'

'Two days with these hands.'

'One,' Sabino said. 'I have another such note in my pocket.' He sat on a sighing sofa and beckoned Ana. 'Now serve us some wine and yourself some ink.'

Ana sat beside Sabino and listened to the dripping of the water released outside by the spring.

They slept on the sofa that night and in the morning Ana put on a thick, heather-coloured dress and a grey shawl and loosened her hair so that it fell softly over her ears and Sabino said, 'You look like a wanton.'

'I have been wanton in the past . . .'

'Once more?'

'Once more,' she said, and took off the shawl and the dress and they lay together on the protesting sofa and at the end the joy was as sharp as pain.

He rode with her on his chestnut mare to the point where the foothills of the Pyrenees finally completed their descent and waited with her in a village in a small square built round a stone cross gnawed by time until the bus for Pamplona arrived. Then she was taken away from him by the passengers boarding the aged bus with their atrophied chickens and vegetables. She watched him from the window as he roped one horse to the other, as he mounted the chestnut and left the square, more upright on a horse than he was on his own feet, on his way to *Euskadi*.

She was a stranger in Madrid this morning. Her city was childhood and courtship and siege. This city was a compromise. If she hadn't been motivated by vengeance, then she would have been disheartened by the complacency of its regal avenues leading to the shanties on its outskirts where peasants fleeing from the unrelenting countryside had pitched camp.

She walked from the bus station to her brother's house. She had money, her share of bandit loot, and she carried a suitcase fastened with a leather strap and she walked proudly. How many of the elegant *gatos* strolling in the spring sunshine had a son training with Real Madrid?

The tall house with the ornamental balconies intimidated

her but it *was* her brother's home and she had come to tell him that neither she nor her daughter needed the charity of a traitor who had fought for the Fascists.

Her brother's appearance shocked her. It was 12 years since she had seen him and in that time he had grown out of the family mould into another identity. The curl of his greying hair was tighter than it had been; his gestures were more considered; his face was taut and guarded.

He led her into a lofty room furnished with carved, chestnut furniture and offered tea. She asked for coffee. He pulled a satin rope, a bell jangled distantly and a maid materialized.

He sat opposite her. 'So tell me everything. What you've been doing, why you're here. Did anyone see you come here?' he asked, too casually.

'Don't worry, I have a new identity.'

'So why are you visiting me, a committed Francoist?' He smiled indulgently.

She stared at him in surprise. 'You must know why.'

He placed the tips of his fingers together. 'Money?'

'You've already done enough,' she said angrily.

'I don't know what you're talking about.'

She leaned forward. 'Rosana is what I'm talking about.'

The maid came in with tea and coffee and a plate of iced cakes.

When she had left, Antonio, frowning, said, 'What has Rosana got to do with anything?'

Fear moved inside her. 'The art school must cost a lot of money.'

'What art school? Has the mountain air addled your brain, Ana?'

'I saw Rosana a year ago. She said you were paying for her to go to college. And for her accommodation.'

Antonio picked up a cake, nibbled the icing and replaced it on the plate. He said, 'I haven't seen Rosana since she was that high.' He held his hand above the coffee table.

Ana heard the traffic outside; somewhere in the house a clock chimed.

Antonio said gently, 'I'm afraid she has lied to you, Ana.'

'Perhaps Martine . . .'

He shook his head at such an absurdity.

'Then where is she?'

'I can't answer that.'

Ana stood up. 'I'm sorry to have bothered you.'

'If I can help . . .'

'That won't be necessary.' She walked towards the door.

There he bent and kissed her on both cheeks and faintly she smelled perfume.

She waited down the street from the British Embassy as the diplomats and staff departed for lunch. In the mountains she had learned how to make herself invisible and no one glanced at her as, grey shawl round her head, battered suitcase beside her, she stood on the pavement consulting what might have been a guide-book but was, in fact, an old copy of *Don Quixote* which she had brought with her from the cave.

What if he drove away? Well, at least she could take the number of the car and come back tomorrow in a taxi.

He looked older than she remembered. Everyone did, of course, but some wore the years with style. Adam Fleming's stride was alert enough, black hair shining in the sunlight healthily enough, but his body was angled and he searched ahead for invisible obstacles.

He turned right on to the Calle de Génova and walked to the Calle Sagasta. He wasn't difficult to follow with his black, diplomat's coat but, mingling with the lunch-time crowds, she employed mountain cunning just the same, using doorways and parked cars as she had once used trees and boulders. He struck left down Calle de San Bernardo which led into the Avenida de José Antonio which had been the Gran Via before Franco won the war. The crowds and their indifference disorientated Ana and she carried her suitcase self-consciously.

Where was he going? He was heading in the general direction of the Royal Palace opposite the Plaza Oriente where Franco made his public appearances. But he turned abruptly at the Calle de los Reyes and she nearly lost him as he turned into a side street and took the steps of a spinsterish block of flats two at a time.

She waited in the doorway of a small shop that sold spices and herbs which, according to the labels on the jars, cured Mankind's every malady. Did Fleming live in the block? All she had to do was ring the bells outside the doors. But who would answer Fleming's? Rosana?

'Señora, can I help you?'

The shopkeeper was fragile and wispy-bearded and he smelled of the Orient.

'Do you know who lives over there?' pointing at the block.

'Many people, señora. They are studio apartments mostly. Students from wealthy families. Fascists,' he whispered.

'Do you know any of them?'

'One or two. They come here when they are cooking meals to impress their friends.'

'Do any girls live there by themselves?'

'Two. One is tall and blonde and well-built and she has many visitors.'

'The other?'

'She has sensitive hands but she drives a hard bargain. She is a painter,' the shopkeeper said. He peered at Ana. 'She looks a little like you.'

The staircase was narrow, steps marble, cold and veined. Ana took her time climbing them, greatly fearing what lay ahead. As she climbed she reviewed the circumstances that had brought her here, distracting herself with them. The Cause which had taken Jesús from her, made her such a bad mother that her son had fended for himself and her daughter had accepted charity – more? – from a foreigner, a Fascist. She felt the cold through the worn soles of her shoes. But what else could I have done? We had to fight, spurred by a history of injustice. But Jesús didn't have to fight: I crucified him, I who never listened to his sculptured words, I who preferred the pistol to the pen. And one day I will take a pistol and listen to the echoes of his words.

The names on the doors on the first two floors were unfamiliar; she rang the bells just the same but there were no replies. On a door on the third floor a hand-written card slotted into a small frame. GOMEZ. She rang the bell.

A pause. Whispered words. Or was that her imagination? Footsteps. 'Who's there?' A man's voice, like a guard demanding a password.

She said, 'Is Rosana there?'

Silence. Then, 'Who wants her?' But he knew, of course.

'Her mother.'

Muffled words reached her. 'Just a minute.'

A bolt slid, a chain fell. 'Come in,' Adam Fleming said.

He had taken off his coat and jacket and was wearing a pin-striped waistcoat with dark silk at the back. His hair was dishevelled.

'Where's Rosana?' she asked.

'I think, perhaps, we should talk,' he said in his educated Spanish.

'I want to see my daughter.'

'In a moment.'

She put down her suitcase and straightened her back. She said, 'It's more than a year since I last saw my daughter. I want to see her now.'

Rosana said, 'Here I am, mama.'

In a year she had become a woman. That happened abruptly, of course, at her age.

They kissed awkwardly and sat opposite each other in the small and somnolent room which burgeoned in one corner into sunlit disarray. In this corner stood an easel with a half-finished portrait of Adam Fleming on it.

Fleming said, 'I wish it hadn't happened this way.'

'And what way would you have preferred it to happen?' Ana asked.

'I wanted to write to you but we hadn't got an address.'

'We?'

'Some coffee? A little wine?'

'I would prefer an explanation,' Ana said.

Rosana stood up and covered the portrait with a paint-daubed cloth. She stood in front of it, arms folded, not wanting to hurt, but unrepentant just the same.

She said, 'Adam has been very good. He is paying my college fees and for this apartment.'

'You told me your uncle was supporting you.'

'He doesn't even know I'm here. I went to see Martine but she didn't want to know me. I don't expect she even told Antonio.'

'You lied to me,' Ana said.

'I had to: you wouldn't have understood.'

'This man,' pointing at Adam Fleming, 'fought against your father.'

'So did thousands of other decent men.'

'You believe in what they were fighting for?' Ana stared uncomprehendingly at her daughter.

'They did.'

'Can't you answer questions honestly any more?'

'I believe that the fight must go on. But not the way you are fighting it. Not with bombs and ambushes. All that is over. You have lost that battle but there will be others. Voices instead of bullets. The voices of the people, protests, demonstrations . . .'

'You truly believe this? That the people can overthrow a dictator who has an army behind him?'

'It has happened before,' Rosana said.

Ana turned to Adam Fleming who was sitting stiffly, hands clasped on his thighs. 'What do you think, Señor Fleming?'

'I believe that the people should have their say.'

'Then why didn't you let them? Why did you fight them?'

'I was young. Everyone in Britain seemed to support the Republicans. I read about priests being murdered, churches being burned. My sister's husband was killed here in Madrid . . .'

'Do you still think you were right, Señor Fleming?'

'Who is the enemy?'

'What is that supposed to mean?'

'I was ordered to shoot a Republican once.'

'And did you?'

'The decision was taken from me.'

Ana said, 'The Fascists killed one of my brothers, having removed his eye first. They killed my parents. And then, for good measure, my husband.'

'I am truly sorry,' Adam Fleming said.

'If you are truly sorry you will leave my daughter alone.'

'And who will pay for her lessons? Where will she live?'

'True artists do not need lessons.'

'A pleasing thought but not true.'

'And she will live with me.'

'Where are you living, mama?' Rosana asked, eyeing the suitcase on the floor.

'I will find a place.'

'That isn't so easy,' Adam Fleming said.

Ana aimed her hatred. 'How would you know? Everything has always been easy for people like you.'

'You're right, but I don't have to apologize for it.'

'What you have to do,' Ana said, firing the words carefully like a marksman, 'is stay away from my daughter.'

'I can't do that, Señora Gomez.'

Ana said, 'You will do it.'

'I'm sorry, Señora Gomez.'

Ana said to her daughter, 'We must go, you and I,' but Rosana didn't move, and Ana said, 'I am your mother.'

'I love you, mama, but you haven't been a mother to me for a long time.'

'That will change,' Ana said, but the years behind the two of them dragged her words.

'It is too late,' Rosana said.

The silence was thick.

Adam said, 'I wish we could talk, the three of us.'

'Three? We don't need you,' Ana said, coldness expanding within her.

Rosana said, 'But we do, mama. Adam and I are getting married.'

Suitcase in hand, Ana ran down the stairs, accelerating involuntarily, pushing at the wall with one hand to stop herself falling, stumbling over the last three steps. Then she was in the street, the vendor of herbs and spices staring at her from his doorway, veering right, aware that she cut an absurd figure, not caring, knowing only that she had to escape from what she had heard.

She heard Rosana's footsteps behind her. Heard her cry out, 'Mama. Stop.' But she ran on, skirts pulling at her legs, shawl flying, towards the Plaza de España. Then she did something that she had never done before. She hailed a taxi. Rosana reached her as she climbed into the back of it. 'Mama, please, we love each other.'

Ana stared at her daughter through the open window, listened to herself as she spoke, 'Rosana, I never want to see you again.' Then she said to the driver, 'Take me to the Puerta del Sol.' And stared ahead as the taxi moved away down the narrow street.

As Adam watched from the window a bird opened its wings within him and took flight. With it flew the guilt that he had harboured since he had fallen in love with Rosana when she was a young girl; with it flew the awkwardness he had felt when, with elaborate diffidence, he had suggested that they might get married; with it went the spectres that had accompanied him since he had fought on the banks of the Jarama.

He listened to her footsteps on the stairs. When the door opened he stretched out his arms and she came to him.

Antonio said: 'Why didn't you tell me?'

'I didn't want to worry you,' Martine said.

'She is my niece.'

'The daughter of a woman high on the wanted list. She would have brought trouble.'

'I could have given her money.'

'She wanted a home.'

Isabel looked up from her homework. 'I didn't like her,' she said. 'She was begging.'

'Not everyone is as lucky as we are,' Antonio said.

Martine said, 'Where will your sister go?'

Antonio shrugged. 'Where all the new arrivals go, I suppose. To a *chabola* on some patch of waste ground on the outskirts of the city.'

'But first she will go to see her children. Do you realize what will happen to Pablo when they find out he's the son of Ana Gomez?'

'They must know already.'

'Gomez is not an uncommon name: Pablo is not stupid.'

'Then we must stop her,' Antonio said.

'Leave it to me,' Martine said. 'One of my father's friends is a director of Real Madrid. I will ask him to warn Pablo and make sure she's not admitted to the ground.'

'And the man at the gate?'

'That can be arranged,' Martine said. 'Just leave it to me; you have enough to worry about.'

Then she went into the bedroom and telephoned the police.

CHAPTER 18

The site of the Valley of the Fallen, the monument to the dead of the Civil War, stood 30 miles north-west of Madrid on a rocky spur guarded on three sides by mountains.

It reminded Tom Canfield, sitting at the wheel of a mud-spattered Dodge in the burgeoning spring of 1948, of a scene from a Biblical movie: the slaves – press-ganged from the defeated Republicans – labouring mechanically at the mouth of the tunnel where, inside the spur, the basilica was to be fashioned; the blue sky and the forests of pine, oak and juniper climbing the mountains. Was it commemorating the dead of the victors *and* the vanquished?

'Well,' Antonio asked in English, 'what do you think?'

'It's going to be something like the Pharaohs might have built.'

'And it's only just begun. Can you imagine what is needed? The tunnel will have to be twice the height to accommodate the nave. They say the cross with its sculptures will weigh 200,000 tons. Think of the materials that will be needed . . .'

'Can't someone else supply them?'

'Think of the money,' Antonio said. He ran the tip of his tongue between his lips. 'Did you know it's going to be hollow, the crosspiece will be big enough to allow two automobiles to pass each other inside?'

'So?'

'It will require an elevator inside to carry the blocks up. Americans make good elevators, don't they? And think what will be needed to build the monastery, the esplanade . . .'

'Your take?'

'The usual,' Antonio said. 'A modest ten per cent.'

'And ten from the contractors?'

'Perhaps more, perhaps less.'

'I often wonder why a middleman is necessary.'

'Because you are in Spain. Everything is achieved through connections. It's protocol. In Spain a businessman would be highly suspicious if it were not done that way.'

'You've got it all set up?'

'Not yet. I wait on your word. We worked well together with wolfram. And perfume and wheat and gasoline . . .'

Tom stared at the embryonic mausoleum and worried. The architect Don Pedro Muguruza Otaño, Director General of Architecture, had fallen ill and progress had faltered. There was a bundle of money to be made and Tom was a businessman and businessmen had to be resolute. And unscrupulous? This is, after all, going to be Franco's Valhalla and I fought against him. He watched a gang of workers emerge from the mouth of the tunnel and collapse exhausted on the rutted ground where marjoram and thyme had once grown.

Antonio said, 'I know what you're thinking. But they're better off than hundreds of thousands of Spaniards. And they're getting remission from their sentences for the time they work here.'

'They fought for what they believed in,' Tom said.

'So did I.'

'Not much of a reward for fighting for your convictions.'

'They knew what to expect.'

'Will Franco ever forgive?'

'You know what Franco said about the murder of José Antonio Primo de Rivera? *May God grant thee eternal rest, and to us may he grant none till we have harvested for Spain the seed sown by his death.* José Antonio was a great man,' Antonio said. 'He will rest here one day.' He pointed to the mouth of the tunnel. 'Alongside Francisco Franco Bahamonde.'

Tom said, 'You really did believe, didn't you?'

'Why not? The Falange was anti-capitalist and anti-Marxist. We wanted an end to class barriers. We wanted unity. We wanted a brave new Spain. Was that so wrong?'

'Maybe no one was wrong,' Tom said.

'The remains of 50,000 people who died in the war will be interred in the basilica.'

'Fascists *and* Republicans?'

'Spaniards,' Antonio said. 'Shall we work together, you and I?'

Tom gazed at the workers lying on the ground. They reminded him of exhausted miners he had seen in the coalfields during the Depression. He shook his head.

'Someone else will get the contracts.'

'Let them.'

Tom started the engine of the Dodge and drove back to Madrid.

As they approached the outskirts of the city, Antonio, anger lightly contained, said, 'I think we can still do business. Wheat and oil and machine parts are still making good profits but we've got to look to the future.'

Tom waited, swaying his body slightly as he guided the Dodge through the sparse traffic.

'Do you know what I'm talking about?'

'Oranges and lemons?'

'Close.' Antonio wound one of his curls round his forefinger. Tom glanced at him: from that angle his face had the beakiness of a predatory bird. 'Where do you find oranges and lemons?'

'On the Mediterranean coast,' Tom said. I should know, he thought.

'Millions of trees between Valencia and Alicante. Fine beaches, too.'

'What the hell are you talking about, Toni?'

'Land,' Antonio said. 'Beside the sea and going for a song. You see,' he said, releasing the watch-spring curl, 'one day soon Spain is going to become the Mecca for tourism. Our greatest asset, perhaps. And when that happens that land is, as you say in America, going to be up for grabs. Interested?'

'Why do you need me to buy real estate?'

'I don't need you,' Antonio said, 'I need your money,' his voice as tight as a guitar string.

'Broke?'

'A few unwise speculations. I overestimated the demand for wolfram after the war.'

'How much?' Tom remembered the trees heavy with blushing fruit stretching from the little railway to the lizard-grey mountains.

'A million,' Antonio said. 'To begin with,' he said. 'You're lucky: it might have been more.'

'Why am I so lucky?'

'I have another source of cash.'

'Another partner?'

'Not exactly.'

'Don't talk in riddles, Toni, you might trip over them. Who is the great benefactor?'

'I will tell you one day.' He lit a cigarette, and Tom noticed the smoke wavering as his hand shook. 'And don't forget you need me – a Spanish name up front.'

'Just you and me?'

'And Adam Fleming. He is your partner isn't he?'

'Junior,' Tom said. 'I pay him.'

'A lot?'

'None of your goddamn business. Why do you want to know about Adam Fleming?'

'None of your goddamn business,' Antonio said.

Adam prepared for his marriage with application and apprehension. He resigned from the Foreign Office because he knew that such a marriage would embarrass diplomats in Madrid or anywhere else – not only was Rosana too young for him but she was the daughter of a wanted terrorist – and from British Intelligence.

And he joined Tom Canfield's import-export business which, in the chaotic aftermath of two wars, one civil and one global, was fast becoming an empire. What helped Tom, he discovered, was Spain's isolation, which was relieved only by the Argentine with pesos and wheat. And when it came to justifying business practices Tom was plausible. 'All the holier-than-thou nations are doing is penalizing the poor and, God knows, there are enough of them. The rich will get richer' – without specifying himself – 'and the poor will get poorer. If the United Nations is so anti-Fascist why take it out on the millions who supported the Republicans? You must see that, Adam.'

And Adam did, truly, and didn't bother to debate the irony that here he was, a Fascist in 1936, who was now employed by Canfield, then a Socialist, who was now – or so he claimed – an unrepentant capitalist.

'And one day soon,' Tom continued, 'Spain will emerge from its isolation. And who will beckon it? The United States, that's who, because Spain is a bastion against Communism, the real enemy of the West. I was never a Communist, Adam, never forget that . . .' He rested his long legs on the desk in his smart new office in the Generalisimo. 'The House of Representatives has already voted to give Marshall Aid to Spain – 149 votes to 52 – and, okay, it was thrown out by a joint committee of the Senate and the House of Representatives but the breakthrough isn't far away.'

Adam thought, 'Who is the enemy?' and departed to complete the purchase of an aristocratic old apartment in a district which he could ill afford, and to see the priest who was to marry them in a cosy grey church nearby.

What astonished Adam about marriage in Spain was its absolute male bias. Article 57 of the Spanish Civil Code: 'The husband must protect his wife and she must obey her husband.' And how! Without his consent Rosana could scarcely breathe outside the marital home. She couldn't work, sue anyone, sign a contract . . . She couldn't even travel any distance unless Adam Fleming said okay. She could not, without his permission, sell any of the possessions that she had contributed to their union, nor could she expect equal control over any children they might have.

But it was the laws of adultery that really astounded him. If Rosana was unfaithful then, whatever the circumstances, she was liable to be gaoled for anything between six months and six years. If he was guilty then he was only culpable if he had fornicated at home, if he was actually living with the other woman or if his infidelity was public knowledge.

Rosana, finishing his portrait in her apartment, told him not to worry: she didn't intend to be unfaithful. He glanced at her, lips pursed, painting a line, as fine as gossamer but a line nonetheless, at the corner of one of his eyes. He searched for the line with his fingertips. How deep would it be in ten years? He would be 43, peering into middle age, and she would be, what, 30? That was more reassuring, an accepted age difference. But it was the years in between that worried him. She loved him, he didn't doubt that; she possessed deep strengths that were unaffected by the surface of life, but he had no idea in which direction they were channelled. He was thinking like a father, he told himself; think like a lover.

But not a lover in the physical sense. In Spain a girl was a virgin until her wedding night. He stood behind her; she was gazing at the portrait, stem of a thin brush resting on her lower lip. Her hair hung down to her shoulders and there was a concentrated vitality about her. She leaned against him; then with one stroke of the brush removed the line from the corner of his eye. He kissed the back of her neck.

She wiped the brush with a cloth and dropped it into a jam-jar in which the colours had blended into the colour of churned-up harbour water. She lit the gas-fire and sat in front of it while blue flames popped. He sat opposite her.

'Are you ready yet?' he asked.

'To paint full-time? I don't know. I didn't realize there were so many artists until I came back to Madrid.'

'Perhaps you should specialize.'

She said, 'I can only paint war.'

'Then paint war.'

'And the minds of leaders as they sign orders to kill children. I see children all the time,' she said, 'even when they're adults. Do you think they're proud, those leaders? Really proud?'

'They see themselves in history books,' Adam said. 'When the children are dust.'

She said, 'Mama will never forgive me; she will never come to see me again.'

'Then you must go to her.'

'After we're married,' Rosana said. 'Then I will try,' and once again Adam was struck by her single-mindedness.

'Did I seem very old to you when we first met?'

'As Methuselah. I wondered if your teeth were your own.'

'Then I would have been cradle-snatching. Now it's not so bad. Soon it will be even better. Time shrinks between two people.'

'When I was born you were thirteen times my age. The following year only seven times. Two years later only four times.'

'When I start talking about the price of cigarettes when I was in my teens I will leave you.'

He hoped she would say, 'Never leave me, Adam,' but instead she said, 'We can never be divorced in Spain. Did you know that?'

Disappointed, he said, 'A marriage can be annulled.'

She shook her head. 'Only if it hasn't been consummated.'

Shocked, he said, 'There are other circumstances. If you were under-age when you got married, for instance.'

'Not quite,' she said and smiled at him, teeth small and even.

'But there are ways around the law. There are ways around everything. I'm just discovering that. At my age.'

'Let's not talk about age.' Rosana said. 'It's boring.'

'If you're rich you can get an annulment.'

'If you're rich you can get anything.'

'But I am not,' Adam said. 'So you will have to stay with me.'

'You will give me permission to work? To paint?'

'As long as you obey me.'

Still smiling, she knelt in front of him. 'I will obey you.'

He kissed the top of her head and thought how warm and sweet her hair smelled and he wished that in Spain sharing rather than obeying was a prerequisite of marriage.

Antonio made his approach to Adam on a cold, sunlit Tuesday afternoon when Tom Canfield was entertaining an Argentinian businessman to lunch at the Cuevas de Luis Candelas.

Adam was sitting at his desk in his sepulchral office debating who to invite to the wedding when Antonio, now Tom's senior partner, came in with a bottle of Vina Pomal and two crystal glasses.

'I want you to try this,' he said. 'We're going to start exporting wine. Vega Sicilia if we're lucky because there isn't much of it around. The best in Spain. And the most expensive.'

'So why have you brought me Pomal?'

'It's very good, too. And I want to test your palate.'

Adam, who had disliked Antonio on sight – he believed that initial responses should never be underestimated – sipped the red wine. It tasted gentle and deliciously woody from its sojourn in a barrel of American oak. He nodded approvingly.

'Year?' Antonio asked.

'No idea.'

'Forty-three,' Antonio said. 'A good year.' He poured more wine into the two glasses. 'How are you settling down?'

'Well enough,' Adam said warily.

'You are very valuable to me. You fought on the right side, unlike Tom.'

'I fought on the winning side,' Adam said.

Antonio shrugged theatrically. 'Business is good,' he said, 'but it could be better. At the moment we benefit from Spain's isolation – in business every obstacle should be converted into a stepping-stone. But think how much bigger we could be if Spain was accepted throughout the world.'

'It will come,' Adam said. His thoughts strayed to the wedding. He wondered where Chimo was: he would like to invite him.

'But first Spain has to change its image. Get rid of the stigma of Nazism.' Antonio sipped his wine stealthily. 'Have you ever heard of an organization called ODESSA?'

'Vaguely.'

'Vaguely. How very English. Well, it stands for *Organisation der SS-Angehörigen*, the Organization of Members of the SS, and it arranges the escape of top Nazis from Germany. There are two routes. Bremen to Rome and Bremen to Genoa. From Italy they sail to South America. And to Spain,' Antonio said.

'What has this got to do with me?' When he had left the embassy, MI6 had been agonizing over ODESSA which had been uncovered too late to prevent the escape of Nazis such as Adolf Eichmann and, possibly, Martin Bormann.

'I'm sure you know I was a member of the Falange.'

'I had heard.'

'Well, I still am. That's how I heard about ODESSA. From a few fanatics who help the Nazis to settle here. It was all laid on years ago, of course, when thinking Germans realized that the war was lost and started smuggling their loot abroad and setting up companies under accomplices' names.'

'Do you know who these accomplices are?'

'No,' Antonio said. 'But I suspect you do.'

Adam, sipping his wine, listened to the waning noises of Madrid adjourning for lunch. Then he said, 'What if I do?'

'If we get rid of the Nazis then we're half-way to being accepted by the rest of the world. Then we can expand our company. And you will be able to keep your wife and family in style,' Antonio said, without recourse to subtlety.

'You can do that?'

'I can make a start. There are a lot of Spaniards who don't want their country to be used as a haven for war criminals. Do you have the names?'

'Some of them,' Adam said.

'Then give them to me. It can't do any harm.'

Well at least he was right in that respect, Adam thought. He went to the safe in the corner of the office and opened it.

Two days later a 45-year-old German, Otto Veit, masquerading in Madrid as a Swiss diamond merchant from Zurich, sat in an outdoor café on the Paseo del Prado drinking black coffee and cognac.

He was debating whether his hair was too obviously dyed brown, whether his features were too gentle for the role he had adopted, when a stranger approached the table.

'Señor Birrer?'

'Who wants him?' Veit asked. He stared warily at the stranger, tall and fussily elegant with a tight-skinned actor's face and curly, greying hair.

'I have a deal you might be interested in.' The stranger eased a small leather bag from the trouser pocket of his pearl-grey suit.

'How many diamonds in there?'

'One, of course. Surely everyone in our business knows that diamond can scratch diamond.' He sat down and Veit could have sworn that he could smell perfume; there was nothing, he felt, that he could admire in this man.

'Very well,' Veit said. 'Let's have a look at it.'

'All in good time, Señor Veit.'

Veit froze. 'Birrer is my name,' he said.

'Otto Kurt Veit, *Sturmbannführer* in the *Waffen* SS, born in Schwabing, the student quarter of Munich, on 23 January 1913. A founder member of the SS. Saw active service in the Rhineland in March 1936, and subsequently in Poland, Holland, France and Russia, where you were decorated with the Knight's Cross. A brave man, Herr Veit.'

Veit said, 'What do you want?'

'Help with an investment in real estate.'

'And if I don't choose to give it?'

'Then I shall report you to the appropriate authority.'

'Which is?'

'Does the name Wiesenthal mean anything to you?'

'A Jewish name?'

'He works with the US Office of Strategic Services. Hunting Nazis.' The stranger smiled charmingly at Veit. 'Last year he set up an office in Linz in Austria. Hunting Nazis. He would be very interested in *Sturmbannführer* Veit and his part in the massacre of 86 American soldiers of Battery B of the 28th Field Artillery Observation Battalion at Malmedy, Belgium, on 17 December 1944.'

'How much?' Veit asked.

For Adam the walk from the office to Rosana's apartment was a celebration. He smelled shy scents – honey and marzipan from a patisserie, water on dust from a dripping balcony of geraniums – touched the trunks of acacia trees and felt their city skins, heard the notes of a piano sprinkled from some leaning garret, tasted rain sidling in from the west. He wanted to dance with two sturdy nuns in pigeon grey, to swing from a candy-striped awning. The noise of gunfire had retreated to the armoury, the spectres to their grave.

Rosana was waiting for him outside the block. She wore her spring coat and a scarf round her hair and her face was smudged with worry. 'It's mama,' she said. 'She's been arrested.'

CHAPTER 19

The two plain-clothes policemen had waited a long time outside the stadium of Real Madrid. A week at least, only leaving to make their daily reports to the *Dirección General de Seguridad* on the Puerta del Sol when the gates were locked for the night.

The elder, whose name was Miguel, was lean and disciplined, the owner of a stiff moustache greyer than his hair; he was married to a loving, soft-fleshed wife and, as he had three hungry children to support, he was grateful for the extra food rations the police received. His colleague, Pedro, was more modestly built and the set of his mouth was more sardonic; he smoked a pipe and, when questioning a suspect, pointed it like a pistol.

They viewed their present assignment without pleasure; shared a furtive hope, in fact, that Ana Gomez would not now visit the stadium. Surely a mother would not leave it so long before she tried to contact her only son?

But still they remained, sometimes in the open, sometimes in a souped-up white Seat, or a San Miguel delivery van, discussing the fortunes of Real Madrid whom Miguel supported, and Atlético Madrid, whom Pedro supported. Or, perhaps, the dignity in the bullring of the great Manolete who had died in hospital after being gored – killed, according to Miguel, by the *aficion* who had taunted him with cowardice.

'I hear,' Pedro said with studied nonchalance as they sat dressed in blue dungarees in the San Miguel van one sunlit Tuesday, 'that you have received an increase. Fifty pesetas, bringing you up to 800 a month.'

'Your turn will come,' Miguel said. 'Think of the peasant who earns 5 pesetas a day, the mechanic who earns 20.'

Pedro took his pipe from his mouth and made a prod with it. 'Do you think she will come? Or do you think she has already made contact with the boy?'

'Not according to the boy. That one will be a great centre-forward some day.'

Pedro said, 'Do you want her to come?'

'I am fatalistic,' Miguel said and Pedro said, 'What sort of an answer is that?'

Miguel, a smile pulling his stiff moustache, said, 'Okay, so neither of us want to arrest this woman. Why should we? She is a heroine, although not many people would like to admit it. So I hope she doesn't come. On the other hand she may have already been here and that will be bad for us.'

'I don't like arresting women.'

'Fantastic. Very articulate. Why not?'

'Because they kick you in the balls,' Pedro said. 'Or squeeze them,' he said, remembering an incident in his career.'

'This woman,' Miguel said, 'won't kick you in the balls. She won't squeeze them even . . . Does that disappoint you?' And when Pedro pulled a face that was a mixture of pain and ecstasy, 'No, this woman will shoot them off.'

'You think she will come armed?'

'Wouldn't you?'

'Perhaps we should be afflicted with blindness when she comes.'

'And get demoted? I thought you wanted 50 pesetas more, not less.'

'I want my balls,' Pedro said.

'She is a good shot, this one.'

'There she is,' Pedro said.

Ana hesitated for many days before going to the stadium because she didn't trust Antonio, still less Martine, and if they had told the police that she was in Madrid then they would be waiting for her there.

She made several telephone calls but each time there was a wariness in the voice of the man on the other end of the line. 'I will get him to call you, señora. Please tell me where you're calling from,' and each time she replaced the receiver.

But she had to see Pablo. Who had she left now that Sabino had gone and Rosana had betrayed her? And when she had seen him, touched him, then she could pursue her mission.

Where were you on that night in Jarama when Jesús Gomez was shot in the back? Where were you and you and you? What sort of gun did you carry? How did he fall? With a poem on his lips?

Finally she went to a second-hand clothes shop where they stocked garments sold by wealthy Madrileños. With some of the money plundered in the mountains she bought a pair of black court shoes, a bottle-green dress of aristocratic but comfortable cut and a stole. Afterwards she had her hair dyed blonde at a salon in Calle de Alcalá.

Then, for the second time in her life, she hailed a taxi, told the driver to take her to the stadium at Chamartín and sat regally in the back looking, she hoped, like the wife of a director of an illustrious football club.

Outside the entrance she told the driver to wait. She looked around. All she could see was a black Citroën beginning to rust, a San Miguel van, its driver asleep at the wheel, and a stiff-backed old man walking a scruffy dog. She stepped out of the cab and made her way to the gate.

The gate-keeper, middle-aged with a pugilist's features, was reading a sports magazine. She handed him a fawn envelope from which a 500 peseta note protruded and said, 'The money is for you. Take it, seal the envelope and give it to Pablo Gomez.'

'Are you –'

'Take it,' she said. 'Do as I say and Pablo will bring you another five hundred.'

'I doubt whether he will be able to,' said the driver of the San Miguel van. 'May I see your papers, señora?'

Ana glanced at his companion. A smaller man, also in blue dungarees, was pointing a smoking pipe at her.

She thrust her hand into her bag.

The smaller policeman said, '*Mi madre*, she is going to shoot them off,' and there was a gun in his hand.

She thought, 'Can it end this way after so long?'

She looked at the gate-keeper. He spread his hands. She heard the taxi move away, accelerate.

The first policeman said: 'You are Señora Ana Gomez?' and when, removing her hand, empty, from her bag, she nodded, he said, 'I am very sorry. Truly.'

As they walked towards the rusting Citroën, Ana looked up at the spring sky and said, 'To think I saved one of your churches once.'

She was imprisoned in Ventas gaol in Madrid where she shared a cell with three other prisoners. What luck, she was told: Spain's 150 prisons were bulging with inmates, convicted or otherwise, some awaiting the firing squad or the garotte. At Yeserias men had to sleep together as tightly as puppies in a kennel.

The weakest of her companions was a half-starved housewife from Vallecas who had supplemented her income from recycling toothbrushes by taking in boarders wanted by the police. She was dying with patience and resolve.

The strongest was a robust black-marketeer from Andalucia with arms like thighs and a tongue curled with oaths, who had been caught throwing food parcels from a train to outwit police waiting at the next station.

Of the relative strength of the third occupant, a young prostitute with pale hair and small breasts, little could be ascertained. At night she cried in her sleep; but she laughed, too, and on occasions simulated orgasms with spectral clients.

Ana tried to isolate herself, to plan escape and vengeance, but it was not easy in a cell three metres by two, in which death was beckoned, sex dispassionately remembered and life grimly celebrated. And the Andaluz, jealous of Ana's fame, did not make it any easier to her.

'We are proud to have you with us,' she said at mealtime one day, filling her mouth with gritty rice. 'Truly we are. The Black Widow. *Hostia!* What an honour. Since you arrived we have had less to eat and a special guard outside the cell. What more can we ask?'

Ana, knowing she would have to conquer this brawny

mobster, said, 'I didn't want to be caught. It isn't my fault I'm here.'

'*Mierda!* Did any of us want to be caught?'

'Exactly. It is none of our faults.'

'But we were caught trying to fill our bellies and the bellies of our families, not fighting for a lost cause. Politics, shit, leave it to the men; it is their weakness, the weakness of Spain.'

'La Pasionaria?'

'That was during the war, when there was hope.'

The woman who was dying offered her bowl to Ana. 'Here, have this, I am not hungry.'

'You see,' said the Andaluz, 'you are indeed honoured. Nothing for the poor little *puta* here,' touching the arm of the dreamy whore. 'Nothing for me.'

Ana, pushing aside the wooden bowl, said, 'Then you are lucky: you have the build of a Miura bull.' She searched her grey prison clothes for the knife she had secreted. 'You need to lose weight for your own good.'

The Andaluz put down her bowl and stood up. 'You are not in the mountains now, Ana Gomez. There are no bandits to protect you here.'

Regretting what was about to happen, Ana, too, put down her bowl. The whore smiled expectantly; the dying woman stared into the hungry past. Ana said, 'I have killed many men; it won't upset me if I kill you.'

'I have killed no one,' the Andaluz said. 'You will be my first.'

Mother of God, there is a lot of this woman, Ana thought, as the Andaluz stood in front of her. What she regretted, she realized, was the lack of necessity of what was about to happen. The crudity. In Madrid, during the siege, and in the mountains, death had been clean and justified.

She thought all these things in the gasp of time before she thrust the small, finely-sharpened knife into the forearm of the Andaluz. Blood flowed immediately. She has more than her ration, Ana thought. The Andaluz stared at the blood with the astonishment of someone who believes that blood is the property of others.

She sat down on her straw palliasse.

'In the neck next time,' Ana said. 'Where the artery pulses,' and thought, 'God, has it come to this?' Then she handed her food bowl to the Andaluz whose face was pale and damp and said, 'From now on, let us share.'

After that she was allowed to roam in her private visions, emerging only when she sought the steadying hand of reality.

She learned that the whore had a *novio* in prison in Asturias who had helped to incite a miners' strike and was lucky to be alive; she believed that she loved him but confessed that she had never been sexually satisfied until she had taken up whoring.

She learned that the Andaluz wasn't sure what satisfaction was, only that she had enjoyed doing it with her husband, four children as a reward. She observed the woman in fatigued pursuit of death smile indulgently at such terrestrial desires.

Six weeks after Ana entered the prison the housewife's wish was granted and a newcomer was ushered into the cell.

She was a shapeless woman in her thirties, of a disposition so negative that Ana, instincts honed by a decade of survival, was immediately suspicious.

Four nights after her arrival, when the Andaluz was snoring and the whore was bucking gently in her dreams, she whispered across the space between their two bunks, 'Are you awake, Ana Gomez?'

Ana said, 'I am now.'

'I have always been an admirer of yours, Ana Gomez.'

'Then you should have joined me.'

'Easy to say. I have two children.'

'You have the exclusive rights to childbirth?'

'My children are young. Yours are almost of age.'

'You seem to know a lot about my children.'

'Everyone knows about Pablo: one day he will score many goals for Madrid.'

'And my daughter?'

'I only know that you have one.' Ana could hear the defensive reflexes in her voice. 'Wasn't she in the mountains with you?'

'And if she was?'

'I heard rumours when I was being interrogated,' the newcomer said.

'Interrogated for what?'

'Robbery,' the newcomer said. 'I stole a loaf.'

'Harsh treatment, Ventas, for stealing bread.'

'It wasn't a first offence: we have to live.'

'And these rumours . . . What were they?'

'That your daughter wants to see you.'

'Isn't it natural, that a daughter should want to see her mother?'

'It can take a long time, weeks, months, for a visitor to see a prisoner.'

'Then I shall wait with great patience. After all, I expect to be here for a long time.'

'But you would like to see your daughter?'

'I am her mother,' Ana said, thinking how ill-informed this nondescript informer was.

'I am to be questioned again tomorrow,' the newcomer said. 'If I hear anything I will let you know.' She turned on her palliasse, dispatching a rat from one corner.

The following night the newcomer, smelling faintly of wine, said softly, 'I heard more rumours today.'

'My daughter?'

'She keeps applying to the authorities for permission to see you.'

And later, after they had eaten their watery stew, when the corners of the prison were filled with snores and whimpers, she whispered, 'I think it can be arranged.'

'I would like to see my daughter,' Ana said, telling the truth but lying at the same time.

'You must know many names, many hiding places.'

'A host of them,' Ana said softly. 'High in the mountains and deep in the valleys.'

'And perhaps the judge will be lenient; perhaps you will be reunited with your daughter sooner than you think. Perhaps you will be able to see your son play, *El Flaco* . . .'

'Anything is possible in this crazy world,' Ana said, turning over, listening to the crackle and slither of the straw and wishing that just once tears would come to her eyes.

The summons came at dawn when light from the small, barred window high in the wall was beginning to explore the cell. Ana had been interrogated many times, although never this early; but it was a good time for the interrogator when dreams were still warm and the day ahead was bleak.

She washed her face in a bowl of cold water, put on her grey overalls, combed her hair that, as the blonde dye spent itself, was black at the roots, and went with the guards to an office, fashioned around a walnut desk, that smelled of cigar smoke.

The desk was too big for the sad-eyed man with the small moustache sitting behind it. He gestured Ana to a chair and began to pace the office, hands clasped behind his back. He coughed a lot – dry gasps that he tried to contain – and the fingers of his right hand were yellow with tobacco tar.

'Coffee, Señora Gomez?' Without waiting for an answer he poured some into a mug from a jug and offered her a bowl of rock-hard sugar. She wondered if he had been trained by the Gestapo during the war; there were still a few of those around, inquisitors who favoured careful foreplay.

She dropped three lumps of sugar into the mug, drained it with strong gulps and handed it back. He replenished it and said: 'I am sorry to disturb you so early, Señora Gomez, but I have to get back to Pamplona.'

So he was a hunter of terrorists. *Sección de Politica Interna* probably. 'How can I help you?' She sipped the coffee; she had not tasted coffee like it since she had left the mountains.

'In many ways. But I understand that so far you haven't been very co-operative.'

'Perhaps I haven't been approached the right way.'

He lit a cigarette and coughed smoke. 'How long were you in the mountains?'

'Eight years. Maybe nine. Quite a bite out of one's life, eh, Señor –'

'Saura,' he said.

'A shark's bite,' she said.

'Imprisonment is another bite, another shark's meal. By the

time you come out the shark will have lost interest because you will be very old and not very appetizing. Unless . . .' He inhaled deeply and with apparent distaste. 'I have read about your son in the newspapers.'

'They must not know that he is the son of Ana Gomez.'

'That won't be necessary.' He smiled and the ripples of the smile reached his hollow cheeks. 'I am a supporter of Madrid. We need that boy.'

She took a cube of sugar from the bowl and placed it in her mouth, felt it dissolve like shifting sand on her tongue. She heard a truck draw up outside, heard a woman screaming.

Saura said, 'You have a daughter, too.' He picked up a sheet of lined paper and she thought how well the newcomer in the cell had done her job and she knew that, whatever happened, she would not be in the cell when she returned. 'She is very pretty, I believe. An artist.'

'Like her father,' Ana said.

Saura consulted the sheet of paper. 'Jesús Gomez? He was a writer?'

'He painted with words,' Ana said.

Saura sauntered round the office, running one finger along the spines of law books on a shelf behind the desk. He treated the desk itself with more respect.

Turning abruptly, he said, 'Your daughter is here waiting to see you.'

She ached suddenly and sweetly. Rosana's hair, the colour mine once was, would be combed tightly and there would be a little paint under her fingernails and for a short while she would be very composed and then I will open my arms and it will be as it was a lifetime ago when the bombers were overhead and Pablo was kicking his shabby ball in the yard and Jesús was arranging his words and we were together.

She stood up. She said, 'You have been misinformed. I do not want to see my daughter.'

As she left the room he was sitting heavily behind the intimidating desk. When she got back to the cell the newcomer had gone.

*   *   *

Rosana walked slowly from the prison. It had taken her two months to be granted permission to see her mother. And then to be told, in between coughs, 'She doesn't want to see you, señorita,' and then to be asked, 'Why?'

'Because I'm going to marry a Fascist,' she had said. 'Does that please you?' And he had pressed the hollows of his cheeks with his fingertips and replied, 'No, señorita, it does not please me,' and walked away from her, coughing gasps of smoke.

From Ventas she caught a bus into the centre of the city. Gazed at the pavements and roofs that were beginning to shimmer lazily in the heat and wished that she had been able to tell her mother that she was getting married tomorrow. But I will have no family at the wedding. No parents. Antonio unavoidably detained in Switzerland – with his wife, thank God. Pablo vacationing in Malaga. Who could blame him? I deserted him. No in-laws either. Adam's sister – one of the reasons he came to Spain – married to a Portuguese and living in Lisbon. Adam's parents too infirm to travel.

So the guests will be impersonal. Tom Canfield, of course – Tom was always around – and a few of Adam's business associates, some art students and the stranger Rosana hadn't yet been able to fathom, Chimo, a war veteran like Adam. Adam had gone to great lengths to trace him through records of the Foreign Legion in Morocco. Why, she couldn't understand. Why bother with a detective in the police force who had been promoted from infiltrating the forced labour battalions in Morocco, to policing the 300,000 Spaniards outside the gaols on the mainland whose liberty was restricted?

Although Chimo dressed thoughtfully, although he was inclined to philosophize, although his greying hair smelled of the barber's shop, Rosana sensed a wildness in him that would never quite be contained by respectability. He frightened her a little and she resented whatever it was that he and Adam shared during the war.

She also resented Tom Canfield. Adam's reliance upon him. His charmed life. The honesty of his avarice. It was this honesty, she supposed, that really fuelled her resentment. Because you, Rosana Gomez, are a fraud.

She alighted from the bus and walked briskly towards her apartment to prepare for her wedding.

The marriage was darkly solemnized in a small church where light had been sacrificed to devotion, and the reception in a nearby hotel burst like a rocket in a twilight sky. Wine flowed, champagne fizzed. Teachers of sombre mien from Rosana's college flirted coyly and partnered each other in bold folk dances. Talk was fired across the table at such a pitch that only the scavenging cats listened. The students clapped martial rhythms and embraced passionately and two policemen dispatched to maintain law, order and decency stole away to the kitchens with jugs of red wine. Mothers wept, husbands of unchallenged probity told dubious stories scantily remembered from their impetuous youth and, at the height of the tumult, Adam and Rosana escaped to the waiting car, their departure scarcely heeded.

Adam drove to a small hotel 5,000 feet high in a pine forest in the Guadarrama mountains to the north of Madrid. In bed in their whitewashed, resin-smelling room he lay quietly beside Rosana, scared by her youth. Then she moved close to him and it occurred to him only fleetingly that even at such a time as this there was about her an air of detachment that was not logically the partner of passion. Then he turned to her and the disturbing thought receded and was lost.

PART IV

1950–1960

CHAPTER 20

Tom Canfield, on his way to view land at a village on the Mediterranean named Benidorm, changed trains at Valencia. And because he had an hour to wait for his connection he ordered a coffee in the buffet of the ornamental station and began to write in his diary.

5 November 1950. Yesterday the United Nations voted to end Spain's isolation, i.e., to annul the diplomatic sanctions imposed in 1946. And it is the Americans that she has to thank. They realize that, with the explosion last year of Russia's first A-bomb, with the outbreak of the war in Korea and with the attrition of the Cold War, that the West needs Spain.

This spells the end of the Republic in exile: not one European country voted against Franco. Come to that it's the end of the old resistance in Spain itself, the final blow to their ideals. I possessed those ideals once. But the Republicans had only themselves to blame.

He put down his pen. He saw himself as a young man cramped in the cockpit of a Polikarpov. He touched his hair at the temples. It was needled with grey. He was 40. He thought: 'Life is so long when you're young and peering forward, so short looking back.' He glanced at his watch: he still had three-quarters of an hour to wait. He ordered another coffee, picked up his pen and began to write again.

What now? There will still be resistance to Franco from the young, the children of the Civil War, but I cannot see it being effective until the Caudillo dies. And then? Don Juan, Pretender to the throne, still sits on the sidelines; but it seems more likely that his son, Juan Carlos, will inherit the throne. He's only 12 but he's at school in San Sebastian and it looks as though Franco is grooming him for stardom.

He screwed the top on his pen. And what of you, Tom Canfield? Have you sold your soul? He shook his head. No, I withdrew from a cause that had been betrayed by bigots. And now through tourism I'm helping to build a prosperous Spain.

Having almost convinced himself, he replaced his diary in his briefcase and walked across the steam-smelling station to the train shuddering at the platform.

He alighted at Gandía and bought a copy of the regional newspaper, *Las Provincias*. It was preoccupied, of course, with the UN vote so, waiting on the platform for the little train on which he had first travelled 13 years ago, he turned to the sports pages. *El Flaco*, he read, would soon be blooded with Real Madrid. He was the *espontáneo*, the writer recalled, who had made his debut against Seville. Would he score now that he was legitimate? The writer hoped so. So did Tom. For the sake of Rosana and her mother languishing in gaol.

The train took him through the orange groves, green fruit beginning to blush, to the station where he had once alighted in search of Josefina. He hesitated, then alighted once again.

He went first to the bar where he had made his inquiries all those years ago. There was an air of stagnancy about it; even the snacks behind the bar seemed to be loitering.

He drank a beer, watched suspiciously by the becalmed customers, paid and left. There was evidence of destitution in the streets but nothing as acute as in the cities. Nothing as abject as Madrid's shanties in the Abronigal or the Nuestra Señora de la Almudena; nothing as obscenely impoverished as the Barrio Chino in Barcelona where beggars and whores, cripples and orphans shared the congested alleys.

He found his way to the house where Josefina had once lived. The fig tree was still there in the white-walled patio, and the sky was the same autumn blue he remembered.

He knocked on the big and tidy door. The blows sounded dull like the rings of an unanswered telephone. He knocked again; in his experience there was always someone at home in a Spanish house.

Dragging footsteps. A shutter in the door opened and rheumy eyes peered through the grille. Tom asked whether Josefina's mother was at home. A voice as faint as moth's wings. Josefina's mother was dead. Who wanted to know? A friend. A breathing silence. Josefina? 'She has not lived here for a long while.' The moth's wings folded, the shutter closed.

The diminutive engine puffed sturdily. Through groves of citrus, along the ledges of lean hills overlooking valleys and windows of sea, through the bowels of mountains. It halted at stations as insubstantial as park benches and it stopped for passengers weighted beside its thin track with fuel, fodder or almonds beaten from trees that bloomed in pink and white clouds in February.

Normally the train kept good time and the occupants of farmhouses and cottages lodged in its environs arranged their lives by it. It had one disadvantage: because it was a single track one train had to withdraw into a siding to allow another to pass on its way.

That afternoon, when the towns of Oliva and Denia were well behind it and the mountain of Mongó had bowed sleepily out of the scene, the oncoming train had withdrawn into its siding, its driver waiting for the signal indicating that Tom's south-bound train had passed by.

As the train approached the siding, Tom was thinking about Irene and how calm and loyal she was and how relieved he was to be away from her for a while.

At that moment the signal at the siding fell and the north-bound train began to move forward to the main line.

Irene was constructive, too, Tom thought, an invaluable help to his business projects. I am a very lucky man, he concluded, to have exorcized youthful passion from my life.

What better relationship could there be? Amiable, sensible, sexually satisfactory.

Dusk was approaching, the horizon fading to saffron, when the driver of the train from the siding noticed the south-bound train approaching at right-angles, lights inside its carriages as cosy as oil-lamps on a winter evening. He braked.

The driver of Tom's train braked too. If he had accelerated the accident might have been avoided. As it was, the train from the siding hit the first of the three coaches behind the sturdy engine of the south-bound train. The impact severed the carriages from the engine. The engine, released from its load, continued on its way at too great a speed, failed to negotiate a curve and sailed over a cliff.

The engine from the siding butted the first coach on to its side, crushing the front and coming to rest among the passengers. A girl in Tom's compartment died and the young man accompanying her lay for a long while with one of his legs trapped beneath a wheel of the expiring engine.

Flames and sparks lit the line for a while, then settled until the rescuers arrived. By that time the moon had lit the track and its wreckage and the stars were sharp in the sky. And by that time Tom had slipped into unconsciousness.

Darkness.

Patterns of coloured light spilling and flattening against the glass of his vision. A shutter slatted luminously.

Some of the lights possess sound. They chime and caterwaul. They have pain, too. Slumberous aches and knife-thrusts.

He tries to part the slats in the shutter but they are obdurate. He opens his mouth to scream but his lips are pinned by his teeth.

The coloured lights linger on the glass. Faces. His mother patiently enduring life's disappointments. Her face is the colour of corn.

His father, mauve-skinned, beckoning him to the engine room of a bucking yacht. He feels sick.

Coloured rain streams down the glass, washing away their

faces. To be replaced by Adam, gun in hand. A shot. A discord of falling glass. Adam's white face turns scarlet and melts.

Josefina peers through the jagged hole in the glass.

The fluorescent colours were more stable now, lingering and coalescing before swimming away. He was not aware of his existence, only what presented itself to him on the dark screen. Sometimes this was a whorl and then a tunnel through which he glimpsed a rich light and heard voices that shone like stars and when this happened he strode cleanly and strongly along the tunnel.

Subsequently he became aware of distractions outside the screen. A thudding, centrally situated. An immobility at extremities. Ballooning voices. Intrusive and clinical scents. At times like this he wanted to join them and he struggled to do so and once the slats of the shutter parted and he became aware of an old and familiar light; then he closed the blinds because he was not sure that he wanted to be exposed to this commonplace radiance. It was early morning; Tom knew this from an inner perception. No birdsong, no breath of yeast or dew or coffee, but it was morning all right. He opened his eyes and Josefina said, 'Welcome back.'

Tom was moved from the Provincial Hospital in Alicante to a clinic at Busot, ten miles from the city, overlooking orange and pine trees.

His skull, he was told, had been fractured; two ribs had punctured his lungs and his femur had been broken in one leg, his tibia and fibula in the other. He was also told many times that he was lucky to be alive – fifteen passengers on the train hadn't been so fortunate.

Josefina visited him one December day when the sun had melted the frost and the waves on the sea in the distance beyond the orange groves skipped like shoals of silver fish.

She wheeled him on to the balcony of his room and kissed him on both cheeks and he held her in such a way that she could not immediately escape and he persuaded himself for that moment that they had never been apart.

She gave him his medicine and sat in front of him on a

rattan chair and he discovered that, despite 13 years of rehearsals, he had forgotten his lines. He examined her face. She was, what, 31? But although the years had pursued her they had not harrassed her. Authority had settled upon her but, even though her chestnut hair was severely combed, the severity was betrayed by tilts of compassion inside her expression. She wore a worn black coat, navy skirt and pale blue jersey.

She said, 'We seem destined to meet in hospitals.'

'I'm accident prone,' Tom said. He moved his plastered legs heavily and touched the hair that was growing, stubble-thick, from his shaven scalp.

'I was on casualty the night of the train crash. I recognized you immediately. I thought you were going to die.'

'I did once or twice.'

'The doctors didn't hold out much hope. But you're tough, you Americans.'

'I was never tough.'

'You used to fight a lot.'

'How do you know that?'

'I sensed it. You had the face of a man who fights.'

'It was only weakness,' he said. 'Fighting is always weakness.'

'And now you have grown strong?'

'Not as weak as I was.'

They listened to the hush of the faraway sea.

He said, 'Can you light me a cigarette?'

She put one between his lips. 'But there's nothing wrong with your hands,' she said.

'I know,' he said.

'Everyone in Spain smokes, but I don't like it,' she said. 'It can't be good for you.'

'What happened?' he said.

'Then?'

'Yes,' he said, 'then.'

'My father died; I had to go to Valencia.'

'Couldn't you have said goodbye?'

'There was no point,' she said.

'Who told you that? The matron?'

'She said it had happened to her. She said love never survived wars. Particularly with foreigners. It seemed to me that she was right and I thought, If he really means what he says he will write.'

'But I did. "I love you very much, do not marry anyone else. I will find a way to reach you. Then we will fly over the orange groves together."'

'Well, you found a way,' she said, and her eyes were moist. 'I never received that letter,' she said.

'I gave it to a nurse to post in Madrid.'

'The matron must have guessed. She must have taken the letter and destroyed it.'

'And read it,' Tom said.

'She meant well.'

'I searched Spain for you.'

'I know,' she said.

'You were in one of the hospitals I visited?'

She nodded and stared at the little waves on the sea.

'Then why –'

'I was married,' she said.

'I know about your marriage,' he said.

'Not everything.'

'I know he's dead.'

'You don't know everything.'

'Your mother would have told me if there had been anything more.'

'We had a son,' Josefina said.

He concentrated on his cigarette. He had not anticipated a child; he couldn't think why.

'How old is he?' Tom asked.

'Twelve. His name is Ernesto. He is a good boy. He goes to school in Alicante and he studies a lot at night. I want him to be a doctor.'

'Can I see him?' he asked.

She stared at her hospital-clean hands. Then she said, 'But you are married.'

'How do you know?'

'Your documents.'

'I thought I had lost you.'

'I am not accusing you,' she said.

'We have an apartment in Spain,' he said for no reason.

'Is she like me?'

'No, she is not like you at all. She's American.'

'Ah.'

'Don't start thinking like that matron.'

'Is she beautiful?'

'She is chic.'

'Then she is beautiful.'

'Yes, she is beautiful,' Tom said. He wanted to say, 'But I don't love her,' but he knew he wouldn't be proud of such a statement. 'We have no children,' he said.

'You would like Ernesto,' she said.

'But I can't see him?'

'There wouldn't be any point.'

'But I should like to see him.' He could have been mine, he thought. His head ached and his legs were heavier than ever.

'You are tired,' she said. 'I must go.'

'You will come again?'

'I don't think it would be a good idea.'

'What do you think is a good idea?'

'That we part now, return to our lives, forget what happened in the war.'

'We will fly over the orange groves together.'

'You must fly with your wife.'

'If you don't return I will have a relapse.'

'You mustn't tire yourself. Then you will get well.'

'I'll strip off the plaster and jump off the balcony.'

'You are happily married,' she said. 'Decently married.'

'There's no harm in sharing the past.'

'You speak very good Spanish now. Like a true Madrileño.'

'I will learn Valenciano,' he said, and he knew that, because she still lingered, there was hope.

She stood up and he felt sad about her threadbare coat.

'I must go,' she said.

'Give me your hand.'

He kissed it; it was dry and smelled of scented soap. 'You will come back?'

'That would be very foolish.'

'A deal?'

'I don't understand.'

'If you come back I will stop smoking.'

'I will think about it,' she said.

He watched her walk down the drive. Heard the crunch of her shoes on the gravel. She didn't turn back. She wore the old coat with style.

For a week he debated the possibilities. She hadn't confirmed that she would return, she hadn't said she wouldn't.

His hair grew and the plaster was cut from his legs to reveal wrinkled flesh; but the bones were knitting.

Irene continued to visit him, flying from Madrid in his Cessna piloted by volunteers from the aero club; Adam paid two visits, quick and eager with marital well-being.

I was the Socialist, Tom thought, watching him sitting beside the bed, and you were the Fascist. Now I am the capitalist and you are my employee. What next?

But Adam's assurance had its effect upon him. He began to regain his own confidence. If she doesn't come to me, he decided, I will go to her.

It was not a decision he would have made in business because it was flawed – he was undermining one of the foundations of his success, his marriage – but he determined to go ahead with it anyway.

Josefina returned the day after he had made the decision. This time she wore a new blue coat and neat shoes and he knew she could afford neither. It was raining softly and relentlessly outside and she sat awkwardly in the rattan chair beside his bed.

She gave him a box of marzipan candies. If there was one candy he detested it was marzipan. He thrust one into his mouth and chewed, bunching his cheeks with pleasure.

She said, 'You look well.'

'Don't tell me I'm lucky to be alive.'

'You're lucky you're not dead.'

'I never forgot you,' he said. 'Not for one day. Were you here all the time?'

'Madrid, Valencia and here. It was very hard at home;

someone had to work. It was impossible for my husband but no one seemed to think of nurses as reds. Then they took him away and, although I didn't know it at the time, I was pregnant. My mother looked after Ernesto at first.'

'They hated me in your town,' Tom said.

'You were asking too many questions. People got marched off the cliffs at gunpoint if they gave the wrong answers. Don't you like marzipan?'

'I thought Ernesto might like it.'

'He hates it,' Josefina said. 'You eat it.'

'So when can I see Ernesto?' he asked, chewing with spirit.

'I told him about you. He wants to see you. He's never met an American. Never met a pilot. That is why I came here today.'

'The only reason?'

'No,' she said, 'not the only reason.'

They watched the rain on the window.

'Once upon a time,' Tom said, 'I thought the Mediterranean was always blue.'

He took her hand and held it on the coverlet.

She said, 'Have you changed very much, Tomás, since we met?'

He considered this intensely, hoping that in some intrinsic way he hadn't. 'Yes,' he said, 'I have changed.'

'For the better?'

'Perhaps one day you will tell me.'

Her hand moved in his; it reminded him of a trapped butterfly.

'I have to go,' she said. 'I took time off from work. But I will come back. If you want me to,' she said.

When she had gone he swung his wasted legs out of the bed and made his way perilously to the window. This time she turned and waved.

Then he dropped the marzipan candies in the basket beside the wash-basin.

She brought Ernesto three days later. He was a thin boy with mutinous hair damped down with water and puzzled eyes behind wire-rimmed spectacles. He spoke carefully and shyly and occasionally his lips trembled when words failed to partner his thoughts.

Tom ordered vanilla and strawberry ice-cream from the kitchen and he ate it on the balcony, slowly, sampling every mouthful.

'I hear,' Tom said, 'that you want to become a doctor.'

Ernesto delayed the answer with a spoonful of ice-cream. Then he said tentatively, 'Mama wants me to become one.'

Tom glanced at Josefina; her lips were compressed. He said, 'It's a wonderful profession,' finding that the boy's shyness was infectious. 'But what do *you* want to be?' and knew immediately that this was a mistake.

'A pilot,' Ernesto said, and Josefina said, 'How can you be a pilot with your eyesight?' and Tom said, 'I knew a pilot once who had bad eyesight,' and he knew that too was a mistake. 'But if I had my life again I'd become a doctor,' he said.

The boy looked at him with polite disbelief.

'Well you couldn't become a commercial pilot with your eyesight. But there's no reason why you shouldn't fly a private plane.'

Josefina said, 'I don't think you understand. We don't even know how we're going to find the money for Ernesto to study medicine.'

Tom, wondering how many more mistakes he could make, said, 'Of course, stupid of me,' thankful that at least he had the good sense not to offer money. 'So where do you go to school?' he asked Ernesto.

'In Alicante.' His voice now had a flatness about it, as though another adult had disappointed him.

'You like it?'

'*Sí*, señor.'

'I went to school in New York,' Tom said.

'That's a long way.'

'To us,' Josefina said, 'America exists in the movies.'

'Well, I promise you it's not like the movies. But I haven't been there for a long time.'

'Would you like to go back?' the boy asked politely.

'Yes,' Tom said, 'I would,' suddenly wanting to go badly. 'Just for a visit. Spain is my home now.' He saw himself strolling down Fifth Avenue with Josefina and Ernesto; the vision surprised him and he shivered.

'Would you like to see America?' he asked the boy.

'And Mars,' Josefina said. She looked at her watch; he imagined her taking patients' pulses with it. 'We have to go.' She stood up.

Ernesto said, 'But you told me we had the whole morning.'

'I've just remembered something,' Josefina said.

Ernesto said, 'What's it like Señor Canfield? Flying, I mean.' He scooped up the last of the melted ice-cream and licked the spoon clean.

'I had a yellow biplane once,' Tom told him. 'In my day-dreams. I used to fly it into great fortresses of cloud.'

'And during the war . . . Did you shoot down many Fascists?'

Josefina said sharply, 'I told you that you must never talk about the war.'

'I think,' Ernesto said carefully, 'that I know when I shouldn't talk about it,' and his voice was wise.

'A few,' Tom said.

'We really have to go,' Josefina said.

'Can we come again?' Ernesto asked.

Tom looked at Josefina.

'Of course,' she said. 'But perhaps next time we can talk about healing instead of killing.'

Tom watched them walk, hand in hand, down the drive. The boy turned first and waved; then Josefina offered one desultory flap of her hand.

A taxi rounding the corner stopped abruptly, tyres spitting gravel. Josefina and Ernesto jumped to one side. He heard the driver swearing and saw Josefina speaking angrily with her hands.

Faintly he heard a third voice, a woman's, from inside the taxi. The invective faltered; the taxi, firing more gravel, took off and stopped below the balcony.

He watched Irene pay off the driver and walk briskly into the clinic.

The bowl that had contained Ernesto's ice-cream stood on the table like an incriminating exhibit in a courtroom. The presence of Josefina and Ernesto lingered too.

He kissed Irene and she sat opposite the wheelchair on the balcony and crossed nylon-clad legs. She wore a ranch mink and Tom remembered the poor black garment that Josefina had worn.

He faced her uneasily. 'Coffee?' He rang the bell before she had time to answer. 'How's Madrid?'

'Madrid is fine,' Irene said. 'Although you are sorely missed at the Balmoral and the Ritz.'

'And at the office?'

'Adam is coping. Under the patronage of Antonio.'

'An unholy alliance. Adam is too straight for Antonio. The sooner I get back the better.'

'Adam glows these days.'

'Good sex,' Tom said.

A nurse brought the coffee and they took their time adding milk and sugar as the atmosphere between them fell into awkward angles.

She took a cigarette from a gold case, made a performance of lighting it, blew a delicate puff of smoke. 'I get the impression,' she said, 'that Rosana is acting a part.'

'Good sexy wife? Nothing wrong with that. I should know.' The words hung thinly between them.

'I hope I'm wrong,' Irene said.

'But you never are.'

'You're in a strange mood,' she said.

'Frustrated, I guess; I want to get back to work.'

'Was that the girl?' she asked.

He contemplated the ice-cream bowl. 'That was the girl,' he said. 'How did you know?'

'The boy, the ice-cream . . . Has she changed much?'

'Thirteen years? Only Dorian Gray would have remained unchanged.'

'Did you know she had a child?'

'How the hell would I have known that?'

'You spent long enough trying to find her. You told me, remember?'

'I only knew she had a husband. He died in a Fascist camp.'

'Couldn't you employ her as a private nurse?'

'Drop it, Irene, there's a good girl.'

From the orange groves there came the lament of an Andaluz song as the pickers plucked the fruit.

She said, 'Did you know that in Spain wives often stay in the clinics with their husbands?'

'Who wants to sleep with a cripple?'

'You're not a cripple,' she said. 'You'll be walking soon.'

'With a limp, so they tell me.'

'There are two beds in your room.'

'Be my guest.'

'You sure know how to sweep a girl off her feet.'

'I'm sorry,' Tom said.

He thought about everything they had shared. How they had been friends, lovers, business associates. He didn't know of a better marriage – everyone envied them.

She stood up abruptly. 'I'll call you from Madrid.' She strode past the two beds, heels tapping briskly on the chipped marble floor.

He sat for a long time after that, listening to the songs of the orange pickers.

He walked on crutches taking some of the weight on one leg then the other. A nurse tore the plaster from his chest. His hair grew, a little greyer than before.

Christmas approached and occasionally there was frost on the lawns outside and once there was a storm and in the morning the fish-grey sea was higher in the sky.

Antonio wanted him back in Madrid, so did Adam, but he stayed on because the specialists in Alicante understood his case and in any case he still had to view the land at Benidorm didn't he?

Josefina and her son visited him twice more. When they were there he was content; when he slept he took their presence with him like a drug; when he awoke he worried, but not agonizingly the way Adam would have done.

Irene telephone twice. He was still as sorely missed as he had been; America, thanks to its support for Franco, was riding high in Spanish Government circles; France was vilified and so was Britain, whose claims to Gibraltar were daily disputed; Antonio thought that now was the time to pull off some big deals so shouldn't Tom think about returning?

'All of a sudden Antonio needs the damn Yankee.'

'He's always needed you,' Irene said.

'Not the way he does now.'

'Shouldn't you come back just the same?'

'After I've bought the land in Benidorm.'

'When's her day off?' Irene asked, and hung up.

The following day he picked up Josefina and Ernesto in a chauffeur-driven car and they drove to Benidorm.

It was the day after the storm and the unmade sea-front was littered with leaves torn from palm fronds and stones and weed tossed over the balustrade from the beach. Sea and sky merged luminously in spume and cloud; the air was salt and wet.

They made their way along the front, deserted except for a couple of beachcombers picking the detritus from the Levante beach, and two *Guardia Civil* watching them impassively through sun-glasses.

Ahead the empty beach, fringed by scrub and cacti, stretched in a scimitar to the haunches of a headland. They stopped beneath an olive tree; the outraged sea was receding and the sand was flat and clean.

Tom put down his crutches and sat on a rock. He gazed at the sea then turned and stared at the khaki-coloured land reaching to the mountains and he thought that anyone who did not invest in this forgotten place deserved to go bankrupt.

He told Josefina what he intended to do and she was not impressed. 'In Calpe a farmer gave away land by the sea because it was no good for farming. Why would anyone want to live here?'

'Have you ever heard of Miami?'

Vaguely, her hands told him.

'This could be Florida before it was developed.'

So what? demanded her hands.

'I could set up offices in Alicante. Or Valencia, perhaps.'

She shrugged.

'Aren't you interested in money?'

'Of course. Without it Ernesto can't study. But what has it got to do with me?'

He picked up his crutches. 'Let's walk back to town.'

Ahead a cluster of white buildings protruding into the sea wore the blue dome of a church like a cap.

They walked through lanes which squeezed the sky to a café called the Gambo. There Josefina ordered a paella which was served half an hour later, rice yellow with saffron, prawns curled pinkly.

'We are lucky on the coast,' Josefina said, peeling a prawn. 'We will never starve. Not like the people inland who eat grass and thistles and wild cauliflower. Sometimes they reach our hospital but they're usually beyond help. They have swollen stomachs, the starving. Did you know that?'

Ernesto said, 'It's air; their stomachs are full of air.'

Ernesto drank Casera and they drank rough red wine from the Jalon valley. The sun shone strongly through wounds in the clouds; a donkey jingling with bells and drawing a cart loaded with firewood stopped outside the café. They ate with great concentration.

Finally Tom put down his spoon. He said to Ernesto, 'Have you ever been to Madrid?'

'No, señor.'

'Would you like to go?'

'I've never thought about it.'

'I met your mother near Madrid.'

'I know,' Ernesto said. He drank his lemonade nervously.

'A long time ago. You must come to Madrid,' Tom said, 'with your mother.'

Josefina held up one hand. 'Please, Tomás.'

Men in Bible-black and women wearing shawls took their places in one corner of the café.

'Would you like to come, Ernesto?'

'It's a long way.'

'Don't tease him,' Josefina said.

Tom drank more wine; he hadn't drunk alcohol since the accident and his reason swam on it. 'Who's teasing? Perhaps one day we'll go to New York. Would you like to go to New York, Ernesto?'

'Tomás!' Josefina's voice was cold with hospital authority. 'It is the wine speaking.'

He stared into his glass. 'I'm sorry. But maybe one day . . .'

'We must go,' she said.

'I'll drop you.'

'In a car driven by a chauffeur?' She shook her head. 'What will the neighbours say?'

'I would be ashamed.'

'I'm sorry,' he said. 'You're right – it's the wine. Remind me to market it and export it to America.' He smiled. 'Coffee?'

'For you, I think.'

'Ice-cream?' to the boy.

'No thank you, señor.'

'Okay, message understood.' Tom placed money on the table. 'Let's go, as the marines say in the movies.' He stood up. Steadied himself against the table. 'Know something? I've never seen a drunk Spaniard.'

He was aware that other diners were staring at him.

Josefina took his arm. 'Don't worry about them,' she said. 'They don't understand.'

'I'm okay.' He reached for his crutches, stumbled, felt her arm strong on his. 'I'm okay.'

He saw Ernesto staring at him, saw his eyes behind his spectacles scared of adult stupidity. He made his way to the door.

The air outside was warmer now but it made him cold inside. He leaned against the wall of the café. Faces floated on the other side of the window. The car drew up.

Josefina and Ernesto got out of the car at the palm-lined promenade in Alicante beneath the Castle of Santa Barbara on its tawny perch.

Tom watched them walk towards the Barrio de Santa Cruz, told the driver to take him back to the clinic and fell asleep in the back of the car.

By Christmas he could walk with a stick. He telephoned Irene and told her that the deal with three land-owners was being clinched today and the papers would be signed in front of a notary on 27 December and felt sanctimoniously pleased that this was true. He had never realized that the *escritura*, the deeds, for land in Spain could be so complicated – four or five brothers jointly owning a cottage and its tract of land.

In the morning he met a dissenting brother who wanted two more pesetas a square metre; he knocked him down to one because that was expected of him and bought the land for next to nothing.

He lunched in a waterfront café beside the lazy palms, took a siesta in the Palas Hotel and in the evening went shopping. But what did you buy the son of a woman who regarded a gift as a slur? He wandered round the small shops beneath the castle heights; some of them were blessed with cribs or hung with tinsel in deference to Christmas but the toy-shops were geared for Epiphany because few could afford two gifts. Toys? Tom didn't think so. He stopped at a bar on the Plaza de la Luceros for a glass of wine and a *tapa*. Books, that was the answer; and faintly he perceived a way in which he might be admitted to Josefina's life; he would have to make the approach tentatively but singlemindedly.

He bought Ernesto four books. A bound volume of comics, *Pequeño Larousse* in colour, an introduction to the human anatomy and a manual on flying. He bought Josefina a bottle of perfume.

He took the presents and two bottles of Monovar red wine to her apartment on Christmas Day, taking care to dismiss the driver two blocks away. The living-room was stiff with pride, chairs straight-backed, two pictures of lugubrious monarchs on the white-washed walls, a branch of pine hung with tinsel and paper decorations in one corner. The room led on to a balcony where geraniums grew in the sunshine beside a pot-bound hibiscus and from it, through lines of washing hung like flags and jumbled roof-tops, he could see the sea.

He poured two glasses of wine while they opened their presents. She pressed the bottle of perfume to her breast, opened it and dabbed some on her wrist. She kissed him on both cheeks and he smelled her warmth and felt as he had once done when he was young.

Ernesto opened his books. He opened the flying manual first. Josefina retired to the kitchen where she clattered angrily.

When she returned, laying plates as though she were dealing cards, she said, 'So, how do you like our grand home?

Fashionable part of town, quaint even, sea views, all modern conveniences. Why, we even have a bath.'

Tom handled his words as carefully as explosives. 'It's just as I imagined it.'

But every word had a fuse. 'Or did you imagine it even more humble?'

'I imagined it as a home.'

'For strays?'

'I know you are not wealthy,' Tom said. 'Does it matter?'

'Don't you ever wonder why life is so unfair?'

'Often,' Tom said. He raised his glass. 'But we're happier here today than most of Mankind.' He raised his glass. *'Feliz Navidad.'* He drank and gazed at the sunshine imprisoned in the wine and it settled his mind.

She served a broth followed by *puchero*, rice with boiled chicken, meat balls and vegetables. He felt Ernesto watching him but now he did not feel awkward under his scrutiny. Turron made from almonds and honey, coffee and glasses of Muscatel followed. Holy music issued from an antique radio; they played parlour games; evening settled gently. Stars glimmered above the roof-tops.

Tom told Ernesto about flying and Josefina let them explore the sky together. Ernesto went to bed at eleven and, when his room was thick with sleep, Tom kissed Josefina, held her face in his hands and said, 'What are we going to do?'

Three days later he returned by train to Madrid, passing through Albacete where he had once lingered on his way to war. Today the small stations where crowds had chanted *'No pasarán!'* were deserted.

The rhythm of wheel on track made him drowsy but blades of unease kept him awake. He had no idea what he was going to say to Irene, only that he didn't want to hurt her. The perfect marriage . . . How we were envied.

Still wondering what to say, he opened the front door of the apartment. He felt the emptiness at once, a silence sealing the past.

The note lay on his pillow.

CHAPTER 21

To the young, the old, venerated, despised or tolerated are a different race. Rosana tried valiantly to include her husband in her generation but she was defeated by the Civil War.

To her contemporaries the war was an obscenity that should be buried in the dust of history. It had devalued their birthright and debased their respect for their elders. But at 37 Adam was a veteran of that conflict. And there was no way in which she could introduce him into the clandestine world she inhabited outside her marriage.

Besides, he would realize that, although she was dutifully fond of him, she had become his wife to occupy a position where she could rally the voice of protest undistracted by the hungry pains of survival. To forge freedom as bright and true as a Toledo blade.

Art was her accomplice, Adam's trust her ally. She told him that modern painting techniques were outstripping her talents and, smiling with indulgent pride, he gave her money to attend classes. She took herself to cellars of dissent and intrigue in the old university quarter of Madrid, San Bernardo. There, beneath a cutlers in the Calle de los Cuchilleros or a second-hand bookshop in the Calle de los Libreros, she listened hungrily to a bearded and tormented young man named Alfonso.

Alfonso raged against capitalism and Fascism and the bourgeois and the Opus Dei and the exploitation of the needy and his anger greatly agitated the young people sitting at his feet sharing cigarettes and *porrónes* of wine.

But his targets were abundant commodities, available by the basket to any orator, and if Alfonso hadn't been driven by an overriding obsession, Rosana might not have listened so acutely. Solidarity was what fuelled Alfonso, curled his tongue like a scorpion's sting, possessed his articulate fingers. An end to schisms and splintered beliefs.

'The Fascists don't have to divide and rule: we do it for them. If we had a single voice,' arms outstretched, beard snapping, '*they* would run, hands clapped to their ears, deafened by truth.'

And Rosana, peering through the cigarette smoke layered like sheets of slate, nodded wisely. An end to divisions. Hadn't her family been devastated by them? If the Republic had been united it would have won the war. Her father might be alive; her mother would be free; her brother would visit her.

After the meetings Alfonso collected money, a few centimos from students and the fee for her non-existent art classes from Rosana; then he took her to smoky cafés where, in the heat of his fervour, he sometimes gripped her wrist so hard that he hurt her fingers. But she didn't object: there was about this man, with high cheekbones and soft black beard faintly streaked the colour of cinnamon, a purpose that she had hitherto only detected in her mother.

'Do you know who rules Spain?' he asked, as he poured rough wine from an earthenware jug.

'The Falange?'

Alfonso shook his head violently. 'Franco keeps their wings neatly clipped: he doesn't tolerate rivals.'

'Who then?'

'The Opus Dei,' Alfonso declared. 'The brains of the Church.'

Rosana, who knew little about the Church, only that a priest had once been kind to her in the village in La Mancha, said, 'They are the enemy, too?'

'They have penetrated the universities, they combine religion with politics, a heady mixture. They may take over one day.'

'I thought you said they ruled Spain now,' Rosana protested. It was not always easy to follow his spiky reasoning.

'If Franco is behind the Church and they are behind the Church then it must be so.'

'And the Monarchists?' Rosana could see no harm in a monarch ruling over a united land of equal opportunity.

'Unless we combine forces we will have another Bourbon on the throne. A puppet of the Fascists.' He clasped her wrist tightly. 'More wine?'

'It is too strong for me,' Rosana said.

'You, too, are strong, like your mother.'

'She is obstinate.'

'Can you blame her? You married a Fascist!'

'Do you hate me for marrying a Fascist?'

'We are using him are we not? He has money. He has the ear of the Fascists. We can learn much from him.'

'I wish I had known him when he was young,' she said.

He drank the rest of the wine. His eyes glowed as he stared at her. He held her wrist more gently.

Alfonso lent her banned novels and introduced her to controversial literature: *La familia de Pascual Duarte* and *La Colmena* by Camilio José Cela, the first invoking the poverty of Extremadura, the second privileged life in Madrid. He took her to the underground theatre and cinema.

Towards the end of February 1951, he asked her to accompany him to Barcelona. 'You will witness a miracle,' he told her. 'The first concerted protest against Francoism. The beginning of the end.' She told Adam that she wanted to attend an art seminar and on 26 February she went by train with Alfonso to Barcelona.

They stayed in a small apartment owned by a friend of Alfonso near the harbour. On the night they arrived half a dozen men who carried themselves intensely and indignantly called at the apartment. They greeted Alfonso affectionately but not, Rosana suspected, with the reverence he had hoped for. What did he expect? He was a mere Madrileño! And they worried about her.

'She has no place here,' said Jordi, a fierce trade unionist with a cast in one eye, as they sat down at a table in a small room piled high with political tracts and Coyote westerns.

'Why? Because I am a woman?'

'We know nothing about you.'

'I am married to an Englishman who fought for the Fascists. Does that satisfy you?'

'Are you serious?'

'Ask Alfonso.'

Their heads turned towards him.

He stroked his soft, cinnamon beard. 'It is true.'

Rosana said, 'In any case, what does it matter? You're only here to discuss tram fares.'

She had been disappointed when Alfonso had told her that the protest was about increased fares.

Jordi, on surer ground, said, 'You don't understand. *"They,"* the ubiquitous enemy, "talk about Spain as an entity. We say, *One Spain? Then equal for all,"'* quoting from the leaflet in Catalan and Castilian that had been strewn and pasted all over Barcelona.

'You're protesting just because the fares are cheaper in Madrid? Couldn't you have found a more noble cause?'

'It is one that appeals to the people. They can identify with it by refusing to take a tram on 1 March. Can you imagine the scene? Hundreds of thousands of workers walking to their factories and offices. The first mass protest by Spaniards from all trades since the end of the Civil War.'

'If you had decided to take over the trams and drive them yourselves I could have understood.'

'You are a foolish woman. Do you want a massacre, a blood-bath?' He glared crookedly at her.

Alfonso held up his hand with the air of someone who has been savouring a revelation. 'Do you know who Rosana's father was?'

They did not.

'Tell them,' Alfonso commanded Rosana.

'Does it matter?'

'That your father fought and died for the Republic? Of course it matters.'

'The Civil War is history,' Jordi said.

'That his anti-Fascist poetry was read all over free Spain?'

'So?'

'That his wife was Ana Gomez, the Black Widow?'

Rosana listened to them breathing, deliberating.

Jordi turned to Rosana. 'Is this true?'

'He does not lie,' Rosana said.

'She fought too long, that one.'

'She had no alternative. They would have thrown her in gaol if she had given herself up.'

'They would have released her after a few years; she wouldn't still be in prison.'

'How is she?' a young revolutionary with a fierce moustache asked Rosana. 'She is a legend, your mother.'

'She is well enough,' Rosana said, lowering her head because she hadn't seen her mother since she was imprisoned.

'Still full of spirit?'

'She will never change.'

Alfonso leaned back in his chair, hands behind his head. Then, with an orator's timing, said, 'Tell them about the rest of your family, Rosana.'

'I don't understand.'

'Your brother.'

'Keep him out of it,' she said angrily.

'Why? Because he will humble mighty Barcelona.'

'Stop talking in riddles,' Jordi said.

'Her brother is *El Flaco*, and he's playing his first game for Real Madrid against Barcelona tomorrow.'

They whistled and shook loose-wristed hands. 'Is this true?' Jordi demanded. 'Are you really so well related?'

'He is my brother,' Rosana told him. 'And there will be more action when he takes the field than there will be during a protest about tram fares.' She stood up abruptly. 'I'm going.'

'I thought you wanted to stay,' Alfonso said.

'What ever gave you that idea?' She grabbed a handful of Coyote westerns and threw them on the table. 'Read those. They might give you some ideas.'

'Where are you going?'

'To buy a ticket to see *El Flaco* play tomorrow,' Rosana said, striding out of the room.

Ernesto Villar settled his bulk in a cane chair in Pablo's studio apartment near the Bernabeu stadium at Chamartín and regarded his protégé fondly.

Pablo was reading an article in a sports magazine about the post-war stars of Spanish football – César, Panizo, Gainza and Zarra – but Villar knew that he wasn't concentrating. How could he? A young man, just 18, about to play his first senior game. And against Barcelona, historic foes.

Ernesto lit a cigarette. His doctor had advised him to cut down smoking but he had been cultivating his perverse image too long. He was grossly overweight but he had no intention of dieting: since he had photographed Pablo Gomez that day in Seville, his bulky presence had acquired a certain majesty, as though it had arranged itself around his new sense of destiny.

Well, that would be fulfilled tomorrow after three years of perseverance. Compiling for Pablo a past that was unconnected with his mother; making sure that he studied, exercised and ate sensibly; processing the girls who wrote and telephoned and lay in ambush; screening him from the perils of fame.

And in Spain today that fame could be overwhelming. Bullfighting was on the wane, its popularity eroded by entrepreneurs boosting indifferent matadors who fought indifferent bulls, often with their horns shaved to make them less lethal. Football was now the sport. Even Franco was said to listen regularly to 'Match of the Day' and those who reached its pinnacles received the same adulation as film stars. Especially if you were skinny with razored good looks and a single-minded determination that scorned adoration.

Ernesto had only betrayed his newly acquired dignity once. That was when he had brought Encarna, the girl with whom Pablo had been staying in Seville, to Madrid, photographed them together outside the stadium and sold the picture extensively in Spain.

Pablo, staring at the photograph in one of the sports journals, had said, 'I didn't realize that was just publicity,' and Ernesto, feeling a cold current of contempt had said defensively, 'What the hell did you think it was?' and Pablo, in a distant voice that frightened Ernesto, had replied, 'I thought it was something special.'

Ernesto stubbed out his cigarette, crossed one plump thigh across the other and said, 'So, how do you feel?'

'Did it have to be Barcelona?'

'It couldn't be helped. Three injured players. Score the winning goal and you'll make history.'

'Miss an open goal and I'll be crucified.'

'Daunted?'

'Maybe.' He felt the soft stubble on his chin. 'But it's not the right word. I just want to score goals, that's all, and when I think about it, I feel a tightness in the chest. I often dream about an open goal and I feel that tightness and I can't breathe . . .'

'Put the ball in the back of the net; then you will start breathing again.'

'Sometimes I can't believe what has happened to me. Was it luck, Ernesto? Are there other young men in villages and towns all over Spain just as good as me? Would I have made it if it hadn't been for you?'

'You would have made it,' Ernesto said. 'Everyone has luck: it's knowing what to do with it that matters. You were lucky to be born with the muscles in the right places, with the right instincts and reflexes. But you knew what to do with that luck: you became an *espontáneo*.'

'Would you have liked to be a football player, Ernesto?'

'I'm one of the world's spectators. There are many of us. And tomorrow they will all be behind you.'

'Even Barca supporters?'

'They might not show it but they will be behind you because you are what we might all have been.'

'And will all the Madrid players be behind me?'

'I think you know the answer,' Ernesto said, shifting his bulk on the chair, making it look fragile. 'It's a tough game. What would you feel like if you were injured and you saw an 18-year-old take your place and score a goal? You would wonder, wouldn't you, if you would ever get your place back.'

'That player should have anticipated what would happen one day. I do already.'

And Ernesto believed him.

This is what the bull feels like, Pablo thinks, as he trots through the tunnel leading on to the pitch at Les Corts stadium in Barcelona in his snow-white strip, as daylight explodes around him, as he hears the baying of the crowds and sees them layer upon layer, staring at him, as fireworks explode, tongues of flame licking the drifting smoke.

The team poses for cameramen; photographers trail him across the pitch, snapping pictures. He kicks a ball about a little, getting the feel of it. Hears his name in the throats of the crowd. The two captains shake hands, the coin is tossed; Barca choose which end they want, Madrid to kick off. Him. Yes, he knows what the bull feels like.

Ball at his feet, he slips two tackles, but is dispossessed by the third. There is a hardness about this game that he has never known before. He falls. Hears the shouts. The stadium erupts. The referee waves play on.

Barcelona in their blue and purple strip converge on Madrid's goal. A diving save by the Madrid keeper. He punts the ball upfield. It's trapped by a half-back. He passes to Pablo who is on-side, just. Pablo misses the pass and hears the collective gasp from the crowd. The ball arrives at the feet of a Barcelona full-back. A long pass upfield. A first-time shot from a Barcelona forward.

Barcelona 1 – Madrid 0.

And if you trace the goal back it began with Pablo's miss.

A Barcelona player ruffles his hair. 'Don't worry *chaval*, it was a lousy pass.'

At half-time that is still the score. Pablo walks off the pitch, staring intently at the grass. The pep-talk from the trainer is harsh and just.

When the players re-emerge the sun has disappeared behind fast clouds coming in from the sea and rain is falling.

He tackles a swift Barcelona forward but it isn't like tackling in training or in the junior games in which he's played – the player rides the tackle and speeds on his way and Pablo hears jeers. He is too young, too skinny.

He chases the ball, captures it and starts a long run upfield. But this isn't his role: he is an instinctive striker, a player who anticipates so that he is there as the long or the chipped pass is fed to him. He is in the team because of this instinct, because of his reflexes, because of his shot.

He dummies, swerves and he is in front of the goal and the

keeper is crouching and, although the crowd is baying, there is an area of quiet in his hearing, a jig-saw piece of clarity in his vision.

Then he is on the ground – felled or fallen, he knows not – but he hears the whistle and the referee is pointing at the penalty spot, waving aside the protests of the Barcelona players.

A veteran half-back takes the kick.

Barcelona 1 – Madrid 1.

One shot at goal. That's all I ask, God.

The ball comes to him. Swerves in the air, bounces badly on the wet pitch, but he has it. He shoots, Straight at the keeper who gathers it against his chest.

The floodlights are on now and the ball soars high into the rain falling in their radiance.

A Barcelona forward traps it, turns, rides a sliding tackle . . .

Barcelona 2 – Madrid 1.

Five minutes before the whistle for full-time. *El Flaco* will not win this one for Real. *El Flaco* will not play again.

The rain thickens, streams down his face. He chests the ball, shoots – wide. The sigh from the stands is anguished.

Two minutes. And Barcelona are on the attack. Pablo goes in for the tackle, wins the ball but crosses the touchline. A throw from a blue-and-purple shirt high into the rain. A Real full-back heads it. The game deteriorates into desultory mid-field skirmishes. And now it's into injury time. There is movement in the crowd as spectators make for the exits. They are wise because there cannot be more than 30 seconds left.

Then Pablo has the ball, it is as old as the leather on the soles of his shoes, and he is making a run across the yard in the Tetuan quarter of Madrid and there are bombers overhead and now he is in the courtyard in the village in La Mancha and there are the gate-posts. And the village kids are coming at him but he wrong-foots one of them, slips a tackle and the quietness is frozen again in his skull and the jig-saw piece is back in his vision, up there in the top left-hand corner of the gate-posts . . .

Barcelona 2 – Madrid 2.

And his eyes are tight shut and he is thankful on this winter day in Les Corts stadium that the players crowding round him can only distinguish the rain streaming down his cheeks.

Still sharing the goal with him, Rosana made her way through the rain to the main gate. Had he felt her willing it? Invoking the closeness that had once accompanied them on the straw mattress in the village in La Mancha so that, staring at the night through the skylight, they had seen the same star? Hardship had given them that, she reflected as she pushed her way to the front of the crowd behind the police. The coach carrying the young gods from Madrid, elevated and exalted, approached the exit. Some smiled, some waved, some appeared unaware of the adoration concentrated on them. Two drenched girls beside Rosana shouted, '*El Flaco.*' They shared a banner, streaked black letters on white. PABLO TE QUEREMOS. Pablo waved hesitantly. Then he noticed her. She saw the recognition on his face and, momentarily, infinite sadness. Then, with one marionette movement, he turned his head and stared ahead. The coach, brake lights stammering, disappeared into the rain and the two girls rolled up their banner and went home.

That night Alfonso tried to make love to Rosana. She wasn't angry. Why should she be? It was a compliment, wasn't it? When he became loud in his avowals, for he was a little drunk, and when she protested equally loudly, Jordi came into the room.

Rosana said, 'He's trying to get into bed with me.'

'He always had good taste,' Jordi said. 'Come on, Alfonso,' putting his arm round his shoulder. 'Save your persuasive oratory for the platform.'

Alfonso walked submissively with him to the door.

Turning, Jordi said, 'Does you husband know you're here?'

She shook her head.

'Do you love him?'

'There has never been anyone else.'

'That wasn't what I asked, but it will do. He should be proud of you. I hope he is.'

March 1, 1951. The hour before dawn is not a time for protest. It is the period, rather, for flight, as dreams and spectres run from the night; any policeman will tell you that this is the time to catch a fugitive. And, indeed, the protest in Barcelona as the stars began to fade was more apologetic than heroic. How can you be mettlesome walking down a slumbering street carrying a *bocadillo* and a bottle of beer in a basket vowing not to go to work by tram? But numbers rally the shrinking spirit. Martial anthems sound down the years, the ring of hob-nailed boots on cobblestones is heard, the snug threat of bolt thrusting into breech. To hell with authority, the devil take your tramcars.

All over the city groups gathered and multiplied and, chanting defiance in the light of the new day, marched to factory and office, shop and stall. But, Rosana thought, there was more than mere protest in their voices, in their strut: these workers were reapers on their way for the first time since the Civil War to harvest a crop of freedom.

She walked with a group of construction workers, many of them members of the PSUC formed in 1936 by the merging of the Catalan Communist and the Catalan branch of the PSOE, the Socialist party. She walked beside Alfonso and she respected him again; his was the voice of fervour and sanity; both he and Jordi had been right about the boycott. Why invoke death and suffering by violence?

The light strengthened and with it the voice of rebellion. She sighed, if her mother could see her now, but she doubted whether Ana would ever forgive: her contempt was armour-plated in a war that had been lost. Nor was she sure that Pablo would ever greet her as a brother. How could he? Their mother had talked to him about Adam as a preacher sermonizes about the devil. And didn't I desert him in La Mancha?

Rosana glanced around her. Banners had unfurled, fists were raised high. The night had been washed away and the day was fresh and there was a smell of baking bread on the air. I will paint this, she thought. And the picture will be exhibited in the Prado when Spain is free and I take my seat in Parliament.

Five days later – the day that the citizens of Barcelona finally won the battle of the tram fares – Rosana went to the Palacio de Oriente in Madrid to hear Franco address the Second Congress of Workers.

She stared curiously at the Caudillo. According to some he was a Christian crusader and arch enemy of Communism who had ushered Spain into an era of stability; according to others he was a Fascist dictator who had brought stagnation to Spain and drowned dissent in blood.

She was a little disappointed. He was smaller than she had anticipated and plumper. His moustache was a postage stamp, his voice high-pitched. But he had become a general at 33! And he had, as far as she could make out, backed the Republic when it was first established in 1931. If Calvo Sotelo, the Finance Minister, hadn't been assassinated in 1936, he might not have joined the Nationalist plot from the Canaries where he had been virtually exiled, flown to Morocco and crossed the Straits of Gibraltar to wage war.

Much to her regret, Rosana found that there was much to admire about Francisco Franco Bahamonde. Rosana wasn't even sure that he was a true Fascist. Hadn't he rebuffed Hitler, given refuge to Jews in World War II and subsequently eroded the strength of the Falange?

What's more he was a family man. Had written a movie script, *Raza*, in which he depicted his mother as the spirit of Spanish womanhood. Enjoyed the company of his wife and daughter and grandchildren.

After Franco's address, Alfonso took Rosana to a conspiratorial bar in the Calle de Toledo where he ordered a *café cortado* for her and a home-produced absinthe for himself.

After his second absinthe he laid his hand on hers. She felt its warmth and the hard shininess of the palm. She examined the way the moustache of his beard swept smoothly and piratically down to its lower reaches. How naked lips appeared in the midst of a beard.

'We make a good pair, you and me,' he said.

'There are some people who shouldn't wear beards,' she said. 'It makes them look ... heavy. Adam is one. A moustache wouldn't suit him either: it would be a stranger on his face.'

'Do you love him?'

Rosana sipped her coffee. Two tables away a couple kissed in the gloom.

She said, 'Tell me what you want to know, Alfonso.'

He ordered another absinthe. He poured water into it and they watched the water turn to yellow milk. Ice tinkled in it like a wind-chime.

'You married him,' Alfonso continued, 'because you needed position. A respectable base from which to operate. I am not talking out of turn – you told me these things.'

'I'm a good wife,' Rosana said.

'In every way?' He tilted his head.

'We live as man and wife.'

'As it should be.'

'I asked you what you wanted to know. Does it take three absinthes to give you the courage?'

'Your husband is well connected. He was, after all, a Fascist. And he is in business. Big business. Now there is no such thing as big business without a few ... considerations.'

'Bribes?'

'Call them what you will.'

'And you want me to . . .'

'It would help our movement,' Alfonso said. 'There is nothing quite as effective as a scandal to demoralize an enemy.'

'I can't do it,' she said.

'You will have to try. You did after all give your word.'

'To betray him?'

'To use him. You can stay happily married – *if* that's what you want – and he will never know that it was you . . .'

'He is a good man,' Rosana said.

'Look,' said Alfonso, moving his hand gently on hers, 'I understand that. We all have ideals. It's the way they're manipulated that matters. The end product. How many thousand idealists are there in prison in Spain at the moment? How many have been tortured and executed because of their ideals? Do you want that to continue?'

She shook her head slowly.

'In six days,' Alfonso said, 'there is going to be a mass protest in Barcelona. A strike, not just a boycott. The beginning of the beginning . . . I want you to come.'

'Impossible.'

'Adam?'

'Two art seminars in Barcelona, within two weeks?'

He spread his hands, acknowledging defeat, but not, she felt, with any deep sense of disappointment. 'But don't forget what I said.'

'About corruption?'

'Even now innocent men and women are being tortured.'

'I can't do it,' she said.

'I understand,' he said. He finished his drink and the cube of ice clicked against his teeth. 'In fact I admire you for your loyalty.'

He paid the bill and left.

Inside the gaol, Ana constructed a life that defied the passing of the years. It had a routine – relieved by the occasional visit from Pablo who came disguised with cap and smoked glasses – as predictable as any housewife's; modest pleasures that gradually engendered a parochial contentment; and a purpose without which even the most ingenious intellects expire.

The purpose was the pursuit of the Fascist who had shot Jesús in the back nearly 20 years ago, and she campaigned from her cell with the diligence of an ambitious but deskbound general.

She had little hope of release under an amnesty, but to each prisoner departing into the intimidating world outside she entrusted an assignment – and a reward from the corner bank in the district of Tetuan where she had deposited money taken at gun-point in the Pyrenees. There hadn't been that many units fighting at Jarama and she instructed some, through their menfolk if necessary, to identify every one.

Then every *general, colonel, capitán, alférez, brigada* and *soldado*.

At the same time she tried to establish what weapons each unit had been using. The bullet that had killed Jesús had been fired by a Star RU 9 mm sub-machine-gun; that helped because it had never been standard issue.

The information her emissaries obtained was relayed either by the prisoners themselves on their return – some had come to prefer disciplined leisure to the rigors of survival – or by newcomers whom they had contacted.

From these assorted couriers, thieves, brawlers, whores, agitators, she learned about the protests – 'as infectious as rabies', according to a strident tart – that were spreading across the country.

She heard, too, about the strike by 300,000 workers in Barcelona who had downed tools and invaded the Ramblas and the Plaza de Cataluña.

'You should have been there,' said the whore who was not renowned for her tact. 'They sang the Internationale and set fire to cars. Then the cavalry charged, scattering us.'

From a thief, a sturdy mother of five who had been caught stealing vegetables in a street market, she learned more about the spread of protest. Student demonstrations in Madrid and strikes in the Basque provinces where a woman protesting about the price of eggs was badly wounded when shots were fired in front of a shoe factory. Hundreds of workers had been arrested, including members of the CNT and UGT and members of the Basque Nationalist movement. Sabino?

But a political agitator with pale, outraged features was not optimistic about the outcome. Churchill was back in power in Britain, he would help Spain become a member of the UN, 75 members of the CNT had been flung into prison for up to 30 years, five of them executed, and tourists were beginning to arrive to help the economy.

'Don't you want the economy helped?' Ana asked curiously.

'Only if it helps the workers.'

'And won't it?'

'Has the Black Widow lost her reason?'

From a woman with the face of a nun who had stabbed her

philandering husband, Ana gleaned the small print of poverty and repression. Shanty towns still festered on the outskirts of Madrid, visas were still needed to leave Spain; you weren't allowed to give a bar or a cinema a foreign name . . .

Is it so different to Russia? Ana wondered.

In the autumn of 1953 the agitator returned to the prison indignantly forecasting prosperity for Spain. The United States with its new president, Dwight Eisenhower, had agreed to give Spain $226 million for the fiscal year of 1954. The price: the establishment of military bases on Spanish soil.

The agitator had been arrested when Franco, Grand Cross of San Fernando on his uniform, had appeared five times on the balcony of the Palacio de Oriente to acknowledge the acclaim of the crowds in the square.

'We have to continue to protest,' the agitator said.

'Even though we are becoming prosperous?'

'Ask the peasants in Extremadura if they are prosperous.'

'Then they should come to the cities.'

'And live in hovels made of packing cases? Only a country priest would get a decent home in a city.'

Ana remembered ancient hatreds. 'Is the Church as unpopular as ever?' Ana attended Mass every Sunday and prayed to her own God, who, as the years melded, came to look more and more like her own Jesús.

'Of course.'

'You forget how out of touch I am.'

'The Church in Spain, Ana Gomez, is a political party. Never forget that. Never forget the power of the Opus Dei – they even tell the Government what to do.'

As Ana lay on her bunk, staring at the familiar landscape of the wall, its rippled dunes and parched river-beds and oases of mould, hope matured into purpose; and by the December of 1955, when Spain was admitted to the United Nations and many of Franco's enemies lost hope, it had achieved a fine numerical exactitude: on the 16th of that month, her 47th birthday, she narrowed down the names of the possible killers of Jesús to 100.

CHAPTER 22

On Adam Fleming's 40th birthday he threw a party. It was a date that he would once have anticipated with misgivings, admission into middle-age. But now he dismissed the calculations of the calendar: he felt as young as he had when he had argued his way from university into war. And the age difference between him and Rosana had shrunk – 27 was an acceptable age for the wife of a 40-year-old.

He played tennis, socialized, debated energetically and travelled – to buy land for Tom Canfield and Antonio Ruiz at the old lace-making town of Blanes on the north-east coast and the small town of Torremolinos, home of Malaga's waterworks, in the south.

He got back from Torremolinos on the morning of the party. It was a hazy June morning, the sun just beginning to burn through blue gauze, and Rosana was supervising the caterers on the sprawling balcony where potted plants grew lushly and birds sang in cages.

Rosana, wearing a blue blouse and skirt, checked the guest list. Tom Canfield, Antonio and Martine, art students from the college where Rosana now taught, a couple of first secretaries from the British Embassy – both, Adam suspected, MI6 – two or three high-ranking Madrid civil servants from the Ministry of Trade, Swiss, German and American businessmen, Chimo . . . Rosana tapped her teeth irritably with her pencil.

'What have you got against Chimo?' Adam asked.

'He was a Fascist.'

'So was I.'

'You've changed. He's still a Fascist. And secret police?'

'Someone has to keep law and order. Look what happened in February last year . . .'

'And what did happen? The Falange candidates were beaten in the student elections at Madrid University. So what did they do? Try and get them elected by force.'

'And what did the others do, the *Sindicato Español Universitario*?' asked Adam, who had been on the streets when the two factions clashed on Alberto Aguilera. Jeeploads of police had arrived, a student had been shot.

'What did you expect them to do? Lie down and be trampled on? The Government has got to realize that times are changing. Strikes, protests, demonstrations . . .'

'The Government does realize it. Franco's appointing younger ministers, pulling the teeth of the Falange, opening up to foreign trade, thanks to pressure from the Americans . . .' Adam frowned. 'Anyway, since when have you been interested in politics?'

'I don't go around with my eyes shut.'

'Then close them today: it's my birthday.'

He opened a bottle of sparkling Spanish wine which was champagne in everything but name. They touched glasses. 'Thank you for the present,' he said.

'You really like it? People don't always like true likenesses. That's why professional portrait painters flatter them – to get paid.'

'It's as you see me. That's what matters. How many men get to know how their wives see them?'

'It's the expression that counts,' she said. 'The looking inwards. You often do that. I sometimes wonder if something is worrying you. Something I don't know about.'

'You know everything there is to know about me.'

'I doubt it. Not even you know that. What is ethical and what isn't, for instance. That must be difficult to judge in business.'

'The difference between business practice and fraud?'

'Bribe or gift . . . Is that the sort of thing you're thinking about when I see you looking in upon yourself?'

'Perhaps,' Adam said. 'Among other things. I didn't know I was so transparent.'

'Look at your portrait,' Rosana said. 'Perhaps you should share some of your worries.'

Adam kissed her. 'I'll do that.' But he experienced a frisson of unease; he couldn't understand why.

He poured more wine. Caterers in white jackets and black trousers laid out plates of smoked salmon, cold meats and potato salad. The birds in their cages sang as though they were free and water dripped from geraniums. The sky, perched on the roof-tops, deepened to hot blue.

The first guest was Chimo. He wore tailored grey trousers, a belt with a Germanic buckle and a waisted blue shirt; his greying hair had been recently barbered, and a dentist had fixed his broken teeth; but to Adam he still looked like a soldier of fortune. A murderer, Adam remembered. Who wasn't in the war?

Chimo put his arms round Adam's shoulders and embraced him, an *abrazo*. 'You don't look a day older than 60,' he said, and gave him a present, a tie with perpendicular silver stripes that he could never wear, a rejected gift, probably, that had offended Chimo's own sartorial taste.

'Champagne?'

'Whisky,' Chimo said. 'Anybody who's anybody in Spain drinks whisky. Didn't you know?'

'I don't mix in the same circles as you.'

Chimo watched Rosana moving away. 'She doesn't like me, does she?'

'You sensitive? I don't believe it.'

'No,' Chimo said, 'she doesn't like me.' He shook his head sadly. 'Is she jealous, Amado?'

'Of you?'

'Of the past.'

'We should all forget the past.'

'And you and I know that is impossible. It always returns, whispering at night.' Chimo drank neat whisky. 'Some family, that. The Black Widow, *El Flaco* – they say he will play for Spain next year. A determined family, Amado. *Mi madre*, how determined they are!'

Tom Canfield, nearing 50, bending only slightly under the weight of the years, came on to the balcony. He punched

Adam on the shoulder. He was very Spanish, Adam thought. He gave Adam a pair of gold cuff-links shaped like pistols. 'For my frustrated executioner,' he said.

'Maybe I should have pulled the trigger.'

'There will be other opportunities.'

'Champagne?'

'French?'

'What happened to those simple tastes?'

'I discovered money.'

'And has it brought you happiness?'

'You know the answer to that,' Tom said.

'How is she?'

'Great. I left Alicante yesterday. You must come to the wedding.'

'Divorce first?'

'Annulment. I have to prove that my marriage wasn't a sacrament.'

'And?'

'The Church is rich. I will make it richer.'

'We've come a long way,' Adam said, 'you and I.'

Other guests arrived. Among them Antonio and Martine and some Germans investing money in property. Waiters circulated with trays of drinks. The sun penetrated the bamboo roof of the terrace in blades of hot light. Food was served. An aircraft droned overhead. The purr and squawk of traffic beneath the apartment faded as siesta approached.

Tom made a speech. Rosana smiled demurely at the allusion to the 'best thing that ever happened to a limey'.

The sparkling wine flowed again while the waiters waited to go home.

Adam was drinking coffee, contemplating making love to Rosana when he was approached by a Swiss. Birrer said he was a diamond merchant from Zurich. He had sensitive features and hair that didn't quite match them and he was a little drunk.

'Congratulations,' he said. 'Forty, huh? You don't look it. Were you a soldier?'

'Briefly,' Adam said. 'Not a very good one.'

'In the last war?'

'The one before,' Adam said.

'Ah, the rehearsal.' He peered at Adam with the patient concentration of the intoxicated. 'On whose side?'

'Mine,' Adam said.

'Is that supposed to be clever?'

'I don't think so,' Adam said. Immediately and instinctively he had disliked Birrer.

'A red?'

'The war,' Adam said, 'was a mistake. For everyone. Let's talk about diamonds.'

'As a matter of fact I know you fought for Franco.'

'Is that supposed to be clever?'

'Not at all,' Birrer said in his over-elaborate English. 'As a matter of fact I know all about you.' He drank brandy from a balloon glass. 'You were in British Intelligence in the last war. The real war,' he said.

'And what were you?' trying to remember the Swiss intelligence agencies. '*Büro Ha?*'

Birrer beckoned him to a corner of the terrace where the birds were taking their siestas, heads tucked into their shoulder feathers. 'As a matter of fact I'm German.'

'And still playing war games?'

'I think you are the one who's playing games, Mr Fleming.'

'And what's that supposed to mean?'

'You had a lot of contacts in the German Embassy during the war.'

'We were all neutral in Madrid,' Adam said. 'Don't you remember?'

'I knew nothing about neutrality. It wasn't a word that we used very much in the SS.'

Adam finished his coffee. As soon as the last guest had left he and Rosana would make love. 'What do you want, Herr –?'

'Veit. Doesn't that ring a conspiratorial bell?'

'Another brandy, Herr Veit?'

'Ironic, really, that we were both on the same side once.'

'Not in the last war.'

'Really? A lot of Germans in our embassy seemed to have other ideas.'

'Then they were extremely gullible.'

'And honourable, perhaps? Not the sort that would stoop to blackmail?'

'I'm afraid I don't understand,' Adam said as Chimo came up and said, 'A word in your ear, Amado.'

'Who the hell is that?' Adam asked as Chimo led him towards the sliding windows of the apartment.

'Who knows. But he looked drunk and boring. I thought I'd rescue you. I'd like to speak to you some time soon,' he added. 'Alone.' He felt for the jagged edges of his teeth with the ball of his thumb but they were no longer there. 'A personal matter.'

'More police work?'

'I've been promoted,' Chimo said enigmatically.

'Congratulations.'

'I'm not confined to Spaniards with restricted freedom any more: I investigate Spaniards with complete freedom.'

'A contradiction in terms?'

'I sometimes think,' Chimo said, tightening his heavily-buckled belt, preparing to leave, 'that we get a permission to live. What if your sister's husband hadn't been killed by the reds, what if . . .' He punched Adam on the shoulder. 'Take care, Amado. You've got permission; don't let it run out.'

Half an hour later, Adam Fleming made love to Rosana with great urgency.

He kissed her. 'It gets better,' he said.

'I love you,' she said.

And yet he still felt vaguely troubled.

Chimo sat in his car, a cream Seat, parked outside the next block. While he waited he made out his report in a red file headed *Dirección de la Seguridad*.

Subject behaved naturally as one would expect in the circumstances. Guests included Thomas Canfield, United States citizen, now Spanish national, former Republican sympathizer, under schedule D surveillance (Ref: Dossier 8543) and 'Swiss-born' Adolf Birrer, alias Otto Veit, a German national residencia authorized 1945 in conjunction with Organisation der SS-Angehörigen.

Chimo licked the tip of his erratic ball-point pen which he had bought from an old woman on the Puerta del Sol who also conducted a lively trade in contraband American cigarettes. What more was there to say? But one miserly paragraph would be regarded by the bureaucrats in the Ministry of the Interior as dereliction of duty.

Glancing from time to time at the entrance to the block where Adam Fleming lived, he continued to write.

Understood from conversation that subject intended to leave the apartment at 19.00 hours. He glanced at the wristwatch with the sun-faded dial that he had worn throughout the civil war: 19.10 hours. *American businessmen well in evidence. They expressed satisfaction at the Government's reaction to the speech by the American ambassador, John Lodge, urging relaxation of foreign capital controls. They hinted that a great deal of American capital would now enter Spain.*

That would reach the top. The Ministry of Trade, too. Maybe even the Pardo Palace. And it *was* true in spirit even though he had made it up. I might even get more promotion, Chimo thought.

He wrote tentatively about Antonio Ruiz and enthusiastically about Adam Fleming, writing Amado in one reference and swearing as he erased it because bureaucrats were always intrigued by erasures. By 7.30 he had filled the page. He yawned. He loathed surveillance; what he fancied was a beer and a snack at a *tasca* on the corner of Calle de Gravina and Calle de Válgame Díos and a visit to a whorehouse behind the Telefónica.

He glanced at the block. It had a somnolent air about it. He wrote: *At 22.28 hours all lights were extinguished in the apartment. I waited until 23.00, then abandoned surveillance until the following morning.*

He started the engine, let in the clutch and drove away. He hoped he would never have to arrest Rosana Fleming.

What Rosana feared most was pregnancy. To be drawn into the great maternal conspiracy of Spain in which every baby is a lamb of God. She saw her life as a single brush stroke of protest and she wanted no distractions.

She continued to confer with Alfonso and his confederates who wanted to unite dissidents – Socialists, Communists and Separatists – and she painted flamboyantly hearing the sound of gunfire and the cries of wounded men.

When she gave an exhibition in the Calle de Serrano the opening was attended by the avant-garde and, over champagne glasses – a curious stimulant for Marxist debate, Rosana thought – the conversation flitted from Picasso, still obdurately in exile, to the poetry of Gabriel Celaya and the movies of Bardem and Berlanga.

She sold only one painting but the next day she received an invitation to meet Franco at the Pardo Palace on the following Wednesday.

Adam drove her to the small palace, guarded by Moroccan cavalry, 15 kilometres from Madrid where, in the ilex forest that had surrounded it, Carlos IV had shot partridges every day during the Battle of Trafalgar. Franco, Rosana had read, also hunted and fished. And painted.

In the library he showed her one of his seascapes. 'What do you think?' he asked.

'It's very competent, Your Excellency,' she said. She was the last of the guests, who had included statesmen, technocrats and a bullfighter, but Franco didn't appear to be fatigued. How old was he? Mid-sixties?

'Competent?' He smiled quizzically and smoothed his small moustache. 'I don't quite know how to take that. Did you know I once painted a self-portrait? In the uniform of an admiral. My father was a naval paymaster and I always wanted to join the navy like my brother Nicholas. What would have happened to Spain if I had become an admiral instead of a general?' He patrolled the library, hands behind his back. 'I have heard some very good reports about your exhibition, Señora Fleming. In the best traditions of Spanish painting. Heroic and bloodthirsty. Where else can you find more corpses than you can in the Prado? But some of those who have seen your paintings are uncertain what exactly it is you are portraying . . .'

'I paint what I feel,' she said, 'and sometimes what I hear; because to me the senses are one.'

'I would like to see the artistic values of the Golden Age

restored,' Franco said. 'The poetry of the Renaissance and the sculptures of the Church and the glories of the architects who designed the Escorial. I don't believe there is a lot wrong with those values, Señora Fleming.' He stopped in front of her. 'You are young, certainly young enough for the very young to heed. Can you help me to disseminate these opinions? After all, art does not have to be heretical to be beautiful.'

'I will try,' Rosana said. Sensing that the audience was coming to an end, she mustered her thoughts for the request that she had phrased and rephrased since she had received the invitation to the palace.

Franco waited.

She said: '*Generalisimo*, do you know who my mother is?'

'The Black Widow? Every Spaniard over the age of 20 knows the name of Ana Gomez.'

She faltered, her rehearsal dried up. 'I wondered –'

'If I can pardon her?'

She nodded, staring at his seascape.

'She didn't ask you this, did she, Señora Fleming? After all you are married to a man who fought for the Nationalists.'

She shook her head.

'How long has she served? Ten years, I believe,' he answered himself.

'She fought for what she believed in.'

'So did we all,' Franco said. 'But Spain is different to other countries: she has too many voices. If we are to emerge once again as a great nation then some of those voices must be quelled. Already this year the treaties establishing the European Economic Community have come into force, de Gaulle has become prime minister of France – soon he'll be president – and we must be prepared to take our place in Europe . . .'

'Will you pardon her?'

'I will consider your request, Señora Fleming.' He bowed slightly. 'Now, if you will excuse me . . .' He paused in front of the seascape. 'What a talented family you are. Where would Real Madrid be without *El Flaco*?'

Rosana's profit from the exhibition after the gallery had taken its cut was 8,000 pesetas. She told Adam she had made

3,000 and, with the balance, opened an account with the Banco Español de Crédito on the Calle de Alcalá.

Her duplicity didn't dismay her. Why should it? It didn't hurt Adam and it made her independent. What did grieve her was the quarrelling within the opposition to Franco, in exile and clandestinely inside Spain. The national malady, she reflected, settling herself in the taxi taking her from the bank to the Central Post Office. Hadn't they learned anything from the Civil War?

True they had organized a Day of National Reconciliation – boycotts and work stoppages – but that had largely been the work of the Communists abroad. And who wanted Communism after the crimes of Stalin had been exposed by Khrushchev? After the Russians had crushed the Hungarian uprising? Odd that they should encourage insurrection in Spain and stifle it when it broke out in one of their own colonies.

There was hope, however. The Socialists, a muted voice at the moment, didn't want any truck with the Communists – it was the Socialists' withdrawal from the exiled government ten years ago that had drawn its teeth.

Rosana's deliberations homed in on Alfonso. Together they would unfurl the banner of the PSOE. 'Unite, unite,' she heard him cry and it seemed to her that it was his soft, cinnamon beard that was rallying dissent.

She glanced out of the window. Behind the taxi she noticed a cream Seat. Its registration was vaguely familiar but her exuberant thoughts dismissed it.

She alighted outside the wedding cake of the Palacio de Communicaciones and looked for Alfonso among the photographers, bootblacks, lottery ticket pedlars, and vendors of budgerigars and black-market cigarettes.

She spotted him and followed him to a rendezvous that was, presumably, not under surveillance. He led her across the park to a café near the children's hospital where, in an empty corner, they conspired over black coffee.

She said, 'We must become united.'

'Of course. But first we must have action. Not just strikes and demonstrations. Real action so that Spain knows we are a force to be reckoned with.'

'We?'

'You and I.' His lips smiled between his moustache and his beard.

'What sort of action?' she asked.

'Assassination?' He sipped his coffee. Steam wreathed his taut features.

'Franco?'

'Who else?'

She peered round the café but the only other occupants were two well-dressed women nibbling *churros* and drinking hot chocolate. Parents, probably, of children in the Hospital del Niño Jesús. There was, Rosana conceded, an inexorable logic about his reply.

The door opened and street noise entered in the wake of a customer. She saw a cream Seat pass the café and remembered the one behind the taxi.

She lowered her voice. 'The Civil War began with an assassination,' she said.

'It would have begun anyway: that was merely the pretext.'

'We don't want another war.'

'That is the attitude that has paralysed Spain for 20 years.'

'We need unity before action.'

'The other way round, *guapa*.'

'Where?' she asked.

'The Valley of the Fallen. The monument to the Fascist victory, the gravestone of the Republican defeat. One thousand million pesetas of grave-digging, 20 years of endeavour. And on 1 April next year it is to be blessed. By Franco. It will be his last appearance.'

Their conversation in the corner of this ordinary place where women ate strips of batter fried in oil and drank chocolate had assumed a grotesque dimension.

'You don't think it's possible?' Alfonso asked.

'Is it?'

'Of course. But we need money to consolidate after the assassination.'

'What will you do, rob a few banks?'

'Far too dangerous. One bank robber hung by his fingers and beaten with rubber truncheons would betray us.'

'So you want me to raise money?'

The women on the other side of the café departed with a screech of chairs and a clucking of maternal condolence. Alfonso rubbed his hands together. He was, he said, sorry to be so brutally practical, but which was more important, theft or the overthrow of tyranny?'

'I have money.'

'Not enough.'

'I will make more.'

'Do you remember I asked you about corruption?'

'I haven't come across any.'

'You mean you haven't recognized it for what it is. Your husband is in business, therefore he is a partner of corruption.'

Adam corrupt? Tom Canfield, perhaps, accepting it in its guise of business practice. Adam never. Obstinate and hard-bargaining perhaps; corrupt never.

'Don't be naïve,' Alfonso said.

'You mustn't judge everyone by the lowest common denominator.'

'I'm single-minded,' Alfonso said. 'Is that a sin?' He stroked her hand. 'Keep your ears open. Not just Adam, his associates. And keep on painting.' He leaned forward abruptly, kissed her on the cheek and was gone.

And she hadn't even mentioned Socialism.

She worried all the way back to the apartment. But that night corruption was handed to her as correctly as a visiting card on a silver tray.

Subject made contact with known political agitator, Alfonso Jiménez outside the Palacio de Communicaciones. She followed him through the Retiro to a café near the Hospital del Niño Jesús. They stayed there for 18 minutes. Jiménez departed first followed three minutes later by subject who walked back through the park and caught a taxi in the Plaza de la Indepencia.

Which is there I lost her, Chimo thought.

I commandeered a taxi and continued surveillance. Subject returned home at 13.08 hours.

Where had she gone? To try once again to see her mother

in gaol? To visit *El Flaco*, whose attitude to her, he understood, was frigid? Adam Fleming, you poor son of a bitch. Chimo wished sincerely that he was back in the Legion where values were honest and the enemy was visible.

Adam first smelled corruption when he scanned a memorandum from Antonio to Tom Canfield, diverted accidentally to his in-tray, confirming the receipt of an investment by Otto Veit in a tract of land at Benidorm.

Veit, the German masquerading as a Swiss diamond merchant who had accosted him at his birthday party. Now why would he suddenly set his sights on Benidorm? Hadn't he been talking drunkenly about blackmail when Chimo had interrupted them?

Adam leaned back in his chair, nudged by a cold presentiment. He remembered giving Antonio the list of Spanish accomplices who had given Nazis sanctuary in Spain through the *Organisation der SS-Angehörigen*, ODESSA. 'If we get rid of the Nazis then we're half-way to being accepted by the rest of the world . . .' Antonio's words.

But no one had got rid of Otto Veit, had they? Instead he has been blackmailed on information laid by me.

Adam strode to Antonio's office but, according to his secretary, he was at home. And Tom was in Alicante where he had opened another office. Adam ran down the stairs into the street and hailed a taxi.

The front door was opened by Isabel. She was just 21, with her father's curly hair and her mother's slim body, and very aware of herself. Her father, she said, was taking his siesta. Like her mother she believed that Tom and Adam were superfluous. Worse, that they were robbing Antonio and thus themselves.

'Then wake him up,' Adam said. 'Do you mind if I come in?'

'I don't –'

'Thank you,' he said, pushing past her.

A ceiling fan rippled the air in the tall living-room, but heat trapped in the city still found its way through the shutters. Adam took off the jacket of his lightweight suit, loosened his tie and sat down.

'I'll see if he's awake,' Isabel said distantly.

'If he's not, wake him.'

Antonio entered the room yawning. He wore a crumpled blue shirt and trousers, but by the time he got back to the office he would be immaculate once more.

He collapsed into a chair and, as Isabel stalked from the room, said, 'So what's the crisis? Couldn't it have waited?'

Adam said, 'You're the crisis.'

'Then it could have waited.' He smiled tightly, the smile intruding into the calculations set bone-deep these days in his face.

Adam said, 'What about all those Nazis you were going to have thrown out of the country for the sake of Spain's image?'

'Tricky,' Antonio said. 'They're here with the cognizance of the regime.'

'Or because they've paid their ransom?'

Antonio hooked one leg over the arm of the chair and swung it rhythmically. 'They're being blackmailed?'

'One certainly is. Otto Veit. How much did he pay?'

'Ask Tom Canfield.'

'Are you suggesting he condoned blackmail?'

'Tom is a businessman.'

'But not a crook.'

Antonio shrugged eloquently. There was a difference? the shrug asked.

'Did you tell him?'

'About Veit? He knew Veit was a German and he knew he was here under a false name therefore he knew exactly what he was – a Nazi on the run who had found a home but would have to pay for it.'

'There was no reason why Veit shouldn't have invested without being blackmailed.'

'If you say so,' Antonio said.

'There is a difference between criminal and business practice.'

'I wonder who defined it.'

'I don't believe Tom knew you had blackmailed Veit.'

'Ask him.'

'If Veit's a war criminal then he should be brought to trial.'

'Kiss my ass,' Antonio said. 'An American expression. Tom taught it to me. And don't bother to report it to anyone in Spain: you'd be the first person to be thrown out.'

'Perhaps I should tell Simon Wiesenthal in Vienna.'

Antonio sprang to his feet. 'Keep your nose out of it.'

'Why? Because you've got more victims lined up?'

Antonio faced him. Adam could see the cobweb lines at the corners of his eyes and the capped teeth and the capillaries at the base of his sculptured and predatory nose. He said, 'I'm warning you: don't meddle. You meddled once before – in someone else's war. And what happened? You were sent home disgraced. It could happen again . . .'

'Disgraced?'

'I met a businessman named Delgado a couple of years ago. Deals in hunting equipment. He remembers you.'

'What did he say?' Adam asked quietly.

'Something about you advancing – in the wrong direction.'

Adam hit him classically on the point of the jaw and Antonio stumbled back, taking with him a coffee table and, with his outstretched hand, a hanging tapestry, until he hit the far wall, arms outstretched.

Adam felt exhilarated, freed. He kept his fist clenched to retain its glow.

Isabel came into the room and screamed. Antonio pushed himself away from the wall. Blood trickled from the corner of his mouth.

He said to Isabel, 'Please show Señor Fleming out. He won't be coming here again. He may not even be staying in Spain . . .'

The exhilaration stayed with Adam as he walked home that evening hearing exasperated home-dwellers calling for the *serenos*, the night-watchmen with whom they had entrusted their keys.

'I don't understand,' Rosana said, sampling partridge stewed in white wine.

'He accused me of being a coward.'

'I understand that, and you were right to hit him. But why did he say it?'

Adam drank wine from the vineyard of *La Rioja Alta* in

Haro. It was old and smooth on his tongue. Everything glowed tonight. 'Because I caught him out.'

'At what?'

'It doesn't matter.'

Fireworks chattered somewhere. A fiesta. Someone's saint's day, perhaps. He looked out of the open window. A rocket burst high above the roof-tops splashing the sky with coloured stars.

'Of course it matters if it made him call you a coward.'

'All right, but this is between you and me . . .'

'Of course.' She laid down her knife and fork precisely, drank some wine and touched her lips with the corner of her napkin.

'I found out he'd been blackmailing German war criminals.'

'I still don't understand.'

'I think he threatened to expose them to the Nazi hunters in Vienna.'

'Unless?'

'They *invested* in our company.'

'I see.' Another burst of coloured stars died in the sky. 'How very corrupt.'

And it seemed to Adam that she held the word on her tongue, tasting it as though it were a wine of an old and rare vintage.

CHAPTER 23

Tom Canfield pursued his courtship of Josefina with the same extrovert application that he brought to business.

He bought her a TV making her the sole possessor in her *barrio* of the phenomenon that had been introduced into Spain in 1956. She sold it two days later for 5,000 pesetas less than he had paid for it.

He bought her furniture for the apartment which she managed to return to the suppliers before his cheque had been paid into their bank.

He paid a deposit on a small house with a garden ripe with orange, lemon and persimmons which she rejected as too remote. Worse, unlike her apartment, it didn't have mains water or electricity.

He bought her clothes for which she thanked him politely, hanging them in her wardrobe where they remained as sought-after as the garments in a family crypt.

He tried to pay for Ernesto's pre-medical education and was repulsed with such acerbity that he momentarily lost hope. After that, conceding that money was more of a barrier than a bond, he changed tack.

He opened an office in Alicante, bought a modest apartment on the Calle de San Francisco, travelled by public transport – except when he was in Madrid – and treated Josefina and Ernesto to *paellas* in a small and sizzling café where the one-legged owner supplemented his takings by trading in cigars smuggled from Majorca that burned incandescently, sometimes bursting into flame, and smelled of autumn bonfires.

At times such as this a sort of fireside contentment settled upon Tom as he drank Alicantan wine and hunted scraps of chicken in the saffron-yellow rice. Until, that was, the conversation led into channels sown with mines. How could she, a nurse, brought up in a cradle of poverty, live with a millionaire? How could they even discuss such an eventuality when he had not yet got his marriage annulled?

'How old are you woman?' he asked her in exasperation one skittish day in the December of 1958.

'Does it matter?' folding her arms and staring through the pine trees at the jostling sea.

'Well, I'm nearly 50 so you must be . . .'

'I'm 38,' she said. 'Not that it's any of your business.'

'We want to share the years left, don't we?'

'We are sharing them.' A stammer of sunshine lit her face through the window; it was scarcely lined and Tom wondered if caring for others took the care away from her.

'And Ernesto. How old is he?'

'He was born in 1945.'

'Then he should be starting college. If he doesn't have a decent education now he'll never be able to study medicine.'

'He'll have a decent education,' Josefina said.

'Can you afford it?'

'You've asked me before and I've told you we don't need charity.'

'Answer the question, for God's sake.'

'I've saved ever since he was born.'

'On your salary?'

'Perhaps *El Gordo* will be good to me.'

'The Christmas lottery? You're as bad as Adam. The chances are a million to one, more . . .'

'Someone has to win.'

'Look,' Tom said, lighting one of the owner's capricious cigars, 'the only thing that must concern us is Ernesto's future. I can help him. Do you think it's right to let your obstinacy endanger his future?'

A muscle moved in her jaw.

Ernesto ran into the café and came to the table. He looked at them comfortably. I am accepted, Tom thought. But if I were his step-father I could pay for him to become a doctor. How much longer?

When Tom got back to his apartment there was a cable awaiting him. It was from his mother. His father was dying after a convalescence lasting more than a quarter of a century. And he was asking for Tom.

Tom flew his Cessna back to Madrid and caught an Iberian flight to New York. The city swooped at him, shouted at him, squeezed him. Since he had gone to war he had been back only once, in 1947. He felt this dull day in the Fall as though he had arrived from the backwoods. He even stared up at skyscrapers.

He booked into the Plaza, hired a Pontiac and drove to the sanatorium in New Jersey. The traffic intimidated him.

His mother greeted him in the lobby of the sanatorium. She was as he had expected her, as fragile as a moth's wing. She settled a brittle-boned hand on his arm. 'He's been waiting for you,' she said.

His father lay in his bed, propped against three pillows, staring into the past or, perhaps, the future. Tom sat beside the bed. Neither of them spoke. Tom felt nothing. These were two elderly strangers; only the parents of his youth were real.

His father said, 'Mind you don't get wind-burn, lying on the deck of the boat the way you do.'

'I'll watch it,' Tom said.

'Always wanted a boat when I was a kid. You're lucky, boy.'

'I've got a plane now,' Tom ventured.

'The sound of the wind snapping the sails in the Sound. Nothing like it, son.'

Tom stayed for an hour, listening to him sailing back through the years. And soon he was not born and his father was young again, talking about a fair-haired girl with a proud head on her shoulders whom he intended to marry. Then, as he reached his own birth, Tom's father closed his eyes and ceased to breathe.

His mother followed him reproachfully two days later and Tom didn't weep until he had returned from the joint funeral to his room in the Plaza.

The following morning he went to look for Seidler. He limped down Fifth Avenue, pausing outside the emporiums of Tiffany's and Saks, buying a bagel from a vendor and giving the change to a panhandler holding the printed legend, I'M BLIND. PLEASE HELP. HAVE A GOOD DAY.

He turned right at the public library and made his way past the tidy oasis of Bryant Park towards Times Square. Cops stood on the street corners and everyone looked as if they knew where they were going.

Ahead lay the strip of cavernous movie theatres. Tom stopped outside a discount bookstore. The window was stacked with novels, cadet versions of classics, travel books about inaccessible paradises and a come-on pile of Saul Bellow's *Adventures of Augie March*.

Tom pushed open the door. An old-fashioned bell tinkled, disturbing the library quiet.

Seidler said, 'What kept you?'

Of course he had changed. But not conclusively. Jowls thicker, hair thinner, but the lines obeying his mind were still lively.

'So what time do you close up shop?' Tom asked.

'Now,' Seidler said.

They went to a morose bar on Broadway where men sat staring into their glasses like fortune tellers.

'So how are you?' Tom asked, sitting at the bar and ordering two beers.

'Twenty years and the man asks me how I am.'

'Okay, so ask me how I am.'

'Not bumming by the look of you.'

Tom told him first about Josefina. Then about business. Then about Irene.

'No shit,' Seidler said. 'I never figured you for a tycoon. Just a lousy flier who mistook farmhouses for hangars. Why didn't you look me up?'

'Likewise,' Tom said. 'You should have stayed in Spain.'

'I like books. In English. I got married, you know. Just like I said. Two kids, too. Then we split.'

Silence settled between them.

'Why don't we take a drive?' Tom said. 'Take a look at Long Island.'

They picked up the Pontiac and drove across Queensboro Bridge, along Northern Boulevard and North Hampstead Turnpike. There were more houses in Nassau than Tom remembered; garages too. But as they made their way east, as the island narrowed and its pastures spread, Tom began to taste the flavours of his childhood.

'It's no good, you know,' Seidler said as they bore south towards the southern prong of the terminal fork.

'What's no good?'

'Opening the packages of the past. They belonged to someone else.'

'Us?'

'Sure us. We tied up the package when I came back to the States and you went back to Spain. But we're still in that package. Nice and cosy.'

Tom drove through the first of the Hamptons to Southampton.

The house was still there, becalmed in the dusk amid shaved lawns reaching for the ocean. But it belonged to a bristling tycoon and a suffering wife and a boy who hated boats.

'Am I right?' Seidler asked.

'You always were,' Tom said.

He concentrated and saw himself walking down the driveway, flicking at the gravel with a branch of scrub pine, and he wondered where he might have been if the creditors hadn't foreclosed on his father, if a clot of blood hadn't lodged in his brain, if a politician named Calvo Sotelo hadn't been assassinated in Madrid . . . But life was an accident, wasn't it?

He turned the Pontiac and drove away.

Neither of them spoke, but the silence was no longer a disappointment.

As they picked up the Brooklyn Shore Parkway, Tom said, 'Do you still fly?'

'Are you kidding? I need field-glasses to sign my name.'

'Where do you want me to drop you off?'

'At the bookstore,' Seidler told him.

'Is that where you live?'

'It doesn't matter where I live.'

Tom pulled up outside the store where the books lay in the street light waiting to be read.

'A beer?'

'Quit trying,' Seidler said. 'This was another package. A small one. Let's tie it up.'

He shook Tom's hand and went into the store.

He met Irene in Central Park. She wore mink and walked like a model and the grey at her temples might have been applied by a beautician. She had opened a florist in the 50s on the East Side and she brought him a red rose which she pinned to the lapel of his grey topcoat.

They walked together easily as though they had a lot of time ahead of them. Squirrels looped among the trees; strolling lovers leaned into each other; cyclists pedalled glumly past.

Tom gestured at the balding grass: 'I lived here once in a hut. The servants from the baronial mansions,' pointing at the guardian blocks of apartments, 'used to bring us scraps.'

'They'd be your servants if you lived in New York now.'

'I'm a foreigner here.'

'I guess I was always a stranger in Spain.'

'But it was good. Wasn't it?' anxiously.

'Sure it was good. A neat, well-scripted episode.'

'A package,' he said.

'Tied and knotted,' she said. 'Congratulations.'

He took her arm. 'What are you talking about?'

'The annulment. I got a cable from Madrid today. Our marriage never happened.'

She stopped. Turned. Faced him. 'Take care, Tom.' She tried a smile but it was spoilt by the trembling of her lips.

She walked briskly and elegantly away and he was ashamed of his happiness.

He went straight to Josefina's apartment in Alicante. Climbed the cold, marble-chip stairs and pushed the bell button. Heard it buzz impotently inside.

Christ, he thought. Not again.

He went down the stairs and found the obese caretaker sitting in his cell hung with keys listening to 'Match of the Day'.

Josefina had left two days ago and he didn't know where she had gone.

An excited gabble from the football commentator. A tinny roar from the radio. 'That *El Flaco*,' said the caretaker, lighting a cigarette from the stub of another. 'Pure genius.'

'Did she go with the boy?'

'How many goals is that this season?'

Tom gave him 500 pesetas.

'They went to the bus station together.'

'Did she say when she'd be back?'

'She didn't say *if* she'd be back.'

'You must have an address.'

He gave the caretaker another 500.

The caretaker unlocked a drawer. It sprang open, pushing at his belly. He took out a creased visiting card. 'That's the only address I've got.' It was Tom's card.

Tom retired to the café and drank black coffee laced with brandy.

He picked up his automobile, a grey and workmanlike Peugeot, and drove north along the line of the coast, razor high above the sea in places, past Benidorm where his first block of apartments was rising beside the beach.

Dusk gathered, night scents reached him – mist drifting in from the Mediterranean, rich earth watered by a recent shower. Lights moved blindly on the sea as the day lingered over the mountains in apricot light. Villages and small towns presented themselves in his headlights, then fled. Altea, Calpe, Javea, Denia . . .

He parked outside the apologetic railway station in the familiar town where he had searched before and made his way through unmade roads to the bar where, long ago, he had been greeted with the wary hostility of the defeated. An old poster announcing a bullfight at Ondara hung from the wall beside an advertisement for a movie, *El Ultimo Cuplé*, at a cinema in Denia.

Once again no one knew anything about Josefina's whereabouts. Why should they? Hadn't she deserted the town to live among the dudes of Alicante? Tom drank an anis and walked along a street where forlorn palms rustled beneath the stars.

He heard delicate footsteps behind him. He turned sharply. Behind him stood a small and apologetic man wearing smart clothes made for someone much bigger than himself. He massaged shrimp-like hands together. The night, he said, was set fair and the breeze coming in from the sea would clear the clouds for the sun in the morning. Was Tom staying in town?

Tom said no, he reckoned he would drive inland to Pego.

Why not try Denia? his pursuer asked, rubbing his fingers together as though he were peeling them. It was the time of the *fallas*, the March fiesta of San José, patron saint of the carpenters, and Denia was a wild and carefree place at such times. Particularly tonight, the climax, when they burned the *fallas*, the statues, made of papier-mâché.

Tom thanked him. But such exuberance, he confessed, was quite the reverse of what he was looking for tonight.

The little man picked at his fingers. 'In these small towns, señor, many of us are related.'

'You have many relatives?'

'Very distantly the señora you are looking for.'

An aching beat of his heart. 'Do you know where she is?'

'She has a relative in Denia.'

'Do you know where?'

His hands writhed in the lamplight. 'In the fishermen's quarter; that's all I know. But tonight she will be out in the streets with her son. She has promised him.'

Tom drove through the orange groves to Denia. He had been there once before. It was a small, tight-clustered port which owed much to raisins. In the century before World War I, when British traders bought ship-loads of dried grapes for their cakes and puddings and casinos and whorehouses nudged each other down the narrow streets. Then the trade withered – British bought from Australia and South Africa – and the traders departed leaving behind a warehouse bearing the legend, COOPERATIVE WHOLESALE SOCIETY OF GREAT BRITAIN – and

a cemetery overlooking the sea. The merchants of Denia,
once the home of Phoenicians, Greeks, Romans and Moors,
continued to trade in fish, oranges, and toys and, by 1959 –
when the British, accompanied by the French, Germans and
Dutch, began to return as tourists – in sun, sea and sand.

Tom parked his Peugeot near the harbour where fishing
boats rubbed shoulders and walked down the main street, the
Generalisimo, beneath the clutching boughs of plane trees.

Girls, *falleras*, in brocade costumes, combs crowning their
polished hair, danced arm in arm in the street; nomadic
bandsmen languished in the bars beside flute and trumpet;
vendors sold liquorice roots, sugar-cane, sliced coconut and
sunflower seeds; firecrackers spat; courtship accelerated. And
in their appointed places the four statues – the *fallas* – waited
to be put to the torch.

But which *falla* would draw Josefina into its embrace? Each
represented a different part of the town and he had no idea
to which part Josefina owed allegiance. He started with the
first one. Each had a satirical theme, bright effigies clustered
beneath the main statue, and each was constructed with a
freedom of expression that was as rare these days as a pardon.

This *falla* concentrated on the advent of tourism.
Englishmen with pink knees, Germans in Tyrolean hats,
lustily-built Swedish girls wearing prohibited bikinis, captions
all in Valenciano. A band played and the young men and girls
in their Valencian costumes danced to their robust music. Of
Josefina or Ernesto there was no sign.

He wandered from *falla* to *falla*. Stopped at the Bar
Benjamin where hams hung like clubs from the ceiling and
shelled mussels lurked in tins on the bar where he met a
knife-grinder who owned a dog with half a tongue, the other
having been cut out when it chewed tent caterpillars on the
march from a pine tree. Moved to the Tropico where he
encountered a snail-minder who stopped his charges from
leaving the table when they were on sale in the market. He
began the circuit again and began to get a little drunk. He met
a boot-black and a secret policeman and a pigeon-keeper and
a town councillor dressed as elegantly as a grandee.

He returned to the first *falla* which, having been adjudged the worst, would be the first to burn. An incendiarist splashed gasoline on it. Fire fighters took up positions.

Perhaps she had left Alicante for ever.

A flame flickered into life and gave birth.

Rubicund knees, a feathered hat and a pair of nuzzling breasts went up in flames. Jets of water from a hose held by firemen splashed nearby buildings and the occupants of their balconies. Sparks flew towards the stars, tourism toppled in ashes. Spectators cheered.

Tom took in another couple of bars and another couple of *fallas*. The fourth was the climax, the best. A satire on real estate and the duping of unworldly landowners. Tom hadn't examined it before. The crowd pressed close; police held them back.

Tom, trapped among the straining spectators, looked around. No sign of her. Despairing, he stared at the *falla*, flame-licked and roaring with its self-ingestion. And saw himself, the king of intrusive developers, standing on a pedestal of fire. At his feet was a caption.

He turned to a youth carrying a guitar. 'What does it say?' He pointed at the caption.

'Go home Yank,' said the youth.

He felt the flames burning his feet.

He turned, pushed through the crowd and made his way through the insomniac streets to the Comercio hotel on the main street.

The following morning he descended the stairs unsteadily from the gallery of the old hostelry in search of breakfast. He ordered coffee, toast and fruit. Through the open door he could see milk-fresh light and hear the rhythmic sweeping of street-cleaners.

She came through the door as he picked up his cup of coffee with a trembling hand.

He put down the cup and, listening to himself, said, 'I was never married.'

'I know,' she said. 'You told everyone in Denia last night.'

In Madrid Rosana agonized. What she wanted was unity not assassination. What would the killing achieve? A great gasp of freedom, according to Alfonso. More logically a stranglehold of repression.

And what was she to do with the evidence of corruption against Tom Canfield's company? Betray Adam? Hand it over to Alfonso to use for blackmail against the company and, perhaps, the Nazi war criminals?

She conveyed her doubts to Alfonso in the basement below the cutlers in the San Bernado district. Outside it was a dreaming March day. He sat at a table in front of a guttered candle drinking San Miguel beer from a bottle. Sunlight entered the basement cautiously through a barred window. A pistol lay on the table. Cigarette ends were scattered over the stone floor and the air smelled of yesterday's tobacco smoke.

She leaned against the wall in a shaft of dusty sunlight. '*If* I found any evidence of corruption,' she said, 'what would you do with it?'

'Fund the Cause, of course.' He stroked his soft beard and regarded her speculatively. 'You're in a strange mood this morning.'

'It's a restless time of the year. What would you buy for the Cause?'

'Weapons,' Alfonso said. He picked up the pistol and weighed it in his hand.

Outside, Chimo deployed his men with care. Two at the front in a black Renault Dauphine. Two at the back on foot. A riot squad of *Policia Armada*, in a truck round the corner. He glanced at his wrist-watch. 11.15 am. He was going in at 11.30. He sat in the back of the Dauphine and lit a cigarette. The sun was growing stronger and a smell of tar reached him from the road. It was very peaceful.

'Why weapons?' she asked. 'What we want is unity.'

'We can't buy unity.'

'We can travel, hold meetings, print pamphlets, rally all the factions.'

'Rally Socialists and Communists? Mate two spitting cats?'

'But that's what you wanted. What you've always talked about.'

'You have to fight for freedom,' Alfonso said. He tipped beer down his throat. 'First the assassination, then the uprising.'

'You've been lying to us all this time,' she said, appalled.

'I know what has to be done.'

'Why didn't you tell us? We believed in you.'

'Because you wouldn't have listened. Now the reality is upon us and you have to listen.'

'What reality? Any uprising would be crushed immediately. There would be reprisals. Innocent people would be jailed, executed.'

'Without El Caudillo? The country would be in chaos. We could take over . . .'

'We?'

'The people,' Alfonso said.

'Another war? Are you crazy?' realizing in a moment of great clarity that he was. 'There will be no more fighting in Spain. The people, your people, have had enough of bloodshed. We can put our house in order peaceably. Show the rest of the world how it can be done.'

'Have you joined the Falange, Rosana Fleming?'

'Are you a Communist, Alfonso Jiménez?'

'The Communists are the only party who are actively helping us.'

'Meddling?'

Alfonso ran one finger down the barrel of the pistol. 'You wouldn't betray us, would you?'

11.25. Chimo tried to think about Adam and their days together at Jarama. There was nothing quite as fulfilling as the camaraderie of war, he thought. He remembered Adam knocking his rifle off aim when he had been about to shoot the Englishman in the International Brigade. I respected him for that. It wasn't a civil war among Englishmen. Adam was the first foreigner I ever knew. So brave and so lost I wanted to protect him. Poor bastard. What will I do about his wife? A stray dog with washboard ribs lay in front of the Dauphine and pointed its nose towards the cutler's premises. Heat rose in waves from the street. 'Two minutes,'

Chimo said to the two plain-clothes policemen sitting in front of him.

She said, 'You didn't answer my question.'

'I think I did.'

'So all the time you've been betraying our trust?'

'Communism is equality. Isn't that what you want?'

'There is only one thing wrong with Communism – it doesn't work. Ask the Russians.'

'If the theories of Marxism are followed truly then it will work.'

She thought, 'My mother would be proud of me. Wouldn't she?'

'Where are your ideals, Rosana Fleming? Did you leave them with your husband today?'

'What would you know about ideals?' She stepped out of the shaft of sunlight. 'Perhaps you had them once. But ideals, like their owners, grow up. They make saints of some people, bigots of others.'

'And I'm not a saint, am I? But I am a realist. Do you have any evidence of corruption?'

She faced him, arms folded across her breast. 'None.' The relief was so intense that she closed her eyes so that he did not see it mirrored in them.

Chimo spoke into his radio handset. 'One minute.' He took his pistol, a Luger, from his shoulder holster. He listened to the breathing of the two men in front of him, fast and shallow. The dog turned sharply to bite its fleas, then subsided again. Chimo smelled the tar and wished it was the smell of mud in the trenches.

A voice from the cutler's shop above the basement. 'Police.'

Alfonso looked at Rosana. 'You?'

'Would I be here?'

'Perhaps . . . But I'm not as stupid as they think.' He picked up the pistol and stuck it in his belt. 'Help me.'

He knelt and began to pull loose bricks from the wall of the cellar. She knelt beside him. The bricks came away easily, two thicknesses of them, the old cement grazed where a chisel had recently been hammered between them.

Chimo led the way, Luger in hand. The van moved up the street. A marksman climbed out, knelt and trained a Karabiner 98K rifle fitted with a telescopic sight on to the roof. The two plain-clothes policemen behind the premises took up positions either side of the rear exit.

Chimo shot out the lock on the front door and shouldered his way inside; ducked instinctively as a line of knives hanging from a wire loomed in front of him. There were blades everywhere – butchers' knives, scalpels, razors, scythes, scissors, shears, cleavers, a couple of swords. The hanging knives moved in the breeze coming through the open door.

Chimo nodded to the two policemen, both armed with machine-pistols, who accompanied him. One made his way upstairs, the other kicked open the door leading to the cellar and began to descend the stone stairs. Chimo picked his way carefully through the cutting edges around him, and fell to one side as the knife flew past, striking the wall and falling to the floor. Chimo fired from the hip through the wooden counter at the far end of the shop. Two shots. A thickset man with a bald patch like a skull-cap reared up, folded across the counter.

Chimo stood up warily.

A burst of machine-pistol fire from upstairs. The sound of a body falling. The armed police were at the door now. The policeman who went upstairs descended the stairs, holding up one finger.

'Jiménez?' Chimo asked.

He shook his head.

'A girl?'

'A man.'

They stared at the top of the stone steps leading to the cellar.

A shout from below. 'They've got away.'

Chimo ran down the steps: time wasted. He peered through the hole in the wall shaped like a piece of a jig-saw puzzle. Another cellar, another hole. How many more?

He shouted up the steps, 'In the street.'

Jiménez and Rosana Fleming were at the end of the street, running. The kneeling marksman took aim as Rosana stumbled and fell to one side. They saw her body jerk as the bullet hit her.

The dog whined and loped away. The engine of a car coughed into life.

Chimo, hand holding the Luger hanging heavily at his side, walked down the street towards the body.

She lay in a private room in La Paz hospital, black hair released from its combs – Chimo had never seen it that way and it made an artist's model of her – dripfeed inserted in one arm. Her face was exhausted, but her eyes were watchful. In good shape, Chimo thought, for a woman who had been wounded just below the rib cage by a bullet that had passed through her body.

She said, 'Will I go to the same prison as my mother?"

'Why, have you committed a crime?'

Her dark eyes appraised him. 'Does it matter?'

'I think you may be able to help us, Señora Fleming.'

'Why should I?'

A nurse stuck her head round the door but she said nothing, head retreating like a snail into its shell.

Chimo said, 'You've been associating with some very dangerous people. One in particular. The one who left you bleeding in the street this morning.'

'He had no choice.'

'Do you think you've been fair to your husband?'

'I've done him no harm.'

'Open? Frank? Honest?'

'Have I ever claimed to be any of those things?'

'We want Alfonso Jiménez,' Chimo said.

'Then find him.'

Chimo sighed. 'Listen to me, Señora Fleming. Jiménez plans to do a great deal of harm to Spain. The sort of harm that will put us back to the dark days after the Civil War. If he succeeds in assassinating General Franco,' watching her carefully, 'then there will be a great deal of misery in the land. Arrests, executions ... many innocent people will suffer. Do you really want that?'

She didn't reply.

He watched a bubble break free and surface in the drip feed bottle.

He tried again. 'Jiménez is no good to anyone. Not even himself. He is a glory-seeker, nothing more. All he believes in is outrage. He knows he will die and he wants to take innocents with him. He doesn't care about them, only his own doom which he sees in headlines.'

'I don't know where he is,' Rosana said.

'You must know the places he frequents.'

'You know them too. In any case he won't go back to them, will he?' She moved on the pillows and winced.

'You puzzle me, Señora Fleming. A martyr like Jiménez? Is that what you're interested in? Your image? Don't you care about your country?'

'That's why I'm here, because I care about my country.'

'Listen,' Chimo said, moving the chair nearer to the bed, 'I believe your intentions were good. But Spain needs stability for a little longer. Your turn will come, believe me. Let Jiménez pull the trigger,' observing the spiderweb lines at the corners of her eyes, 'and Spain is doomed. I don't think you want that.'

Another bubble in the bottle. Slower this time.

The nurse put her head round the door again. Chimo held up his hand. 'I know,' he said, 'she's had enough for today.'

'She's very tired,' the nurse said. She had a healthy, friendly face and Chimo wondered if he could make a date with her.

Rosana said, 'What do you want to know?'

Chimo had two appointments the following day. One with Solana, his superior at police headquarters in the Puerta del Sol, the other with Adam Fleming in his apartment. He relished neither. He went first to the Puerta del Sol.

Solana listened to his proposition with exaggerated patience. He was small for a policeman with starved features and dyed hair that shone the colour of plum juice in strong light. He was left-handed and he blamed many of his frustrations on his sinistral tendency.

The proposition was very simple and to the advantage of everyone concerned, Chimo stated boldly. Well, everyone except Jiménez, that was. Rosana Fleming had infiltrated a dangerous anti-Francoist organization in order to lay information that would lead to the apprehension of the assassin.

Solana lit a cigarette, striking the match with his left hand, and blew smoke across the desk as though it disgusted him. And had she laid any such information? he asked. Not yet, Chimo confessed, but it would come. And why was Chimo so concerned about the fate of the daughter of the Black Widow? Had it anything to do with the fact that she was the wife of Adam Fleming with whom Chimo had served in the war?

'As a matter of fact,' said Solana, 'I have always taken a personal interest in Señor Fleming. I met his business associate many years ago. Tomás Canfield. He gave me a false identity. What policeman could resist keeping an eye on him and his colleagues?' He sucked down cigarette smoke, wincing at the impact on his lungs. 'He has done well, Señor Canfield. What could I do about him? We depended on the Americans . . . Can you give me any good reasons why we should take pity on Señora Fleming?'

'A couple,' Chimo said.

'Name them.'

'Nail the assassin and you'll get promoted.'

'Supposing I don't agree to a deal.'

'Then we won't get the information that will lead us to the assassin,' said Chimo, who already had the information.

'And the other reason?'

'She has the ear of Franco.'

Chimo sat back and watched Solana concede. A tight grimace, a great exhalation of smoke through his nostrils.

He made his way on foot to Adam's apartment. The morning was beginning to pick up from the intermission after the rush-hour. A waking murmur like a second dawn. He walked down Alcalá where baronial insurance houses and banks had trampled upon the cafés of old in which *tertulias*, specialized groups of customers, had met. Chimo sighed for the past because it reminded him of the small town in Extremadura where little had changed.

He walked slowly to the Plaza de la Cibeles and bought a newspaper opposite the fountain. He scanned its pages but there was no mention of yesterday's shooting – the censor would have seen to that.

He strolled on, finding many diversions to delay his arrival at the apartment. He stood enthralled outside the window of a shop selling guitars although he had never plucked a note; he bought a carnation and pinned it in his lapel and a tenth part of a ticket for the national lottery held every ten days – as the draw was on the 25th, the cheap end of the month, it cost him only ten pesetas. Next Christmas he planned to gamble 400 pesetas which could win him one and a half million.

He neared Adam's apartment block. Should he forget the whole thing? Chimo wavered, stopped on a street corner. No, a man should know from a friend how it came to be that his wife was lying in La Paz with a bullet hole through her belly.

He ignored the lift and mounted the stairs. Pressed the bell, felt a scrutiny through the Judas Eye. The door opened. A maid. Mr Fleming offered his apologies but he had flown to Valencia on urgent business; he would be back in two days. Chimo smiled; two days was an eternity. He walked briskly to a call box and telephoned the nurse at La Paz. Yes, Señora Fleming was better and yes, tonight was her night off.

Adam took a taxi from the airport into Valencia, holding his anger as carefully as the briefcase on his knees.

Perhaps he was mistaken; perhaps the property deal on the Costa Brava wasn't as dubious as it appeared. But Tom would have to be more forthright than he had been in the Madrid office last summer.

'Okay, so a little pressure was brought to bear on Herr Veit. But he would have invested anyway,' he had said.

'How the hell do you know that?'

'Because he told me so.'

'You'll have to do better than that,' Adam had said.

'Do you want to hear it from the man himself? Herr Veit should be here any minute now.'

When he materialized he shook Adam's hand and said in English, 'I'm sorry I was so obnoxious at your birthday party. I have to keep up pretences.'

'Swiss diamond dealers have to be obnoxious?'

'Mass murderers do.'

Tom said, 'You'd better explain, Otto.'

Veit sat down, hand straying to his dyed brown hair. 'The trouble is,' he said, 'that when most people think about the part Germany played in the Spanish Civil War they only remember the Condor Legion. Guernica. They've forgotten – if they ever wanted to know – that a hell of a lot of us fought on the other side. Have you ever heard of the Thaelmann Centuria?'

'The German contribution to the International Brigades?'

'You surprise me, Mr Fleming.' He smiled. 'But, of course, you did fight against them.'

'They fought well,' Adam said.

'Their commissar was Hans Beimler, a former deputy in the Reichstag and a Communist. He had been gaoled in Dachau – yes, it existed in those days – but had escaped by strangling his guard and putting on his clothes. The unit was named after Ernst Thaelmann, a dock worker from Hamburg, who was encouraged by Stalin to become a Communist leader in Germany. He, too, was imprisoned at the time but he didn't escape.'

'He was murdered in 1944,' Tom said.

'You, too, are well informed,' said Veit. 'But you would be – you fought on the right side.'

Adam stared at him in astonishment. 'You, a former SS officer, think the Republicans were right?'

'Let him finish,' Tom said.

'The Thaelmann,' Veit went on, 'was actually led by a novelist, Ludwig Renn. A pacifist, would you believe. That must be the greatest contradiction of our civilization – that you have to fight for peace.'

'The whole Civil War was a contradiction,' Adam said. 'It

wasn't just Spaniards fighting Spaniards. Germans fought Germans, Italians fought Italians. The Garibaldi Battalion . . .'

'And British fought British?'

'There weren't many of us on the Fascist side.'

'The Thaelmann was here in Madrid,' Veit said. 'Defending it against you Fascists. That's when Hans Beimler was killed. Murdered according to some because of disagreements with Moscow. A tangled web, eh, Mr Fleming?'

'And *you* fought with them?'

'Oh yes,' Veit said, 'I fought with them all right.'

Tom said, 'Otto is a modest man. One place he fought was Las Rozas outside Madrid. The Thaelmann had been told to hold, not to retreat an inch.'

'A centimetre,' Veit said.

'They were bombed, attacked round the clock by Moors . . .'

'Those bastards,' Veit said. 'They bayonneted the wounded.'

'. . . but they held out.'

'And I found the body of a German pilot who had been bombing us. I went to school with him in Munich. Then do you know what happened?'

Adam shook his head.

'We got orders to advance. Advance! Can you imagine? We sent back a reply: "Impossible. The Thaelmann Battalion has been destroyed."'

'But you hadn't?'

'I am indestructable.'

Tom said, 'He broke through the lines with a wounded soldier. Then broke back in again and rescued two more.'

'And then?'

'A little more bloodshed. Then, as you know, the International Brigades were pulled out in the autumn of 1938.'

'And you joined the SS?' Adam stared at him incredulously.

'One of the finest fighting forces the world has ever known but, no, I didn't join them. I still had my ideals, you see.'

'Ah, those,' Adam said.

'But they don't preclude patriotism. I kept my head down – only a few people in Germany know I fought with the Thaelmann and they were nearly all dead – and joined a less glamorous regiment.'

Adam sighed. 'So can you now explain what you're doing in Spain posing as a Swiss diamond merchant?'

'I felt that I belonged here. I wanted to come back. To help. Now can you tell me how a German who fought for the Republicans can get back into Francoist Spain?'

'By posing as an ex-member of the SS?'

'I had the money. My family is rich – that's why I fought for the Republicans. The rebellion of youth. Those ideals again . . . it was the only way.'

'And ODESSA fell for it?'

'Their Spanish collaborators fell for it.'

'Then if you weren't in the SS how could Antonio Ruiz blackmail you?'

'Wiesenthal would have told him that I wasn't in the SS. Then I would have been thrown out of Spain. Or thrown in gaol as a Communist spy.'

'But in any case,' Tom said, 'he was going to give us the money whatever happened.'

'Why?' Adam said.

'For the same reasons that Tom is investing here. To help Spain emerge from bankruptcy. I did help to save Madrid once . . .'

Later that day Adam asked Tom how many others had been blackmailed by Antonio.

'A few.'

'Don't tell me they're all phoney members of the SS too.'

'C'mon, Adam. Don't play the preacher with me – you knew about the gold all along.'

'That was wartime.'

'That makes a heist legal? Don't bullshit me, Adam. Maybe you should stay in the perfume side of the business.'

'Maybe I should quit the business.'

'For Christ's sake. Now you listen to me. Some of these guys investing in our companies were Nazis, right. But that isn't the point. They're going to make money, buckets of it. Now supposing someone decided to expose this method of raising funds . . .'

'Me?'

'Anybody. Spain is just emerging from the Hungry Years.

What would happen to all the men we employ if there was a scandal and we went bust? They'd go back to the Hungry Years, that's what, and their families with them.'

Yes, he would have to be much more forthright, Adam thought, as the taxi burrowed through the streets of Valencia, bursting into the sunlight and the flower stalls of the Plaza del Pais Valencia. He paid off the cab outside the dignified old Reina Victoria hotel and walked up the stairs to the first-floor bar.

Tom was waiting for him. They ordered two beers and sat at a table. There were no books around but Adam felt as though he were sitting in a library: you expected to hear the scratch of quill on parchment.

'So, how's Rosana?' Tom asked.

'She's great. Housewife, eminent artist, confidante of Franco . . . Josefina?'

'We're getting married in the summer.' Tom smiled contentedly. 'A long courtship, huh?'

'Congratulations,' Adam said.

'And you're best man.'

Adam sipped his beer. 'I've got a few questions to ask.'

'Shoot,' Tom said.

Adam opened his briefcase. 'It's about the land on the Costa Brava.'

'I guessed it might be.'

'We have some very unhappy investors.'

'They took the risk,' Tom said. 'That's their problem.'

'They claim they were misled.'

'They always do.'

'Twenty thousand acres, a lot of land.' Adam opened a green file and read from it. 'Superior development, houses with pools, et cetera . . . Capital to be raised by investors who will get a cut of the profits after the land has been sold off in plots, after water, electricity, et cetera have been installed.'

'Or a slice of the pie for themselves,' Tom said.

'Except that there isn't any pie. And they each paid 100,000 pesetas.'

'You know what happened,' Tom said. 'We didn't get the

investment. We couldn't proceed. But it's not too late. Tell them to be patient, Adam.'

'Their patience is exhausted.'

'Then tell them to get screwed. They knew what they were getting into. Can't you see the fat-cat smiles if the gamble had paid off?'

He limped to the bar and ordered two more beers. When he came back Adam asked quietly, 'What happened to the money, Tom?'

'We bought land with it.'

'And the amenities?'

'Like I told you, there wasn't enough cash.'

Adam tapped the file. 'The investment would have paid for more than twice the land we bought.'

'So I'm a crook?'

'You're out of touch,' Adam said. 'How the hell can you know what's going on when you spend all your time in Alicante?'

'Antonio knows what's going on.'

'Is that the best you can do?'

'I don't have to do any better. I employ you, remember?'

'I would like you to do better,' Adam said.

'I don't have to.'

'Try.'

'The balance of money has been spent paying the contractors.'

'Who were contracted to do what?'

'Build access roads for a start.'

'There aren't any access roads,' Adam said quietly.

'There will be.' Tom rifled his fingers through his grey-blond hair. 'Look, I don't like any of this any more than you do, but we've known each other a long time and we've been through a lot together. I'm not a crook, I'm a businessman. What we're talking about is common business practice in real estate. You have to pay architects, attorneys . . . Everyone will be paid, Adam, I promise you.'

Adam took a plan of the development from his briefcase. He pointed at some fine-nibbed lines. 'Those access roads,' he said, 'were going into the sea.'

'So why didn't you shoot me that day at Jarama?'

Adam stretched out his hand. 'I quit, Tom. We're on different sides, just as we were at the beginning.'

Adam's liberated thoughts took wing on the flight back to Madrid. He would start his own business. Language schools, perhaps, in the big cities, because Spain was emerging energetically from its isolation and words had always been his strength.

But first he would take Rosana to England. To Cambridge to see Magdalene, his white-walled room above the Pepysian Library overlooking the Cam on one side and the garden of the Master's Lodge on another, the quadrangle which he had traversed shivering in pyjamas and overcoat to take a bath, the Pitt Club where the élite such as Old Etonians dined, the Pickerel where you ordered pints, nothing less, at the old wooden bar. And, of course, the Backs to regale her with memories of May Balls and punting on the river, music blaring scratchily from a gramophone with a cornucopian horn. It would be deeply satisfying to present his youth to someone who now shared his life . . .

He caught a taxi from Barajas airport to his apartment. Bounded up the stairs, opened the door and came face to face with Chimo who was standing with his back to the window, glass of beer in his hand. A snowflake settled in his soul.

Chimo said, 'The maid let me in. I hope you don't mind.' He held up the glass. 'I helped myself.'

'Of course not. Where's Rosana?'

Chimo sat down and stared into his glass.

'Is she ill? An accident . . .?'

'She's all right, Amado. She's in hospital but she's okay, I promise you.'

'What happened, for God's sake?'

'She was shot,' Chimo said.

'A burglar? Bank robber?'

'A policeman,' Chimo said, staring into his beer as though it contained some hitherto unfathomed secret of life.

'Why?' Adam sat down as cold gathered within him.

'She was running away.'

'From you?'

'I'm not good with words,' Chimo said carefully. 'But I thought it was better if I told you. From the beginning, that is.' He swallowed some beer, tasting it elaborately. 'It's not the sort of thing you want to tell someone who fought by your side . . .'

'Get on with it,' Adam said harshly.

'Those art lessons, those seminars, they didn't exist. When she left this apartment she met a man named Alfonso Jiménez, a known political agitator. Stayed with him,' Chimo said reluctantly.

'You mean she was unfaithful?'

'She stayed with him, that's all I'm saying.'

'I don't believe it.'

Chimo leaned forward and took a clip of carbon-copies from his briefcase. 'Surveillance reports. No point in making them up.' He read three extracts, dates, times, assignations, time spent with Jiménez. At night. Till dawn. In Barcelona, three days.

Adam walked to the kitchen, opened an Aguila beer and drank it from the bottle. His serenity surprised him.

He picked up a photograph of Rosana when she was much younger. She was smiling. At him. Afterwards, he remembered, he had kissed her; he could smell the lemon-scent of her hair.

'Why are you framing her?' he asked.

'No frame, Amado. All true. I'm sorry.'

'The shooting,' Adam said. 'Tell me about the shooting.'

'We raided the house where she was staying with Jiménez while you were in Valencia. But he was too smart – they got away through the cellars. He got away,' Chimo corrected himself. 'Rosana caught the bullet. Just below the chest. A good clean wound – she's out of danger.'

'Nice shooting,' Adam said. 'You let the "known political agitator" escape and shoot an innocent woman. Were you in charge?'

'It was my operation, yes.'

'You realize I'll have to make a formal complaint?'

'Don't Amado. Don't make a fool of yourself. It's all true.'

'Why would Rosana get mixed up with a man like that?'

'I don't know why. You'll have to work it out for yourself. Do you mind if I search her room?'

'Our room,' Adam said.

'A dressing-table? A locked drawer?'

'Go ahead,' Adam said. 'It will all go in the formal complaint.'

The pastel-blue bedroom with the gold-painted headboard was undisturbed. An amber necklace lay curled on the glass top of the dressing-table, a dusting of face powder beside it like pink pollen. He touched the amber beads; they felt warm but that was an illusion. He remembered the way her shoulder muscles moved as she sat, wearing a slip, making up her face in the mirror.

Chimo tried the drawers. The bottom right-hand one was locked. He took a clasp-knife from his pocket. 'Do you mind? It won't cause much damage.'

'Do what the hell you want.'

Adam sat on the edge of the bed where they had made love the night before he flew to Valencia. The door of the wardrobe was open and he could see her clothes hanging there.

Chimo inserted the blade of the knife above the drawer near the lock and twisted it. The wood splintered, the drawer opened.

Inside were a few papers and a diary. Adam didn't know she kept one. And what were the papers?

'Bills,' Chimo said.

'What for?'

Chimo leafed through them. 'Paints, mostly. A few hotels.'

'Very incriminating,' said Adam.

Chimo opened the diary, black leather embossed with gold-leaf.

'Eighteenth of January. JA, 2.30, Plaza de la Independencia.'

'Who's JA?'

'AJ backwards,' Chimo said. 'An old trick. Amateurish.' He handed Adam a copy of a surveillance report. It recorded that at 14.33 hours on 18 January the subject had met the known political agitator Alfonso Jiménez.'

Chimo turned to the back of the diary to the pages reserved for addresses and telephone numbers. He pointed at the initials JA and a number ending in 61. He selected a surveillance report containing a phone number. The initial digits were the same but the number ended in 16.

'Another reversal,' Chimo said.

Adam let his clenched hands fall. They felt heavy, someone else's hands. 'I won't be making that report,' he said.

'I'm sorry, Amado, I really am.'

'But why?'

'Maybe she wanted to change the world. You did once.'

Adam smoothed the blue coverlet on the bed. He saw her, as though in a transparency, lying naked beside a faceless man with a hard-muscled body.

He said, 'Why did you leave it so long?'

'The raid? We would have left it longer. Widened the net. But we didn't have much time left. You see Jiménez intends to assassinate Franco. And what better place than the opening of the Valley of the Fallen tomorrow, 1 April?'

'You knew that when you raided the house?'

'We had a good idea. All that was missing was the details.'

'And now you're missing Jiménez.'

'But we have the details,' Chimo said. 'Your wife gave them to us.'

They brought the bones from all over the country. The remains of 50,000 Spaniards who died in the Civil War to be interred in burial niches in the great basilica of Santa Cruz del Valle de los Caidos. Among the remains to be exhumed and brought there were these of José Antonio Primo de Rivera whose coffin, still covered by a Falange flag, was removed from the Escorial, Philip II's gloomy palace nearby, at 20.05 hours on 31 March.

On 1 April, 20 years after the end of the war, 8,000 army subalterns and many thousand children from the Youth Front assembled to greet General Francisco Franco Bahamonde who was, at 11 am, to open the monument that had cost 1,000 million pesetas.

The marksman lay on a patch of thyme on a rocky outcrop, overlooking the esplanade and the mouth of the crypt contained between the jaws of two classical arcades.

He wore the uniform of a *Guardia Civil*, just a little too small for him. The body of the uniform's true owner lay concealed beneath holm oak and brambles 100 metres away. A few deposits of black and cinnamon beard that had fallen tardily from his hastily-shaven chin and cheeks lay on the olive-green tunic.

He was armed with a Russian World War II rifle, a Mosin-Nagant, fitted with a PE telescopic sight which was supposed to be accurate up to 1,400 metres. Well, it would have to extend its accuracy today. He stroked the trigger with his index finger.

So what has brought you to this hill that has been here since the world was created? Indignation certainly. About assumption and arrogance. You have dimly perceived a kind of sharing and you have fuelled it with eloquence.

But how much martyrdom is there in all this, for as surely as the bull in the ring dies in the contest or its sequel I will face the firing squad or the strangle-hold of the garotte.

Jiménez, peering through the cross-hairs of the telescopic sight, squeezed his eyes together and kept them shut for a long moment.

What of the girl? You left her bleeding in the dust.

But I had no choice. A sacrifice to the Cause.

He wished he had made love to her just once, that she hadn't been so loyal to her Fascist husband, the *inglés*. What beliefs had driven *him* to fight in a foreign land all those years ago? Had they become as indistinct as mine are now becoming as I lie on a hill outside Madrid waiting to kill the Chief of State and Generalisimo of Spain?

He smelled the pungency of the thyme. And the oil on the rifle. And the flinty earth. Of all the senses smell is the most evocative, he thought. As I die I will smell the thyme and the oil and the earth.

Thousands, ranks of ex-servicemen among them, stood hushed on the great esplanade as Franco addressed them. 'Our war was clearly not a civil war but a real crusade . . .'

Above him the cross, with the four evangelists, St John, St Mark, St Luke and St Matthew at the base, reached into the sky. Behind him the echoing crypt led to the High Altar and the tomb of José Antonio and the site where he himself would one day be laid to rest.

At the opening of the Seminary for Social Studies adjoining the monument, Franco spoke about the evils of Communism. From the crowd came the chant, '*Arriba España! Viva Franco!*'

At his vantage point, Alfonso Jiménez waited. One shot as Franco made his way to his car.

As he waited, a detached part of his mind, as sharp and cold as an icicle, concentrated on what lay ahead; another part melted and spread in rivulets of incomprehension.

He saw Franco as a child in Galicia and he saw himself playing in the garden of a small but not impoverished house on the outskirts of Madrid. What had brought them together in this valley, leader and inconsequential orator, victim and assassin? Was it all circumstance? One great unfathomable accident?

An eagle hovered above the basilica. He felt the crust of the world with his elbows, heard its heartbeat. As he heard the voice of the *guardia*, 'Don't move,' as he moved, trying to redirect the aim of the rifle, as one bullet hit him in the chest, the other in the back of the head.

And then the smell of thyme and oil and earth was strong in his nostrils.

Rosana read about the inaugural ceremony in *ABC* and *Ya*. No mention of an assassination bid; but there wouldn't have been anyway – the censors would have seen to that. Not that it mattered: Franco was still alive so Alfonso had failed.

A knock on the door. Chimo entered. He handed her purple grapes powdered with mauve bloom and sat beside the bed. 'How are you feeling?'

'A little pain. Nothing much. Did you tell Adam?'

'I had to,' Chimo said.

'How did he take it?'

'I don't know. He locked it inside himself.'

'Does he think I was unfaithful?'

'He's not stupid,' Chimo said.

'I wasn't,' Rosana said. 'I wasn't unfaithful to myself either.'

Chimo shrugged. 'The point is you have earned the undying gratitude of my superior officer. You saved Franco's life and he is going to be promoted and I am going to get his job. It showed great initiative, Señora Fleming, to penetrate a dangerous terrorist organization and prise their secrets from them.' He grinned and took one of her grapes.

'Alfonso?'

'Dead. I scarcely recognized him without his beard.'

'And what will happen to me?'

'That depends on Adam.'

'And me,' she said.

'Well, good luck, Señora Fleming, even though we never really liked each other.'

He took another grape and left the room. Rosana glimpsed the nurse in the corridor outside, heard her talking to Chimo.

When she came into the room she was smiling smugly.

'How are we today?' she asked Rosana. Rosana said she was fine.

'We must thank God that we saved the baby.'

'What baby?'

The nurse stared at her. 'You mean you didn't know you were pregnant?'

CHAPTER 24

On 30 May 1964, Pablo Gomez, aged 27, better known as *El Flaco*, went to see Manuel Benitez, aged 28, better known as *El Cordobés*, perform at Las Ventas bullring in Madrid.

In many ways Pablo identified with the orphan from Andalucia who, with his abbreviated *banderillas* and his sword, had fought his way up from unrelenting poverty to become the charismatic star of the *fiestas bravas*.

Both had been *espontáneos*. Both had been projected by mentors. I had Ernesto Villar, *El Cordobés* had Rafael Sanchez, *El Pipo*. He has been gored many times; I have been injured – kept out of the Spanish team by my injuries.

Today *El Cordobés*, watched by millions on television, was to make his first appearance in the Madrid bullring as a fully-fledged matador. And next month I will play for Spain in the European Nations Cup.

Rain pattered steadily on the sand as *El Cordobés* in his Suit of Lights, handsome urchin face beneath his Beatles haircut locked in concentration, faced a black bull named Impulsivo. He should now have been preparing for the kill. Instead, with his *muleta*, he was engaging the bull in one more flirtation with death.

Such crazy courage, Pablo thought. Even now purists were still outraged by his unorthodoxy. In Pablo's book it was originality. How could you qualify the style of a matador as he held a bull's horns in his hands and kissed its forehead?

But there was no kissing now as the bull followed the cape, refused to leave its thrall, creating a long, spinning pass with *El Cordobés* at its axis. And Pablo knew it was one pass too many. One manoeuvre too many in front of the goal-mouth . . .

Impulsivo got him in the thigh. He fell. Impulsivo moved in for his revenge and thrust again at his thigh, his horn gouging it open.

Pablo thrust his way out of the bullring. In his apartment he switched on the television and followed *El Cordobés*'s fight for life in Room 9 of the Toreros' Hospital after the chief surgeon of the Madrid *corrida*, Dr Maximo de la Torre, had operated on his thigh in the bullring infirmary.

Forty-eight hours later, Pablo and the rest of Spain learned that *El Cordobés* was going to live. And with Pablo's relief came outrage composed of comparison – the rejection the penniless vagrant had suffered and the adulation he now received from those who had treated him as an outcast.

The outrage grew like a mutating cell until it embraced all the injustices of life and, three days after the goring, he sat down at the table while Encarna was visiting friends and wrote a letter to Franco about the biggest injustice of all, his mother's continuing imprisonment.

It was a muddled letter, but he hoped that his sincerity would imbue it with a special lucidity. He invoked youth and ideals and the inherited circumstances that set men and women on course for their destinies. He cited *El Cordobés* who might still be a vagrant if it hadn't been for certain circumstances. *My mother has surely suffered enough for the circumstances of her birth and I plead with you to release her remembering that, like you, she fought for what, rightly or wrongly, she believed in.*

He posted the letter, reflecting that there were three possible outcomes to it. My mother will be released. I will be thrown into gaol. Or, the situation will continue as though the letter had never been written.

During the next couple of weeks it seemed to Pablo that he had invoked the wrath of a vindictive fate. Ernesto Villar died of a heart attack half-way through a *paella* cooked for four and Pablo broke his leg while practising, thus precluding him from playing for Spain in the European Nations Cup.

As he heard the bone snap he thought of *El Cordobés* lying on the wet sand of Las Ventas bullring.

Most news from the outside world reached Ana who, by 1964, had been in prison for 16 years, through a dumpy wardress named Angela. Angela had been at the gaol a mere nine years but, as the two longest serving occupants, they struck up a friendship that owed much to boredom.

In Angela's room where they drank bitter cocoa and ate magdalenas, she told Ana about the tourists swarming on to the beaches of the Mediterranean, of the poverty those tourists never saw – the hovels at La Chanca in Almería, for instance, the strikes and the bombs that had exploded in Madrid in 1960, the Basque and Catalan dissent, the minimum wage set at 36 pesetas a day, the growing voice of the Church – the Archbishop of Seville asserting that no one could live on less than 110 pesetas.

Angela told Ana about the speculation as to when Franco, 70 in December 1962, would nominate Juan Carlos as future king of Spain while his father still languished in Portugal; and she told her about the marriage of the young prince to Princess Sofia of Greece. 'A beautiful couple,' she said, sipping her cocoa and staring at the grubby walls unadorned by any photographs of gallant suitors.

And when the young couple's daughter was christened two days after Christmas Day 1963, she brought the newspapers into the room and stared at the pictures of the baby as though it were her own.

'Do you think Juan Carlos will ever become king?' she asked Ana, and Ana thought he would. Hoped he would, because, even though she was a Republican, Spain needed dignity.

'And will we still be here?'

'It is up to you whether you stay. I have no choice.'

'There will be another amnesty,' Angela said. 'You will be released.' She took a small bite from her magdalena and chewed methodically, squirrel-pouch cheeks moving busily. 'And then I will be sad.'

'You can't expect me to visit you,' said Ana, reflecting that she needed to get away from the prison soon because she had narrowed the list of those who might have shot Jesús to 48 and there was nothing more she could do here.

'Then I shall visit you.'

'You will be welcome in my home. If I get a pardon, which I doubt.' But Angela's words had made a possibility of it and she smelled the streets of Madrid and saw white clouds drifting high across its turrets; but mostly she saw the light over the city that is polished by the winds from the mountains. 'Why did you become a wardress?' she asked. 'You know what they say – a prisoner gets a sentence, a warder gets life.'

'It's a living. There are worse jobs. For many there are no jobs at all. I am performing a duty,' she assured herself. 'I am good at my job.'

'The best,' Ana said.

'It will seem a strange place to you when you get out, Ana Gomez.'

'Madrid is still Madrid.'

'But attitudes have changed. Everyone is waiting, just as El Caudillo has always done.'

'For what? The second coming?'

'For Franco to die,' Angela said.

'He could live another 20 years.'

'They say he is ill.'

'You showed me a paper in which his doctor said he was in good health.'

'What else would he say?' Angela took another disciplined bite of magdalena. 'No, it will be a foreign land to you, Ana Gomez. How old are you?'

'Fifty-five,' Ana said. And I look older, she thought, although, with her sense of purpose, she did not consider the years. 'Old enough to be your mother.'

'And you haven't even seen your grandson. He's a beautiful boy,' said Angela, who had seen Rosana when she had brought her son to the prison. 'Aren't you interested?'

'I am more interested in my son and his wife. What will they do now?'

'It's only a broken bone. He will play again.'

'He isn't young,' Ana said. 'Not for football.'

'I can't understand,' said Angela, a spinster, 'why you don't want to see your own grandson.'

'Why should I? I have never seen him. Why should I want to see him any more than the son of a peasant in Siberia?'

'Because he's flesh and blood.'

'The Civil War taught us that is nonsense. Father killed son, brother killed brother.'

'He asked why you wouldn't see him.'

'And what did you say?'

'That you were ill.'

'Did he believe you?'

'His mother didn't. She's a famous painter now,' Angela said. 'She exhibits all over the world. I wonder if her husband sees them in London.'

'It is of no interest to me,' Ana said.

'I don't know how he could live without that little boy.' Angela, who had heard about most of life's iniquities, shook her head sadly.

That night Ana was more restless in her bunk than she had been for a long time. Life outside the prison walls breathed into the cell. Because her work inside the prison was finished?

The summons finally came on 22 June.

Glumly, Angela took her to the office. At the big desk which she had last seen more than a decade ago sat a thin-faced man with dyed hair. He was holding a copy of *Marca* in his left hand. 'A famous victory,' he remarked, 'Spain 2, Russia 1. Goals by Pereda and Marcelino. What a pity your son couldn't have played. *El Flaco*, a well kept secret, eh, Ana Gomez?'

'But not from you,' Ana said.

'And your daughter, a famous painter. Did you know she once had an audience with General Franco?'

Nothing surprised Ana any more; her emotions had become polarized.

'She has become quite influential,' the plain-clothes policeman said. 'She is very lucky,' he added, but he didn't elaborate. 'Why won't you see her?'

'You know why.' Ana sat on the opposite side of the desk. She guessed she might be released.

He chewed the inside of his lip and gazed at her
speculatively. He looked like a man waiting for a nip from a
stomach ulcer that never came. He said his name was Solana.

'Do you know anyone named Chimo?' he asked.

'There are many Chimos. Ask me if I know a Paco or a
Pepe.'

This unrevealing answer seemed to satisfy him, as though
he hadn't much cared anyway – a throw-away, a distraction
from the mainstream of interrogation. He picked up a pink
file bearing her name. It was surprisingly bulky considering
the number of years she had been inoperative.

He said, '*El Sentido* is dead.'

This time he found a nerve. 'How?'

'He worked closely with the Basques in France, trying to
unite them with the Basques in Spain. He was responsible for
many bank raids in Spain. He was clever, always striking far
away from his homeland.'

'Homeland? You recognize that?'

'He did,' Solana said. 'That is enough. Me, I administer the
law.'

'What happened?'

'At last you have come alive, Ana Gomez.' He shuffled the
contents of the file. 'In January 1963 he was ambushed by
the *Guardia Civil* near Gerona. He escaped but he died from
his wounds.'

So even while I was lying in my bunk feeling the hardness
of his body, the curve of his bandy legs, he was dead.

Tears gathered in her eyes. She couldn't remember when
she had last cried.

'I'm sorry,' Solana said.

'Why should I care whether you are sorry or not?'

Solana flicked his thumb against the fingers of his left
hand; the hand seemed to irritate him as though it were a
stranger's encroaching on to his desk.

Solana lit a cigarette. Where would inquisitors be without
cigarettes? Offering them, exhaling their smoke insolently,
seeking a pause by the ritual of lighting-up.

Solana said, 'Madrid has changed a lot since you were out
there,' pointing over the prison walls. 'You wouldn't recognize

what was the front line in your day. Great blocks of apartments at Rosales and Argüellas. Battlements of them at Chamartín, Cuatro Caminos . . .'

'You are trying to persuade me to stay in gaol?'

'I'm merely warning you.'

'You're releasing me?'

'It depends.' Everything depended with him, she thought.

'On what?'

'Your intentions. We know, of course, that you have a vendetta to pursue. That doesn't bother us.'

'Because you think I'll fail?'

'Nineteen thirty-seven? Twenty-seven years ago?'

She let it ride: it was better that they thought she was merely nursing a prison obsession – they were common enough.

Solana said, 'What we don't want is the Return of the Heroine. Which is why exiles stay exiled. No interviews, no platform speeches. Spend the autumn of your life in comfortable obscurity.'

'What I don't understand,' Ana said, 'is why you're releasing me at all if I'm still a threat.'

'Compassion?'

She let that one ride, too.

'You have influential children,' Solana told her.

'A painter and a football player?'

'Both interests close to the heart of El Caudillo.'

'They petitioned for my release?'

'I ask the questions, Ana Gomez. Can you give me those assurances?'

Why not? She wasn't going to exhume political skeletons.

'You have my promise,' she said.

'In writing,' pushing a four-paragraph statement in triplicate across the desk.

She signed with a stuttering pen and he dried the ink with a sheet of blotting-paper.

'When can I go?'

'Whenever you please.' He stood up, looking as though he were going to shake hands; instead he held his left hand with his right. 'Good luck, but remember it's a different world out there.'

Angela accompanied Ana back to the cell. 'I know,' she said, as Ana rummaged through her belongings, 'I'm in for life.'

'You must visit me,' Ana said. 'Cocoa and magdalenas.'

'I think I'll quit. They're moving the prison to Delicias, next to the railway station. It won't be the same . . .'

Carrying her old suitcase, wearing the mould-smelling black dress that she had worn when she was admitted, Ana made her way towards the exit, trailing behind her the stale odours of confinement.

She didn't experience any surge of relief; sadness, rather, at leaving familiar contours. Angela's hand lingered heavily on her arm. Then the gate opened and she was a child emerging from a darkened cinema into dazzling light.

Tom Canfield also had to re-assess, to handle gingerly the fragile contradictions that had assembled in his middle-age.

Who would have thought that a man in his fifties would approach sex as nervously as a virginal youth? But that was the effect the long-delayed marriage and consummation had upon him and it was Josefina who guided them. Instinctively and competently but not, thank God, clinically. Soon they made love with the familiarity of a long-wedded couple and the freshness of honeymoon novices.

His affluence, too, was a paradox. It should have been the seal of success, a security for their marriage. Instead it was, Josefina intimated, his shame. Profits on such a scale could only be ill-gotten and should, like a robber's loot, be disposed of.

He took her on a tour of his properties stretching down the Mediterranean coast from the Costa Brava to the Costa del Sol. Wherever they went, concrete climbed from sand to sky, while Spain's latest army of insurgents, the tourists – 14 million of them in 1964 – occupied the beaches. Spain – thanks largely to the Minister of Information and Tourism, Mañuel Fraga, who was also busily expanding freedom of expression – was now part of Europe: even the French conceded that.

Tom, pointing at a block rising skeletally opposite Benidorm's Levante beach – once as lonely as a seagull's cry, now packed with grilling bodies – said with quiet desperation: 'Look, I'm helping to accommodate vacationers and bring prosperity to Spain. What's so wrong with that?'

'The profits,' Josefina said.

In a promenade café filled with bare-chested men and girls in bikinis which, ten years earlier, would have provoked the police to arrest them for indecent exposure, Tom, wily businessman, approached the subject from a devious angle.

'You've got to accept that any successful business makes profits,' he said, looking at a flushed girl at the next table who had sand on her bosom and was drinking sangria as though it were lemonade.

'It's what you do with them that matters.'

'Some of it has to be reinvested.'

Josefina sucked Coca Cola through a straw.

'As for the rest . . . You wouldn't object if it was given to charity, would you?'

A slight shake of the head as she continued to siphon Coke.

'Medicine?'

An infinitesimal nod. The girl drinking sangria began to giggle as a man with a thatch of sandy hair on his chest massaged a nipple stiffening beneath cerise nylon. Not so long ago he would have been thrown into gaol.

'It may interest you to know I'm financing a new wing of a hospital.'

'Gangsters do that sort of thing,' she said, pushing the bent straw aside; but her voice had lost its edge.

'And philanthropists,' said Tom who had anticipated just such a retort. 'Ernesto might operate there one day.'

She glanced at him warily.

The girl at the next table brushed ineffectually at the hairy hand at her breast and drank thirstily, ice and fruit bobbing against her teeth.

'But he's got a long way to go,' Tom said casually. 'How old is he?'

'You know how old he is, 18.'

'That means he will be at least 24 before he qualifies as a doctor.'

'And another three or four before he becomes a heart specialist,' said Josefina, supplying his ammunition for him.

'During which time he'll earn scarcely any money.'

'We'll manage.'

'Josefina,' Tom said, laying his hand over hers, 'the time has come to stop being a martyr. Of course we'll manage. I'm his step-father.'

'He doesn't need your money.'

'What's he going to live on studying in Valencia for ten years?'

'I've put money aside. He can work during the vacation. And when he's working as an assistant to a heart specialist he'll earn some money.'

'Peanuts,' Tom said in English. And gently, because Spanish pride is a delicate fabric, 'I don't think you would have been able to make it. Honestly I don't. I know you would have tried . . . but ten years . . .'

She tied the straw into a knot with her capable fingers.

'So doesn't it make sense,' Tom went on, 'to help him? Why deprive him of his future just because you don't like the way your husband earns his money? It isn't fair to him is it?' he asked softly. 'And one day he'll be a fine doctor . . .'

Lips compressed, she pulled the two ends of the straw so abruptly that it broke at the knot. 'You're right, of course,' she said and, although Tom didn't rejoice at the small victory, he was satisfied that in their modest household he had established his credentials.

Despite the compromise Tom found that he still had to display his wealth modestly and manoeuvre it tactfully. He bought a larger but unpretentious apartment in Alicante in a venerable square overlooking the beach, and a smaller flat in Madrid to neutralize any suspicions that there he worshipped at the altar of Mammon. He encouraged purchasers of his properties to pay him in other currencies in other countries and kept accounts in banks in Switzerland, Andorra, Gibraltar and New York. He thought it was crazy to be so self-effacing about his riches – where was the yacht, the Ferrari, the chateau? – but he was at peace and there was no value that you could put on that.

While he built, while he manoeuvred, while he settled thankfully into domesticity – he watered the geraniums on the balcony and squeezed the orange juice – he continued to keep his diary, which now filled a cupboard with its years, the early entries faded to the colour of dried blood.

It was those early entries that prompted him to re-introduce Adam into his diary. It was a warm May evening and through the open windows he could see the milky sea cat-licking the beach, hear the rustle of indolent palms. Josefina was preparing supper in the kitchen, Ernesto was studying in his room – an aeronautical manual, probably, hidden between the covers of *Gray's Anatomy*. Tom unscrewed his fountain-pen and began to write in the 1964 volume of his collected works.

5 May. Remembered the instant camaraderie that sprang up between Adam Fleming and myself. Destroyed more than two decades later by a stupid quarrel over business ethics. Or was it? Even though he's in England I can feel the tug of those bonds, particularly in the early hours of the morning. I think maybe we might have gotten together again if it hadn't been for . . . what?

Tom laid down his pen and gazed across the sea where the lights of ships moved like wandering stars. What had occurred between Adam and Rosana? What could be so heinous that a man of Adam's integrity could abandon a pregnant wife, only seeing his small son at legally arranged intervals? Adultery was the obvious culprit but Tom found that difficult to accept. Certainly not Adam; he had felt about Rosana as I do about Josefina. Rosana? That didn't quite fit either. Resourceful she was, an opportunist too, but an adulteress?

Josefina brought him a beer. 'Am I in it today?' she asked, pointing at the diary.

'You've been in it ever since you first took my temperature.' She smiled secretly and returned to the kitchen.

Tom began to write again with concentration and anger that fuelled upon itself.

What really bugs me is that he left without even consulting me. Egotistical, I guess, but we did share. And already it's a lifetime ago, his son's lifetime.

He replaced the diary on top of the years stacked in the cupboard.

Ernesto came into the room, stretching and yawning cavernously. He had a lanky basketball player's physique and he assessed life analytically through his spectacles; when he took a break from analysis he was cheerfully good-looking in a rumpled sort of way.

Tom, often the subject of measured scrutiny, said, 'So, at what altitude have you been flying?'

Ernesto grinned abruptly, put his finger conspiratorially to his lips. '*Principles of Resuscitation*,' he said, and Tom grinned back at him – such conspiracy was the soul of family life.

The entries he made in his diary in his offices in Alicante and Madrid were more the stuff of history.

12 June. Spain is developing at a gallop. A new working-class as relatively well-off as the bourgeoisie is emerging, owning or sharing TVs, fridges, automobiles. But, by God, they have to work for them. Twelve hours a day on a building site for instance – and you can't walk ten paces without falling into one of those. Factories and housing estates shooting up at Zaragoza, Valladolid, Vigo, Huelva . . . The countryside is being bled of its people as they flock to the cities. Most people work so damn hard these days that they don't have time to protest. Although, of course, dissent can still be heard among students and, more significantly, the clergy. And in the regions, in particular in the Basque country where *Euskadi Ta Askatasuna*, ETA, is taking hold.

In October the diary lapsed for a few weeks while Tom and his partner, Antonio Ruiz, went to war.

Following the best business traditions, the battles were fought in restaurants, the fare varying from *haute cuisine* to wholesome according to the quality of the invective.

The first range-finding shots were fired in English in the Casa Ciriaco on the Calle Mayor beneath the balcony from which, appositely, a bomb was thrown in 1906 in an abortive attempt to assassinate Alfonso XIII on his wedding day.

Antonio aimed first – over pigeon and beans.

'The attitude to foreigners,' he said chewing delicately, 'has changed a lot in the past few years.'

'I guess the attitude to everything has changed,' Tom said, slicing his pigeon breast.

'We aren't so dependent on them any more.'

'No?' Tom rolled velvety Rioja wine round his mouth. Such restaurants still surprised him – from the outside the Ciriaco looked like a forgotten milk bar; inside, despite the pictures of bullfighters on the walls, it was as intimate as a confessional. 'What about the tourists? Americans, British, Germans, French, Dutch, Belgians, Scandinavians, Italians . . .'

'We feed off them,' Antonio said. 'We are not dependent upon them as we once were on Americans.'

A warning sounded distantly. 'Not dependent maybe, but they are helpful . . . the Madrid-Washington renewal? More economic aid for Spain, the Grand Cross of Carlos III for the Spanish ambassador in the States for his contribution to American-Hispanic relations?'

'We're in the driving-seat. That's the difference. America needs its bases here. We're the bulwark against Soviet expansion,' Antonio recited.

'You mean Spain doesn't need that aid?'

'Payment due. Why not?' Antonio shrugged. His hair was quite grey now, coaxed to a fashionable shade by his hairdresser, curls still springily virile; only the whites of his eyes, that were the colour of his teeth, and the tightening skin on his cheekbones betrayed him.

'So Spain can do without America?'

'That's not what I'm saying. No one in the West can do without America. It was a sad day for all of us when Kennedy was killed . . . All I'm saying is that these days we're not reliant only on the States – there are other countries who have consigned the Civil War to history.'

'You can forget Britain,' Tom said. 'They got themselves a Labour government yesterday. They still believe George Orwell should have led the Republicans to victory.'

Antonio removed the meat from a fragile bone. 'Let me put it more directly,' he said, nibbling. 'We don't need *you* as much as we once did. You were important to the company because you were American. You could buy, sell, negotiate, move freely, cut a few corners, duck a few regulations . . . No one wanted to upset you.'

'And now?'

'Let's face it, Tom, you haven't been giving the business your undivided attention recently. How can you from Alicante?'

The second skirmish occurred in the restaurant on the 26th floor of the Edificio España. From there you could view the display case of Madrid. The wrinkled rooftops of the old city, the oasis greens of the Retiro, the Telefónica tower, apartment blocks on the march, spires and towers, domes like sprightly fungi in the autumn mist.

'We would, of course, pay handsome compensation,' Antonio said, as though he had omitted the introduction to an overture.

'We?'

'My daughter, Isabel, is joining the company.' Antonio cut the corner of a wholesome steak.

'Compensation for what?'

'Your services in the past.'

'As of now?'

'I'm sorry,' Antonio said. 'But you have been neglecting your duties.'

'Duties?'

'Responsibilities.' Antonio dabbed at the corners of his mouth with a napkin.

'Supposing I said I had no intention of quitting?'

'Then I would say you were stupid. You will still be a wealthy man. You enjoy home life and you will be able to spend even *more* time with your wife and step-son.'

'Or maybe I should tell you to get lost.'

'That would be inadvisable.'

'A threat?'

'Statement of fact. Almost all the recent contracts have been negotiated by me – while you've been picking oranges in Alicante. They're mine, Tom; all we share is our letterhead.'

'*Our* company. In law you wouldn't have a leg to stand on.'

Antonio leaned forward. Tom felt that they were alone together in a capsule suspended over Madrid. Antonio said, 'Have you ever heard of a man named Belov?'

So that was it. Tom shivered inwardly as he had once done before doing battle in the skies. 'Sure I remember him. Is he still alive? Stalin executed most of the advisers when they got back to Russia.'

'He's alive all right,' Antonio said. He drank some beer. 'He reckons you defrauded him.'

'Of what?'

'Gold,' Antonio said.

'What gold?' Tom pushed aside his plate and leaned back in his chair.

'You know what gold. The gold the Republicans handed over to Russia in the Civil War. The bullion that prompted Stalin to say, "The Spaniards will never see their gold again, just as one cannot see one's own ears." The missing gold that Spain heard about in 1956 when Negrin died leaving the receipts to the Spanish government. But the Russians didn't get it all, did they Tom?'

'Didn't they?'

'You know damn well they didn't because you stole some of it.'

'Who says I did?'

'Belov says you did.'

'And where's Comrade Belov?'

'In Madrid,' Antonio said. 'In the Hostal Fontela. He says you promised him a cut but you never paid him.'

'And what has all this got to do with you?' Tom pushed aside his plate and stared across the city emerging from its chrysalis of mist in the fragile sunshine.

'I don't think the Ministry of the Interior would like to

hear that you stole Spanish gold,' Antonio said, staring at Tom with his yellowing eyes.

Tom said, 'If anyone stole any gold it must have been from the Russians.'

'Spanish gold just the same. The Francoists didn't hand it over, did they? According to their reckoning it still belongs to Spain. I honestly think it's time you retired, Tom,' Antonio said.

'Honestly?'

Antonio shrugged; he had made a language of shrugs.

Tom asked the waiter for the bill. When it arrived, folded on a saucer, he pushed it across the table to Antonio. 'Your treat,' he said.

The following day he sought out Belov in his hotel. His eyes were still sad and beautiful but his muscles had retired and his belly had fallen victim to gravity.

'Okay,' Belov said, 'where do you want to talk?'

'In the military museum,' Tom said. 'For old times' sake.'

'I tried to find you,' Tom said, as they entered a petrified chapter of Spanish history.

'Not as hard as you tried to find the gold. Fifteen per cent you promised me.'

'I went to the address you gave me. No one knew where the hell you were.'

'Not a forwarding address you like to leave,' Belov said.

Flags and banners hung pacifically above them; lances of sunlight struck sightless visors. There was even a suit of armour worn by a dog which children would remember long after they had forgotten the dates of conflict.

'What address?' Tom asked.

'A labour camp,' Belov said.

'You went back to Russia?'

'I was thrown out of France.'

'Forged passports?'

Belov nodded and his cheeks wobbled.

'Why didn't the Russians shoot you?'

'Not what you know, who you know.'

'Forged passports?'

'Better than gold. In the circumstances,' he added. 'I got 25 years instead of a bullet in the back of the neck.'

'And you got out . . .'

'Sixty-two, with remission. You really tried to find me?'

'Has anyone told you differently?'

'Your partner,' Belov said, staring at a gallery of pistols, Webleys, Smith & Wessons, Colts . . .

The Aroca tavern lies on the Plaza de los Carros. Step into its whitewashed interior and you step into pre-Republic Madrid. Sit at a table as dark as history and you sit at an altar to an ancient cuisine. Langouste from the mouth of the Ebro, wedges of hake from the Atlantic, snips of chicken fried with garlic, milk-fed lamb cutlets . . . washed down with robust wine from La Mancha.

Tom invited Antonio there because invective would be minimal, on his part anyway, and therefore good food was protocol. They both carried briefcases bulging with importance and they placed them carefully beside their chairs. They both drank a fino, consulted the menu with lingering concentration and, having made awesome decisions, leaned back in their chairs and gazed at each other with the rapport of familiar enemies.

'I gather,' Antonio said – a little prematurely, Tom thought – 'that you've reached a decision.'

'All in good time,' Tom said, pouring himself some of the wine which was reputed to be matured in a pig-skin. 'Let's enjoy the food.'

Simultaneously they attacked their langouste. Antonio finished first, returning briskly to business. 'The parting of the ways,' he said, as though they had been conversing inaudibly. 'To be regretted but inevitable.'

'Certainly inevitable,' Tom said.

They both reached for their briefcases.

Tom got his papers out first. He said, 'I want to talk about that deal on the Costa Brava.'

'Which deal?' Antonio frowned. 'We've got a lot of deals. In any case I don't see –'

'That deal.' Tom laid an old brochure on the table between the excavated langouste shells. 'Invest in sunshine, Spain's gilt-edged security . . . Remember?'

'That was years ago,' Antonio said. 'And it's got nothing to do with what we've come here to discuss.'

'Should have been guilt-edged,' Tom said, spelling out 'guilt' in English. 'Nice brochure, though. Look at that swimming pool. Where did you find that, Florida? Look at the grass, straight from Wimbledon. And look at that sunshine . . . practically burns your fingers as you hold the brochure. And a lot of investors did get their fingers burned, didn't they, Toni?'

'There are thousands of developments like that in Spain,' Antonio said.

'Sure, but this one was never finished. Scarcely started. A cut of the profits after water and electricity were installed? What water, what electricity?'

Antonio said, 'We came here to discuss gold.'

'A lot of people lost a lot of money on that deal.'

'Are you going to quit or do I go to the Ministry of the Interior?'

The waiter served *flan*.

Tom said, 'You handled the contracts, Toni. Right?'

'On our joint behalf.'

'But it's your name on them. As you so rightly pointed out I've become a little lax in recent years. Too busy growing oranges in Alicante . . .'

'You can't confuse business practice with robbery. You stole bullion.'

'I consulted my lawyer,' Tom lied. 'Here's a copy of the denouncement.' He tossed a type-written document on top of the brochure.

Antonio grabbed it.

Tom spooned *flan*.

'You've got a nerve,' Antonio said, still reading.

'And another document. This one needs your signature.' Tom delved into his briefcase again. 'It's simple enough. You resign and renounce all interest in the company.'

'On the contrary,' said Antonio, 'it's you who have to sign a document like that.'

'In your briefcase? Leave it there, Toni. It's not worth the paper, et cetera . . . I want that,' pointing at the resignation and renunciation, 'signed in front of witnesses in my office by six o'clock this evening.'

'You've got to be out of your mind,' Antonio said, ignoring his *flan*. 'What about the gold?'

'What gold is that, Toni?'

'You know what gold. The gold Belov told me about.'

'Ah, Belov, my new partner. I forgot to tell you – he's moving into your office tomorrow. Odd, he didn't mention anything about any gold . . .'

Abandoning any pretence of business-lunch protocol, Antonio stood up abruptly, knocking over his chair, and made for the door. Tom called out after him, 'My treat, Toni. My pleasure.'

CHAPTER 25

Adam's school stood close to the Thames in a terrace of tall Georgian houses. Most of his students were middle-aged members of the professional classes contemplating retirement in Spain and the turnover was brisk because, although the cheese and wine parties where everyone spoke English were popular, few persevered beyond the winter when Spanish verbs had warmed the bleak evenings. Having 'mastered the basics', they took off on holiday to the Costas in the spring, returning with silver bottles of orange liqueur and Lladro figurines to Richmond but rarely to the classrooms. When Adam met them by chance and inquired after their health in Spanish they replied in English and crossed the street.

In high summer, when the school catered for Spaniards learning English, Adam left assistants in charge and flew to Spain to be with his son. Or was Eduardo his son? he wondered, as he watched him playing in the garden of the rented villa at Estepona on the Costa del Sol or watching television in the living-room furnished with rickety cane and scattered with holiday reading.

He was certainly black-haired, quick to laugh and quick to argue, but maybe Jiménez had been too. He was ashamed of the way he scrutinized Eduardo but the revulsion at what Rosana had done was still strong and quick. And when he had put the boy to bed, read him a story aware that his role was more avuncular than paternal, he drank whisky in the insect-humming garden and reopened the timeless debate with himself.

Had Rosana really been an active dissident? Why hadn't

she confided in him? He would hardly have shopped her to the authorities. Had she ever really loved him or had she used him all the time?

At this point disgust leaped and he tried to drown it with his third or fourth glass of whisky. The molten sea glimmered on the horizon; lizards pulsed on the balding grass.

How much of the disgust was ego? Humiliation? You should have realized what was going on under your nose. Seminars, exhibitions . . . How naïve can you be?

A fifth whisky, thoughts slurring round a single question. Did he sleep with her?

And then he thought of the little boy lying in the frugal bedroom, sweat beading his lip, trust locked in sleep, and he patrolled the garden with wandering footsteps assuring himself that, whatever the truth, the disgust should be concealed from him.

Sometimes, as Eduardo stood beside the pool shaking the water from his cropped blue-black hair or building with Lego bricks, he questioned Adam.

'Why do you live in London?'

'Because I work there.'

'Then why don't *we* live there, too?'

'Because you're Spanish.'

'Aren't we a family?'

'Of course.'

'Then why don't we live together?' testing his springy hair with the flat of his hand. 'They ask me at school,' he explained.

'One day I'll explain.'

'Why not now?'

'Because now it's time for bed.'

'What shall I tell them at school?'

'You don't have to tell them anything.'

'They laugh at me.'

'Already? Tell them you're luckier than they are. Two homes, one in Madrid, one in London.'

'When am I coming to London?'

'Soon.'

'Promise?'

'Promise.'

And the dark eyes beneath Rosana's strong eyebrows looked at him and saw through adult promises. Were his eyes the same shade as those of Alfonso Jiménez, known political agitator?

In the evenings, when the bats took over from the swooping swallows, Adam drank even more industriously beside the cascades of morning glory which, during the day, faded from bright blue to exhausted mauve.

He gambled, too, on any game that was going. Poker in home-spun casinos behind nondescript bars while the sighing maid looked after Eduardo or, through his bookmaker in London, horse-racing. And he lost with abandon.

Occasionally, perhaps twice during a vacation, Rosana joined them from Madrid, acting, it seemed to Adam, as though she were the injured party. As though distrust was a greater crime than infidelity.

While Eduardo was with them during the day they behaved like unnaturally polite parents. In the evenings they prolonged the courtesy until one of them provoked the other with words of apparent tolerance.

She was, she told him one night as they sat in rocking chairs on the terrace gazing at the distant lights spilling on to the sea, making a lot of money from her painting. Exhibiting shortly in Paris.

He congratulated her, glass of whisky held in one hand.

'But, of course, the pictures will be different in France. The theme is the Civil War.'

'Is that wise?'

'Why not? There was a civil war, you know.'

'Depends who's winning it in your collection.'

'It's about those who lost.'

'Everyone lost,' Adam said. He drank some whisky. 'Are you still fighting?'

'Planning,' she said.

She wore a long yellow dress and she was fanning herself, a figure from the traditional past; but Rosana was a creature of emergent Spain – she held herself differently these days and, hair released from its tortoiseshell combs, moved with unconscious arrogance.

'Planning what?'

'The future,' she said.

'The way Jiménez was planning it?'

'The way I thought he was planning it. He preached unity.'

'Unity? In Spanish politics?'

'Unity of purpose.'

'Which is?'

'Practical Socialism,' she said. 'Sharing prosperity instead of poverty. Communism isn't for Spain, never was. The climate's not right.' He picked up a smile in the uncertain light.

'I don't think Santiago Carillo would agree with you.'

'He's sincere but he's nailed to the cross of the past.'

'Nice phrase. Are you going to take your place on the political platform?'

'One day,' she said.

'Who would have believed it? The little girl who wanted a roof over her head . . . Were you planning even then?'

'To marry you, yes.'

'But you didn't love me?'

'I knew you'd be a good husband. I grew very fond of you.'

'Which is more than a lot of husbands can hope for.'

'But I could never confide in you. You were the great protector, the benefactor . . .'

A bead of light from a glow-worm appeared in the tangle of the bougainvillaea. Crickets chirped, mosquitoes whined.

'Did Jiménez listen to you?'

'I listened to him.'

'Did you sleep with him?' The words burst out as though they had been clamouring for release for a long time.

She stood up and slapped him.

The insect noise stopped but the glow-worm continued to glow.

Inside the house the boy began to cry.

In Richmond, Adam continued to teach and drink and gamble. When he wasn't doing any of these things he walked. He was an all-seasons walker but he preferred the late afternoons of winter, promenading the banks of the Thames, breathing the lonely scents of mud and mist and wet leaves.

On one such walk he was joined by one of his students, a widow stranded in her thirties, whose black, bust-filled jerseys were never quite free of strands of the thick blonde hair which she wore in a pony-tail. After the walk, as actors bound for the West End were leaving Richmond and businessmen were returning to it, they lingered on the green opposite Maids of Honour Row waiting for opening-time.

They then visited several different pubs in Richmond, and washed down an Italian meal with a bottle of vinegary Barolo. She accompanied him back to his cramped apartment above the classrooms, initiating a routine which endured on Wednesdays and Saturdays long after her studies had lapsed. She also displayed a sustained interest in gambling, helping him, with the collaboration of bookies' runners who called at the Orange Tree and the Roebuck, to dissipate most of the profits from the school.

Thus occupied, he thought minimally about Rosana and Eduardo. Except in the early hours of the morning when he was awoken by his dreams or when he stood on the Terrace gazing across the riverine landscape imagining small boys walking there with their dogs.

In Madrid, Rosana applied herself to politics, painting and motherhood. In that order. Not that she was a bad mother. Indeed, with the help of her maid and family, Eduardo was pampered, educated and disciplined as determinedly as any small boy in the capital.

What worried Rosana was that he might become aware, subconsciously, that she was not as devoted as other mothers. Why this was so she was not sure. Was there, perhaps, a blank in her brain that had not been filled because the war had separated her from her own parents, one dead and one in exile? She was inclined to doubt this: a deprived childhood was too handy an excuse for adult inadequacy. Hadn't both she and Pablo risen triumphantly from the ashes of war?

No, there was an inexorable quality in her make-up that excluded conventional emotions. This quality may have been honed by the survival lessons of the war but it had been there nonetheless. God knows, if it hadn't been for the war she might have grown up trying to cultivate emotions that she didn't possess. The war had bequeathed her honesty – with herself at least – and for that she was grateful.

Armed with this she examined her feelings towards her mother, husband and brother. She didn't know whether she loved her mother. Was never, in fact, comfortable with the word love, which embraced so many different emotions. What she did know was that she grieved over the stupidity of their estrangement.

Once she visited the small apartment that Pablo had bought Ana in a crowded block off the Paseo del Marqués de Zafra to the east of the city. She knocked on the door on the communal first-floor balcony and waited outside nervously, as if she had committed some misdemeanour in their home in the Tetuan district.

The door opened. Her mother had been diminished by the years but preserved by confinement. She was dressed in black and her hair was grey but her skin was softer, more pliant, than Rosana remembered it during the Hungry Years.

Rosana had no idea what to say to her. If only she would open her arms, offer one hand, utter her name. But she did none of these things. Instead she stood, arms folded and said, 'What do you want?'

'To see you.'

'Well, you've done that.' She began to close the door.

'For God's sake, I'm your daughter.' Rosana held the door with one hand.

'I haven't forgotten.'

A door opened along the balcony. Rosana could feel people listening in the somnolent heat.

'Don't you think this has gone on long enough?'

'You betrayed your father,' Ana said. 'That is all there is to it.'

'By marrying a man who believed in what he fought for?'

'Believed? An Englishman in a foreign country?'

'Can't you remember what it's like to be young? To believe, even though you are subsequently proved wrong. When you're young belief is everything.'

'They were the enemy,' Ana said. 'They had exploited us for centuries.'

'I know that,' Rosana said. 'I know that . . . But all Adam heard about was the killing of priests, the burning of churches, the "Irresponsibles" . . . His sister's husband was killed by the "Irresponsibles".'

'And where is she now?'

'Does that matter? All that matters is that young people have ideals; it doesn't matter if they contradict each other.'

'Your husband's ideals killed your father,' Ana said.

Behind the shutters along the balcony the listening quickened. At the same time Rosana's feelings hardened.

She said, 'The war was no one's fault and it was everyone's fault.'

'And what is that supposed to mean?'

'That whatever happened was your fault as much as anyone else's. Did my father want to go to war?'

'You have no right –'

'He was a poet.' *Stop this*, she told herself.

'And a soldier,' but there was rust in Ana's voice.

'Did he want to fight?'

Ana backed into the dusk of the apartment. She unfolded her arms. Her hands reached for each other in prayer. She said, 'He did what he had to.'

A church bell began to chime. Children's voices reached them from the park.

Another door on the balcony opened.

'What I'm trying to say,' Rosana said softly and urgently, 'is that you were as much to blame as Adam. That everyone was to blame then and we should stop blaming each other now.'

Ana, hands tightly clasped, knuckles bone white, said, 'I have the names of nearly 50 men who may have killed Jesús. Adam Fleming is one of those names.'

The door closed, squeezing, so it seemed to Rosana, some of the dusk into the daylight.

Her feelings for her husband and brother were tidier.

Adam had left her. She wished he hadn't. But she didn't grieve. If he returned one day then they might rediscover their orderly contentment once again; she hoped they would.

If she mourned at all it was for Adam. His aloneness, even when he was in company.

As for Pablo . . . They had occupied a period of time together. Then she had stepped out of it. She had almost stepped back once, when he passed her in the coach in Barcelona, but that had been an anachronism. She regarded him fondly, as she would have done if he had lived on another continent.

Acquaintances, she knew, were shocked by her attitudes, but they forgave her because she was an artist – they wanted to believe that her true passion was painting and in this she encouraged them, talking pensively about her inspiration and nodding wisely when collectors noted the influence of particular schools on her work. In truth she believed that she was neither inspired nor influenced. She sat before an empty canvas and waited while visions assembled in her mind; then she mixed her paints and transferred them to the canvas. Once she had seen the roof-tops of Madrid and they had become playing cards, politicians substituted for royalty, swirling towards a vortex of dissent; this had become her most famous picture.

She exhibited in New York, Paris and London and was photographed in *¡Hola!* and *Semana*; but painting was her escape, not her passion.

That was politics. Her platform: Socialism stripped of Marxism. Her obsession: unity. Her enemies: Francoists and Communists. Her heroes in the late 60s: the young bloods of the PSOE in Andalucia, Felipe Gonzalez and Alfonso Guerra.

So she plotted and preached and helped to organize the demonstration on 27 January 1967, protesting against high prices and low wages. In Madrid, despite police precautions and the boycott on public transport, legions of workers assembled at the Plaza de Castilla, Las Ventas and Cuatro Caminos.

Elsewhere protests erupted in Barcelona, Bilbao, Seville and Valencia. ETA interrupted a television football match between Real Madrid and Inter Milan by sabotaging a pylon; workers clashed with police in Franco's home town, El Ferrol.

But all the time she campaigned, Rosana felt as though she

were striding through stagnant water, thick with weeds. However impressive the protests, only a minority of Spaniards was involved, the majority paralysed by the belief that nothing would really change until Franco died. On 4 December, when he celebrated his 75th birthday, it was recalled in a newspaper that his father had lived to be 82, his mother's father 96.

One spring evening she went to a concert given by a young protest singer whose messages were similar to those of Raimón, the Valenciano, whose repertoire, which included verses by the poet Salvador Espriu, had been so emasculated that he had taken it to France.

The concert was held in a warehouse in Vallecas, Madrid, and most of the audience were students. Police – uniformed *greys* and plain-clothes members of the *Cuerpo Superior de la Policia* – were thick on the ground too.

Chimo, promoted to second-in-command of the *Cuerpo*, warned Rosana about attending.

'It could get rough,' he said.

'Why? The man's only singing.'

'You know why,' said Chimo, stopping in front of one of her pictures in a gallery on Serrano and pointing at it. 'What the hell's that?'

It was a painting of a bomb exploding, children fragmenting inside it.

'What does it look like?'

'It looks gruesome.'

'The Civil War wasn't a picnic.'

'Why would anyone want to buy that?'

'To remind them?'

'Spaniards want to forget,' Chimo said. 'And I strongly advise you not to go to this concert.'

'Are you going to break it up?'

'Only if it gets out of hand. Think what the Press would make of it. Society beauty and painter arrested at red concert.'

'Ignacio isn't a Communist.'

'So?' Chimo moved to another painting, a roofless church with a congregation of one, a soldier with hollow eyes, praying before a blood-stained cross on the altar.

'My mother spoke in a church like that,' Rosana said.

'Do you want to go to prison too? The sister of *El Flaco*, daughter of the Black Widow . . .'

'Confidante of General Franco?'

'One audience with him? Don't imagine that would help you.'

'Police informer? Heroine who saved Franco's life?'

'When? There has never been an attempt on Franco's life . . .'

They walked to the door of the gallery opposite a café where Madrileños were eating their first snack of the day. The quivering sunlight was gathering heat.

Rosana said, 'It *was* you who told Adam, wasn't it?'

'About Alfonso? Someone had to explain what you were doing in hospital with a bullet hole through you.'

'I suppose,' Rosana said carefully, 'that I should be grateful to you.'

'For telling Adam about you?'

'For making up my mind for me. I hadn't made up my mind about the concert until you came. Now I have: I'm going.'

She went with a gangling young French painter who was a friend of the singer. He parked his car, a Volkswagen beetle, in the Avenida de la Albufera and they walked to the warehouse. It was ringed by police, some on horseback. Inside, plain-clothes members of the squad assigned to Madrid University mingled conspicuously with the students.

Red flags bloomed among the audience seated on fold-up chairs; pictures of Fidel Castro and Che Guevara adorned the breeze-block walls. A voice rose above the babble, 'Stand up the police spies.'

The painter led Rosana to an office behind the improvised platform. Furniture catalogues were stacked against one wall and a vase of long-dead freesias stood on the desk. Ignacio was sitting on a chair, feet on the desk, plucking sad chords from his guitar. As she entered the office he stood up and she was instantly and astonishingly attracted to him.

He was slightly built with longish hair and Slavic angles to his face. He was noted for his disarming smile and when he switched it on for her she wanted to say, 'Don't. Not with me. I know all about you.' He wore flared black trousers and a white shirt with his name embroidered in red on the pocket. She sensed that this was deliberate, an antithesis to the unkempt school of protest, and she wanted to know what he saw when he looked at her.

He brushed his fingers across his mouth taking the smile with them. He knows I know, she thought. How old was he? Twenty-five? And I'm nearly 40, exposed for the first time to the potency of immediate attraction.

'I like your paintings,' he said.

True or calculated charm? 'Have you bought any?' she asked, discovering that instant attraction can generate ill-considered words.

'I can't afford them.' He plucked a lingering note on the guitar.

'Anything he gets,' the painter said, 'he gives to the cause.'

'And which cause is that?'

'Socialism,' Ignacio said. 'I'm not unconventional.'

'We all are,' she said.

He smiled and the smile spread from his lips to his eyes and this time it wasn't contrived.

He cradled the guitar and played a ripple of notes. 'My advice to you,' he said to Rosana, 'is to get out of here. There's going to be trouble.'

'You really think I'd go?'

'No,' he said, and she knew that he saw more than just a society painter standing in front of him.

'Come on,' the painter said, 'the show's about to begin.'

He and Rosana stood at the back of the warehouse, behind the students and plain-clothes police. To each song, protesting about dictatorship or poverty or repression there was a rapturous response.

The trouble started half-way through the programme. Ignacio had recited a poem, each verse separated by a few chords on the guitar. It was about two meals, one eaten by a gourmet, the other by a peasant in Extremadura. Each course of the gourmet's repast merited a verse, whereas the peasant's bean stew comprised interludes; it ended as the gourmet contested the vintage of his port and the peasant squeezed his empty wineskin.

The reaction from one pocket of the audience was raucous and not quite apposite. 'Down with the oligarchy,' and, 'To hell with Franco and the CIA.' Rehearsed, Rosana thought, at the behest of Chimo. A fight broke out and the grey-uniformed police moved in.

Ignacio grabbed the microphone. 'For God's sake,' he shouted, 'this isn't the way. This isn't 1936. What do you want? Fascism for another quarter of a century?'

Police, batons in hand, moved towards the stage.

The fighting spread and Rosana saw blood flowing down students' faces and she knew that this painting was filed in her inner visions – flowers with frightened eyes and bloody petals.

'Come on,' the painter shouted. 'Let's get out of here.'

'What about Ignacio?'

'He's old enough to look after himself,' the painter said, gripping her arm.

'Has he got a car?'

'Who cares?'

'I'm not going to leave him.'

'I told you, he can take care of himself.'

She broke free from his grip and made for the platform. Chairs were being smashed, the wreckage wielded as clubs. The police went about their business inexorably; students falling or fleeing before them.

Then the lights went out.

Rosana reached the platform. Heard the voice of the painter behind her. 'I'll bring the car.'

And now she was on the platform. 'Ignacio?'

'Over here composing a poem,' his voice theatrically amused.

'You've got to get out of here.'

'Have you brought a helicopter with you?'

'Don't act with me,' she shouted. 'Is there a window in the office?'

A discord of notes from his guitar.

Where was the office? Behind the platform, to the right.

She felt the boots of the police thudding on the platform. Heard the wood rupture. Leaped as it collapsed.

'Where are you?'

'Here,' he said beside her. 'Not acting any more.'

She heard his key slot into the lock of the office door.

Flashlights swept the darkness behind them. 'Stay where you are. Don't move and no one else will get hurt.'

He shut the door behind them. Then he kissed her. And something leaped inside her.

He opened the window, jumped out and helped her while she climbed out. When she dropped beside him he put his arm round her waist. Ragged fighting was going on around them. Sirens squawked. The moon shone fitfully, animating the scene like an old movie.

She smelled refuse, she kicked a can. His hand, holding hers, was dry and warm, as she had known it would be.

She saw the silhouette of the Volkswagen as it mounted the pavement and stopped on a patch of waste ground.

She ran ahead, pulling his arm, but he pulled her back.

He said, 'Do you love me?'

'Are you crazy?'

'Tell me or I won't get in the car.'

'Then stay here.'

'Do you?'

'You know I do,' she said.

One hour later he stood on the balcony of her apartment in the moonlight. Behind him the caged birds grumbled in their feathered dreams.

He said, 'I know I can only be natural with you and that scares me. We all act, don't we? To impress other people. And ourselves. What are we if we're deprived of our pretences?'

'Vulnerable?' She sat in a cane chair staring at his silhouette.

'Or innocents without personality?'

'I should like to make being natural an obligatory subject at school.'

'So no one must be sophisticated?'

'Only when it's natural,' she said.

She stood beside him. They smelled jasmine and saw a star move. She felt his warmth.

He went to bed first. She undressed slowly in her own room then, naked, joined him. He was the second man who had ever made love to her.

CHAPTER 26

Ana pursued her vendetta with resolute application. She installed filing cabinets in the gloomy living-room of her apartment, pinned maps of the provinces of Spain on the walls and sat for long periods at a gate-legged table honing down the list of suspects.

Many of them proved to be dead, but Ana did not believe that the man who had killed Jesús was among them: she had lived with him too long in gaol, had injected his veins with blood, covered his bones with flesh. Besides, anyone who shot another in the back was a survivor.

When she had completed the preliminary process of elimination she was left with 15 names. Adam Fleming was 15th but, so regulated was she by the inflexible routines of prison, so steadied by the disciplines of the huntress, that she didn't promote him for immediate attention.

On the May morning when she wrote his name at the end of the list, she took the bus to San Martin de la Vega to the south-east of Madrid and walked along the banks of the Jarama to Pindoque bridge, a nondescript concrete ruin circumvented by the thick waters of the small river. To one side, across wheatfields and vineyards, she could just make out the old gun emplacements in the mauve hills that sparkled with crystal in the sunlight.

She walked slowly towards the heights of Pingarrón which, more than 30 years earlier, had been taken and retaken by Nationalists and Republicans seeking to dominate the valley. Beneath it she found the small hill where Jesús had died. From her string bag she took a sketch map, drawn from information provided by survivors, and followed its arrows to a vantage point overlooking a sprawl of pine trees. Trenches had been gouged long ago from the soft rock and their knuckles were scattered with tiny pink and yellow weeds as bright as confectionery on an iced cake. She sat on the edge of one, legs dangling like a puppet's. If her calculations were right Jesús had died here and the trenches must have been dug after his death. She tried to recreate the scene but her mind was obstructed by the present. A hawk hovered far above her, a breeze sang in the pines.

She closed her eyes and waited for the gunfire, the thrust of steel, the vision of death perceived by men in battle, but she saw only pink shadows, heard only birdsong. She opened them again and let in the sunlight. Her imaginative powers, she understood, had long since departed; most of her emotions, too, shouldered aside by her mission.

As she deliberated she unconsciously scrabbled with her fingers in the pulverized rock thrown up long ago by soldiers burrowing for safety. Her fingers touched sun-warmed metal. A brass cartridge case, intact except for a pock-mark of verdigris where the exploded percussion-cap had been. She knew only that Jesús had been killed by a bullet fired by a little-used Star RU 9 mm sub-machine-gun; she had no idea what bullet this case had contained. Nevertheless, she slipped it into the pocket of her skirt.

She took a last look around the forgotten battle-field and walked back to San Martin de la Vega beside the canal running ruler-straight beside the river.

The following day she went to the bank where her capital had been earning interest while she had been in gaol, withdrew 5,000 pesetas and caught a train to Malaga to investigate the first suspect, a former corporal in the Nationalist infantry. She had a black-and-white photograph of him wearing his *granadero* trousers, flared at the thigh, and his *gorillo* forage cap with tassel. He looked self-consciously brave and Ana wondered what the years had done to him. She also wondered what sort of gun he had carried in 1937.

Sitting in a corner of the carriage, watched curiously by a

plump man with wiry hair plastered across his scalp from ear to ear, she opened her file on Miguel Garcia.

Born 10 October 1910. Enlisted in the Army 1928. Served in Madrid in the Cuartel de la Montana until 1934. Seconded to the Legion in Morocco as an instructor in small arms. Acknowledged marksman. Returned to the mainland in October 1934 to take part with the 111 Bandera *in the suppression of the Asturian miners,* Los Dinamiteros, *at Gijon and Oviedo. In August 1936, participated in the massacre at Badajoz . . .*

The plump man beamed at her over a copy of *ABC*. She ignored him but read the headlines. Franco had at last named Juan Carlos as his successor. She must have been too obvious because the man handed her the newspaper.

She read Franco's proclamation. *Conscious of my responsibility before God and before History and having weighed with due objectivity the qualities united in the person of Prince Juan Carlos de Bourbón, I have decided to propose him to the nation as my successor.*

Her companion said, 'So what do you think, king or puppet?'

'I have no idea,' Ana said and went on reading. *When, by the laws of nature, I shall no longer be able to steer the ship of state, which must inexorably happen, the decision we are to take today will prove to have been a wise one.*

Franco dead? It required considerable concentration to imagine Spain without him: he was a portrait that had always been on the wall. She stared at a photograph of Juan Carlos. Had his mentors instilled Francoism in him so thoroughly that it could never be eradicated?

'Odd, isn't it,' the plump man said, checking with one hand to see if his strands of hair were still in place, 'that his father is still next in line? Don't you think Don Juan should become king?'

Ana shook her head emphatically. 'He was alive during the Civil War. Juan Carlos is untainted.' The prince continued to regard her steadily from the pages of *ABC* and for a moment she glimpsed hope beyond the brief of her own life.

'Well, it's put paid to all the other schools of thought,' the man said. 'The Carlists, the old order of Falangists, the supporters of Don Juan . . .'

Ana returned the newspaper and read her reasons for placing Miguel Garcia at the top of her list. *Had access to, and tested, different types of weapons.* A little-used Star RU submachine-gun? *Campaigned at Jarama under José Asensio and took part in the fighting on 12 February when Asensio stormed Pingarrón. Subsequently fought on the hill below where Jesús died . . .*

Ana stared through the window at an ancient shepherd gazing paternally at his flock of goats cropping invisible sustenance on the khaki-coloured plain. According to inquiries carried out – and paid for – by the friends, husbands and pimps of five inmates of the prison, Garcia would have been in the unit that had attacked the position which Jesus was defending. One had found a soldier who had fought in the Republican 15th Brigade who claimed to have seen Garcia aim his gun at the retreating troops. But Ana was well aware of the national characteristic of wanting to please. Had this keen-eyed observer noted what sort of weapon Garcia was holding? No, he had, after all, been in full retreat himself and it had been misty . . . However Garcia merited his place at the head of the list.

The plump man offered her half a *bocadillo*. 'Tuna,' he said. 'With olive oil.'

'No thank you,' she said.

She tried to imagine Garcia as he was now, aware that the years changed the countenance as well as the flesh. But she would be able to recognize the truth in his attitudes. Prison had done that for her: she could identify deceit as surely as a surgeon can diagnose malignancy. And she had evolved an approach for each name on her list.

Her companion bit as daintily as it was possible into the tough-crusted bread-roll. Olive oil dribbled down his chin. 'I bet your pupils don't realize how hard you work during the vacation.'

She looked at him blankly.

'You are a school teacher, aren't you?'

'How clever of you,' Ana said, and returned to Miguel Garcia.

Married with three children. Owner of a small hotel off the Calle del Marqués de Larios in Malaga favoured by old commercial travellers, who fought with the Fascists. Still inclined to reminisce about the war.

The hotel was a genteel and slightly soiled establishment that had turned its face away from Costa del Sol tourists. Its windows were amost clean and through them in the lobby Ana glimpsed a potted palm.

She walked briskly past on the opposite side of the street and booked into a small *pensión*. In her room – a single complaining bed and a wardrobe that smelled of coffins – she unpinned her hair and changed into a heavy skirt and eggshell-blue blouse. Then she returned to the hotel.

The receptionist wore a black jacket with wrinkled lapels and his face, once sharply handsome, had been sucked in by the years. He was juggling names with pencil and india-rubber on a plan of the rooms.

Ana said, 'I want to see Señor Miguel Garcia.'

With his rubber the receptionist ousted a Fernandez from his room and replaced him with a Pastor. 'Who wants to see him?'

Ana fumbled in her new black handbag and produced one of the visiting cards that had been printed for her in Madrid. 'I'm from *Triunfo*.' She placed the card on the counter.

He picked it up and examined it beside the chart as though trying to fit her into a slot. 'A woman working for a magazine? And why would you want to see Señor Garcia?'

'It's the 30th anniversary of the end of the Civil War next year and we're doing a series of interviews with veterans who fought in it.'

'And why should Señor Garcia be so important?'

'You should know, Señor Garcia.'

He tightened a smile round his lips and Ana was gratified to observe it because it confirmed conceit which made him vulnerable. 'You are very perceptive, señora.'

'Everyone gets older, but some retain their youth at the same time. You are one of those, Señor Garcia.' And indeed, now that he had been identified, he did seem younger, as though he had preserved some distant vitality. He straightened up and ran a small comb through his grey hair.

'I still don't understand how you identified me.'

She showed him the photograph.

'Who gave you that?'

'Does the name Pepe Alvarez mean anything to you?'

'It should do, we fought together.' He gave her back the photograph. 'A glass of wine?'

He escorted her to a marble-topped table beneath the forlorn fronds of the palm, returning with a bottle of sweet Malaga wine. He poured two glasses and raised his. 'To Pepe Alvarez, a brave man.'

'He said the same about you.'

'He used to be a great boxer.'

'With one arm?'

'I was testing you. He lost it at Jarama.'

Ana took a notebook and ball-point pen from her bag. 'You fought there?'

'Beside Pepe. I was luckier than him.'

If you are the one, she thought, I shall return tonight and shoot you as you stand behind your reception desk. She shivered.

'So what do you want to know?' he asked.

'Why you joined the army. What life was like in the trenches. Your emotions when you had to kill fellow Spaniards . . .'

He placed his glass carefully on the table. 'I was a soldier; I carried out orders. Where were you during the war, señora?'

'In Madrid. Hiding from the reds most of the time.' She made some notes, thankful that her handwriting had improved in gaol. 'You were a marksman, I believe.'

'I was a good shot, yes. I was gifted with good eyesight and my hand didn't shake. Do you know the greatest gift a sniper can have?'

She saw the back of Jesús's head in a gun-sight; she remained silent.

'Anticipation. Put yourself in your victim's place. What you would do . . .'

'Do you have any photographs?'

'An album of them.'

He went to the office behind the reception desk, returning with a worn, green and gold album. Soldiers with their arms round shy girls, soldiers giving the Fascist salute, soldiers receiving decorations, soldiers grinning at death, one soldier astride a goat – Garcia. She studied the photograph; he was glossily swashbuckling and probably drunk. 'Weren't you ever photographed with your gun?'

'You want to see my gun?'

'You still have it?'

'It wasn't difficult to win trophies after a battle. When I knew the war was almost over I took a rifle from a dead man and stored my own away.'

He took her into the cluttered office. The desk was littered with evidence of bureaucracy on the rampage; bills, paid and unpaid, were bunched on hooks on a shelf. There was a portrait of Franco on the wall and a sepia photograph of José Antonio on the desk.

The armoury was in one corner. A rifle, grenades, shell-caps, a pistol . . . all in much better repair than the office.

Garcia picked up a grenade, weighed it in his hand, looking as if he might lob it. 'A Lafitte,' he told her. 'The most common grenade used in the war.' He grinned. 'Don't worry, it's been defused.'

He was much younger now, eyes peering through the dust of battle.

'What sort of rifle is that?'

He picked it up, stroked the butt lovingly. 'A Mauser. Maximum range about 2,700 metres. Effective, about 550.'

'I should imagine you were always effective.'

'Usually.' He worked the bolt of the rifle.

'What was the effective range of your sub-machine-gun?' fingers tight on her pen.

He looked up from the rifle. 'I don't understand.'

'Wasn't your unit equipped with sub-machine-guns?'

He frowned. 'What a strange question. I never fired a sub-machine-gun at any time during the war. Why would I? I'm a marksman. Was,' he corrected himself. 'Sub-machine-guns, machine-pistols if you like, are for soldiers with white sticks.'

She believed him.

She replaced her notebook and pen in her bag.

'Is that it?'

'Just a few quotes from each veteran I interview. You've been very helpful, Señor Garcia.'

'I've got more photographs.'

'They won't be necessary.'

'You've lost interest already?'

'A few quotes, that was all I needed.'

'And you came all the way from Madrid for them?'

'There are others,' Ana said. 'In Estepona and Algeciras,' she said vaguely.

'Pepe deserves a write-up too.'

'You all do,' Ana said. 'Everyone who fought.'

She walked across the lobby. When she turned at the door, Garcia was standing behind the reception desk still holding his rifle, and for a moment she saw him leaning against the wall of a trench carved from soft rock.

When she got back to the *pensión* she crossed his name from the list. Fourteen more. She opened her suitcase and placed the list on top of the pistol.

Then she paid her bill and walked to the railway station to catch a train back to Madrid to watch Pablo play football against Seville.

Pablo stood in his den in the third-floor apartment of the block near the stadium at Chamartín watching his son play football with a group of boys on the lawns below. He played well enough, with application and energy. What he lacked was instinct. This didn't disappoint Pablo: he would be able to embark on a career – law, perhaps – that didn't end in your thirties.

Pablo turned away from his son's enthusiastic endeavours and surveyed the adornments of his own 20-year-old career. Cups, pennants, statuettes, sweat-stained shirts, team photographs . . . And yet Pablo couldn't accept his age. The past was as vibrant as the present, the roar of the crowd, the thud of the ball on boot, the mud smell of wet turf . . .

He walked from the den into the living-room, his leg aching a little where he had broken it long ago just before Spain played Russia. The ache disappeared when he played but sometimes the leg felt weak towards the end of a game and he had to disguise this by falling theatrically when he was tackled and thus sometimes winning a free kick.

'Is it troubling you?' Encarna asked. She was sitting at the table making a dress with her new sewing-machine.

'Is what troubling me?'

'You know what.'

'Maybe it's going to rain. It always plays up when rain is on the way.'

She pushed the material away from her towards a bowl of oranges. 'How much longer?' she asked.

'Playing?' Pablo shrugged with feigned nonchalance. 'God knows. Two years, maybe three.'

'And then what?'

'We haven't any worries. I've earned enough.' He gazed fondly upon his wife who had remained resolutely unimpressed by his success and the adulation it attracted. Her face and body had settled comfortably with the years but her mind was still as nimble as the needle of her new machine.

'But you will have to do something. You can't go out to grass. What do other players do?'

'Some become managers,' Pablo said, 'if they have the aptitude. Others who have studied while they were playing take up a profession.'

'And what have you studied?'

'You,' he said, grinning.

'We could go back to Seville,' she said.

'Why would we want to do that?'

'Open a hotel, perhaps. Near the ground,' she added craftily.

'Give me one good reason why I should want to be near Seville's stadium.'

'Because Real Madrid play there?'

'Once a year,' Pablo said.

He selected an orange and began to peel it with a knife the way the peasants do, finishing with an unbroken circle of peel, once again postponing the time when he would have to tell her about his plan to find a small team and become its trainer and scout. Believing that when a club bought players it lost some of its identity – he admired the Basque clubs

Bilbao and Real Sociedad for their regional pride – he wanted to mould it into a local unit of talent and loyalty and lead it into the company of the aristocrats of football. He already had a club in Catalonia in mind.

The door burst open and his son came into the room, hair damp with sweat, cheeks flushed.

'Coming to the game?' Pablo asked.

'Not today, papa. Exams.' He went to his room, trailing behind him a slipstream of healthy effort.

'Someone in this family has to study,' Encarna said, standing up and replacing the cover on the sewing-machine.

'It never occurred to me that I would get old.'

'You're not old.'

'No footballer over 30 is young.' He picked up his bag. 'May the best team win,' he said.

'Seville?'

He patted her on the rump, kissed her and went downstairs to his car.

The trainer took him aside in the changing-room. 'Change of plans,' he said. 'Hope you don't mind – we're going to try out the new kid. We'll bring you on in the second-half.'

'Why should I mind? I was a *chaval* myself once.'

From the substitutes' bench he viewed the stadium. The crowd already baying, police in position, fireworks exploding as the two teams trotted on to the pitch. How many of the players, he wondered, were truly aware of the lucky combination of sinew and reflex that made them the focus of so much worship?

His leg ached.

At half-time the score was one-all.

The trainer said, 'I'll give him another fifteen minutes, then bring you on.'

After ten minutes he heard a chant from the crowd, 'We want *El Flaco*.' Just as the new *chaval* scored. An opportunist goal, the ball passed to him from the wing, an instant shot, the ball in the top right-hand corner of the net.

How could the trainer bring him off now?

Pablo stared across the pitch. What if I run on to the pitch into the goal-mouth mêlée, an *espontáneo*? A fitting way to make my exit.

Seville equalized.

How could the kid go off now? He could still win the game for them. Fast, instinctive, tigerish reflexes . . . Saliva swam in Pablo's mouth.

Five minutes left.

From the crowd, '*El Flaco* . . .'

He glanced at the trainer but he was staring across the pitch, fists tightly balled.

Two minutes.

The kid, the *chaval*, rose to a centre. Headed it down. Into the bottom of the net.

The spectators rose to him.

How skinny he is, Pablo thought, as the *chaval* extricated himself from the mobbing players and trotted back to the centre of the pitch. How old was he? Eighteen?

Ana was waiting for Pablo beside his car. She put one arm round his shoulders. They didn't speak.

Near Ana's apartment he noticed a crowd of boys kicking a patched football on a waste plot of land. He stopped the car as a boy with gypsy features trapped the ball, slipped two tackles, sent another boy sprawling, dummied and shot the ball between the posts painted on the wall.

Pablo climbed out of the car and beckoned the boy. 'Do you know who I am?'

The boy nodded and kicked a stone; he was the sort of boy who would always be kicking something. 'You were on the substitutes' bench today – I heard it on the radio.' He spoke with a strong Catalan accent.

'What's your name?'

'Nacho,' the boy told him.

'From now on you're *El Santo*. Not because you look like a saint: because you look like a sinner.'

Pablo called for the ball and collected the pass. 'Now see if you can get it away from me.' Hearing the fading cheers of the crowds on the terraces, Pablo made for the posts painted on the wall, ball at his feet.

Every morning, wherever her mission took her, Ana went to church and prayed to God to help her find the murderer of

Jesús. She came to know God very well and regarded him as a collaborator. In their conversations vengeance was never mentioned, only justice.

In Segovia, where Jesús had been born, she prayed in the cathedral where storks perched on the honey-coloured masonry. Kneeling in the incense twilight, she reminded God that the list of suspects was now reduced to ten; that today she intended to interrogate a factory-owner who every morning drank a glass of anis on the pavement terrace of a bar across the square from the cathedral.

A candle spluttered and died and she made her way out of the cathedral into the pure light of the ancient city that, accompanied by its Roman aqueduct, sails on a crag above the plain of Castile, and walked across the square to the bar, La Concepción, opposite the bandstand.

The factory owner was sitting at his usual table, drink in one hand, following the music of an invisible orchestra in the bandstand with the other. He was in his late sixties with islands of brown pigmentation on his noble, well-nourished features and dyed hair that faded into silver wings above his ears. What Ana noticed most clearly was the fat bulge of his thighs beneath the trousers of his fawn suit.

She waited down the street outside the old theatre. This man had occupied five months of her crusade. Too arrogantly established to succumb to any of her routine artifices, he had merited special attention.

The factory-owner paid his bill, leaving a tip on the table – one peseta if the character assessment in her file was accurate – and strolled along the square, turning right in the general direction of the Alcazar. She followed him at a distance, the way the private detective she had hired must have followed him. When he was set on course she dodged round a side street and hurried along another so that she would be waiting outside the studded doors of his house when he arrived.

As she positioned herself she saw him round the corner and head towards her at an amiable pace. She knew him well. A lieutenant in the Nationalist army, he had fought with distinction in several battles in the Civil War, including

Jarama. He had been then, as now, something of a fop – she
had a photograph of him wearing a flashy, non-regulation
sahariana jacket favoured by Italian officers fighting in Spain.
After the war he had prospered and now owned factories in
Bilbao, Valladolid and Barcelona.

He stopped in front of her. 'Can I help you?'

She took the letter from her bag and gave it to him. He
handled it tentatively, feeling it between thumb and forefinger
as though it might contain a bribe. 'Who is this from?'

'It doesn't matter who it's from, it's what it contains.'

He looked at her inquisitively, noble head slightly tilted;
then he opened the envelope. She knew the contents by
heart.

*It has come to our notice that you have involvements in what has
become known as the Matesa Scandal, details of which have not yet
been made available to the investigating authorities.*

She had consulted the newspapers for details of the Matesa
affair and discovered that on 10 August 1969 the government
had admitted that credits totalling 10,000 million pesetas,
given to Matesa, a textile firm, to export machinery, had
been used for private investment overseas. It was Spain's
biggest-ever financial scandal.

*We have four witnesses who will testify to this involvement but we
do not, in fact; wish to implicate you. What we seek is co-operation . . .*

He finished reading the letter, folded it carefully and
replaced it in the envelope which he slipped into the inside
pocket of his jacket. 'Money?' He seemed in some perverse
way to be enjoying the clandestine meeting.

She shook her head. 'Information.'

'Then you must come with me,' talking as he inserted a
huge key into the lock of the door. 'And perhaps take a glass
of wine while I telephone the police.'

She followed him through a patio, so cool and green that
it might have been under water, along a corridor paved with
flagstones and into a high-ceilinged room that still smelled of
winter fires.

He sat on a leather-backed chair beside the telephone.
'Blackmail? A hefty sentence, señora.' He picked up the
receiver and held it to his ear. 'What sort of information?'

'About a battle.'

He dialled two digits. 'A battle? Blackmail and history? A curious combination.'

'Jarama.'

'Ah, Jarama.' One more digit. 'Why would you want information about Jarama?'

'Because you were there,' Ana said, sitting on a leather sofa opposite the cavernous fireplace.

'Ah.' He replaced the receiver. 'What do you want to know?'

'A few details.'

'Worth blackmail?'

'Tell me about the battle,' she said, looking into his brown eyes, one of which was clouded with an incipient cataract.

'Not much to tell.' He paused for effect. 'You see I wasn't there.'

She rode this easily because she had become more used to lies than truth since her odyssey had begun. 'I have the evidence.' She took an extract from his file from her bag and read out his rank, unit and service record.

He listened attentively, then said, 'Odd, because I served in the Navy.'

'I have a photograph.' She took it from her bag. And there he was in his red and gold piped *gorillo* cap with its tassel, his Sam Browne, leggings and ankle boots, posing with youthful arrogance in front of an army truck.

'Let me see that.'

Ana gave him the cracked snapshot. He held it away from him, half closing his cloudy eye. 'There was a quite remarkable likeness,' he said finally.

Cold began to occupy Ana's body. She said, 'Are you trying to tell me that isn't you?'

'Wait here a moment.' He disappeared into an ante-room. Was he getting a gun? She should have brought her pistol but her missions had fallen into a routine in which execution was envisaged after interrogation. He returned with two framed photographs. 'There. Quite dashing, wasn't I?'

He was very young, a teenager, wearing in a high-buttoned tunic, white cap and sitting with a sword across his knees.

'But –'

'My brother fought at Jarama.' He passed Ana the other photograph; the face was the same as the one in her snapshot.

She knew it was the truth.

'You see we both have the same initials. Juan and Josef. You should shoot your researcher.'

'I was going to shoot you.'

'I don't doubt it; you have a formidable air about you. But why?'

'Where is your brother now?'

'In heaven if you take the Nationalist point of view. He was killed at the Ebro. At Gandesa, Hill 481.'

Ana believed this too.

She said, 'I won't trouble you any further,' and made for the door.

He opened it for her and bowed stiffly. 'Two questions, señora,' one arm barring her. 'Why did you want to kill me if I had been at Jarama?'

She told him, hearing a weariness in her voice that she had not detected before.

'And Matesa?'

'That is the concern of the government, not mine.'

He bowed again, features in aristocratic repose.

When she got back to Madrid she went to the church with the blue dome near the Marqués de Zafra and confessed to the crime of attempted blackmail. But she didn't tell the priest that her accomplice had been God.

In the four years that followed Ana reduced her list of suspects to two. A former legionnaire, now police officer, known as Chimo, and Adam Fleming.

CHAPTER 27

For much of the year the sun shines over the Costa Blanca from a blameless sky. But reminders that this benvolence should not be taken for granted are extreme. Fires roar hungrily through the hills, especially where they are fed by pine, and in churches, kneeling beside beaches and orange groves, priests pray for rain. When their prayers are answered, when lightning zips open the sky for the deluge and streets become canals and hailstones pock-mark becalmed automobiles, they beg for deliverance from the fruits of their prayers. Once every 25 years or so snow falls, knee-deep sometimes, and children are led from school to touch it and the oranges on the trees look like giant holly berries.

At the time that Tom and Josefina stood on a small airstrip watching Ernesto make his maiden solo flight in Tom's Cessna, the countryside was poised between fire and water. Flames, unchastened by firemen's hoses, were making their way busily through a pine forest on a lion-shaped hill, the smoke clouding the sun, while to the west storm clouds were on the march.

Josefina, holding Tom's arm, pointed at the small plane breezing through the sky. 'He shouldn't be up there,' she said. 'The heat from the fire will make air currents, won't it?' Her fingers tightened on his arm.

Tom who, seeing the storm approaching, had called the aero club and advised Ernesto not to take off, placed his hand on hers. 'He'll be okay. He's a good pilot.'

'You encouraged him,' she said.

'He wanted to fly; I couldn't stop him.'

'Of course not – you made it sound like poetry.'

'He'll be a fine doctor too,' Tom said.

A cold breeze came sniffing in from the direction of the storm clouds. The wind-sock straightened, moving like the tail of a waking dog.

The Cessna, flying through the thick orange light beneath the smoke, dipped.

Josefina said, 'Can't they radio to him to come down?'

'They have,' Tom said. 'Maybe that's what he's doing now.'

The breeze, strengthening, blew a cartwheel of dust and leaves across the runway.

The Cessna gained height and circled the strip. Was he about to land? Tom considered what he would do up there. Drop from the narrowing gap of smoke-smudged sky, of course, get the hell out of it and touch down. Or, if he was as young as Ernesto, would he make a last defiant circuit?

The little plane banked. Too sharply, Tom decided. He saw it deviate as the hot air or the vanguard of the storm pushed it. He moved away from Josefina and signalled to Ernesto to land.

The breeze, fast becoming a wind, fashioned another spiral of dust and spun it across the runway.

Josefina said, 'Is he all right?'

Tom said, 'He should bring it down now.'

The Cessna bucketed and Tom thought, 'Sweet Jesus touch down.'

The Cessna, wobbling, flew round the airfield and turned, lining up with the strip. Tom tried to put his arm round Josefina but she moved away from him.

Lightning stuttered, thunder grumbled.

The Cessna was descending, wings jittery.

Tom looked at Josefina. Her face was praying; nurse's hands – she hated anyone to call them capable – tight-fisted. He saw faces at the observation window of the control tower. A streak of lightning fizzed across the advancing clouds and thunder chased it close on its heels.

The Cessna veered to one side. He could see Ernesto in the cockpit. Feel his hands, oily with sweat, gripping the control column.

The Cessna was over the strip again. Josefina's hands went

to her mouth. The wheels touched. The Cessna sprang into the air again. Bumped. Rose again. Tilted. Touched. Stopped. A few feet from the end of the strip.

Fat drops of rain fell in the dust.

Ernesto climbed from the Cessna and walked towards them, hands spread apologetically.

He said, 'I suppose now is as good a time as any to tell you: I've decided to give up medicine and become a pilot.

When the flood waters had receded from the roads, Tom took his diary to the smuggler's café overlooking the sea through a mask of pine trees and pondered the future of Adam Fleming and the future of Spain. Both were uncertain.

On 11 August of that year he had written;

Government shaken by the Matesa scandal. But my guess is that Franco will, as always, emerge unscathed. Get rid of any members of the Opus Dei involved *and* their enemies seeking to exploit the scandal. His old buddy Carrero Blanco will emerge stronger then ever and, although no spring chicken himself, will still be there to keep Juan Carlos in the Francoist flock. Or will the young prince prove to be a black sheep?

20 August. Antonio and Isabel now going from strength to strength in the tourist industry. Hotels, travel agents, you name it. A bank next?

Tom glanced at the entries with desultory interest, his mind occupied with the crisis that had arisen in his own household since Ernesto had renounced medicine. It distressed him all the more because Josefina blamed him; it angered him because, since he had taken out Spanish citizenship, his business interests had prospered and he had planned to delegate more responsibility to Belov and spend more time with his family – some chance with a martyred wife and an errant step-son.

The one-legged smuggler left his vantage point behind the pines and joined Tom at the unsteady table on the terrace, bringing with him a fawning cat and a whiff of his terrible cigars.

He ordered two brandies as rough as his cigars and said, 'You look as though you prefer death to life, my friend.'

'Anything is better than smoking your cigars,' Tom said.

'Woman trouble?' He inhaled hot smoke from his moulting cigar. 'The worst kind,' without waiting for a reply.

'Not really. Ernesto is the trouble.'

'A good boy. How old is he, twenty-two? He will make a fine doctor.'

'Pilot,' Tom said.

'I thought –'

'He's changed his mind.'

'And Josefina . . .?'

'Exactly.'

The tip of the cigar flamed briefly. 'No problem, surely. Can't he be both?'

Tom cornered Ernesto in his bedroom while Josefina was shopping and talked to him urgently.

When Josefina returned he said, 'I have news for you.'

She began to unload the basket on the kitchen table, tomatoes, lettuce, peppers and purple, polished aubergines. 'About your business interests?'

'About Ernesto,' Tom said. 'He's going to be a flying doctor.'

And when, after an inordinately long pause, she blinked, then smiled tremulously, he thought, 'Now that leaves Adam.'

Gazing over the stone parapet of a bridge spanning the Thames, Adam Fleming saw in the languid water another face, warped by the jostling waves, but young and argu— mentative just the same, one of those quick and rare faces that would not be made foolish by a judicial wig. He smoothed his greying hair and the young man smoothed his; he trailed his finger over his confused features and the young man touched his.

Adam straightened up. It was a warm, exhausted evening, the air languorous with the scent of dying blossom and the fumes of homeward traffic, and, although the pubs had only been open for an hour, he was amiably intoxicated. He walked with the determined gait of those who are familiar with this condition, only attracting the attention of the most perspicacious and those with whom he collided.

He caught a bus to Richmond and, head down, aimed himself in the direction of the towpath. No longer did he admonish himself for over-indulgence; no longer did he try and convince himself that he would cut down. Why deceive yourself? He never became roaring drunk: alcohol harmlessly buttered each day.

He bore left and began the ascent of the lawns that climb from the river to the statue known as Bulging Bessie. When he was half-way up he remembered that he had an evening class and increased his stride. But the thrust of his thighs was laboured, as though he were paddling in deep water, and when he reached the summit a slight pain needled his chest.

The class was not a success, containing as it did a trio of remorselessly humorous young bloods, awaiting postings from the City to Madrid who, with their puns and linguistic double-meanings, upset the studious pupils nervously contemplating emigration to Spain. Normally Adam, with indulgent repartee of his own, was able to defuse hostilities, but this evening his tongue was thick in his mouth.

Half-way through the class one of the bloods, a beefy young man with a phlegmy voice, asked him what the Spanish for drunk was. And when Adam told him *borracho* he asked how to say 'I am drunk', and when Adam told him it was too elementary to explain he said, with change of emphasis: 'Or "You are drunk",' nudging another member of the trio.

Adam tried to think of a rapier response; when nothing occurred he made his way, observed furtively by his more serious students, to his desk beside the blackboard on which he had conjugated several irregular verbs. On his way he stumbled and, steadying himself, toppled a pile of books into the lap of a pale girl whose complexion would be no match for the Spanish sun. The young men elaborately suppressed their mirth while their class-mates frowned into their books.

After the class a sturdy woman with laundered white hair

approached Adam purposefully. She said, 'I have to tell you, Mr Fleming, that a number of us are not satisfied with the way these classes are being conducted.'

'Then you will have to find another teacher.'

'That's what we intend to do.' She braced her militant legs. 'But there is the question of our fees.'

'Don't worry about them,' Adam said, 'I've spent them.'

'On drink no doubt.'

'And fast women and slow horses.'

'We want our money back.'

'Then sue me,' Adam said.

'That we will.'

She marched from the room, white curls springing briskly.

In his office Adam poured himself a respectable measure of whisky and opened his mail. Mostly bills, all final demands. One letter from Rosana: Eduardo, running out of school, had been knocked down by a car. He hadn't been seriously injured but he was at home, one leg in plaster, one arm in a sling. Adam smiled sadly and poured another measure of whisky.

In the bedroom the widow was asleep between the sheets, still wearing a soiled and inadequate brassiere. The room smelled of gin and perfumed deodorant. He washed in cold water, taking care not to catch sight of his flushed features in the mirror, and brushed his teeth so vigorously that blood appeared on the brush. Then he undressed, dropping his clothes on the floor, and climbed into bed, distancing himself from the widow.

He was awakened at three by the return of the spectres of war. He stared wide-eyed at the faint luminosity beyond the curtains and the spectres lengthened ghoulishly; he shut his eyes tight and they shrank into squatting corpses. When finally he slept he saw Eduardo as a marionette, splinted limbs jerking on strings.

In the morning he walked down Richmond Hill to an estate agents and put the school up for sale. Then he persuaded a dreamy girl in a travel agency to change his flight so that he could fly to Spain the following day, four days before he was due to see Eduardo.

When he arrived in Estepona he telephoned Rosana in Madrid. Two days later while he was drinking a bottle of wine on the terrace – he had renounced whisky on the day he left Richmond, but had to drink a substitute otherwise his limbs jerked him from sleep – he received a visitor, a resolute and compact Catalan with a cast in one eye who said his name was Jordi.

Adam fetched him a glass. 'What can I do for you?' he asked, filling the glass with a cheap Rioja.

The Catalan spoke English. 'I've come from Madrid,' he said, 'to tell you that you're a bloody fool.'

Adam sat in his rocking chair. Palm trees whispered and, above him, mosquitoes sizzled as they committed suicide in a mauve-glowing lamp. 'You're not the first person to have told me that,' he said.

The Catalan sipped his wine and grimaced. 'I wonder if you know how big a bloody fool.'

'I have no doubt you will enlighten me. But perhaps you would also be good enough to tell me who the hell you are.'

'A fellow conspirator with your wife.' A mosquito zipped to its death. 'A long time ago.'

'And Alfonso?'

'All piss and wind.' The Catalan smiled, sunlight on a craggy hillside. 'I learned my English at the London School of Economics.'

'Apparently he had a way with him,' Adam said.

'And what's that supposed to mean?'

'Make what you like of it. What are you, a Communist?'

'I'm a Catalan. That's all you need to know. Rosana and I have gone our separate ways. She is a Socialist, a member of the PSOE. And a worthy one. When Franco dies, when we have free elections, she will become a member of the Cortes.'

Adam said, 'Why am I such a bloody fool?'

The Catalan drank more wine with the air of an orator loosening his words with a glass of water.

'I will tell you,' he said, leaning back in his cane chair, fingers entwined. 'First of all you treated your wife as a child. Perhaps because when you first met that's what she was. Perhaps you fell in love with her then, harboured some sort of guilt even when she was grown-up . . .'

Adam wanted to interrupt, tell this bold interloper to mind his tongue, but there was a good deal of truth in what the Catalan was saying. He remained silent.

'. . . Even when she became a successful painter you treated her as a child prodigy. And as for political leanings, well, she was a child *and* a woman.'

'I didn't know she was interested in politics.'

'Of course you didn't. Do you think she would have told you? Run the risk of your English male indulgence?'

His English is excellent, Adam thought. But where is it leading us? Something moved inside him, like sand shifting on a child's castle on a beach.

'So what did she do? She entered politics secretly and became intoxicated by conspiracy. There is nothing, you know, quite as addictive. Nothing quite so compelling. Not even hunger. Not even sex.'

Adam got the impression that sex had been introduced deliberately. That it was part of a prepared script. There was a tightness in his chest and he breathed deeply of the jasmine-smelling night air.

The Catalan finished his glass of wine and replenished it. 'I spent many nights under the same roof as them,' he went on. 'Conspiracy has its own camaraderie. We used to drink and talk and plan and go to bed exhausted at four in the morning . . .'

Adam said nothing.

Angered, the Catalan said, 'Do you really care what happened – or didn't happen – to your wife, or are you such a prig that you care only about your hurt pride?'

Adam said, 'You should know about pride: you're a Catalan.'

'I know about trust,' the Catalan said. 'But that's a stranger to you, isn't it?'

'Did Rosana send you?'

The Catalan shook his head, a slight but authoritative movement. 'But she told me you thought she had been unfaithful.'

Adam realized that the small movement he had experienced in his reasoning had been hope. That was certainly a stranger. 'And?'

The stars pressed down. A mosquito whined and died.

The Catalan said, 'I was there when Alfonso tried to climb into bed with her. I heard her protesting. Alfonso left quietly . . .' The Catalan finished his wine. 'I can promise you that your wife was never unfaithful. That, you see, is why you're a bloody fool, and a big one at that.'

It was then, to his intense surprise, that Adam felt tears making their way down his cheeks.

Said the Catalan, also surprised, 'Why, you're more of a man than I thought you were.'

It was Rosana who suggested to Ignacio that he should leave the apartment. She loved him in her way, carnally and companionably, but he was, nevertheless, an obstacle to her intentions. How could a woman in her forties stand for election to the Cortes when she was living with a strolling player in his twenties?

He accepted her decision philosophically. He could, she reflected, have been a little more distressed.

'So now I have to return to acting?' folding his engaging smile.

'You act every time you go on the stage.'

'But not with you. I shall miss absolute honesty: not many men have even a casual encounter with it. Tell me, did it make you feel vulnerable?'

'And alive. But sometimes it scared me. Honesty isn't the currency of the human race.'

'Then try introducing it into the Cortes.'

He packed carelessly, kissed her and departed.

In the weeks that followed she painted several canvasses. And cheated, she decided. Lacking her former purity of vision, she took to staring at brightly lit subjects, closing her eyes tightly and painting the images photographed on the retinas – cubes and triangles and diagonals of rust-red and gentian and copper penetrated sparingly by revelations of light. Sometimes she even copied trembling shadows on the walls of her studio.

She knew the culprit for her lack of inspiration well enough. The delight and torment of every Spaniard – politics.

They absorbed her utterly. Every division, every speculation
– predominantly about when Franco was going to die –
every nuance. The ETA kidnappings and hold-ups; the
strikes; the burgeoning freedom of expression in such
newspapers as *Ya* and *Informaciones* and the new and pungent
magazine *Cambio 16;* the possibility that Spain might at last
be approaching the road to democracy. Hadn't Franco in his
Christmas speech in 1972 declared, 'We have to depart from
any closed criterion . . .'?

To her surprise she found that, after the Socialist leaders
of the PSOE, the politician she most admired was Manuel
Fraga, former minister under Franco and currently Spanish
ambassador in London, who had written a book advocating
reform. And in her clandestine way she admired Franco too.

With her political future in mind, Rosana was cautious
when Adam called at the apartment suggesting that they live
together again. Would a continuing marriage to a former
Fascist, a foreigner and an alcoholic at that, damage her
credibility?

She served coffee on the balcony. His hand holding the
cup shook a little. His grey hair was lifeless, his features had
loosened and lost purpose.

She said 'We've been apart a long time. Our lives have
become self-contained . . .'

'I should have trusted you,' he said.

'Why? I was deceiving you. You see I can't resist conspiracy.
That's why I want to be a politician.' She smiled. 'What would
you do in Madrid?'

'What I was doing in England. Teach English to Spaniards,
Spanish to foreigners.'

She considered her feelings for him. Dipped into the past
and reviewed the respect and affection she had once felt for
him. But we are two different people, she thought.

She heard a key in the door of the apartment. Eduardo,
almost a teenager, limped on to the balcony on his crutches.
He shook hands with Adam, spoke in halting English and
called him sir. Then he sat down, one arm cradled, plastered
leg sticking out as though it belonged to someone else.

It was, she later conceded, the leg that did it. So detached did it seem that it was a symbol of family estrangement. The bleak distance between her and her mother.

And, as she listened to father and son awkwardly discussing the road accident, she was visited by a sense of unity, hitherto a stranger, that was as comforting as shifting embers on a fire.

The sensation expanded luxuriously, although it was not devoid of calculation. Could not the marriage of a one-time Fascist and a Socialist be interpreted as the settling of the ancient rifts of Spain?

Smiling, she stepped down from a distant platform.

Her husband and her son looked at her questioningly. She changed the angle of her smile. 'I was thinking about tomorrow,' she said. 'The three of us going to the coast together.'

When she returned from holiday, Rosana went to see Tom Canfield. Belov was ponderously present in the outer office and she had to wait until Tom returned from a meeting.

He greeted her cordially, his movements a little stiffer than she remembered, but he was a man who had entered his sixties with composure. The fairness of his hair disguised the grey and he exuded the tolerance of someone nursing a private satisfaction.

She said, 'I've come to ask a favour.'

'And that doesn't come easily to you, does it Rosana? How about a walk? In the Retiro, maybe. What I like about parks is they never change.'

They stopped at an outdoor café beside the lake opposite the statue of Alfonso XII. Rowing-boats sent indolent ripples across the water; a vendor sold liquorice roots, spinning tops and windmills on sticks. Tom ordered a Coke for Rosana and a beer for himself. He stretched, as settled as the venerable and summer-dusted foliage around them.

'So what are you after?' he asked. 'Contributions for the Party?'

'I want you to swallow your pride,' she said.

'Adam?'

'You're very shrewd.'

'Am I? I never thought of myself as that. I've always seen

myself as an expansionist. Part of my British heritage, I guess. Wherever they go the British colonize. Look at the *costas*. The Spanish should have diplomatic representatives there.'

'You're shrewd,' Rosana said, 'because while you were making that speech you were deliberating.' She sucked Coke through a straw. 'Adam's back.'

'I know.'

'Chimo?'

'It doesn't matter how I know. He wants his job back?'

'He doesn't want anything: it's I who want something for him.' She watched a couple embrace precariously in a rowing-boat. 'Did you say his *job*?'

'Partnership then.'

'Did you always patronize him?'

Tom shook his head lazily. 'That wasn't possible – we were a unit. From our first meeting. When he was ordered to shoot me. We shared ideals, you know, even though we were supposed to be enemies.' He raised his head and stared at the blue sky bisected by the white chalk stroke of an aircraft. 'Who is the enemy?'

'And what's that supposed to mean?'

'The enemy,' Tom said, 'is the one you're taught to hate. Sad, isn't it?'

'Will you help him? Without telling him that I asked you?'

'It was written,' Tom said, 'a long time ago.'

Above them the trail of the aircraft blurred and spread.

Tom walked slowly through the park, marvelling at the way in which decisions can be delivered to you. He had been contemplating retirement, staying in Alicante, putting an end to Josefina's guilt about all the money he earned. Taking her on vacation to America . . . He emerged from the park on Alcalá and telephoned Adam from the Palacio de Communicaciones.

He met him outside the umbrella shop, the Casa de Diego, on the Puerto del Sol. 'I have a proposition to put to you,' he said, as they walked past the busy kiosks towards Madrid's most famous lottery establishment, La Hermana de Doña Manolita. 'I want to sell my partnership in the business.'

'To me?' Adam laughed bleakly. 'I'm broke.'

'Payable over five years from the profits you make with Belov. Or.' glancing at his watch, 'buy a lottery ticket. It's Saturday – you've got five minutes before they call a halt.' He propelled him towards the lottery shop.

Adam bought one ticket, 01439. He showed it to Tom. 'The first of April nineteen thirty-nine, the day the Civil War ended.'

'You won't win,' Tom said. 'No one did.'

'But if the last digit's correct I get my money back. Is that enough for my first payment?'

Outside the shop they shook hands, keeping them clasped for several moments. Then Adam grinned. 'I was wrong last time you asked,' he said. 'I would have shot you.'

CHAPTER 28

November 1975. Franco lay in La Paz hospital, dying. In her dark apartment Ana Gomez scarcely heeded the manner of his prolonged suffering. Nor had she dwelled deeply on any of the formidable events of the past two years.

The assassination in December 1973 of the Prime Minister, Carrero Blanco, blown up in his armour-plated Dodge on his way from Mass to his office by an ETA commando group, and the bomb explosion the following year that killed 11 in Madrid, both incidents arresting the fledgling wing-beat of reform. The speech by Blanco's successor, Carlos Arias Navarro, promising that political associations would be tolerated – a promise subsequently hedged by qualifications that disbarred regional groups. The temporary six-week reign of Juan Carlos in the summer of 1974 when Franco was suffering from phlebitis. The recent executions of two members of ETA and three of FRAP, an urban guerrilla movement, that had provoked worldwide protest.

Nor would the imminent death of Franco, still inconceivable to many Spaniards, affect Ana, because in truth, since Chimo had proved that neither he nor Adam could have killed Jesús because they weren't fighting at the time he died, thus leaving a void once peopled by suspects, she was not aware of anything outside her cocoon of introspection.

Then late on the evening of 19 November she was visited by the hotel owner in Malaga who had once been a prime suspect. His face had withered and his eyes looked into the past. He sat opposite her as she see-sawed gently in her rocking chair. She regarded him without interest; he had been eliminated long ago and there was no one else.

'You must,' he said, 'be wondering why I've come here.'

She gave a fragile shrug.

'When you came to see me you mentioned sub-machine-guns. I wondered why and I have wondered ever since.'

She blinked and it seemed to her that her eyes shed a layer of skin.

He hesitated, waiting for a response. Getting none, he said, 'It has worried me. I am dying you see.'

'We all are,' she said, 'from the moment we are born.'

'And I do not want to leave behind injustices. You don't by any chance think that Pepe Alvarez used the machine-gun you referred to?'

Her eyes focused. 'Who did?'

'I don't know his name. Only that he shot many Spaniards in the back.'

'Who?' She regarded him with great clarity, felt her heartbeat quicken.

'I told you, I don't know. Only that he was armed with a Star RU sub-machine-gun.'

'No one else saw him. I have interviewed many people.'

'I was beside him. The mist was very thick. Then it lifted for a moment. That's when he shot them. Then the mist came down again. He disappeared in it. I think he was sickened by what he had done.'

'You must have some idea who he was.'

MUST.

'Only,' the hotel owner said, 'that he smelled faintly of perfume.'

The following morning she walked past the blue-domed church near the Marqués de Zafra, scarcely giving it a thought, pistol heavy in her bag where, at this time of day, her Bible normally rested.

When she emerged, oblivious to the razored cold, on a main thoroughfare, she hailed a taxi and told the driver to take her to an address outside Madrid on the road to La Coruña.

'It will cost money,' the driver said, looking at her unkempt clothes.

'A million wouldn't be enough.'

He spread his hands. Crossed himself. Steered his taxi through the traffic of Madrid with suicidal aplomb.

He spoke only once. 'So it has happened,' he said, but she didn't reply.

Antonio was standing beside his empty swimming pool, frail shoulders draped with a tartan blanket.

She said, 'So, it was you.'

'It took you a long time, my sister.'

'It doesn't matter how long: the ending is the same.' She took the pistol from her bag and pointed it at his head, vaguely noticing how old he looked, grey curls on his scalp unwinding, expression untouched by colours or sounds or scents.

'These things happen in war,' he said. 'Supposing Jesús had shot me?'

'In the back?'

'It was a long time ago. Do you know what happened today?'

'Franco died?'

'At five o'clock this morning. The end of the Civil War. It lasted longer than most people think. Now perhaps there will be peace and, God willing, prosperity.'

He pointed at the cross above the Valley of the Fallen, its silhouette small and sharp on the horizon. 'Maybe Jesús is there.'

She eased back the trigger of the pistol.

Antonio offered her his outstretched hands. 'Do you think this is what Jesús would have wanted?'

She kept the pistol levelled unwaveringly at his head, then lowered it.

She sat in the rocking chair in the balm of the apartment's perpetual dusk. He was right, of course: Jesús would have killed him with words. She cradled the spent cartridge case in the palm of one hand. It felt warm. The dusk settled comfortably around her. She heard the bombers overhead. The chair continued to rock for a few moments, then stopped.

Angels in the Snow

Angels in the Snow is a vivid and tense novel which gives the first comprehensive picture of this Western community forced to live in selected blocks of looming flats guarded by militia men, living an existence in which the tensions and hostility of the Soviet Union sometimes prove intolerable. The three main characters are Westerners: the American who works for the US Embassy and the CIA; the young Englishman at the British Embassy who gradually cracks under the strain of Moscow life; a member of the Twilight Brigade which includes such conscripts as Philby and Maclean. In an alien land these three lives become inextricably joined against a background in which the bugging of flats and the photographing of couples in compromising circumstances are accepted hazards of life. It peers behind the diplomatic front at the embassies of America and Britain, and finds the jealousies and rivalries underneath the surface.

'A novel of terrifying atmosphere' *Daily Express*

'Excitingly real' *Sunday Telegraph*

'An eminently readable and poignant documentary novel' *Sunday Express*

I, Said the Spy

Each year a nucleus of the wealthiest and most influential members of the Western world meet to discuss the future of the world's superpowers at a secret conference called Bilderberg. A glamorous millionaire just sighting loneliness from the foothills of middle age, a French industrialist whose wealthy matches his masochism, a whizz-kid conducting a lifelong love affair with diamonds – these are just three of the Bilderbergers who have grown to confuse position with invulnerability. A mistake which could prove lethal when a crazed assassin is on the loose. *I, Said the Spy* is a novel on a grand scale which sweeps the reader along on a wave of all-out excitement and suspense until the final stunning climax.

'Lambert certainly keeps the action moving with surprise plot twists thrown in every now and again to unsettle the reader' *Liverpool Daily Post*

'Could put ideas into the head of many a spy' *Sunday Telegraph*

BY THE SAME AUTHOR

The Red Dove

As the Soviet space shuttle Dove orbits 150 miles above the earth on its maiden flight, Warsaw Pact troops crash into Poland. What is the deadly connection between the soaring bird and the shattering fist? The 72-year-old President of America wants to be re-elected, and for that he needs a spectacle. He needs to win the first stage of the war in space: he needs to capture the Soviet space shuttle. But as the President plans his coup a nuclear-armed shuttle speeds towards target America – and only defection in space can stop it.

'Writing as crisp as the Moscow winter ... magically evocative' *New York Times*

'Lambert, author of many intelligent political thrillers, has another in this fast-paced, complex, and timely novel. Highly recommended' *Library Journal*

'A most satisfying thriller with a highly dramatic finish' *Publishers Weekly*

BY THE SAME AUTHOR

The Judas Code

In June 1941, Stalin was warned of Hitler's intention to mount a mighty offensive codenamed Barbarossa, aimed at dealing a death-blow to Soviet Russia. Stalin could have saved the lives of millions – yet he ignored the warnings. Why? The answer lies in the Judas Code. In neutral Lisbon, British Intelligence have concocted a ruthless double-cross to lure Russia and Germany into a hellish war of attrition on the Eastern Front and so buy Britain the most precious commodity of all – time. That plot now hinges on one man, Josef Hoffman, a humble Red Cross worker. But who is Hoffman? And where do his loyalties really lie? Brilliantly turning history on its head, *The Judas Code* is a gripping tale of betrayal, passion, hurtling action and knife-edge suspense.

'Charged with action and tension from start to finish'
John Barkham Reviews

'For unbearable suspense, for chapter-by-chapter fascination, nothing I've read equals this one' *Los Angeles Times*

'A World War II "what if" that's great fun. Lots of suspense and a bang-up climax' *Publishers Weekly*